WAKEFIELD'S COURSE

BOOKS BY

MAZO DE LA ROCHE

*

YOUNG RENNY (JALNA–1906)

WHITEOAK HERITAGE

JALNA

WHITEOAKS OF JALNA

FINCH'S FORTUNE

THE MASTER OF JALNA

WHITEOAK HARVEST

WAKEFIELD'S COURSE

*

LOW LIFE AND OTHER PLAYS

PORTRAIT OF A DOG

LARK ASCENDING

BESIDE A NORMAN TOWER

THE VERY HOUSE

GROWTH OF A MAN

THE SACRED BULLOCK AND OTHER STORIES

WAKEFIELD'S COURSE

BY
MAZO DE LA ROCHE

Whiteoak Edition

BOSTON
LITTLE, BROWN, AND COMPANY
1941

FIRST EDITION

Published September 1941

ATLANTIC–LITTLE, BROWN BOOKS
ARE PUBLISHED BY
LITTLE, BROWN AND COMPANY
IN ASSOCIATION WITH
THE ATLANTIC MONTHLY PRESS

PRINTED IN THE UNITED STATES OF AMERICA

TO CAROLINE

CONTENTS

WAKEFIELD'S COURSE

The Whiteoak Family

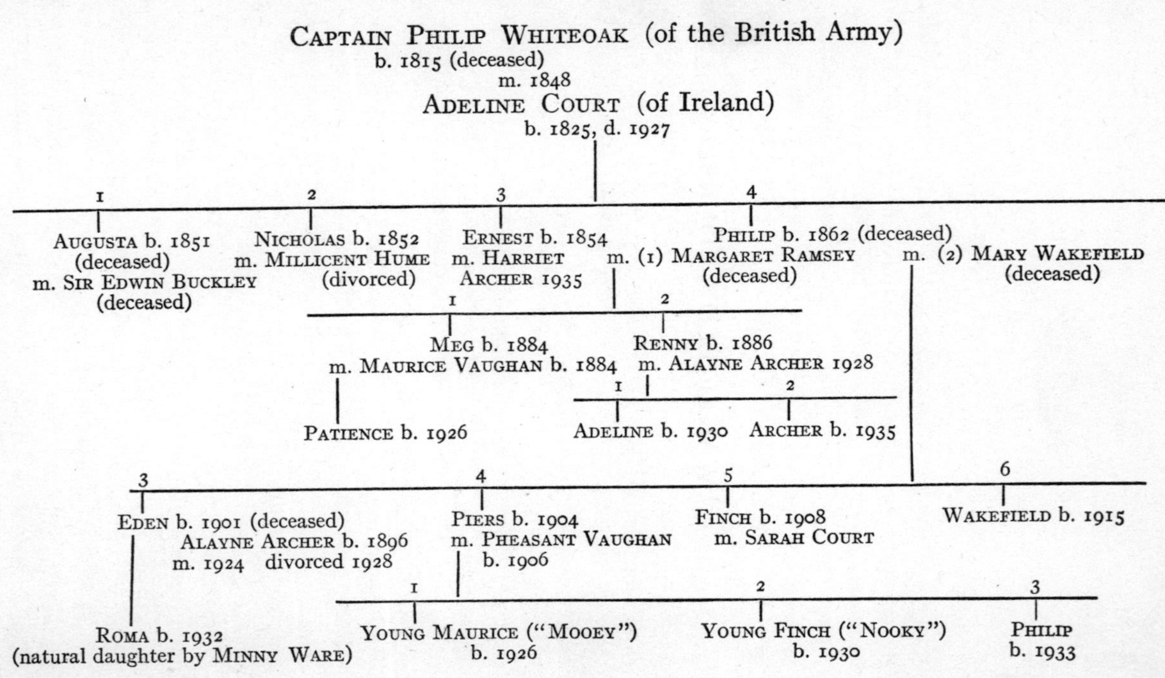

I
AT JALNA

RENNY WHITEOAK had done well to provide himself against the weather for, though it was now March, the wind was as icy as in winter and it needed his rubber boots to keep out the icy slush of the road. He had thrust his bare hands into his pockets, pulled a battered felt hat over his eyes, and drawn his chin into the shelter of his coat collar, so that the only parts of him exposed to the elements were his ears, which were somewhat pointed, and his bony, aquiline nose. The wind and the sleet did their worst to these so that his ears were whipped to a bright red. His nose, however, showed an invincible defiance and looked only a little more weatherbeaten than usual.

He walked with bent head, in a state of almost ecstatic concentration, so that the time it took him to walk from his own stable to his brother Piers's house might be estimated as a few moments or half a lifetime. His mind was concentrated on one problem — should he respond to Wakefield's cablegram, and to another which he had received from his cousin Dermot Court, or should he not? Common sense and a keen sense of duty told him no. But what were they compared to the wild clamor that shook his soul when the idea of acquiring a grand new horse possessed it? If an observer watching his progress along the country road could have looked at the same time into his mind he would have seen there a strange conglomeration of shapes, a strange and antagonistic medley of shapes — the shape of a bankbook, the outline of a wife's accusing face, a steamship ploughing across the sea, innumerable hurdles and hedges over which flew, in hypnotic leapings, the shape of the unknown horse.

He was so intent that he had overtaken two small boys before he saw them. They belonged to his brother Piers and were on their way home after their day at a school in the town. It was a long walk from the railway station and the younger, Nook, looked tired. He was barely nine. Renny took his hand and remarked: —

" Drifts too high for the car, eh? That 's why I 'm walking, too."

Nook nodded. " Mummie says she 's never known such a March and she 's lived a long time."

" Not nearly so long as I, and I 've never seen such a one. But it 's still early in the month. Any day you will wake to find a warm sun and the snow going off in a hurry. Is your father at home ? "

" I don't know."

" Of course you don't. That was a damned silly question, but then I 'm in a damned silly mood." He grinned down at them. "What 's the matter, Mooey? Have n't you anything to say for yourself? "

" Not specially, except that I have a blister on my heel and I think one of my toes is frozen and I 'm hungry." Being tired and somewhat disgruntled, he added — " I 'll bet there 's something for dinner I don't like."

" I 'll bet," said Nook, " that Philip has taken my train apart. I just had it on my birthday but it does n't matter !"

" He smashes all my things," said Mooey. " But it does n't matter."

" What a pair of grousers! Here we are! We 'll go in and find what damage is done."

The house was of wood, painted white with green shutters, pointed gables, and long sloping roof. Though it was nearly a hundred years old it had a spruce, youthful appearance. In summer it was surrounded by a charming old-fashioned garden, but at this time of year it looked rather bare. The two boys darted ahead and threw open the door.

Renny could hear them heralding his approach at the top of their voices.

His sister-in-law, Pheasant, slender, brown-haired and brown-eyed, came eagerly down the stairs to meet him.

" How nice of you to come! It 's been such a dull day. Wind and rain and sleet. I 've lived a good many years and I 've never known such a March."

" So your boys were telling me." He touched her cheek with his cold one and asked — " Where 's Piers? They told me at the stables he 'd come home and of course the phone 's out of order."

" He has n't come. But probably he soon will."

Her youngest son, Philip, came prancing in from the kitchen. He wore a toy leather harness with bells and was eating a rosy apple. He was six years old, fair-haired, pink-cheeked, with bright blue eyes. His eyes still had the wonder of the cradle in them but he carried himself with an air of purpose and even pugnacity. He demanded at once: —

" Have you brought the lollipops you promised me, Uncle Renny? "

Renny pulled a wry face. " I 've forgotten them! But I 'll buy them to-morrow and send them by your dad. I promise you."

" Has Philip played with my train? " Nook asked of his mother.

" Yes," answered Philip for himself. " I did play with your train and the funnel came off."

Nook waited to hear no more. He fled from the room and up the stairs to investigate the damage for himself.

" What I go through with these boys! " exclaimed Pheasant. " Nook values his things so, yet he leaves them about where Philip can get them."

" You can't hide away a locomotive like you can a thimble," said Mooey, sternly.

Philip was astride of Renny's knee, taking small quick bites of the red apple. " I busted it but it was n't my fault," he said. He gave a shout of joy. " Here comes Daddy! "

Piers came in, shining in oilskins and his own fresh complexion. At sight of him Renny's face assumed a look of great gravity. He fixed his brilliant brown gaze on his brother's face.

" I have had a most important cable," he said.

Piers stared. " Who from? The boys? Is anything wrong? "

" Yes. From Wakefield. Nothing wrong. It 's about a horse."

" My God! " said Piers. He went out into the hall and removed his wet outer garments.

Pheasant looked uncomfortable. Renny joggled the child on his knee and whistled softly between his teeth. In a moment he said: —

" That was silly of Piers. Surely he does n't imagine that I will do anything without due consideration."

" He thinks you are impulsive where horses are concerned."

Piers returned, wearing an expression of defense. But he knew he was not proof against Renny's urge to buy a horse. He said: —

" May I read the cablegram? "

Renny handed it to him.

" Certainly," said Piers, " Wake has gone to a lot of trouble to make this animal sound enticing. But Malahide! Surely you would n't trust him! "

" I 've had another cable. It 's from Cousin Dermot. Read it." He fished it from a pocket and gave it to Piers, who passed both on to Pheasant.

" How thrilling! " she exclaimed. " Of course you 'll buy him! "

Renny beamed at her. " You think I ought? "

" Well — it seems a marvelous opportunity."

Piers struck his fist on the table. " *Never* — never without seeing him first! You 'll have to go over. No — you can't possibly — it will make the horse too damned expensive. Upon my word, I think it 's a harebrained scheme. Neither Finch nor Wake is capable of judging a horse. And how do you know what Malahide or that old Dermot Court has up his sleeve? It may be a put-up job to fleece you."

" On Malahide's part it might. On Cousin Dermot's, never. He 's a grand old boy. I absolutely trust him. Both as a judge of horses and as a kinsman."

" I do love to hear you use that old-fashioned word! " cried Pheasant. " It might be your grandmother speaking."

" If Gran were here," said Piers, " she 'd counsel you not to take such a risk. Just think! Either you buy this horse without seeing him or you take an expensive journey to see him — "

" I shall cross tourist — "

" I can picture *you* doing that! "

" You 're not denying that I can be economical, are you? "

" In some ways you can be as close as bark to a tree."

" *What?* "

Renny's color rose. He stared hard at Piers.

" I only mean — "

" Well — go on."

" You know yourself that you won't buy the new farm implements we need."

" I know that the old ones are adequate."

" You are the only one who thinks so."

Pheasant's pacifying voice broke in. " Surely if Renny trusts Cousin Dermot's judgment and thinks well of Wake's — "

" I do indeed."

" Then surely it 's worth considering. If the horse

should win the Grand National, Renny could sell him for a stupendous sum. It may be a gamble, but what a glorious one!"

"Piers would prefer," said Renny, "that I should take any extra money I have for farm implements, in order that he can make a few dollars extra on the crops — which I don't believe he could."

"I could do with less hired help."

"If I win the Grand National," said Renny, "I 'll buy you anything you want."

"Thanks." Piers gave an unbelieving laugh.

"Then you are dead against the project?"

"No. I 'm not. I 'm keen about it. But — I think the risks are too great. You would have to depend on other people to superintend the training. Then you 'd make a second trip across the ocean to see the race. You 'd want to see your horse win, would n't you?"

His elder brother had listened to him with the color deepening in his already high-colored face. Now he tilted Philip from his knee and rose in anger to his feet. He strode up and down the room.

"Am I," he asked passionately, "to spend the rest of my days at Jalna and never go anywhere? Am I to rusticate here like a vegetable? I tell you I 've got to have a change!"

"I never get a change," said Piers, doggedly.

"You never want one."

"How do you know?"

"You 're welcome to go anywhere at any time you want. Why, you were in Montreal just before Christmas, about that consignment of apples!"

"You were all over the place during the polo season."

"Yes," returned Renny bitterly, "and generally came back with a pulled tendon or a broken collarbone!"

"You did that just once! Also, you rode in the New York Horse Show."

Renny's tone was almost plaintive. "Yes, and got a flu germ that laid me up for a fortnight! I can tell you that I made up my mind months ago to go to Ireland this spring to see my Cousin Dermot. I visited his father, old Dermot, in 1919. I 've always promised myself I 'd go back. Now the son is an old man and if I delay it may be too late. He must be nearly eighty."

"Oh," cried Pheasant, "I do think you ought to go!"

The passion in his eyes melted to an enfolding warmth as he looked at her.

"Do you really?" he asked.

"Yes, I do."

Philip shouted — "Go to Ireland and buy the horse!"

His uncle picked him up, hugged him, and gave him a kiss. He said: —

"If I do go I 'll buy you a present. Choose whatever you like." Renny then turned to Piers. "Well, what do you say?" he asked.

Piers's bright blue eyes smiled up at him.

"Well," he said, "if you 're going over in any case, you might as well drop in and have a look at the nag."

"You know," said Renny to Pheasant, "I think it 's damned disagreeable of Piers to be sarcastic about this."

Piers lighted a cigarette and laughed. "I 'm just being philosophical. I only hope that Alayne will be equally so."

"I don't think Alayne will oppose me in this. She knows that financially things are much better with me than they were a few years ago. Some of her own investments are recovering. I think myself that things are looking up with us from every side. As for that new reaper you want, go ahead and buy it. I dare say we need it." He gave a sigh and picked up his hat from the top of the coal box where he had laid it. A rivulet of water ran from its brim.

"Don't go," said Pheasant. "Stay and have supper with us."

"Thanks very much but I must go. I must get this thing settled."

Nook had returned to the room. There was a haziness in his eyes as though he had been crying. Piers gave him a quick look.

"How did you get on at school to-day?" he asked.

"All right, Daddy. But I wish I could have lessons with Adeline, the way I used to."

Piers looked almost pathetically at Renny. "Where did I get such a son?" he demanded. "He'd rather have lessons with little girls than go to a good boys' school."

"I don't think it's that, Piers," said his wife. "I think it's because he is naturally studious and Alayne makes lessons so interesting."

"It's unnatural," said Piers, and looked sternly down into the little face. "Why were you crying?"

"W-wasn't crying, Daddy."

"Come — don't lie!"

"It's his locomotive," said Pheasant. "I'm afraid Philip has broken it."

Piers looked more kindly at Nook. "If he has broken it you should give him a good punch. Bring it here and I'll see if I can mend it."

Nook flew upstairs, followed by Philip, shouting — "I'll get there first!"

"Well, I must be off," said Renny.

"It's getting dark and blowing harder than ever. Do stay to supper."

"Yes," added Piers. "Then I'll drive you home. I'd like to be there when you break the news."

"Thanks. I'd rather walk, with the roads like this."

He had an unaccountable nervousness of motorcars and, as he strode homeward through the early dusk, he found the exercise in the biting wind not unpleasant. There was a clear saffron streak in the sky and, above it, a pale blue radiance, a promise that Spring was soon to draw back the curtain from her wonders. It seemed to Renny that there was a different quality to the wind in the last hour. It was biting as ever but there was a certain erratic playfulness in it, as though it had new ideas in its head. Then, out of the sky, came the loud cawing of crows. He saw their black shapes blown from a grove of pines and scattered like leaves across the pale clear space. They were the first birds of spring, reckless and rowdy. Whatever sweet-singing birds came after, these were the heralds and bore the soul-piercing news.

"It is spring!" thought Renny, tramping through the icy slush with his ears tingling and his nose almost raw. Every branch was as bare as a bone, the ground was frozen to a depth of two feet, but the crows never lied.

"Caw — caw — caw!" they shouted and swung on the wind, made flails of their wings and fairly threshed the floor of the sky, took beak-dives, then strained their lungs to shout, "Caw — caw — caw — caw!" Night was falling and it was time they had found a perch, but they did not care. They streamed along the wind, rioting sable gangsters, with all heaven open to them.

"God," thought Renny, "I shall see spring in Ireland!"

The whole icy, windy, slippery scene about him vanished and he saw himself in County Meath, with billowy clouds floating low, the hawthorn in bloom, a bright-green paddock surrounded by white railings and his Cousin Dermot coming across it to meet him, leading Johnny the Bird. A tender smile softened his features. A quick fire of exhilaration pierced his being and the smile became a grin.

Down in a hollow, overflowing with evergreen trees, he could see the orange squares which were the windows of his sister's house. For a moment he had a mind to go there and tell Meg and Maurice the news. He had a feeling that they would be sympathetic, but then, his feelings were not always right and he decided to go home. He was far from certain that he would meet with sympathy *there* but go he must eventually, so, with the grin still lightening his face, he turned his steps in that direction.

He heard a small scrabbling on the road behind him and looked round to see Piers's wire-haired terrier, Biddy, at his heels. Since puppyhood she had had an infatuation for him, greatly to Piers's chagrin. She had tried to follow him when he left the house but Piers had stopped her. Renny could imagine how, at the first opening of the door, she had slid out into the dusk. She was panting violently but delighted with her achievement. He bent to pet her. "Little devil," he said.

But her companionship was pleasant. It was a lonely thing to be on a road without a dog. She kept up a methodical jog trot at his heels. It was as though she were tied to him. He opened a gate and crossed a field so rough with snow which had melted and frozen again that he picked up the terrier and tucked her under his arm. She gave his nose a quick lick of gratitude.

It was the first time this year he had taken the short cut and the walking was even worse than he had expected. But he had the feeling of spring in his blood and this was his gesture of welcome to it.

From the field he entered a bare oakwood and from there, quite suddenly, charming grounds surrounding the small house where his uncle, Ernest Whiteoak, lived. Ernest's wife was Renny's wife's aunt, so the relationship was doubly close. He had a mind to go in and see them but he knew that, once he got inside the door, their interest in what he had to tell them would be so great and Uncle Ernest would have so many reminiscences of bygone meetings with Dermot Court that it would be a long time before he could get out again. Instinct told him to be on time for dinner that night.

He drew near the lighted window of the living room and could see the two sitting happily by a table where tea things were placed. Uncle Ernest's long fair face was animated as he talked, while Aunt Harriet regarded him admiringly out of round, intelligent eyes. The waves of her silvery hair looked lovely in the lamplight. Biddy ran on to the porch and began to scratch at the door. With a stride Renny had her by the scruff, tucked her under his arm once more, and half walked, half slithered and slipped, down the steep path into the ravine where the stream lay curled beneath a bolster of snow. Pillows of snow propped the rustic bridge that spanned the stream and, as the snow pressed in over the tops of his boots, he said to the terrier: —

"I guess you wish you 'd stayed at home, Biddy."

Not she. She strained upward to reach his face with her cold little muzzle. She was excited and pleased. She was no longer young but she had a great zest for life. He hugged her to him.

At the top of the rise on the far side of the ravine he stood for a moment to get his breath. A low wicket gate was in front of him and beyond it his own house standing among its trees, the wide lawn showing patches of earth through the snow, the windows shining in the dark bulk of the house. He never came on it suddenly like this without his inmost being dilating, as it were, to receive that sight in its fullness. The house, though substantial, might have been unimpressive to many a man and no more than the solid residence of solid people, but it was to him the very distillation of all that his life and the lives of his forbears had stood for. Here they had been born, had lived, loved, and suffered. Here they had carried on their traditions in a changing world. Here he would live as long as he had life in him and, if he had his way, his children after him. Even a multimillionaire with half-a-dozen mansions might, after his first glance, have discovered something unique in the old house. For it was certain that the highly individualistic people who had lived there had left some mark of their sojourn. There was something in the way its chimneys gave their smoke, in the way the roof leaned down to the porch and the porch raised itself to shield the front door from intrusion, in the way the staunch network of the old Virginia creeper clasped the brick walls, marking the place where every new leaf would spread its greenness, in the very way in which two bare branches of a pine played an unmusical but stubbornly vigorous tune, that spoke of character and continuance.

When he stepped into the hall he was met by a very old spaniel, a young sheep dog, and a bulldog who rose from their happy roasting by the almost red-hot stove to welcome him. He bent to touch their heads and Biddy, whom he still held under his arm, bared her small teeth in a grimace of warning. She could not bear at that moment to share his affection.

Renny heard his wife's step. She appeared at the top of the stairs and began slowly to descend.

"Oh, hullo," he said, and moved to the side of the banister, holding up his face for a kiss.

She leant over and gave him one, with the air of depositing it lightly on his cheek. There was something faintly defensive about her as though she were not certain what the tone of their meeting would be.

Casting his mind quickly back to their last meeting he remembered some slight disagreement, though what it was he could not recall. Nothing very serious, he was sure. He set down Biddy. She moved growling among the larger dogs, who sniffed her with tolerant amusement.

Alayne scanned his face with an almost fierce pleasure in having him back in the house with her, for the day had been long and uneventful and she had had trouble with the children. She pretended that she did not notice the large clots of snow that had come in on his boots. He saw, however, that she did and exclaimed: —

" By George, I forgot to wipe my boots! I came home through the ravine and the snow is deep, I can tell you. It was right over their tops."

He sat down on the step below her and pulled off his boots. Fresh clots of snow fell out of them and she could see that his gray woolen stockings were wet. She said: —

" It does n't help things to take them off here, does it?"

Quickly he snatched up the clots of snow and returned them to the empty boots. He then padded to the front door, opened it, and deposited them in the porch. The four dogs, thinking he was going out again, jostled each other through the door and he closed it on them.

" How is Uncle Nick?" he asked.

A shadow darkened her eyes. It was strange that his first question should be about his uncle and not as to how she had spent *her* day.

" Very well, I think," she answered, coolly. " Uncle Ernest spent most of the afternoon with him. Then some papers came from England and a letter from Wakefield."

" Good." He came back to her and took her in his arms, holding her close. She clung to him, feeling at once passionate love and a kind of anger. She passed her hand over her hair, smoothing it. He saw the silver among its bright fairness, and gave it a quick caress with his lips.

" Sweet girl," he murmured.

Linked together, they went into the drawing-room, where a fire was burning low on the hearth. Nicholas had left his newspapers scattered about. To Alayne the room looked uninviting and felt chilly, but to Renny it was a haven of exemplary neatness and warmth. He sat down and stretched his feet toward the fire.

" I 'll run up and get your shoes," she said.

He caught at her skirt but she eluded him.

"No, no," he said, "I'll get them myself."

She was back with them in a moment and put them on him one after the other.

"You have feet just like your grandmother," she said.

He was pleased. "Have I?"

She sat down beside him and he asked the question she had been waiting for.

"What have you been doing this afternoon?"

Because it was at the end of a long winter and because her activities were seldom of the intellectual sort she would have liked, a note of complaint came into her voice.

"No need to ask me what I have been doing. The same old round. How thankful I shall be when this slush and sleet are over and the children can play outside. The noise they have made to-day has been appalling, and as for lessons — well, I feel sometimes that I must just throw up the job. It takes too much out of me. When Nook was here it was often quite fun for he enjoyed the work. I really think we shall have to send Adeline to boarding school."

He gave her a horrified look. "But Meg never went to boarding school!"

"I don't see what that has to do with Adeline. She's an entirely different type."

At this moment he did not want to oppose Alayne in any way so he sat silent, looking into the fire, his mouth down at the corners.

"Oh, well," she said, "I suppose I can go on for a while longer. Spring will soon be here. As a matter of fact, Adeline did not give me as much trouble to-day as Archer." She saw his stern look and added hastily — "It was mostly a matter of fidgeting. He just could n't keep still."

Renny took one of her smooth white hands in his. "If the kids bother you," he said, "I'll skin them alive"

The barbaric threat comforted her, though to see him lay a hand on them was dreadful to her.

He asked rather abruptly — "Is there anything decent on at the theatre? We might go. Or would you rather see a picture?"

"*Candida* is being played. I was going to speak of it, but I know you hate Shaw."

"Well, I should like to see that one, as Wake has played in it. Let 's get tickets. I 'll ring up the theatre now."

He sprang up impulsively and crossed the hall to the sitting room. She heard him talking loudly over the telephone and she ran into the room and shut the door so the children could not hear his voice and come running down to him. She stood behind him. She saw the admirable set of his head on his shoulders as he telephoned, and how his close-cut red hair was not yet even touched by gray. She heard him order five of the best seats and would have rushed to stop him but, possibly conscious of this contingency, he hung up the receiver with a triumphant bang and turned to face her.

"Are you crazy?" she asked.

"Not at all. I want to give a little theatre party. That 's all. I 've been thinking of it for some time. Uncle Nicholas loves a good play. Aunt Harriet and Uncle Ernest both admire Shaw. We 'll have dinner in town and make an evening of it."

"But those seats! You need not have bought such expensive ones."

"No use in taking Uncle Nick anywhere but in front. He 'd not hear a word."

"Yes, that 's so."

He looked at her anxiously.

"You 're pleased, are n't you?"

"Of course." But she had a sharp stab of disappointment. She wanted to go alone with him. Just the two of them! His solicitude for these old people was sometimes deeply irritating to her. But she forced herself to conceal it.

They had barely reseated themselves in front of the fire when the dogs began to scratch on the front door and raise their voices in complaint. Renny sprang up to let them in. Alayne never had got used to his way of turning repose into lively action at a moment's notice, just the way the children did, and felt that she never could.

The dogs came in, talking of the cold and wet outside. Biddy looked in at the drawing-room door but when Alayne cried "No!" she turned away and leaped on to a chair in the hall. Uncle Nicholas could be heard coming heavily down the stairs. He came slowly and carefully, leaning on the banister, for he would be eighty-eight on his next birthday and had been a victim of gout for many years. In truth none of the family but himself remembered the time when his knee had not troubled him. His brother, Ernest, could have remembered but it was easier to think of Nicholas so afflicted because he had somehow fitted this affliction into his strong personality.

Renny went to meet him and the old man leaned heavily as he made his way to his accustomed chair.

"Hullo, dogs," he mumbled under his drooping gray moustache. "Hullo, dogs! Been out in the fresh air, eh? Lucky dogs! Hullo, Biddy! Over here again? Your master will have it in for you, old girl. Now then — let me down, Renny! Ha — this weather plays the devil with me!"

He smiled at Alayne, who had to smile back, though the moment before she had been thinking somewhat grudgingly of his presence at the theatre party.

"Well, and what have you been doing this afternoon, sir?" he demanded of his nephew.

"I've had a busy day. One thing on top of another. I think I have a likely purchaser for the bay colt. Alayne and I have just arranged a theatre party for to-morrow night.

I hope you 'll enjoy seeing *Candida.* It 's the play Wakefield acted in, you know."

"Yes," said Nicholas, gravely, "I remember."

"Mr. Shaw would be flattered!" exclaimed Alayne.

Nicholas beamed. "I shall be delighted to go. How kind of you two!"

"It was Renny's thought."

"No it was n't! You said yourself you 'd been thinking of it."

How generous he was! Any irritation she had felt toward him was gone. She had a sudden exhilaration in the prospect of to-morrow night. She smiled happily at the two men. Though she had lived so many years at Jalna she had not made friends in the neighborhood. She had begun by considering it a backwater and feeling impatient of its Victorian traditions. The old neighbors were not intellectual and, when newcomers did appear among them, the Whiteoaks held themselves aloof and she did not meet them. Nor did she want to. She had always been of a reserved nature and though she deplored the self-sufficiency of the Whiteoaks, it suited her better than she knew. Yet it was her fate often to be longing for what she would not put out her hand to acquire.

A sound of rushing steps and a clamor of children's voices came from the top of the stairs. It grew nearer like a rushing wind, inexorable and boisterous, till the three children were in the room. They were Alayne's and Renny's two children and the child of Renny's brother, Eden, who was dead and who had been Alayne's first husband. She had divorced him and married Renny. Now the presence of his child in her home was an unhappy reminder to Alayne, of Eden. The child had his coloring and his smile that sat oddly on her little face. Though Alayne thought of herself as modern and widely tolerant, her upbringing had been somewhat puritanical and she judged others, more often than she guessed, by the standards of her forbears. So little Roma's irregular birth would have made a barrier between her and Alayne if nothing else had. Alayne saw her as set apart from her own children — first as Eden's child, second as the offspring of Eden's connection with that laughing English girl of few morals, Minny Ware.

The boy of the little group was four-year-old Archer. That had been Alayne's maiden name and it was an annoyance to her that Renny should call him Archie. And of course, since Renny did, Adeline imitated and was being constantly reprimanded for it. He himself, proud of his name and wishing to emphasize it, pronounced it with a strong accent on the last syllable which was almost as irritating to his mother as the abbreviation.

As the greater part of his days was spent with girls much older than himself Archer had to make the most of his masculinity. He was very straight and the straightness was exaggerated by his carrying his chest high and his neck rigid. His face was inclined to thinness but his arms and legs were sturdy, so that the pedestal of his small being looked firm indeed. He had fair hair, not sleek and glossy like Nook's or fluffy like Roma's, but dry and rather stiff. His forehead was high and white and beneath it his blue eyes looked out with an expression almost piercing. This expression seldom changed. He seemed to be searching for something and determined not to rest till he found it. His lips were thin and his mouth wide and usually turned down at the corners. When he did smile his look was sweet and rather surprised, as though he had not believed himself capable of being amused. He was the apple of Alayne's eye and her constant annoyance. As an infant he had been perfect. She had thought of him as the reincarnation of her beloved father. But, as he developed, he was often an enigma. She could not believe that her father had ever behaved in such a way. She could only believe that he had inherited some perverse strain from the Whiteoaks or the Courts, and she spent many of her waking hours in trying gently to eradicate it and lost sleep over it at night. However Archer went his own way with a kind of blind persistence. He apparently had some scheme of life, known only to himself, which he felt obliged to follow, no matter what suffering it caused to himself or others.

He was a source of amusement to nine-year-old Adeline, partly as a human being and partly because she saw that his behavior was the cause of grave concern to their mother. This was not so much from cruelty as from a mischievous pleasure in the antics of the little brother who, till he was nearly four, had been held up to her as a paragon of goodness and on whom endearments were lavished which had never been bestowed on her.

She was her father's darling and she knew it. She knew that she was the image of the great-grandmother whose portrait, in a yellow satin evening dress, hung in the dining room. Her great-uncles never let her forget that she had the same dark red hair, the same brilliant brown eyes, the same milk-white skin and scarlet lips as were depicted in the portrait. She had the same nose, too, and the same temper. She did not know from where she had got her abounding vitality, for she did not know that she possessed it. She only knew that she could ride for hours on a spirited horse and at the end be ready for any kind of wildness. Yet she could on occasion be quiet and even contemplative and sometimes showed real self-restraint. Toward the younger, weaker Roma, she was generous and protective.

"Children! Children!" exclaimed Alayne. "I wish you would n't come into the room like that."

"But it 's the first time I 've seen Daddy since early morning," said Adeline. She got on to his knee and clasped his neck tightly. She kissed him again and again on the mouth. Roma went and sat on one of the beaded ottomans near the fire. She moved constantly on it as though it were her will to rub the beads off.

"Roma!" cried Alayne. "Please get off that ottoman. It has a lovely covering and it is being ruined."

"Little rascal," said Nicholas, looking sternly at the child.

Roma held herself suspended above a chair. "Has this a lovely covering?" she asked.

"Come and sit on my other knee," said Renny. "Nothing can hurt it." He looked sternly at his son. "And what have you been up to to-day?"

Archer, for a reason known only to himself, had lately decided that he wanted to be a baby again. Now he held up both hands, in a feeble, flapping kind of way, and tottered across the room. He lisped, in a nasal whine:—

"Can't walk yet. Somebody help Archer walk."

This was painful to Alayne but Renny grinned from ear to ear. He asked:—

"How old are you, then?"

"Don't know," whined Archer. "Can't walk yet. Want a bottle to thuck."

"Archer," said Alayne sternly, "come here." She reached out and drew him to her. He took one of her hands and began to gnaw at it in a toothless way. "Thumthing to thuck," he urged.

"Do you want to go straight back upstairs?" she asked.

He began an affected imitation of an infant's wail.

Renny stretched out a leg and poked him in the seat with his toe. "Come," he said, "enough of that!"

Archer continued to make infantile noises and mouth Alayne's hand. She rose and took him by the arm. "Very well," she said, "you must go upstairs, I am afraid."

"Archer can't walk. Give Archer a pickaback."

She bent over him and whispered in his ear.

"Give him a good smack," suggested Nicholas.

Archer, propelled by Alayne, took a few wobbling steps into the hall. Out there he shouted in his own loud voice: —

"I won't go up! I want to stay with Daddy!"

"If I come after you, you 'll be sorry," called out Renny.

From the drawing-room they could hear Archer stamping up the stairs, yelling as he went.

Renny scarcely knew what was going on about him, his mind was so occupied by the problem of how he should break the news of his proposed trip to Ireland. He heard Nicholas's voice rumbling on and on. He felt the two little girls snuggling warm against his breast.

Adeline said — "I do like the smell of you when you 've been in the stables, washed your hands with Windsor soap, then walked in the frosty air."

Roma snuffed, and declared — "I like your smell best when you 've just shaved and had a smoke."

Renny hugged them to him. "What would you think of me if I won the Grand National?"

"It would be the happiest day of my life," said Adeline.

"What is the Grand National?" asked Roma.

"It 's the greatest race in the world, little silly," said Adeline.

Suddenly Renny pushed them from him and leaned toward his uncle.

"Look here, Uncle Nick. Read these. I had them to-day." He handed him the two cablegrams.

Nicholas put on his spectacles and read them. It took him some minutes to absorb their import.

"What 's it all about? Oh yes, a horse. Dermot Court, eh? Wants to sell you a horse, eh? No, no, don't you do it! I would n't trust any Court, when it comes to a horse deal."

"My God, Uncle — he does n't want to sell me a horse! He 's recommending one to me."

"Who owns it? Malahide? Worse still."

"No. A farmer named Madigan."

"What a cable that boy Wakefield sent! It's like a letter. He could have said it in half the words."

Renny replied testily — "He had to make it clear and he had to make it urgent. What do you think of the idea?"

Nicholas took off his spectacles and stared at Renny from under his shaggy brows.

"I think it's a very foolish scheme. I don't like it at all. Five hundred guineas is a lot to risk."

"I know. And I'd never do it without seeing the horse first."

As he said these words Alayne returned to the room leading Archer by the hand. She said: —

"Archer says he will be quiet and good, if someone will play a game of dominoes with him. Will you, Adeline?"

"I want to hear about the horse."

"I'll play with him," said Roma.

"Thank you, dear," said Alayne, but her eyes were cold as they rested on the child's face.

"Archie!" exclaimed Renny.

Archer turned his piercing gaze on him.

"Do you know what the Grand National is?"

"It's a steeplechase!" He began to gallop about the room, leaping imaginary obstacles.

"Good legs, has n't he?" observed Renny. "Go it, old boy!"

"Roma, will you *please* take him to play dominoes?" said Alayne.

"Yes, Auntie Alayne."

But Archer prostrated himself on the floor.

"I'm down," he said, "I'm hurt."

Alayne went to him, her face tense but her voice gentle.

"Archer, darling, you must get up."

He began to rock rhythmically on the floor, as in a cradle.

"I 'm a baby," he lisped. "Ca-an't walk. Give me pickaback!"

Adeline stood smiling.

"You make him worse," said Alayne angrily. "Stop smiling at him instantly. You do it purposely."

Renny sprang up. "Come, Archie!" He caught up his son and threw him to his shoulder. "Come, Roma." He took the children to the sitting room.

"Adeline has such a tormenting spirit," said Alayne to Nicholas.

"She inherited it from Mamma," he answered complacently. "Mamma always enjoyed the discomfiture of weaker natures."

Alayne thought — "Smug old man! Everything the family does is right. I feel half-suffocated by them all tonight." She passed her hand across her forehead.

"Headache, my dear?" inquired Nicholas, solicitously. "No wonder. This weather is appalling."

Renny returned with Adeline clinging to his arm. He had overheard his uncle's words and he too gave Alayne a sympathetic look. He said: —

"I quite agree. For my part I 've never been so affected by weather. I don't know what is the matter with me." He sat down, rested an elbow on a knee and his head on his hand.

If the cast-iron stove in the hall had come into the room and announced that the weather was affecting it, Nicholas and Alayne could scarcely have been more surprised. Alayne asked: —

"When did you begin to feel like this? Does your head ache? Do you think you have a temperature?"

"I just feel seedy. A sort of lassitude." The word, on his lips, was terrible.

Alayne sprang up, came to him and put her hand on his forehead.

Nicholas remarked — "You ate a hearty lunch."

"Yes. I did."

"When did you have tea?" asked Alayne.

"I had none."

"Would you like some now?"

"No, thanks. I believe I 'll have a whiskey and soda."

"Have you got a chill?" asked Nicholas.

"No. There 's not much wrong with me. I guess I need a change. I 've thought so for some time. Do you know, —" he turned to Alayne, with an ingratiating smile, — "I have it in my mind to go to Ireland."

"To Ireland!" she repeated, on a suddenly suspicious note. "But why?"

He tightened his arm about her. "Well, for one thing, the climate agrees with me and for another I promised dear old Dermot Court, in 1919, that I 'd go back to see him before he died. I 've just heard from him and he wants me, most particularly, to go over soon." His eyes had a deep light of sincerity in them. His mouth took on the lines of classic truth.

Nicholas made deep unintelligible noises inside himself. He made as though to hand the cablegrams to Alayne, then changed his mind and stuffed them into his pocket. After all, they were n't his to show and if Renny chose to approach the matter from a sentimental angle, let him.

"Is Daddy ill?" asked Adeline.

"Ask him," answered Nicholas. "I 'm inclined to think it 's a kind of horse fever."

"Did he catch it in the stables?"

"Partly. And partly inherited it. It 's incurable but not fatal. Except to the family of the afflicted one."

"Now you 're talking rubbish," Adeline said.

Alayne firmly detached herself from Renny.

"Really," she said. "I wish you would tell me what all this is about."

Renny answered, "It 's quite true that I need a change.

It 's quite true that I promised Dermot Court I would go back to Ireland to see him. It is also true that there is a horse for sale who has got it in him to win the Grand National."

The sympathy that had softened her features fled, leaving them sharpened, her eyes intense.

" I do wish," she said, " that you would be candid."

" I am candid."

" You made me believe that you were not well, when all that was wrong was your craving to see this horse. Uncle Nicholas, do help me persuade him not to do this! It 's insane. How much do they ask you to pay for the horse? "

" Only five hundred guineas," he answered.

" Five hundred guineas! " Angry color flooded her face and she added bitterly — " I have seen you at your wit's end for five hundred *dollars*."

" I know," he answered quietly. " But things are better now and I count myself fortunate that I can spare the money to buy this horse. Now listen, Alayne, let me read these cables to you. When you hear them you 'll understand — "

" I 'll not listen to them," she retorted. " I know only too well what they contain. If you go to Ireland and see this horse, you will buy it. It 's as certain as that I am standing here. You will spend any amount of money in having it trained. But it won't win the race. It will break its leg or its neck or some woman will kill it — like that other one was killed! "

He looked at her, speechless, too astonished for words. Then he said, his lip trembling a little: —

" That was unkind of you, Alayne."

She turned away and went to the window. There was blackness outside, and the sound of rain. Wragge, the houseman, came in and put coals on the fire. He went about drawing curtains. She moved from the window and went to the mantelpiece and laid her hands on it.

When Wragge had gone, Renny said — " Now I 'll tell you what I 'll do. The family is coming to dinner on Sunday. This is Friday. We 'll talk the thing over and, if the majority is set against it, I 'll give up the idea. But I warn you I shall be throwing away one of the best chances of my life."

Already Nicholas was beginning to weaken. He said: —

" By gad, I never knew Dermot to back a horse that was not a sound one! The only timc Ernest ever won a pot of money at the races was on a tip he got from Dermot. Does Ernest know about this horse? "

Affection for his uncles shone in Renny's eyes. He felt that they would be on his side. Pheasant already was. Piers could be won over. Meg was easily caught up by his enthusiasms. That left just Maurice and Aunt Harriet and he anticipated little opposition from them.

"I don't want any family conclave about the matter," said Alayne. "If you 've made up your mind to go, go."

" I have not made up my mind and I want to hear what the family thinks about it."

With her back still toward him she said: —

" All the family knows that when your mind is made up to buy a horse nothing will stop you. Adeline, run off to the other children."

Adeline spoke breathlessly. " Daddy, if you go to Ireland, may I go with you? "

" I 'm not at all sure if I 'm going," he returned.

" Adeline, I asked you to leave the room."

" I think I might be answered that one little question."

" Really, you are ridiculous."

" Why? "

" To speak of an ocean voyage as a little thing."

" I did n't."

" *Will* you leave the room? " There was such tension

in Alayne's voice that both men were startled. When the child had gone, Nicholas rumbled: —

" End of a long winter. Hard on nerves."

Alayne thought — " I cannot have a few words with my husband in private. And I 'm losing all my self-restraint. But it 's no wonder. Adeline is exactly like them. She 's unbearable. That look she gave Renny before she left the room . . ."

" I 'm willing to bet," said Renny, " that Uncle Ernest and Aunt Harriet will say I ought at least to see the horse — to say nothing of keeping my promise to Dermot Court. I 'll say nothing more about my need of a change of air. I 've survived a good many winters and I dare say I shall survive this."

Alayne laid her forehead against the mantelpiece and began to laugh. Nicholas joined in.

" You think," said Renny, " that because I look as hard as nails I have no feeling. Well, perhaps I shall surprise you some day."

Alayne turned and faced him.

" How can you say such things ! "

" I think I 'm justified."

" Nonsense ! " said Nicholas. " Alayne and I are merely envious of your health."

Wragge sounded the gong in the hall. The dogs, once more established about the stove, rose to their feet as one and stretched. The noise of the gong had hurt Biddy's head. She raised her high soprano in a howl. The bobtailed sheep dog joined in, his voice seeming to emanate through all his shaggy coat. But the bulldog, his under jaw projecting in an expression of intensely masculine scorn, led the way toward the dining room. Alayne forestalled them.

" No," she said, firmly, " I can't have you in here. Your coats smell in this weather. Please don't let them in, Wragge."

She said nothing, however, against Renny's sixteen-year-old blind spaniel Merlin, already lying by the side of his chair.

Adeline was the only one of the children who shared the evening meal with the grownups. She sat very upright, facing Nicholas, whose gaze frequently was raised from her small face, surrounded by its mass of dark red hair, to the portrait of his mother behind her. Her eyes flew from the face of one parent to the other, her partisanship of Renny showing in the smile that curved her lips when she looked at him, and the wary look that came into her eyes when they met her mother's.

Alayne was determined there should be no discussion at the table. Mealtime at Jalna had too often been the field of heated argument and she was striving to uproot this long-established habit while her children were still young. Renny knew what was in her mind and somewhat taciturnly applied himself to his broiled chop. He gave it the extra dose of Worcester sauce which Adeline had learned to associate with the mood he was now in. She stretched out a leg that was growing long, and gave him a little poke with her toe beneath the table. He flashed her a look of understanding and, as their eyes met, an electric vibration caused Alayne to give them both a cool, detached glance. But she began to talk cheerfully of an article she had been reading, in an American weekly, on the situation in Europe. Nicholas was interested and they bore the conversation between them. Wragge waited solicitously on Renny as he always did in crises such as this.

The telephone rang in the next room. Wragge hurried to answer it. It was Aunt Harriet wanting to speak to Renny. He rose with alacrity as though a telephone talk in the middle of this meal were a relief. Those sitting at table could hear all he said.

"Oh, yes, Aunt Harriet," he was saying, "I'll have the roof attended to at once. A pity it leaked on your best bed.

Yes, I 'll come round and look at it myself. I want to talk to you in any case. I want Uncle Ernie's opinion — and of course yours too — about two cables I 've had from the Old Country. One is from Wakefield. He 's getting on fine. He 's been to Ireland to see a most extraordinary horse. It has a great future ahead of it. . . . Yes, it is interesting, is n't it? Our cousin, Dermot Court, — Uncle Ernie must have spoken of him to you, — is frightfully keen about this horse. He urges me to let nothing stand in the way of my seeing it — not even the ocean! Ha, ha! But I don't expect to go across — even though it 's the chance of a lifetime. . . . Would you? But of course you 're one woman in a thousand. Ha! Ha! Yes, I know you would. What do you suppose young Adeline wants? She wants to go with me, *if* I go! But there 's not much likelihood of a change for yours truly. . . . Yes, I still have a bit of a cough. But it 's nothing. I 'm as strong as a horse. It 's Alayne who needs a change. I wish she would go South. You and she might go together, eh? . . . Yes, it would be a wonderful thing for Adeline to go to the Old Country. She 's old enough now to appreciate it. Oh, well, perhaps the day will come. It 's lucky you rang up. I was wanting to speak to you. Alayne and I are having a little theatre party to-morrow night and we want you and Uncle Ernie to join us. *Candida.* Is that highbrow enough for you? You 're a New England intellectual, are n't you? Or once were. . . . No longer one, eh! No wonder, living among us! Well, whatever you are, you suit me!" There was a long silence while Aunt Harriet apparently relieved herself of much pent-up desire for conversation. Occasionally he made small noises of appreciation or gave a chuckle. Wragge had removed his plate from the table to keep his chop warm. Nicholas had made no attempt to eat but had sat with his hand curved about his ear determined to hear what was being said in the next room. Drops of moisture gleamed on the ends of his gray moustache and the shapely old hand lying on the tablecloth trembled a little.

Leaning toward Alayne, he asked — "Are they coming? Is he going?"

"I have no idea," she returned remotely.

Adeline answered, "Yes, they 're coming, Uncle Nick, and I think — I 'm pretty sure — he 's going."

"You have no reason for making either statement," said Alayne.

"I guessed by the way he spoke."

"Please don't speak of your father as *he*."

Adeline looked daring. "Renny, then."

"Now you 're being just silly."

Renny returned to the room.

Nicholas demanded, without waiting to swallow a mouthful of peas, "Are they pleased about the play? And what do they think of your going to Ireland?"

"Aunt Harriet is delighted to go to *Candida*. As to the other, well — she 's not unsympathetic. Rags, my dinner!"

Wragge placed it before him as though he were an invalid. Renny shot a quick glance at Alayne. "Sorry to have interrupted the meal," he said.

"It does n't matter." She was thinking, with a good deal of irritation, of her Aunt Harriet. Just a few years ago Harriet Archer had been a typical New England spinster of the intellectual sort, elderly, well-turned-out, with an admirable, though not stiff-necked, loyalty to her traditions. Her investments had gone wrong. She had lost almost all she had. Renny Whiteoak had invited her to spend the rest of her life at Jalna. There she had met Ernest and he and she had found each other so congenial that they had made a match of it.

This was all very well and Alayne had been happy for her aunt's sake. What she could not understand was her aunt's desire to remodel herself on the Whiteoak design. Aunt Harriet, of course, denied that she had. She simply said that her new environment had brought out a latent something in herself. The very traits in the family which most irritated Alayne were interesting or amusing or even admirable to her aunt. To Alayne there was something affected in this. She did not believe in Aunt Harriet's sincerity. She thought Harriet was posing and she hated poseurs.

So their relations, though affectionate, were not so sympathetic as they once had been. Alayne was quite prepared to find her aunt favorable to Renny's scheme and surprised at her own opposition to it.

The theatre party was to have dinner in town. Uncle Ernest and Aunt Harriet appeared at Jalna promptly at five o'clock. Ernest was always glad of the opportunity to wear evening clothes, and he wore them extremely well. A man of sixty might well have been proud of the slender, upright figure of him, at eighty-five. His wife, many years younger, was a pretty sight in a black velvet evening gown, with jade necklace and earrings which had once graced the person of old Adeline Whiteoak. Her silvery hair was charmingly curled and her neat features and clear blue eyes expressed almost girlish anticipation.

Nicholas, Renny, and Alayne rose to greet them. There was a pleasant flutter of excitement in the room. Alayne put aside her misgivings and prepared to enjoy the evening.

"Well, my boy," Ernest said to his brother, "and how are you? You 're looking very well, considering the weather."

Nicholas drew him aside. He said — "Alayne 's greatly upset over the Irish Question. If he takes that trip and buys that horse and loses that race, she 'll be a sick woman, and no wonder!"

Ernest smiled tolerantly. "He 'll not lose the race. I

have implicit trust in Dermot Court. I shall never forget the tip he gave me. I should not hesitate, if I were a few years younger, to buy the horse myself."

Nicholas was impressed. "Well, well, you 'd better say something like that to Alayne."

Harriet took Renny's hands in hers and stood on tiptoe to kiss him on the chin.

"All our good wishes go with you, my dear!" she exclaimed.

Renny was embarrassed. "Nothing is settled yet."

"Oh, yes, it is," put in Alayne, with a sharp tremor in her voice. "Everything is settled. Everything was settled from the moment the cables came. Don't let any qualms of mine cramp your style!"

"Alayne, darling," said Harriet earnestly, "you must not feel like that."

"I should try to feel that all is for the best, eh?"

Harriet colored slightly. "I never could stand up against sarcasm. But I do feel that, from what I know of Dermot Court, we owe it to ourselves to take his advice."

"Yes, indeed," agreed her husband, "it 's the chance of a lifetime."

"Hmph, well," mumbled Nicholas, "it 's a big step to take. Quite a sum involved. Egad, I 've lost my opera glasses! Wherever can they be?"

They were found for him. Coats and wraps were put on. The car was waiting and Rags ushered them out to it with his grandest air. A bright new moon was just hesitating between rising and setting above the treetops. Harriet saw to it that she was beside Renny, asking him innumerable questions about horse racing, strengthening him, as Alayne thought, in his wrongheadedness. But she had given up struggling against it. If he had made up his mind to do this thing, let him do it. There must not be coldness between them. Better anything than that. A mistiness dimmed her eyes. As he was helping her from the car she said softly: —

" If your heart is set on this trip I want you to go."

He gave a delighted smile. He drew her for a second against his side.

" Really? "

" Yes."

" And you will come with me? You must! "

"At this time of year! Nothing would induce me. You know what a bad sailor I am."

Ernest was saying — " There 's a new feeling in the air to-night. Spring is certainly on the way. I hear an orchestra playing. I do enjoy a dinner party in an hotel, don't you, Harriet? "

" There 's nothing I like better," she said stoutly.

Nicholas exclaimed, " My opera glasses! Egad, I 've left 'em in the car! "

Renny tore after the car, bareheaded. Looking after him, Alayne thought: —

" The darling! "

II

THE MEETING AT THE PREYDE THEATRE

A MONTH before Wakefield sent the cable, he had not even known of the horse's existence. He was *entirely* concerned with his determination to be interviewed by Ninian Fox — Fox of the Preyde, as he was generally called.

The Preyde Theatre was in one of the network of streets all of which seem eventually to lead into the Strand. It was small but not obscure, for its manager was enterprising and, while he often had failures, Ninian Fox occasionally produced a West End success. At this moment he was precariously recovering from two failures, one of them the translation of a macabre foreign play, the other an ambitious historical drama by a new author. He was consequently, so he said, almost bankrupt and was about to risk his all on another play by an unknown author.

He was sitting in his inner office drinking a glass of whiskey and soda and looking anxiously at the well-thumbed manuscript of the play on the desk before him while his secretary, a tiny, harassed-looking young woman with a remarkably intelligent face, scanned the letters she had just typed. The month was February. Mr. Fox stretched out his hand, took a vase of hyacinths and daffodils from the window sill, and sniffed it.

" I 'm half dead," he remarked.

There was something effeminate in his way of doing this but, in his tall angular frame and straight clear-cut profile, he was entirely masculine. He had a fine head covered with thick iron-gray hair, cold blue eyes and a smile that was consciously genial but without warmth.

Miss Waite was used to his saying he was half dead and

waited politely to hear if he had anything more important to declare. He went on, "Unless I can get the right sort of young fellow to play Frederick, the thing 's a failure."

Miss Waite already knew this. She said: —

"There 's that boy I interviewed last week. He 's been here every day since. Had you perhaps better see him?"

"Do you think he might be possible?"

"He certainly would look the part. And he has a clever face but he 's not had much experience."

"You say he 's in the lobby?"

"Yes."

"H'm. Well — bring him in."

In the lobby Miss Waite found the young man walking nervously up and down. A young girl was sitting very upright on a small chair, by a small table, her handbag clasped tightly in her thin hands. She started and half rose when she saw Miss Waite.

"Does Mr. Fox want to see me?" she asked.

"Not yet. He wants to see the young man. What did you say your name is?" She turned from the girl's tense pale face to his eager one.

"Whiteoak. Wakefield Whiteoak. I 'm terribly anxious to play the part of Frederick. I 'm sure I can do it. I feel that I *am* Frederick."

Miss Waite had often heard this sort of thing from young actors and a look of pessimism on her small face chilled his warmth. But she said politely, "Please come this way. Mr. Fox is waiting."

The young girl pressed forward.

"Do you think there 's any chance of his seeing me?"

"Not this morning." Miss Waite's voice was dry. Then something in the girl's eyes touched her and she added, "I 'll find out if there 's any possibility and let you know."

"Oh, thank you. Thank you."

Young Wakefield Whiteoak threw her a swift look. It

was not the first he had given her. He had even tried to talk to her but she had been too nervous and too shy for conversation with a stranger. But now she met his look that was so full of friendliness and admiration, and she smiled in return.

"Good luck," she said.

Mr. Fox's glance was appraising as he shook hands with Wakefield. He looked coldly pleased.

"Physically," he said, "you are all right for the part. But so many young men are. What experience have you had?"

"Not a great deal. I still —"

"How could you have had much, at your age?" interrupted Mr. Fox impatiently, but with his genial smile. "Just tell me what parts you 've played."

"I 've done the usual thing at the Dramatic School. I played Romeo with a company in Cornwall last summer. And I played the tutor in *A Month in the Country* at the Portal Theatre."

"Quite a good beginning! You come from Canada?"

"Yes."

"You have an interesting accent. How did you come by it?"

"As a child I lived in the house with my uncles, who were educated at Oxford, and my grandmother, who was an Irishwoman. I was educated by a clergyman but I have got something from my brother and guardian, who is a horse breeder."

Mr. Fox looked at him sharply. Was the young fellow being humorous? No, he was quite serious and evidently certain that any details concerning himself would be interesting.

"H'm, well — Miss Waite, will you please give Mr. Whiteoak Frederick's part? Let him read the bit where he discovers his sister's relations with Ransome." To

Wakefield he remarked — " This is a very fine play but it 's a terrible risk for me. No one knows what a risk. I stand to make well out of it or be ruined. I can't afford to pay much in the way of salary, you understand."

" Of course," said Wakefield sympathetically.

Mr. Fox's brow cleared a little. Miss Waite handed Wakefield the typescript. She noticed how steady his hand was and how his gravity barely concealed a look of mischief.

" I think we 'll go on to the stage," interrupted Mr. Fox. " I think both producer and author are in the theatre. We might as well have their opinion."

He finished his whiskey and soda with a sigh, bent to smell his hyacinths, then led the way in a measured walk. Just as Miss Waite and Wakefield passed through the door the telephone rang and she darted back to answer it. Mr. Fox, with an irritated frown, stopped and stared at the young girl who waited in the lobby. He remarked: —

" The telephone is a nuisance. It provides ceaseless interruptions and little convenience. Were you waiting to see me, my dear? "

The young girl had already sprung to her feet.

" Yes. Yes — please, I should very much like to see you. I mean I want terribly to do the part of Catherine. I've had quite a lot of experience. If you 'd just give me — "

Mr. Fox interrupted testily — " I 've all but engaged Geraldine Bland for the part. I 'm sorry, my dear. Perhaps in some other play I might use you. I like your looks. How old are you? "

" Eighteen."

" And your name? "

" Molly Griffith."

She spoke almost breathlessly in her eagerness. She was tall, thin, and very fair. The fineness of the bones of her face was visible because of her thinness, which approached emaciation, but her profile had a daring tilt, and her thick hair and the scatter of bronze-colored freckles on her nose gave her a look of boyish virility.

Miss Waite appeared from the lobby. Mr. Fox at once approached her and they whispered together.

"It 's that Geraldine Bland," she said. "She does n't like the part now that she 's read it carefully. There is n't enough in it for her, she says."

"Damn her," said Mr. Fox. "She seemed keen enough when I interviewed her. Damn her, and her pretensions. Take a look at this girl. Do you think she looks the part? I do. And she 's a lady, — much as I hate to use the word, — which Geraldine Thingumbob is n't."

"I like her looks," said Miss Waite. "And after all, the part of Catherine is n't frightfully important. I dare say we could get this girl for even less salary."

Mr. Fox turned briskly back to Wakefield and the girl, who stood holding themselves meekly, in readiness for his commands.

"Well, my dear," he said, "things have turned out fortunately for you. I 've just had a message from Miss Bland. She tells me that she has had another part offered her which is more in her line. I myself was n't quite satisfied with her, so I 'll give you an audition, if you 'll come along with us. You and this young man can try that bit together — where Frederick discovers his sister's affair. You should look very well together."

Cheerfully he led the way through the darkened theatre, along the aisle to some shallow steps which mounted to a doorway. Beyond it was backstage confusion, men working with ropes, lights, and props. There was pulling about and hammering, of an apparently senseless nature. Wakefield could see the girl's jaw set, in an effort to control her excitement.

"Don't be frightened," he whispered. "Everything will be all right."

"If only I thought so!" she breathed. "But so much depends on my getting this job. I've had nothing for months."

In the hard light he discovered the shabbiness of her clothes, the sharpness of her features. With a pang he thought, "She looks half-fed. When this is over I'll ask her to lunch." He whispered—"We'll get the job. You'll see."

Mr. Fox's progress was slow. Everybody wanted to ask him something. He answered all these with a pained look, as though he were convinced that the questioner was out to rob and cheat him. His ascetic profile was outlined against the dark green of a screen but his protruding corporation disclosed his fleshly tastes.

A short man, with dark hair curling about a bald spot and a top coat that reached almost to his heels, was talking to a man with sandy hair and a cigarette between his lips. They were Robert Fielding, actor and producer, and George Trimble, journalist and author of the play.

Finally Mr. Fox led the two young people to them. He said, after a formal introduction, "I want you to hear these two read a scene from the play. I want you to see what you think of them for the parts of Frederick and Catherine. I've had so many disappointments about these parts that I'm at my wit's end and willing to try anyone."

The boy and girl stood, meek and untried, looking the personification of youth and biddableness. Mr. Fielding gave them a kindly, yet pessimistic look. The author's face was a blank.

Fielding said—"Well, it's time we got things settled. The principals are getting uneasy. They want their salaries and the rehearsals to begin."

Mr. Fox groaned, as though in pain.

The author lighted a fresh cigarette from the stump of the last. Miss Waite handed some sheets of typescript to Wakefield and Molly Griffith.

" Just read those as naturally as you can," said Mr. Fox.

He, the producer and the author descended into the stalls. Miss Waite retired to the wings. One of the workmen began loudly to hammer on metal behind the scenes.

" Stop that noise! " ordered Mr. Fox.

Miss Waite appeared and disappeared. They had one glimpse of her clever, wizened face distorted by worry. Then the noise ceased.

Wakefield and the girl stood awkwardly side by side on the stage.

" This is poisonous," Wakefield said, under his breath.

" Yes," she returned. " Having to do it together, you mean."

" Well, I 'm terribly afraid I shall spoil your chances."

" I guess that we 'll stand or fall together, but my nerves are a curse."

It was true that she was shaking all over. He wondered how she would be able to make out the words on the paper that trembled in her hand. He was self-possessed on the surface but apprehensive underneath. He found the place marked by Miss Waite. The scene they had before them concerned the discovery by a youth that the sister he idealized was no better than the mother he hated. The principal part, that of the mother, was to be taken by a well-known middle-aged actress who dominated the entire play.

" Begin," said Mr. Fox.

" ' Oh, Frederick,' " the girl got out, in a small voice, " ' don't look like that! ' "

" ' Don't look like what, Cathie? ' " Wakefield's voice had a tremor of emotion in it.

" ' As though you 'd never seen me before. As though I were a kind of frightening stranger.' "

" 'You are a stranger, Cathie.' "

" 'No, no — I won't have you say that! I 'm not a stranger! I 'm just the same — only —' "

" 'I know. Don't explain. You 're like Mother.' "

" 'I 'm not! I 'm not! This is different!' "

Mr. Fox interrupted from the stalls. "Young lady! Unless you can raise your voice and speak more distinctly, there is no object in our going any further with this."

"Yes, Mr. Fox. I 'll try."

"Please begin the scene again."

The manager's shoulders and head rose imposing in the stalls. The producer slumped in his greatcoat that was too large for him. The author sat tense, his chin on his clenched hands, his sandy hair almost in his eyes. Several scenes were tried. Then, with a wave of dismissal to the young actors, Mr. Fox turned to his companions.

"Well, what do you think?"

"They might do," said Robert Fielding, warily. "What do you think yourself?"

"The girl will never be really good unless we can hammer some emotion into her. But she looks the part and has a lovely voice. The boy has good stuff in him. And, with his looks, I 'll wager he 'll end on the screen. What do you think, Mr. Trimble?"

"I think they 're perfect," he exclaimed enthusiastically.

As he had been far from enthusiastic about the casting of the play so far, even to the choice of Robert Fielding for the comic part, Mr. Fox was surprised. He was one of the few London managers with whom the opinion of the author carried weight.

"Perfect!" he repeated. "This is surprising from you."

"What I mean is, they 're convincing. They 're just fumbling with their parts, of course, but they look real — authentic. I feel that, if we searched London over, we could n't find a better Frederick and Cathie."

" I don't see it," put in Fielding, " but I think we might do worse than try them."

" I 've reached the end of my tether," said Mr. Fox. " I can't struggle any more over the casting of this play. I 'll take these two on if you want me to, but as I 've said before, it 's a play that, if not perfectly cast, can never be anything but a failure."

This was the only remark in the nature of a compliment which he ever paid to the play. A flicker of gratitude passed over the author's face. He said: —

" I don't believe we can make a mistake in engaging these two."

" And, after all, they 're minor parts," said Fielding.

" There are no unimportant parts in the play," said Mr. Fox.

" Well," said Fielding, " we might have had Clive Rogers and Peggy Ardale."

" At ruinous salaries," snapped Mr. Fox.

He rose irritably and moved, with his slightly pompous gait, toward the stage.

" He 's a mean old dog," said Fielding. " He 'll offer those poor kids starvation salaries and they 'll jump at the offer."

Trimble looked worried. " A damned shame ! "

" I could never manage if I did n't both act and produce. I 've somehow got on with him through a good many productions."

" He 's taking them into his office. I wonder when we shall have a rehearsal."

" In a few days, I hope."

Wakefield and Molly Griffith looked into each other's eyes and laughed as they passed through the stage door of the Preyde Theatre on to the pavement.

" Is n't it grand," he exclaimed, " that we 're both taken on ? "

" Yes. I *am* glad. I 'm so nervous and you 're not a bit. I think you 're going to be splendid as Frederick."

" Is n't it extraordinary the way we 've just hopped into the theatre, hopped into two good parts and hopped out again — hand in hand — like two old friends? " He caught her hand in his.

" We sound rather like frogs — all that hopping, I mean."

" Will you have some lunch with me? I know of a nice place. We 'll talk over our parts."

" I 'd love to."

" We 'll tell each other about our pasts and boast about our futures." He hailed a passing taxi.

" Why — you 're not taking a taxi, are you? "

" Why not? "

" Goodness — you 're affluent! "

" I 'm the sort who would spend his last shilling on a taxi."

" Please don't. I 'm terribly hungry."

" Don't worry. I 've just got my allowance from home."

They were in the taxicab.

He examined her profile outlined against the window. " How happy you look since we 've got these jobs."

" It means a lot to me. I 'd have had to go home — otherwise."

" Where is home? "

" Wales."

" Wales! I 've never been there."

" Where is your home? "

" Canada. But my mother was a Londoner."

" Have n't you any relatives over here? "

" I 've cousins in Ireland. I 'm part Irish. And I 've a brother in London. I live with him."

" Is he like you? "

" Not a bit. He 's a pianist. Let 's talk about the play."

They did and were so absorbed that they were surprised

to find themselves at their destination. She looked up at the sign over the door.

"L'Écu de France! How grand you are! I thought it would be — no, I won't say that."

"An A.B.C.! I 'll bet that 's the impression I gave you." He paid the driver.

She colored. Then she gave a happy little laugh. "This is my lucky day."

They put their heads together over the menu. "I like everything." She folded her hands in her lap, like a well-behaved little girl, and gazed at the people at near-by tables. The order was given and they broke the crusty rolls and ate them while they waited. A bottle of white wine appeared with the sole.

"We must drink," said Wakefield, "to the success of the play and to our friendship."

They touched glasses and their eyes met in a look in which he revealed the warmth and self-confidence of his nature and his sensitive, yet resilient egotism, and she nothing but a girl's interest in the male, and her pleasure in the moment.

She ate more than Wakefield did. In truth she seemed so hungry that he judged that she had been cooking her own meals over a gas ring and not spending a penny more than necessary on them. She wore her clothes well and he liked that. He quite probably would not have invited her to lunch had she not. He noticed that other men were looking at her. He noticed the lovely curve of her short upper lip that was oddly combined with a look of physical courage.

They talked of the play and their parts in it. They poured out confidences of their professional past. If he had been an actor grown old in the profession he could scarcely have seemed to have had greater experience. She drank in every word.

Over coffee he said — "It 's a wonder your family would let you come so far from home alone."

She stared. " Why not? I 've been acting since I was sixteen. I 'm able to take care of myself. I 've been in London a year."

" And we 've never met till to-day! What a waste of time."

" I 'm glad."

" Why?"

" Because to-day would n't have been such a nice surprise."

" I do think that was a charming thing to say. Molly — Molly Griffith. I like your name. I'll bet your parents are proud of you."

" My mother 's dead. I don't think my father is particularly proud of me."

" Why?"

" Well, he 's not that sort."

Wakefield considered this and took an instant dislike to Mr. Griffith.

" Have you brothers and sisters?" he asked.

" A brother and three sisters."

" Four girls! What a lot! Do you get on well together?"

" Yes . . . not always."

" And your brother? What about him?"

" He 's a darling. I love him better than anyone else in the world." Her face flushed and she tapped with her finger tips on the table. She added — " We 're awfully poor."

" The Welsh generally are. But they are recompensed by being picturesque and musical, are n't they?"

She considered this gravely. " I think my family is rather picturesque. At any rate the place we live in is. But we 're not musical. One of my sisters paints. I don't know how good her pictures are. She 's never had any lessons." She was disinclined to say anything more of her family and asked him about his.

" My mother is dead too. Also my father. I was a posthumous child. My eldest brother and my sister brought me up — with help from my grandmother, my aunt, and my two uncles."

" That partly explains you."

" How? "

" You 're so well-brought-up."

" Am I? "

" What I mean is, you seem as though you 'd been the centre of a lot of attention."

Wakefield's face lighted in mischief.

" I wish you could have seen them about me, when I was a kid. I had them all going. There was Grandmother, nearly a hundred. She was a bit fierce but really full of love. There was Aunt Augusta, dignity personified, haughty and covered with bracelets and brooches but with a heart of gold. There was Uncle Nicholas, a grand-looking old fellow, with a lot of gray hair and a drooping moustache. When I was on his shoulder I felt as though nothing in the world could hurt me. Then Uncle Ernest, very careful of my manners, very fastidious about his person, very much absorbed in the family. My eldest brother, Renny — he 's been a father to me. He breeds horses. You ought to see him ride. He 's married now and has two children. Then there 's Piers, my next brother. He farms and helps Renny with the horses. The brother next me is Finch, who is here in London. My only sister is married and lives next door to us."

" What a family! Are all living? "

" Gran and Aunt Augusta are dead, and one of my brothers — Eden."

" Funny. You have three brothers and a sister and I have three sisters and a brother."

" Tell me about them."

She frowned a little. "Some other time. Just now I want only to enjoy myself."

Her family must be different from his, Wakefield thought, for it was always a pleasure to him to talk of his family. She was a good listener and the time went quickly as he poured out stories of the idiosyncrasies of his kin. She exclaimed, "I can just see that house and those people! You 're such a good one at describing."

"You must come out some time and visit us. They 'd make you very welcome. Supposing the play is a great success! I 'll tell you what will happen. It will go to New York. They 'll take us too and, at the end of the run, we 'll go to Canada and visit Jalna."

"If only we could!"

"I 'm a prophet. I feel it in my bones."

They exchanged a look of happy expectancy.

III

IN GAYFERE STREET

THE February sunshine was warm over London. The sky was a mild blue and small ethereal clouds were barely moved by the light breeze. People in the streets walked slowly, enjoying the warmth of the sun. The windows of the lumbering buses were open and people peered out, as though expecting to see some palpable sign of spring, such as lambs frisking along Piccadilly or a milkmaid milking a cow in the Green Park. Wakefield stopped to buy a bunch of daffodils from a flower seller just outside St. James's Palace. He felt a new confidence in life and in his ability to make himself a place here in London. It was not only that he had got a part in a West End theatre but that his meeting with Molly Griffith had, in some way, intensified all his feelings. If he were to become suddenly sad or depressed he knew that such emotions would be the more keenly felt because of her, and he felt that this was because of some quality in her rather than in him.

He could scarcely wait for to-morrow when he would meet her again, possibly again take her out to lunch. He could scarcely wait till he got back to Gayfere Street, so that he might tell his brother, Finch, about her. He could scarcely wait till he might sit down in his own room and learn his part. Yet in the midst of his straining forward he found himself loitering in the street to stare at the black Arab steed on which one of the Horse Guards sat immobile in his niche outside the Palace. The man was lean, ruddy, and his eyes looked straight ahead of him into space beyond the people who stood staring. His silver helmet, with its white plume, his silver breastplate, gleamed in the sun. The close-curled sheepskin lay soft on the horse's muscular back. Its eyes too looked straight ahead and, in their depths, Wakefield thought he saw reflected deserts with waving palm trees and galloping Arab hordes. It stood rigid on its four slender legs, as though carved out of ebony.

He walked on, past the Houses of Parliament, on and on into Smith Square and turned at last into Gayfere Street. He knocked on the door of one of the smallest houses and it was opened by an enormous elderly woman, with a face that looked too large even for her body. But her hand resting on the side of the door looked massive, beyond proportion, even for that face. She greeted Wakefield with a melancholy smile.

"I 'ope you don't find the 'eat of this sun too much for you, sir. It does take it out of one when it first opens up in the spring."

"I think it 's glorious," said Wakefield. "There can't be too much of it for me. Will you please put these daffodils in water. Is my brother in?" He entered the narrow hall.

"Yes, sir. 'E 's just done 'is practising. 'E looks tired, poor young man."

She took the flowers and disappeared into the basement. Wakefield could hear the drag of her heavy cloth skirt from step to step. She was Henriette, the half-Cockney, half-French housekeeper. The brothers had leased the tiny house for a term, Henriette being left in charge. The one room on the ground floor was the sitting room, an end of which was used as a dining room, half-drawn curtains dividing it. On the floor above were two bedrooms, and on the next floor, another bedroom and a bathroom, while Henriette had her being in the basement.

Wakefield opened the door of the sitting room and went in. No sunlight entered here and, for a moment, he did not see Finch. He saw the hired piano, strewn with music, the untidy room. Then he discovered Finch lying face down on the sofa, his fair head pillowed on his arms. He raised his head and turned his long, gray-blue eyes on Wakefield, with a dazed look.

"Hullo," said the younger. "Did I wake you?"

"No. I was just thinking. Did you get the job?"

"What do you guess?"

"I'll bet you did, to judge by your face."

"Yes, I got it. I've my part here. We're to begin rehearsals in a few days. Finch, I'm going to make a success of it. You'll see. God, how glad I am. The old boy — Ninian Fox, I mean — is a queer egg, but I like him. And I've met the producer and the author and the girl who's going to take the part of Catherine. She's Welsh. We had lunch together. I want you to meet her. I don't know when I've admired a girl so much. Not since Pauline."

Finch had been listening to him only half tolerantly. He was skeptical of Wakefield's enthusiasms, his eager outpourings. Wakefield was too articulate, as he himself was too reticent. If he had been Wakefield it would have been impossible to speak casually of Pauline. As it was, he could bring himself to utter her name only with difficulty. Yet it was Wakefield who had been engaged to her, who had broken off the engagement because he had made up his mind to enter a monastery, and so been the cause of her entering a convent. The monastery had not lasted. It had been a boy's impulse, Finch thought scornfully, yet had to admit that Wakefield's sojourn there had made a man of him. He would never forget how kind Wakefield had been to him when his nerves had gone to pieces. Wakefield had comforted and controlled him. But now, in London, far away from home, their boyhood relations had been more or less re-established: Finch the older, half scornful, half admiring of Wakefield's ease with himself and with the world; Wakefield pouring out his experiences to Finch, wanting his approval, yet a little contemptuous of Finch's awkwardness and self-depreciation.

Looking at Finch stretched on the sofa, his head once more pillowed on his arm, the thought came to him, and not for the first time, that perhaps poor old Finch had been a little in love with Pauline himself. God knew she would have been a thousand times better as a wife for him than the one he had chosen — his distant cousin, Sarah Court. She had been a devil, thought Wakefield, and before he could stop himself had exclaimed: —

"I wonder where Sarah is!"

Finch shrank almost more from the sound of Sarah's name than Pauline's. Pauline's name brought a tender sadness, a heartache at the thought of her in nun's robes; but Sarah's, a picture of what his life with her had been, how her cold, calculating, devouring passion for him had made that life unbearable.

"I don't know and I don't care," he muttered.

Wakefield looked at him speculatively. "Being a Catholic," he said, "I don't believe in divorce but I can't help wishing you were free of her and might marry again. It would be good for you, I believe."

"I hate marriage," broke in Finch. "There is n't a girl living who would tempt me to it."

"Perhaps you 're right. I feel pretty shy of it myself, though I 've had no experience. Still, we can have friends. I 'd like to invite this girl — Molly Griffith is her name — to tea here. Do you think it would be all right?"

"I don't see anything against it excepting that Henriette might frighten her."

The brothers knew little of the so-called Bohemian life of London, its free-and-easy parties. They had been brought up in a conventional atmosphere. They had few friends in London and generally were content in each other's company. Finch was to give a series of recitals and the preparation for those took all his energy. But he loved the theatre and often thought he would like to be an actor. Wakefield's work was a new bond between them. Finch sat up and stretched out his hand.

"Let 's see your part," he said.

Wakefield gave him the sheets of typescript. He said:—

"It 's a good part. I 'm lucky to get it. And I was just as glad for the girl as for myself. She looked hard-up, I can tell you. I think I 'll send a line home to tell them the news. There 's a ship sailing to-morrow."

He sat down at the writing bureau and began rapidly to cover a sheet of notepaper with his small firm handwriting. He was orderly in his habits and he hated the way Finch had stuffed letters, musical scores, accounts, and newspaper cuttings into the pigeonholes. He hated the disorder of the room. But he said nothing. He had always had self-control and during his stay in the monastery he had cultivated it.

Finch searched for and found a pair of spectacles he had dropped on the floor, and began to read the typescript. In his college days he had loved play-acting next to music and he had shown such talent that the producer of the amateur company he had worked with had prophesied a fine future for him. But music had come first. Now, reading Wakefield's part, the feel of the lines tingled through his nerves and he wanted to do the part himself. The thought came to him that acting might not have, surely would not have, taken such toll of his strength as did music. He was strong enough, he thought, yet surely there must be something wrong with him when he could not practise for five hours, as he had to-day, without feeling exhausted. He did not believe it was the actual practising, but the thought of what it led up to, the cold, waiting lights of the platform, the row upon row of ears — all waiting for him to falter once, waiting to catch the falter of that left hand of his, faintly behind the right. Yet why should this matter so when sometimes he could bring his audience to their feet in the passion of his playing! Still he continued to imagine all the ears as antagonistic to him, straining their drums to catch him in a fault, caring nothing for his passion.

After a while he said — "It 's a pretty good part."

Wakefield turned to face him.

"You can't imagine how good till you have read the whole play. And I 'm going to make it an important part. You 'll see."

He sealed and stamped his letter.

"You might have read me your letter," said Finch.

The idea of home was such a living bond to him, though he barely remembered his parents, that the sight of an envelope addressed to Jalna made him want to guess what its effect would be on each member of that circle.

"You would have found it too enthusiastic. You make me shy."

"Good God! *You* shy! Let 's have a look at you."

"I don't always show my feelings."

"You dramatize them almost before they 're born."

"And yours arrive through a sort of Caesarean operation that devastates you and everyone around you."

They were angry and it was a relief that Henriette appeared carrying a tray loaded with their tea things. She said, in her doleful voice: —

"It was the best I could do. By the time I 'ad my work done and got to the shop all the best cakes were gone. The market was very poor at Strutton Ground, so I could n't get very nice salad stuff for your dinner. I 'm afraid you 'll not like it." She looked at them lugubriously, her huge hands folded on her black cashmere stomach.

"It 's all right," said Finch, coming to the table.

Wakefield snatched up a small cake filled with custard. "This is just the sort I like!" He put it whole into his mouth. " As for dinner, if we have your good soup, Henriette, it 's all that matters. Everything tastes marvelous to-day."

Henriette sighed heavily and trailed her skirt down the stairs to the kitchen. She had just reached the bottom when the doorbell rang. They could hear her groan as she began again to climb the stairs.

" I 'll go! " shouted Wakefield. He ran to the door and opened it. A soft rain had begun to fall. His cousin, Paris Court, stood on the threshold. Wakefield swallowed the last of his cake and made him welcome.

" We 're just sitting down to tea," he said.

" I hope there 's plenty of it," said Paris. " I 'm starving."

Paris always said he was starving and indeed behaved so, but looked well-nourished. He was so typically the young Irishman of tradition, lighthearted and irresponsible, black-haired, blue-eyed and fresh-skinned, with a dimple in his cheek, that it made you smile to look at him. He was a distant cousin whom the brothers had met only in the last months but already he seemed a near relation. He understood them very well, their weaknesses, their generosities, and how they had brought the atmosphere of their own home with them. He was about twenty-eight and was the only son of Malahide Court, both friend and enemy to old Adeline Whiteoak. At the end of his resources Malahide had made a last desperate visit to the Riviera and there become engaged to, and in Paris married, an American girl. He had been convinced that, being an American, she was rich. She had imagined she was marrying an aristocratic Irishman of means. Each had told the other singularly little of the past. When he took her to his dilapidated mansion, where the green moss was encroaching on some of the inner walls, and discovered that she had scarcely a dollar to bless herself with, the fat was indeed in the fire. It was a marvel that they both had survived that scene. But they had survived it and the marriage had turned out better than could have been hoped for. Paris was always talking about his parents. Finch and Wakefield remembered how, at Jalna, his father was generally referred to as " that snake, Malahide."

Paris had had one position after another in London but was seldom able to do more than keep body and soul together. Body was healthy and soul was cheerful, yet he asked more. He wanted luxury and freedom from care and did not much mind how he got them, so long as he did.

Wakefield could not have asked for a better listener than his cousin. Paris was delighted that he had got a part in the new play at the Preyde Theatre. He was delighted with Wakefield's imitations of Ninian Fox. He listened, with knit forehead and pouting lips, to Wakefield's description of Molly Griffith. Finch said little but his nerves relaxed in the careless flow of their talk. He pulled at his pipe, while his large-pupiled eyes rested on them in amusement and envy.

" Let 's hear your part," said Paris.

Wakefield eagerly unfolded the manuscript and sketched the outline of the play. He read bits of his part aloud. Paris was enthusiastic.

" It 's a grand part," he said, " and I envy you doing it with the girl you describe. I 'd like to meet her. So far I can't think that English girls compare well with the Irish."

" Wait till you see Molly Griffith." He began once more to rave over her.

Finch yawned. " I 'm going for a walk," he said. " Do you mind, Parry? I 've got to have air."

" It 's raining."

" I like the rain." Finch rose to his long, loosely made length.

"Sure I don't mind," answered Paris. "Wake will put up with me for a bit."

"I want the rain on my face. I'm going to walk by the river."

"I dare say I'll still be here when you come back."

"Good." Finch touched his cousin's shoulder affectionately in passing.

When he had left the house Paris remarked: —

"I always feel that Finch is unhappy, even though he's so talented. Do you think maybe he still hankers after that wife of his?"

"You don't know Finch. He'd run the other way if she appeared on the scene. He hates her and fears her too."

"Well," Paris spoke musingly, "that does n't mean that he may not hanker after her. She may have done something to him that he can't get over."

"I believe that 's true. I mean that she did something to him — just as you say. But no power on earth could make him go back to her. What Finch has always wanted is peace and somehow the poor devil has never been able to get it."

"I wish I'd had his chance with that rich cousin of ours. To think of a Court having money! And such masses of money! It's incredible. I can't tell you how poor my family is. I *can* tell you we've nearly reached the point of bringing the family skeleton out of the cupboard and putting him in the pot for the juice that may still be in him."

Wakefield's mind flew back to the stories he had heard at home of how Malahide Court had come to visit at Jalna and stayed so long he had had to be ejected almost by force. He said: —

"You'll do something for the family fortunes some day. I'm certain of that, Parry."

Paris turned his blue gaze ingenuously on Wakefield. "Please God, I shall," he said solemnly. He drew his chair confidentially closer. "I've just had a letter from my father. In it he tells me of a beautiful young horse he can buy at a great bargain. He says that it has no end of possibilities as a racer. It 's a rare beauty on the track. My father knows that your brother Renny has had the ambition to win the Grand National and he says there is n't a likelier horse in these Islands than this one. And I myself say that there is n't a finer judge of horseflesh in these Islands than my father. Now he says that he could buy this horse for your brother, have him trained, and your brother could come over for the glorious finish of it and reap the profits. After this horse has won the Grand National he 'll be worth his weight in gold, mind you."

Wakefield's eyes shone. If only such a triumph could be achieved for that eldest brother who had done so much for him and who had had so much hard luck!

"Renny did train a horse for the Grand National," he said, "when I was n't much more than a baby. But it never ran. It got killed. Young as I was I can still remember the excitement and how wild Renny looked and how he got drunk and came into the house singing."

"Poor man," said Paris. "But this would be different. This horse would n't get killed and my father says it can win any race it 's put into. He says he 's willing to back it with all he has and that 's saying a good deal for a man of his age."

Wakefield was swept along by the idea. He walked eagerly up and down the room.

"I 've just been writing to Renny," he exclaimed. "I 'll open the letter and put in another sheet telling him about the horse. You must give me all the details you can."

Paris shook his head. "I don't think that 's the way to go about it. What my father wants you to do is to come straight over to Ireland and see the horse for yourself. Then, when you 've got an eyeful, you can write and tell your brother what you think. He might n't take my father's word for it and I expect you could n't grow up at Jalna without knowing a good deal about horses."

"I 'll do it," said Wakefield. "Could we go to-morrow? Rehearsals are to begin in a few days. Then it will be impossible to get away. I wonder what Finch will say."

"Don't let him stand in your way," said Paris.

IV

AT COUSIN MALAHIDE'S

FINCH had felt only misgivings at this proposal by Paris to inspect an unknown horse on Renny's behalf. He had no confidence in his own opinion and he distrusted Wakefield's enthusiasms. He liked Paris and believed him to be sincere, but he had heard Cousin Malahide called a sneak, a traitor and a sponge, as long as he could remember. Yet the thought of going to Ireland came as a lovely surprise. If he went he would throw aside, for a few days, the strain of preparation for his recital. He believed that, in the long run, it would do him good. His eyes, the nerves in his head, were feeling the strain. His sleep was broken. He felt himself nearing one of those periods of despair and bitter doubts of his future. He found himself envying the men working at the side of the road, eating their lunch there in easy contempt of the traffic, joking as they ate their bread and cheese.

He decided to go to Ireland but to make no promises. He would write all details to Renny and let him decide if he would be willing to take such a risk. He felt in himself such a snatching at those few days of respite that they began to seem of vital importance to all his future. Wakefield, Paris, and he could talk of nothing else.

Then, one misty evening, they found themselves in a mud-splashed car bumping along a country road in County Meath, with rooks sailing dark against the sky and the cattle raising their heads, with the young grass tender in their mouths, to see them go by. A rough-haired young man called Leo was driving the car and Paris kept asking him questions about his father and mother.

" How is my mother's rheumatism, Leo? "

" A bit betther, sor."

" Is she having any luck with her poultry? "

" Aye. She have forty young pullets as plump as pigeons."

" Has my father had the drains attended to? "

" No, sor, fur the plumber has been dead this three months and no other dare succeed him, he was so unpopular."

" Are there any visitors in the house? "

" There was a young lady, a cousin, but she 've gone. I never heard her name."

Wakefield's eyes sparkled at Finch. " I can scarcely bear to wait to see Cousin Malahide," he whispered. " What a letter I shall write home! "

Paris looked over his shoulder. " Did I hear you say you can scarcely wait to see my father? No wonder. He 's a wonderful man and the best judge of horses in the county. And you should see him jump the tallest hedges at the Hunt and he well past seventy."

The dark clouds, massed in the western sky, let only a dim shaft of sunlight down to the moist earth. The brown thatch of the cottages by the roadside looked no more than humps of the earth itself. On a rise of ground, with a slow stream encircling it, stood a long low house. A double row of linden trees led to the front door.

A small light in an ancient lantern was hung at the side of the door, and of the long rows of windows only one was lighted. A stone turret at a corner of the house had fallen and lay crumbled. Enough earth had collected among the shattered stones to make a foothold for tall ferns and a graceful fuchsia the size of a tree. The place was enfolded in an air of melancholy and decay. The hollow ringing of a cowbell on the marshy land below only increased this. The air was mild and moist, like the kiss of a person in tears.

Paris did not appear depressed by all this. He sprang

from the car and ran lightly up the steps. Before he could open the door it was opened from within and an old man-servant poked out a bony bald head.

"Lord bless us, Mr. Paris, 't is glad I am to see you," he said and showed the rest of himself. He wore a mulberry-colored livery, very faded, and he had not a tooth in his head.

"Hello, Jamesie," said Paris. "How are things going with you?"

"Ah, I 've no more than me share of throubles! But we shall all be aisier in our minds for this sight of you."

"These are cousins from Canada," said Paris. "They 've come all the way from London to look at the horse my father has told us of."

"My God in Heaven!" exclaimed Jamesie. "You could n't find a lovelier horse in the length and breadth of Ireland. He runs so fast that the shweat dries on him between one shtride and the next. He 's halfway to the goal before the rest of the beasts has left the starting p'int."

"I believe you," said Parry, "but we 're standing out in the rain. Are my parents in the drawing-room?"

"Aye. With their eyes fairly dropping out of their sockets with watching for you. Come away in."

The hall was so large that it made the one at Jalna seem small and cozy in Wakefield's memory. Two lighted candles on a carved oak chest dimly illumined the paneled walls. From it they went through a small, still dimmer room into the drawing-room. It was lighted by an ornate and ghostly chandelier, the crystals of which were too dim with dust to reflect the light. They hung cold and motionless, like frozen fog. On a gilded sofa, by the side of a small fire, sat two dark figures who rose and came forward eagerly to meet the three young men.

As Paris embraced his mother, Wakefield's eyes swept the room and the bent figure of Malahide Court. He saw the brocaded upholstery in holes, the pictures dim in their tarnished frames, the piece of embroidery hanging on the wall worn into ribbons by age and damp. If Paris Court was the traditional gay young Irishman, Malahide was the traditional decadent aristocrat. His long, ivory-colored face was like the face of a mediæval Spanish portrait. His large dark eyes looked from under arched black brows but his hair, which he wore rather long, was silvery white. His expression, as he came forward with outstretched hand, seemed to Wakefield both sneering and conciliatory, as though he had forgotten nothing of the past but was determined that his visitors should.

His voice was soft and he had a slight sibilant lisp.

"My dear young cousins, how glad I am to welcome you here. Our son's letters have been full of his pleasure in meeting you. Having you here brings back to me my visit to Jalna, which was one of the happiest times in my life."

His hand lay silken and relaxed in Wakefield's. It was difficult to think of him as controlling a horse or taking a jump, yet Wakefield knew he could do both. He replied with deference to Malahide. He had an air that always drew elderly men to him.

Finch was shaking hands with Mrs. Court. It was easy to see where Paris had got his looks. She was of compact build and quite fifteen years younger than her husband. Her black hair was gray at the temples but her skin was smooth and her blue eyes had a determined and cheerful light in them. There was a wryness to her smile as though many a time her laughter had been inward and bitter. She made the brothers very welcome and sat down with Paris at her side. It was clear that both parents doted on him.

She said to her husband — "These young men have a strong look of the Courts, have n't they?"

"Especially Wakefield," answered Malahide. "He bears a certain resemblance to his dear grandmother, though, if I remember rightly, it was Renny who inherited her red hair."

As he said the name "Renny" he gave a smile that was almost a simper.

"Gosh," thought Finch, "I don't like that smile! It makes me feel that he has something nasty up his sleeve."

"When I visited at Jalna," went on Malahide, "the baby of the family was Piers. He was a perfect Whiteoak and a great pet of mine. But I admired Eden even more. I looked on him as the flower of the flock."

The sudden mention of Eden's name brought a contraction of the heart to Finch. He drew down his sensitive upper lip and stared at Malahide in silence.

"I quite agree," said Wakefield. "It has always been a grief to me that Eden died. I feel that he and I would have been such friends."

"Did he leave any children?" asked Mrs. Court.

"A girl who is being brought up with Renny's children. She 's a dear little thing."

"And your uncles," inquired Malahide. "I hope they flourish. I fagged for Nicholas, as a boy at school in England, and I must say he was pretty hard on me. But Ernest was a charming fellow, a dear man. He married late in life, did n't he?"

"Yes. We think a lot of our aunt by marriage. She 's an American and so is Renny's wife."

"And so am I," laughed Mrs. Court. "Your family seems to like my countrywomen. But the truth is I 've lost all connection with America. I 've never been there since my marriage. I have no relations there. I feel myself Irish, through and through."

Wakefield noticed then that she spoke with a slight Irish accent which Malahide did not. Paris held one of his mother's hands in his and stroked it, and now and again raised it to his lips. Now he spoke to his father.

"Tell the boys about the lovely horse, Dada," he said. "And must we dress for dinner?"

" No dressing for dinner to-night," put in Mrs. Court. " It is getting late and you three boys must be very hungry. What sort of crossing did you have? "

" Vile. All our English food is at the bottom of the Irish Sea. We 're starving. Shall I go and urge on the dinner? "

" There is plenty of time," said Malahide. He proceeded to question Wakefield about his new profession and, once drawn on to talk of that, Wakefield forgot all about food and poured out his London experiences. Something he said led to the discovery of his conversion to Catholicism and his stay in the monastery.

" I 'm very sympathetic indeed to that," said Malahide, " for, though the Courts have always been members of the Church of England, there is much in the Catholic faith that I admire and I 've often thought that, with my sensitive nature, I would have found real sanctuary in a monastery."

His wife and son looked at him and it was impossible to tell what was in their minds. He talked of monasteries in Spain and France as though he were deeply familiar with them. Finch felt dizzy with hunger and fatigue. He wished he had let Wakefield make this visit alone — but no, he could not wish himself back in London. The strange unreality of this house would lift him out of himself — once he was rested. Rest — that was what he needed.

Old Jamesie came in carrying a tray on which were four small glasses, a small decanter half full of sherry, and a silver basket of biscuits.

The sherry slid down Finch's throat like a burning sweet caress. He took a biscuit. It was flabby as flannel but he ate it. Mrs. Court also took one but she did not touch the sherry. " It gives me a headache," she explained, but Finch thought she looked longingly at the decanter.

Wakefield was enjoying himself. He had lived such a sequestered life at Jalna, his one excursion his sojourn in the monastery, that each new experience was an unfolding of vital interest to him. The tiny glasses of sherry had long been emptied when dinner was announced. Malahide led the way with his wife on his arm. His willowy figure, his drooping back, slightly bowed legs, and affected walk, filled Finch with a sudden hilarity. He found himself suffocating a laugh. He dared not meet Wakefield's eyes. Wakefield so fitted himself into the scene that he might have spent his days in this house. "Damned little play-actor," muttered Finch to himself.

Their footsteps sounded melancholy on the stone flagging of the hall. The double doors of the dining room stood open. The table was lighted by six candles.

"There is no need for such an illumination," said Mrs. Court. She took a heavy silver extinguisher from a drawer and extinguished two of the candles. Finch remembered how he had seen her draw aside a lump of coal, not yet ignited, before they had left the drawing-room. He noticed her small, bony, capable hands and the set of her lips.

The silver on the long table bore a resemblance to the silver at Jalna. Some of it bore the same crest. But there resemblance ended. When Jamesie lifted the heavy silver cover from the platter in front of Malahide, the chicken disclosed was so small that Finch felt he could have eaten it all himself. He remembered the prodigality that weighted the table at Jalna and wished he might have seen the face of the master of Jalna had he been set down to this.

The room was very large, the walls covered by portraits, some too dim to be clear in candlelight. One, a man in armor just behind Malahide, showed a startling resemblance to him.

Malahide took up the carving knife and fork and smiled across the table at his wife. He looked like a dastardly pirate, thought Finch, ready to knife you in the back. But he spoke in his soft voice.

"What part of the bird would you like, my dear?"

"A very thin slice from the breast," she answered, "and a little of the stuffing. You know I must eat lightly at night."

But she did not eat lightly of potatoes and artichokes. She mounded her plate with these, drowning them in the watery gravy. Malahide gave Finch and Wakefield a drumstick each and to his son the neck and the parson's nose. As he did this he said simperingly: —

"Ever since Paris was a little fellow he has firmly demanded these tidbits and now, though it looks childish, I must humor him."

Paris smiled good-humoredly and he also helped himself liberally to vegetables and gravy.

Now Malahide transferred the remainder of the bird, almost shyly, to his own plate. "It is for me," he said, "to pick the bones. But it is surprising what can be got from a little carcass like this when there is a will and, I might almost add, necessity."

One of Finch's long legs moved beneath the table toward Wakefield. He pressed his brother's foot with his. Their eyes met. Malahide drew on his guests to talk. Before Finch was aware of it he found himself talking about music. Malahide divided his attention between Finch and his own plate. When the bones were cleaned he wiped his fingers delicately and, while the plates were being changed, talked of great pianists he had heard and of orchestras which had given him pleasure. When he could possibly bring in a kindly remark about one of the family at Jalna he never failed to do so. Wakefield began to think that Malahide had been badly used by the family and that they were unjustly prejudiced against him.

There was a salad of a few limp leaves of lettuce, some spongy radishes and cucumbers. Then came a raspberry flan which Malahide meticulously divided into five equal portions. Then a dish of green apples and pears was placed on the table and flanked by smaller dishes of nuts and raisins. Still, at the end of the meal, Finch felt ravenous. Nerves and weariness always made him hungry, but Wakefield was one of those happy people who can eat little or much, as occasion offers.

The dining room grew colder and colder. There was a draught through it that toyed with the hair on Wakefield's forehead. He felt a shiver down his back yet he was strangely happy and could not understand Finch's expression of melancholy as he looked across the dimly lighted expanse of table to him.

In the black-paneled hall their heads turned, in one movement, to look at the small portrait of a little girl of eight whose laughing face was clustered about by waves of dark red hair. Finch exclaimed: —

"Why, she 's the image of Adeline! Look, Wake! It might be her portrait."

"Who is Adeline?" asked Paris.

"She 's my brother Renny's child. She 's just the age of this one. Lord, it makes me feel strange!"

"This is your grandmother, Adeline Court," said Malahide. "I 'm very fond of the picture. It was given by her father in part payment of a debt to mine. Only part payment, mind you, and that was all my father ever got. Yet, when your grandmother visited here, just before she sailed for Canada, — that was more than eighty years ago, — she took that picture off the wall, after everyone was in bed, and hid it in one of her trunks. She was leaving early the next morning. But my mother discovered the loss and refused to let her take her trunks from the house. I believe that there was quite a scene, for both ladies had violent tempers. Your grandfather offered to pay for the painting but my mother refused. Finally he persuaded your grandmother to return it, but you can imagine the parting. I 'm very fond of that portrait. I greatly admired your grandmother."

He took up a candle from the chest near by and held it close to the smiling child face.

"What a skin!" he said. "I wonder if it was as milky white as that!"

"I'm sure of it," said Wakefield, "for little Adeline's is just the same. Finch, would n't Renny love to have this picture?"

"I'm afraid you would never part with it," Finch said to Malahide.

Malahide's hand, so nearly the color of the candle wax that they seemed one, began to tremble.

"I'll tell you what I'll do," he said. "The day your brother buys the horse I'm interested in, I'll send him the portrait as a token of friendship, as a charm to bring good luck."

"He would be delighted," said Wakefield. "When shall we see the horse?"

"The first thing after breakfast."

Finch did not speak. He was wrapped in the strangeness of life that had turned that red-lipped child, with the flowerlike flesh, into the old, old woman he had called grandmother, who had left him her fortune, now all disappeared. He lingered behind the others, fascinated by the picture.

"And this was you, Gran," he murmured.

As they sat over coffee in the drawing-room Malahide told them of the horse. It had been bred and was now owned by a Mr. Madigan, who was in dire straits financially and would take a low price for the horse.

"He has little idea," said Malahide, "of its glorious potentialities. He knows it can run, and run fast, for that has been proved. But I can see deeper than he can and I warn you that, if your brother misses this opportunity, he would miss the greatest in his life so far as racing is concerned."

" How much do you think Mr. Madigan is asking for the horse?" asked Wakefield.

" I believe," said Malahide solemnly, " that he would take as little as five hundred guineas for him. You probably have some idea of what he will be worth when he has won the Grand National."

Wakefield drew a deep sigh. He knew that such a sum would be very hard for Renny to lay hands on. Then there would be the training of the horse and his keep. And always there was the chance of failure. He looked anxiously at Finch.

" I don't think we ought to do it," said Finch.

" There is no need to decide in a hurry," said Malahide. " When you have seen the horse, write to your brother. Get him to come over to Ireland and see for himself. There 'd be no harm in that, surely. We 'll have photographs taken and sent to him. Come now, let us put it out of our minds till the morning. There is so much to talk over."

" It is a great joy," said Mrs. Court, " to have you three young people here. It makes us believe that spring has come."

They asked Finch to play for them and half reluctantly he went across to the piano seat. He had practised so much in the past weeks that he shrank from the very voice of the piano, yet the potent attraction of the keyboard drew him. He longed to put his hands on it as a man might long to touch a loved one. There was a violin lying on the piano. The sight of it brought back the memory of Sarah and the summer when he had first met her. Far clearer and more real than the moment he was living in came the recollection of those days in Devon when they had played Chopin and Brahms together. He could see her standing by the piano, her white still face slanting across the violin, her chin holding it close as though inexorably. He could see her narrow green eyes and the glossy braids of her black hair encircling her small head which he afterward came to think of as snake-like. And those pale hands, with their unguessed strength! The sweetness of her kisses, her warm sweet breath on his face! This dim, moist landscape beyond the windows became for him the sunny Devon fields, the rolling moors. Surely their first love had been the happiest time of his life! Yet, before the honeymoon, he was afraid of something in her. And after — her all-possessing passion for him, that left him no freedom, had sickened him, thrown a sickly light over all they did. Yet — now he wondered if the fault were not in himself. He knew he was not the sort of man Sarah should have loved. She should have loved a man like Renny. Indeed she had once said to him that, if she did not so hate Renny, she could have loved him. Certainly she had no attraction for Renny. Finch laid his hand on the violin to feel its vibrant smoothness. He heard Wakefield's voice.

"He 's dreaming. But I believe he is in the mood to play. He 's good, I can tell you."

That roused him and he sat down on the faded yellow velvet seat. He began softly to play — not the pieces he was preparing for his recital but some of those he had played with Sarah. As he played he kept looking at the violin and he fancied that it would speak to him. It seemed in some delicate and subtle fashion to respond to the vibration of the piano beneath it. The figures in the room became more and more dreamlike. He had a glimpse of Cousin Malahide's ivory hand shielding his face, as though something in the music had made it vulnerable. He saw Mrs. Court, still as a statue, the candlelight shining on her forehead and in her fixed blue gaze. There was Paris, his face no longer laughing and gay but drawn together, as though he were searching his mind for something lost there. Wakefield sat with bent head and arms folded, his darkness not sparkling and rich-hued now, but sombre. Of what did he dream? "Oh, my darling Sarah," thought Finch, over and over, "why did I drive you away from me? Why did my love turn to hate?"

As the three young men went along an upstairs corridor to their rooms, Paris held a hand curved about the candle he carried, yet the draught almost blew it out.

"It 's at this corner," he said, "where the bit of wall is fallen down."

Finch could see a jagged aperture at the corner and the wall all green and discolored.

"It does n't trouble us at all," said Paris, "except in the worst weather and then we hang a blanket over it."

"Have you no electric light?" asked Wakefield. "For my own part I love the candlelight, but I was just wondering."

"We did have electricity," said Paris, "but my mother found that the servants wasted it, so she had it turned off at the main. Well, here we are, and if you 're anything like I am, you 're ready to tumble into bed at once." He laid his hand on Finch's arm. "Good Lord, I wish I could play like you! It wrings the heart out of one. Now, is there anything you want? Would you like some food on a tray? You might be hungry in the night."

There was something unconvincing in this invitation and both brothers declared they could take nothing more till breakfast. Then they found themselves alone. Wakefield faced Finch with a little laugh.

"What a house!" he exclaimed. "And what people! Yet in some curious way I feel very near them. Of course, I 'm very fond of Parry. His mother is an enigma but I like her. And I can't help thinking that Cousin Malahide has been maligned by the family. You know, I can't keep my eyes off him. He 's beautiful in an unholy sort of way. What do you feel about buying that horse, Finch? They 've given you by far the better room. Mine is little and bare but I don't mind. It takes me back to the monastery. Look at your bed hangings. Be careful they don't fall down in the night and smother you."

Finch answered him in monosyllables. He was tired and Wakefield's manner of leaping from one subject to another always made him close up. He went to see Wakefield's room to be rid of him, and so was.

As he shut his own door behind him he drew a deep breath of relief. He wanted to be alone. He took off his jacket and hung it up, stretched his arms and lighted a last cigarette. The casement was open and a musical drip of rain came from an eave. It was so damp he thought he would close the casement but found he could not because ivy had so strongly entwined itself about the hinges that they would not move. As he turned away he faced his own reflection in a tall pierglass whose tarnished gilt frame was topped by an eagle. He stood motionless, straining every nerve to discover what it was in the room that made him feel uneasy, as though he were not alone. He thought: —

"It 's exactly the setting for a ghost story. All that is needed is a headless monk or something of the sort to come from that cupboard."

The thought had barely come into his mind when the door of the cupboard actually did move. He felt a creeping down his spine. He felt sick with fright. He riveted his eyes, brilliant with fright, on the moving door. It opened softly and his wife stepped into the room.

So often his imaginings had been fantastic that he did not for a moment think of her as real. He just stared at her, awaiting what might happen next.

But her voice, when it came, dispelled all thoughts of the supernatural. He had thought that Sarah must be dead and her spirit come to reproach him, but that voice, sweeter than any he had ever heard, with the sweetness of the muted notes of a violin, was warm and vibrant with life.

"Finch," she said, "don't be angry! I had to see you — just for a moment. I did not go down to dinner because I was afraid it would anger you. I hid here to have the joy of being near you for one little moment. Don't be angry, Finch. Say you don't hate me!"

"Sarah!" He said her name in a voice not his own but like the voice of a sleepwalker. "Was that your violin I saw?"

"Yes. I forgot to hide it."

"I felt that you were near. But — not in the flesh."

"Finch, my little one, say you don't hate me."

"I think — I 'm not sure — but — oh, Sarah, I could not get you out of my mind."

"You wanted me!" She gave a cry of delight and glided to him. How familiar was that gliding walk, in which the legs seemed scarcely to move but the whole body to swim forward.

Without his volition his arms were raised. He closed his eyes, then felt the weight of her against his breast. He felt the sweetness of her breath on his mouth. Strength surged into his body and a delirious wildness into his soul. He carried her to the four-poster, with its tattered brocade canopy, and laid her on it and knelt beside her.

"Finch," she whispered, "say that we are to be united again. Oh, if you knew what an abyss of loneliness I have been through! Oh, your lovely eyes — let me kiss them!" She drew down his head and laid her lips first on one eyelid, then on another.

The door handle turned softly and Wakefield stood silhouetted against the light in the corridor.

"Did you call me, Finch?" he asked. "I thought I heard your voice." He peered toward the bed and saw Finch kneeling there.

"Oh, I 'm so sorry!" he said. "Finch, you are praying

and I interrupted you! God bless you, Finch." He closed the door gently and was gone.

In his own room he stood motionless, his dark head bent in thought. What a queer fellow Finch was! He never seemed to be religious — not outwardly — but in his heart he must be deeply so.

V

JOHNNY THE BIRD

WAKEFIELD slept soundly, almost dreamlessly. Perhaps it was being in the country again, perhaps it was talking of the purchase of a horse for Renny, but whatever it was his one short dream was about his eldest brother. In it he was himself a child again and sleeping with Renny, as he had been accustomed to do. He had pains in his legs, as he had often had in those years of his delicacy, and Renny was rubbing them with his thin muscular hands. Lying on his back he looked up into that weather-bitten, highly-colored face, with the lean flat cheeks and the hair growing in a russet peak on the forehead, and noted the concern for him written there. But he felt no gratitude or affection, just anger, and he heard himself say: " I 've found you out! You can't deceive me. You 're going to be married! You 've got her hidden in this room!"

He had dreamed this in the moment before waking. He smiled as he remembered the dream and he looked up still smiling into the face of the pink-cheeked maid who had brought him early tea. He sat up in bed, his hair tousled, while she placed before him the tea and a plate of thin bread and butter.

" What sort of weather is it? " he asked.

" Sure 't is the loveliest you ever seen. And one of the sheep in the pasture has a little new lamb."

The air coming in at the window was mild and mistily sunny. Wakefield turned the two slices of bread together and rolled them into a cylinder. He took a large mouthful of tea and gayly greeted Finch when he opened the door.

" Hullo! How did you sleep? I believe the weather has changed."

Finch closed the door behind him and came to the side of the bed. He looked at Wakefield almost sombrely. He said: —

" Wake, I 've something to tell you. When you came into my room last night I was n't praying. I was kneeling beside Sarah. She was on the bed."

Wakefield was for a moment astonished into immobility. He sat transfixed. Then he was frightened. He was afraid for Finch's mind. Something terrible had happened to it. Coming to Ireland, into a house where she might well have visited sometime, had unhinged Finch. He was very tired. His nerves had been troubling him. Wakefield set the tray to one side and moved, with childlike swiftness, to his brother. He gripped his hand.

" It 's all right," he said. " She has n't come back. You 've been dreaming. You 'll never need to see her again, Finch."

" I had need," said Finch harshly. " She is in that room across the passage. She was with me all night. I slept with her."

" That 's impossible." Wakefield spoke sternly. " You dreamed it, Finch. You know you did. Sarah is not in this house."

" If you don't believe me, come and see her! She is there now, in the flesh. In the flesh, by God!"

Wakefield's incredulity began to weaken. After all it was not impossible that Sarah should be in the house. She was a cousin of Malahide's and might visit him, quite probably *would* visit him, if she thought it might lead to a meeting with Finch. His anger rose.

" Are you telling me in truth," he said, " that that woman came to your room last night and that you slept with her?"

" Yes," said Finch, in the same harsh voice, " I did. Not

because she tempted me to but because I wanted to. I tell you, Wake, I am mad about her. And the reason everything has gone wrong with me, the reason I am not well, is because I would not live with her. I sent her away from me when I knew she was my salvation."

"That is preposterous. And you know it. Sarah always sapped the vitality from you and tortured you by her very presence. Did n't you beg Renny to keep her away from you? Did n't you run up two flights of stairs and hide yourself in your room when she came into the house? You 've said with your own lips, to me, that you hated her. This is just the madness of a moment, Finch. Tell me where she is and I will find her and talk to her. You must not see her again."

Finch began to walk up and down the room, his arms tense at his sides. "I tell you, Wake, it 's no use. I know what I 've got to do. It 's not a moment's madness. It 's going back to where I dropped the thread of my life and picking it up again. It 's finishing a composition I threw down in despair but now know has got to be finished or I am lost."

"There 's no truth in this and no balance. Sarah is not the woman for you. Just now she 's made you feel that she is. She 's got a kind of hypnotic influence over you. If she had n't, you would n't have begged Renny to keep her away from you when you were ill. You were afraid of what she 'd do to you. I tell you, Finch, I shall look on this visit as one of our greatest misfortunes, if it gives you back to Sarah!"

The door opened and she stood before them.

"I 've been listening," she said.

"Very well," said Wakefield. "I 'm glad. You know what I feel without my telling you."

"I also know what Finch feels and that means infinitely more to me — to hear from his own lips — in confidence to you — that life is meaningless to him — if I am not with him." She entered and closed the door, standing against it, as though in a frame. "You loved a girl once and broke off your engagement to go into a monastery. What can a man of your type know of a great passion such as Finch and I know! There 's nothing of the monk about him! He 's flesh and fire. And if he and I separated once, it was because our love had consumed us and we parted to gain more fuel for it."

As she spoke, Wakefield's features had taken on a chiseled severity. "Finch left you," he said, "because he was exhausted spiritually. He was n't seeking fresh fuel for passion but forgetfulness of the harm it had done him. And it 's not only a matter of passion, Sarah, it 's just you — the woman that you are. There 's something in you that cannot be accepted — perhaps that 's not the right word but it 's the best I can think of — it cannot be accepted. It 's as though your soul were a pillar of salt. No man could be happy with you. Finch least of all."

She brought her hands from where they had rested against the door, and clapped them before her. "Ask Finch! Ask Finch if he was happy last night! Ask him if there was anything in me he could not accept."

"Finch is not in his sane mind this morning." Wakefield's voice softened persuasively. "Can't you see, Sarah, that, as an artist, he 's got to be his own man? He 's got to respect the thing in him that makes him able to play?"

She laughed triumphantly. "Finch told me last night that the sight of my violin on the piano had filled him with a strange joy."

Wakefield spoke with solemnity. "Yes, Sarah. I don't doubt it. A *strange* joy. That 's what you would inspire. But Finch needs normality. He needs naturalness and all that 's wholesome and sane."

"You sound like a preacher," sneered Sarah.

"I am preaching. I'm preaching what's right and true."

Finch broke out, "I've had enough of this! There's no use in your trying to stop me. I don't want your interference. Sarah and I —"

He was interrupted by a knocking on the door. Paris called out, "Hullo, in there! May I come in?"

Sarah moved from the door and he threw it open. He stood astonished. "Why — why —" he stammered.

She smiled. "I suppose you are Paris. I'm your fourth or fifth cousin — Sarah Whiteoak. Have n't your parents mentioned me?"

He came to her and took her hand. "My mother did tell me that a distant cousin was here but —" his eyes swept over her admiringly — "I never thought of anyone so charming."

"Sarah is my wife," said Finch. "I've told you of her."

"Yes, but upon my word, Sarah, he did n't give me any idea of your looks. I expect he's jealous." Paris wondered greatly what the raised voices had signified. He suspected that Sarah had been brought there in the hope of a reconciliation between her and Finch. He thought what a fool Finch was to have parted with a woman of such wealth and such looks. His candid face expressed this as he turned to Wakefield when they were alone together.

"What a sweet face!" he exclaimed. "Oh, I could love that girl! Surely you are mistaken about her temper. Do you think she and Finch are going to come together again? God, I hope not!"

As Wakefield went down to breakfast his mind was deeply disturbed. He had looked forward to the visit to Ireland as a happy adventure. But this meeting with Sarah, her recapture of Finch, for Wakefield looked on it as nothing but a shameless recapture, had darkened his sky. What was going to happen? Would she return to London with them?

It was impossible to think of living with her in the house in Gayfere Street. If she came, he would go. He would find other lodgings. Then anger against Finch flamed up in him. He hesitated, his hand on the banister, almost ready to go back and begin the feverish discussion once more. But he knew that would be hopeless. There had been a light in Finch's eyes that told of an invincible resolve to go his own way at this moment. Well — let him go his own way! It would ruin him but let him go! What would Renny say? He would be furious, that was certain. Wakefield turned again down the stairway. Now the thought of the horse troubled him. Had he any right to encourage Renny to take such a risk? He was easily excited about a horse. An enthusiastic letter about this one would probably result in his moving heaven and earth to acquire it; Renny's wife, Alayne, would feel that his family had little to do to encourage him in such a risk. The buying of a race horse was only the beginning of the outlay it would entail. He had a mind to tell Cousin Malahide that he would not even look at the horse.

He found the family collected in the dining room. Mrs. Court asked him kindly how he had slept. Sarah sat close beside her, as though trying to hide behind the coffee urn.

"She was brazen enough," thought Wakefield, "up in my room. Now she 's being demure. She 's as two-faced as the devil."

"What a nice morning," said Malahide. He wore riding things and was helping himself to sausages and bacon from a dish on the sideboard. "Do have some of this, Wakefield."

Finch, on Wakefield's other side, said in a low voice: —

"Don't look as though the end of the world had come, Wake. I don't know when I 've felt so happy as I do this morning. So don't worry!"

"I 'm thinking about the horse, too." Wakefield felt

sudden embarrassment. " I think we ought to back down before it 's too late."

" After coming over here? "

" Yes. There was ill luck in it."

Finch gave a sudden relentless grin at him. " You call it ill luck! Not I. Let 's have the horse! All omens are good. He 'll win the Grand National, you 'll see! " He lifted the dish cover and disclosed two sausages and a lonely rasher of bacon. " Here, you have them, Wake! I 'll take some of that cold meat."

Wakefield gave him a look of hurt. " I 'm not hungry. I want only some coffee."

" Tck! " said Malahide, as Wakefield returned to the table. " No appetite! What a pity! But you 'll enjoy your lunch all the more. Now look at Parry, how he fills himself up."

He beamed at his son, who had a large dish of porridge before him, his mother having the same.

Finch and Paris were laughing and talking as they ate. Finch's eyes were bright and he had a fair color in his cheeks. His unruly lock hung across his forehead. Sarah sat demure, speaking to no one. She seemed hungry.

The pale sunlight slanted across the room. The bleating of newborn lambs came from the meadow.

" To me there is no sweeter sound," said Malahide. " The dear little lambs! " He placed a scrap of bread on his fork and collected on it the bacon gravy from his plate.

" Do you remember my pet lamb? " asked Paris.

" Can I ever forget her? " answered his mother. " We could n't keep her out of the house when she 'd grown to a sheep. She was devoted to Parry and would follow him upstairs to his room, bunting her head against the door and bleating till he opened it. Eventually we all hated her."

Wakefield's eyes met Sarah's.

" Poor lamb! " she exclaimed.

"It ended by my sending her to the butcher," said Malahide.

"The proper place for her," said Wakefield, grimly.

At eleven o'clock Malahide was waiting in the hall for the young men. In his riding clothes he had a look of vitality in contrast to his white hair and sallow, sunken cheeks. Wakefield and Paris were riding with him but Finch and Sarah were going in the car with Mrs. Court.

Malahide rode a good bay mare but the other horses were old and the one ridden by Wakefield was stiff in the hindquarters. He rode side by side with Paris, seeing, as in a dream, the new tender greenness of the countryside, the white thatched cottages with women standing in the doorways and little children and hens in and out of the doors. A delicate mist still hung in the hills and in the hollows and here and there was the silver flash of a pond with ducks on it.

"I can tell you, Paris," said Wakefield, in a low voice, "this is one of the unhappiest days of my life."

"I think I can guess why." Paris threw him a sympathetic look. "It 's the reconciliation between those two. I can see through her, I think. But how I wish she'd taken a fancy to me! Oh, I could love her fierce enough to satisfy even her! Do you think maybe I could cut Finch out?"

"Never. He fascinates her. Everything he does or says is wonderful to her. She told me so herself. Years ago."

"Well, well," said Paris, "that 's queer. Now I should say that you 'd be far more fascinating to a woman."

Wakefield turned to look at him in surprise.

"You don't know Finch. He 's an artist and he has all that implies — where women are concerned. But something happened to him — something went wrong — I don't know just what it was. It was n't altogether marrying Sarah. There have been other things. I think my brother Eden's death was a great shock to him. Then — when my grandmother died — she left all her money to Finch and the family thought — that is, *some* of them thought — he 'd been scheming and underhand about it. That hurt him terribly."

"What became of the money?" asked Paris. "He does n't seem to have much now."

"He has n't. He gave a lot of it away — to different members of the family. He made some bad investments. He has to work hard. Sometimes I think it would have been better for Finch if he 'd not been a musician. I mean, not devoted his life to music. What I 'm certain of is that he should never have been reconciled to Sarah!"

They rode on in silence for a space, then Parry said: —

"As Sarah is so much in love with Finch maybe she 'd like to buy the horse for your eldest brother, as a sort of bid for his good will. What do you think?"

"Renny would never accept it from her. Moreover she 'd not raise a finger to help him. She once held a mortgage on Jalna and Renny had the devil's own time to pay it off. She was going to foreclose. But he got the best of her and she 's hated him ever since."

"How did he get the best of her?" A subtle resemblance to his father came into Parry's handsome face.

Wakefield grinned. "With the last of Finch's fortune!"

Malahide's horse was trotting on ahead. Now he turned in a gateway almost hidden by tall holly bushes whose prickly leaves glittered in the pale sunlight.

"This is Madigan's," said Paris.

They dismounted and a young boy, with a reckless air and his head bandaged, took their horses.

"What 's the matter, Shaun?" asked Parry.

"I was just helpin' a friend, Mister Parry, and a fella came along and hit me with the tailboard of a cart."

Paris seemed to consider this a satisfactory explanation. He and Wakefield followed Malahide to the door. He turned to them with a secretive air.

"Now I warn you not to be too enthusiastic about this horse. You especially, Wakefield, must be very knowing and a bit skeptical. It is possible we may get him for even less than I said."

Wakefield felt as though he were being drawn into a net. He wished with all his heart that Renny were here.

The door opened and a maid, with large staring eyes, gave them one startled look and retreated, showing her bare pink heels at every step through the holes in her stockings.

Wakefield thought he had never felt anything like the frozen mustiness of that hall. A row of muddy boots stood along the wall and a mackintosh and whip lay on the floor beside them.

A short square man came cheerfully from the back premises to meet them. He had a square forehead and a look of spurious intensity in his small eyes.

"Good morning, Mr. Court!" he exclaimed. "And Mr. Paris! Is it come to see Johnny the Bird, ye have?"

"We have," agreed Malahide languidly. "This young gentleman is our cousin, Mr. Wakefield Whiteoak, from Canada. I 've had a time to persuade him to come, for he thinks his brother has given up steeplechasing and also he 'd not want to buy a horse by proxy."

Wakefield's spirits rose and Mr. Madigan's face fell. He said regretfully, as they shook hands — "Well, your brother is missing the chance of a lifetime. The devil himself could n't persuade me to part with this horse but that I 'm in desperate need of cash. Will you come along and look at him then?"

"Yes," agreed Wakefield, "I 'd like to see him." He felt sorry for Mr. Madigan for he knew what it was to be in need of cash and had heard of such need from his earliest days.

Outside, the car had just driven up. Mrs. Court had been

to the village to shop. Mr. Madigan greeted her with effusion.

"I 've been buying a leg of mutton," she announced, as though it were a piece of news worth repeating.

"Well now," said Mr. Madigan, "there 's a coincidence! My wife brought some glasses of red currant jelly out from the storeroom this morning, and a bottle of our cherry brandy. I hope you 'll give me the pleasure of accepting one of each — the jelly will go well with the mutton and the brandy will give a fillip to it all."

"Well, that is kind of you!" said Mrs. Court. She looked much gratified.

Finch and Sarah, after the introduction, followed the others toward the stables, she with her hand in his like a child's, he giving Wakefield a look of mingled anger and pleading.

"You 'd think," he said, as they jostled each other in the stable doorway, "that I 'd committed a crime, when all I 've done is to return to the woman I love, the woman I need."

"For God's sake," said Wakefield, "don't try to talk about it here! They 'll hear you."

"But it 's your expression that drives me to it. If only you 'd let me do this normally and naturally."

"There 's nothing normal or natural about it." Wakefield shouldered past him into the clean whitewashed stable.

The boy with the bandaged head led the way to a loose box at the far end.

"Here 's himself," he said, "waitin' to greet ye! Look pretty for the gentlemen, Johnny the Bird!"

The horse regarded the approaching group with curiosity but his expression was not friendly. He was big-boned and gray, with head and ears that were iron in their stark decisive outline.

"Now is n't he a darlin'?" asked Mr. Madigan.

Nobody answered. All were gazing in acute concentration at the tall, unfriendly, beautiful animal who now nonchalantly turned from them and helped himself to a mouthful of hay. With hay bristling from his lips he looked contemptuously over his steel-gray shoulder at the weak humans gathered there.

Mr. Madigan began to extol his value. From point to point, from ears to rump, he loosed fiery words in his praise, while Malahide stood pulling at his flexible underlip, Paris stretched his mouth in a grin of delight and the two Whiteoaks mentally collected all they knew of horses and trained it on Johnny the Bird. The stableboy kept fingering the sore spot under his bandage.

Then, bidden by Mr. Madigan, he led the horse to a very poor track behind the stables and the owner himself mounted him. Just as he started, a scatter of mud flying from his hoofs, an old man mounted on a sober bay gelding rode into the yard. Two others rode with him. Malahide gave a start of obvious anger.

" It 's that old rascal, Dermot Court," he said to Paris. " What in hell is he doing here? "

But he went to meet him with a smile.

" Cousin Dermot," he said, " what an unexpected pleasure! "

Mr. Madigan drew in the horse and trotted back to the starting point.

Dermot Court leaned from the saddle to shake hands testily with his kinsman.

" How d' do," he said. " Here, some of you, help me down."

Paris and Wakefield were at his side. What an arresting face he had, Wakefield thought. He was the Dermot Court he had heard his grandmother talk of as a " dashing young fellow." Renny too had told of visiting him and his old father at their home in County Meath, after the War. Dermot would know all about horses, he had been prominent in the racing world in his day. Surely he had been sent here by Providence to help them in their decision.

"I 'm Wakefield Whiteoak, sir," he said, flushing. "My brother Renny has talked of you, and my grandmother too."

"Yes, yes," broke in Malahide, "these two youngsters are our dear Cousin Adeline's grandsons. They 're here to look at a horse — a perfect wonder — with a view to buying him. I 'm delighted you 've come, for now we can have your invaluable opinion."

"Aye, that 's why I came," answered old Dermot, in his harsh voice. "I 'm staying with Colonel McCarthy, him yonder with the eyeglass, and I heard you were trying to sell these lads a *race* horse. I thought too much of their grandmother and liked their brother too well to want them to be fleeced. So I came over."

"I 'm *so* glad," said Malahide. "There is no one whose opinion I value more. You have met my wife, have n't you? And Sarah?"

"I have and admire them both." He bowed over Mrs. Court's hand and gave Sarah a pat on the shoulder. "What are you doing here, my dear? I thought you and your husband were separated."

"No longer, and never again," answered Sarah, with her small, secret smile.

"I don't believe in these marital reunions. I 've tried 'em myself and I say that, if a husband and wife once come to the point of parting, they were never meant for each other. Now which of you young fellows is the husband?"

Finch gave a boyish and rather tremulous smile. The smile, Wakefield thought, showed Finch's weakness, for in repose his face was distinguished and bore a look of experience. Dermot shook him by the hand.

"Well, well, any girl ought to get on with you. I hear that you were your grandmother's favorite."

"Oh, no," answered Finch hurriedly. "No. Not at all. That is —" He flushed painfully.

Malahide said suavely — "Women are unaccountable in their decisions, and our dear Adeline was no exception. But, Dermot, Mr. Madigan is anxious to show you the horse. I do hope you and your friends will come to my place afterward. Then we can talk."

"Yes, yes," agreed Dermot Court amiably. "But first let me shake hands with this lad." He took Wakefield's hand in his strong clasp.

Wakefield thought — "Why, it 's as though Gran held my hand!" He smiled and said: —

"You are like my grandmother, sir."

Dermot was delighted. "You could not pay me a higher compliment. As for you — you certainly bear a resemblance to her. In fact both you lads have the Court nose. How beautiful she still was when first I saw her! She was fifty and I fifteen. I followed her about like a dog." He made a wry face. "Well, she 's been long in her grave and was a centenarian when she went there. Sure, I have no business to be on the face of the earth. Come, let 's see the horse. I must tell you that I saw him in his last race and that 's why I asked Colonel McCarthy to bring me over."

All the while he inspected the horse, all the while he held the stop watch in his hand, he never ceased talking, but when they were in the Madigans' best room, with a decanter of whiskey and a syphon of soda before them, he was silent.

"What had we better do?" Finch whispered to Wakefield.

"Just what he says," answered Wakefield stiffly.

Colonel McCarthy was holding the floor, in a very wheezy voice.

"If there 's a man in Ireland," he said, "whose opinion you can depend on, it is Dermot Court. It 's in his blood.

And what a man old Renny Court was! That would be your great-grandfather. He spent everything he could get his hands on in steeplechasing. I expect he lost money but he had a lot of fun. Steeplechasing was n't too respectable then. It was nobody's child. But he and his father-in-law, the Marquis of Killiekeggan, and of course the famous Marquis of Waterford — they put it on its feet. Made it fashionable."

He ran on about the old days, Finch feeling that he could listen forever, feeling his grandmother in the room with him, as he heard the exploits of her father and grandfather; Wakefield impatient to hear Dermot's verdict on Johnny the Bird. At last he moved to a chair behind him and leaning forward whispered: —

"What shall I write to Renny, sir?"

Dermot spoke out of the side of his mouth but almost inaudibly. "Don't let that horse get away from you. That horse dealer and Malahide don't realize how good he is. Nobody does but me. I 'd buy him in a minute if I were n't so old. However, I 'd like to do your brother a good turn. I like him. Malahide is getting a commission on this sale. That 's why he 's so keen. But urge Renny to buy the horse. He can be trained in my stable. You cable Renny to come and see the horse himself, if he 's skeptical."

VI

THE TRIO IN GAYFERE STREET

THE passage to Ireland had been rough but the return calm and tranquil. Wakefield and Paris kept somewhat to themselves. Wakefield because of his anger and disappointment toward Finch, Paris because he could see that the married pair wished to be alone. Finch had asked Wakefield if he would object to his bringing Sarah to Gayfere Street. Wakefield had answered that he did not mind but he promised himself that, if he found her presence as unbearable as he expected to find it, he would get another lodging.

It was surprising how Sarah, who always traveled with much luggage and who seemed incapable of doing anything for herself, was ready to leave Ireland with so little preparation. It seemed to Wakefield that she had held herself ready to follow Finch wherever he went, at a moment's notice. She was conciliatory towards both Paris and Wakefield, she used the charm of her voice and her smile on them as though she would force them to speak well of her to Finch.

In London they had parted from Paris and stood waiting on the doorstep of the house in Gayfere Street, the rain falling steadily, driven slantwise by an east wind. Henriette opened the door but the smile faded from her large yellow face when she saw Sarah. She half closed it again as though they were peddlers. Finch had prepared himself for this moment but the words went out of his head and he stammered helplessly. Sarah stood smiling, waiting to be taken care of. Wakefield said, in a matter-of-fact voice: —

"Hullo, Henriette, are n't you going to let us in? I hope you have some of your good soup waiting for us. This lady is my brother's wife, who has come back with him from Ireland." As he said the words he had a complete disbelief in the reality of their import. Surely this thing had not happened! Surely they were not to have Sarah like a millstone about their necks from now on! They had been so happy in this little house. He had been so happy at getting a part in a play, at making a friend of Molly Griffith. Now there was this still, closed-in pale face between him and Finch, a barrier against their candid intercourse.

"I did n't know as the gentleman were married," said Henriette. "I 'ope the lady does n't intend to stop 'ere. There 's scarcely room."

"I may not be staying," answered Wakefield.

Henriette looked more doleful than ever. "I 'd be sorry to see *you* go, sir."

Finch spoke with exasperation. "We 'll settle all this for ourselves. Please get us something hot to eat."

Henriette retired groaning to the basement. Wakefield thought — "There he goes — either too shy to speak at all or speaking aggressively! Now he 's hurt the poor old thing's feelings."

"What a lovely little house!" exclaimed Sarah. "I 've never seen another like it. It must be terribly old. Did you hear the boats on the river while we waited at the door? Which is our room, Finch?"

They went up the stairs.

In his own room Wakefield set down his suitcase, contemplated it bitterly, then gave it a kick that sent it right across the floor. "Hell!" he said. Then added, "God forgive me for using bad language but I just can't help it. This thing is all wrong!"

He felt tired and disgruntled and he told himself that it was because Sarah's coming had spoilt his privacy. It was just as much a selfish resentment of that as a generous defense of Finch's integrity. Then he denied this, almost fiercely, and said out loud, " No, I do not mind for myself! It 's for Finch that it 's all wrong."

He had time for a hot bath before the meal. He got into his dressing gown and ran up the steep stairs to their single bathroom. The water was running and he heard Sarah softly humming. He sharply turned the door handle to express incredulity at her presence there. She sang out: —

" Is that you, darling? "

" No," growled Wakefield, " it 's me."

" I shall be finished soon."

" It's all right."

He retreated to his own room and poured cold water from a ewer into the basin. He took off his dressing gown and began, in an angry Spartan spirit, to sponge his upper half.

Finch came into the room. " Look here, Wake," he said, " I think you might at least *try* to understand."

" I understand only too well."

" But you can't understand how long I 've been troubled and what a strain I 've been under. Sarah has brought me tranquillity. Just for an example — I was terribly worried about my recital, you know. I felt exhausted after a few hours' practising. Now I 'm quite different."

Wakefield faced him, sponge in hand. " You must think I 'm blind not to know what you were like before we left London. But you 're always like that before a recital. I 'll bet anything that if you had met Sarah after it was over and you were elated by your success, this would never have happened. She 's having an hypnotic effect on you. But it won't last, and it seems hard to give up all your freedom in exchange for an hypnotic sexual content to carry you through a recital! "

" God, what a smug little beast you are! " Finch exclaimed, hotly. " You 've always been the same — damned pleased with yourself and your glibness! "

Wakefield had a moment's desire to throw the wet sponge

in Finch's face but he turned back to the washing stand without answering. He was shivering with cold.

They could hear Henriette coming heavily up the stairs. Finch wheeled and went out of the room. Henriette regarded Wakefield with a lugubrious motherliness.

"You 'll 'ave your death of cold," she said. "If you must wash, why don't you 'ave a 'ot bath?"

"Oh, I 'm hardening my body, Henriette. It 's good for the soul."

"You 'ave a lovely shape," said Henriette. "You 'd ought to take care of yourself. Do come now and have some hot soup."

Finch and Sarah were waiting for him when he went into the dining room. The daffodils he had bought were on the table. They were a little droopy. He bent to sniff them and Molly Griffith's face came before him, with that daring tilt to her profile and the golden freckles on her nose. "Everything was going to be so nice," he thought, "but Sarah has spoilt it all."

Sarah had evidently made up her mind to become an acceptable third. She smiled at Wakefield and touched his hand with hers.

"How cold you are!" she said. "We must arrange the baths so we shall not interfere with each other. I 'll have mine when you boys are out."

Wakefield was surprised at the shrinking he had from her hand. Involuntarily he put his under the table and rubbed it with his table napkin. He said rather precisely: —

"It 's quite all right, Sarah. I 'm not really cold."

"Henriette might have put a fire here," said Finch, eagerness to make it up with Wakefield trembling in his voice. "I 'll build one myself after dinner."

"What delicious soup!" exclaimed Sarah. "Not much like the watery broth at Cousin Malahide's. This Henriette is an excellent cook."

The sole that followed the soup was indeed perfectly cooked. Finch produced a bottle of wine from the sideboard. Suddenly excited and passionately eager to make things go well, he would not wait till the end of the meal for the fire. He found a bundle of lightings and some coals in the bottom of the hall cupboard and laid them in the grate. A bright blaze sprang up.

They sat about it drinking their coffee. Sarah wore a bright-colored shawl and placed herself so as to get the full glow of the fire. With feline abandon she luxuriated in its warmth and in that strange brightness in Finch's eyes. Wakefield rested his head on the back of his chair, his gaze speculatively on Sarah, and resigned himself to the new life.

Sarah also was determined that things should go well. With a strange ingenuousness she tried to make herself as small as possible, as though to take up less room in a chair were to make her brother-in-law less conscious of her presence. So that, even while she abandoned herself to the joy of the glowing fire and that brightness in Finch's eyes, she did so in a *small* way and spoke almost in a whisper. "I have never met anyone," thought Wakefield, "at once so sly and so transparent. She 's like a crystal figure of a cat. You can see through it all right but it 's a cat nevertheless."

"Old Cousin Dermot," said Finch, "reminds me of Uncle Nick. I 'd like to see them together."

"Yes," agreed Wakefield. "And whom does Cousin Malahide remind you of?"

"Don't say me!" exclaimed Sarah, in a little voice. "Don't dare to say me!"

"I 've never seen two people less alike," said Finch, but dared not meet Wakefield's eyes, for the laughter in them.

"He is a snake," said Sarah. "I 've heard your family say so."

Wakefield thought — "Heavens, if she knew what they say about her!"

" Our family is too intolerant," said Finch.

" But they 're generally right."

" They would approve of Parry."

" How could they help? "

" They approved of me at first," said Sarah. " They were very nice to me — at first."

Wakefield pulled himself together. " First impressions are always right." He smiled at Sarah.

Finch gave him a look of gratitude that hurt Wake. He said, to change the subject: —

" I must write home to-night and tell Renny about the horse."

" Yes, yes," said Finch, and pulled nervously at his lip.

" Shall you tell him about Finch and me too? " asked Sarah.

" Yes, Sarah, and I 'll give Finch the letter to read, so he 'll know exactly what I 've said."

" Thank you." There was irony in her voice and he hastened to add: —

" Not that anything I can say will alter Renny's opinion."

There was silence for a space, then Finch asked: —

" Should you like us to play for you, Wake? "

" Yes. I 'd like that." He did not really want to hear them play, to be the spectator of this particular form of their intimacy, but it would be easier than making conversation.

He kept his eyes on the fire as Finch went to the piano and Sarah took her violin from its case. The fire was making patterns of sparkling leaves and flowers only to wither them in the instant of their perfection. As the first note sounded he glanced furtively at Finch and Sarah. Somehow he wanted them to feel as unconscious of his presence as possible. Might he divine if they were truly happy in their coming together? Or was Finch feeling no more than a release of his troubled spirit?

But they baffled him again. They played only light, gay, charming little pieces, throwing themselves into the playing with zest and as though with the purpose of charming away his hostility to their reunion.

He could not but enjoy their playing. However terribly they might be unsuited to each other in their inner life, he must grant that in their playing they were one. When at last they paused, he said: —

" I think you two ought to have a recital together. I think you 'd make a great success of it."

" Oh, I 'm not good enough!" said Sarah. "I can't play anything really difficult. I only play the things I learned years ago."

" She is good enough, is n't she, Finch?"

" She could be but she 'd never work hard enough. She 'd have to work like hell for a year. Besides I 'd not want her to do it. She 's not made for that sort of thing."

Sarah laid her violin on the piano and took two short gliding steps to his side. She put a hand on each of his cheeks. He raised his face to hers; Wakefield saw her pale profile with its thin arched nose, small mouth and pointed chin, bend to him like a menace. He turned his eyes again to the fire. It was making little blue flames that were dying and soon to droop into the ash.

He moved restlessly in his chair.

" Well," he said, " if I 'm going to write that letter to-night I must begin."

There was no answer for a moment, then Finch said, with some constraint in his voice: —

" Why be in haste to write?"

" He 'll want to hear from us."

" He has your cable."

" Put yourself in his place. You can imagine how the cable will excite him."

" Of course."

Sarah said — " I 'm tired. I must go to bed." She moved toward the door, then turned to pick up her shawl. " What a lovely evening! Good night, little Wake."

" Good night, Sarah." He opened the door for her. As she passed she turned her cheek to be kissed. Wakefield just touched it with his lips.

" This is such a dear little house," she said. " To-morrow I 'm going to explore the streets all about. I shall love this part of London."

" Oh, no, you 'll not," Wakefield said to himself, as the door closed behind them. " You 'll stay indoors, reading and eating sweets till Finch takes you somewhere — just the way you used to. I remember what the family used to say about that." He opened the writing bureau and sat down before it, his young mouth set in firmness and disapproval. " I don't like you, Sarah, and never shall. I would n't give Molly Griffith's little finger for the whole of your slinky body."

It was some time before he could find his pen. Finch had been using it. It was empty and when it was filled and Wakefield began to write he found the nib somehow different and less suited to him. He frowned and wrote: —

My dear Renny,

By now you will have had my cablegram from Ireland and I guess that you and all the family are excited. I expect you will meet with more disapproval than encouragement in the scheme. But from all I can learn about him, and from Finch's and my own judgment, and from the opinion of Cousin Dermot who came all the way to Ballyside when he heard we were there to inspect Johnny the Bird, I do firmly believe he is a wonderful horse. Naturally I did not accept Malahide Court's opinions. I gather that he will get a commission on the sale. He was very nice to us, in that slightly slimy way so delicately described by the family. Mrs. Court was very nice too. I fancy she has had a hard time of it. I have told you how much I think of Paris. He 's a fine fellow and the apple of his parents' eyes.

They are terribly *poor*. (I find myself in this letter wanting to underline certain words the way Aunt Augusta used to. Do you remember?)

I enclose a copy of Johnny the Bird's pedigree and a record of his accomplishments. Cousin Dermot thinks you ought to go to Ireland to see him. He is going to write to you and I leave it to him to press down the balance in Johnny's favor.

My mind is in fact full of another matter. I have news for you which I am afraid will trouble you greatly, as it has troubled me. It is about Finch. He and Sarah have *come together* again! She was waiting for him at Cousin Malahide's and he was n't proof against that something in her which first fascinated him. I think it is a great mistake but Finch seems to be very happy. Sarah is with us in Gayfere Street. What will be the outcome of all this remains to be seen. I expect that Finch will write to you.

Rehearsals begin to-morrow morning. Did I tell you that I have met a charming young actress named Molly Griffith?

My fond love to all the family. Tell Adeline that I shall send her a necklet for her birthday.

Your affectionate brother,

WAKE

"Poor old boy," he murmured, as he blotted the letter. "I pity him when he reads this."

He went slowly up the stairs and at the top gave a low whistle for Finch. He appeared in shirt and trousers, with tousled hair.

"Want to read this?"

"If you like." Finch's tone was defensive. He took the sheet of notepaper in his bony, yet beautifully articulated hand. He read it without change of expression.

"It 's brief and to the point," he said. "I mean the part about me."

"If I had written down my feelings I should have been at the desk half the night."

"It 's sufficient that you registered your disapproval."

"I think I was very moderate."

"You were cold and rather smug."

Wake's voice trembled. "Point to one sentence that suggests either quality."

"I can't. It 's just the whole tone of it."

"The trouble with you is that you 're self-centred and supercritical."

"Well, this letter is about me, is n't it? After the horse has been disposed of."

"Is that what you think is cold? Writing first about the horse?"

"Partly. No — it 's the whole tone."

"Very well. I 'll not send it. I 'll tear it up."

He snatched the letter from Finch's hand and would have torn it across had not Finch caught him by the wrists. The feel of their flesh at grips sent a hot desire for violence through both. Wakefield's eyes flashed. He drew back his lips from his teeth and wrenched to free his hands. Finch realized that Wakefield had lived a harder, more outdoor life than he — that he actually was stronger. He said loudly: —

"You 're not to tear up that letter!"

"I will! I 'll not have you say what you did!"

They struggled over the letter.

Sarah glided on to the landing. She peered over at them. She had unplaited her hair and it hung over each shoulder in a silky river. Like the pale reflection of the moon her face hung above them.

"Are you quarreling?" she asked. "Can't you see the stairs below you? You 'll fall if you go on like that."

The crushed letter fluttered to the floor. Wakefield said: —

"Finch does n't like what I wrote to Renny. I want to tear it up."

"Let me read it."

He handed it to her.

Standing beneath the gaslight she read the letter.

"I don't see anything wrong with it — from your point of view. After all, you 're writing what you think. Let me smooth it out and you can post it the first thing in the morning."

"Very well, Sarah." He gave an accusing look at Finch and went down the stairs.

Alone, Sarah reread the letter. She smoothed it as well as she could, then wrote at the bottom, in pencil: —

You thought you could keep us apart. But I knew Finch better than you knew him and better than he knew himself. I never gave up hope. Now that there is no longer any need for hating you I give that up. I even forgive you for all the harm you tried to do me. That horse is a good one. Don't be afraid to buy it.

SARAH

She glided down the stairs and into the living room. She found an envelope and addressed it to R. C. Whiteoak, Esq., in her large black handwriting. She found Finch's mackintosh and put it on to cover her loosely hanging hair. She took an umbrella and let herself cautiously into the street.

From there she could see Finch silhouetted against the window blind. She laughed, thinking how frightened he would be if he could not find her. It was raining so lightly that she did not put up the umbrella but hastened past the little houses, with their bright-colored doors, toward Marsham Street. She kept on walking and dropped her letter into a pillar box. The streets were full of a slow-moving, quiet life. The lights were blurred by the misty rain. People glanced at her as they passed. She felt strangely happy. She thought of the two Whiteoaks in the house in Gayfere Street and how they had struggled together at the top of the stairs. What a lovely head Wakefield had! And those eyes! She felt drawn toward him but with no feeling of sex. All that feeling was for Finch. She thought of her nights with him in rapture, their isolation in the night, the immensity of the moving universe and they at its heart.

She turned into the passage that leads into Dean's Yard. She had never been there before and was filled with delight by the seclusion of the lovely old houses, the towering bulk of the Abbey. She discovered the cavern of the cloisters and went into them. Between pillars she saw the greenness of spring grass but she was in the blackness of the cloisters, half drowned in the dark well of the past. Her footsteps echoed on the flagstones. ("Beneath my feet bishops are buried," she thought.) Then another sound came — other footsteps running after her.

She had a moment's terror. A madman — some grotesque figure that haunted these walls — the ghost of a monk — was pursuing her! She clutched her throat and pressed her body against a pillar. In an instant she would shriek. Then she saw that it was Finch who was following her.

"Sarah!" he cried. "You've given me a terrible fright. Why did you come here?"

She saw that he was ghostly pale and that, like hers, his wet hair was plastered on his forehead.

"I could not bear," she said, "that you and Wakefield should quarrel about me — so I left."

"We were not quarreling about you."

"I am the cause of it."

"Sarah, you will drive me mad, if you do such things! Come, my darling, my precious one. Come home." He led her back through the streets.

VII
WAKEFIELD AND MOLLY GRIFFITH

THE rehearsal was over and a pretty scramble it had been. Wakefield and Molly Griffith were the only two who knew their lines and hers went out of her head the moment she opened her mouth. That was in the first hour, when she was so nervous. But she got over that and she and Wakefield began to enjoy themselves. It was a good cast. The middle-aged actress who took the part of the delinquent mother would be splendid later on. Now she read her lines from the script in mystifying mumbles. She and Ninian Fox had several small quarrels which promised to develop into real wrangles. But in between these they paid each other charming compliments. Robert Fielding was everywhere, his bowler hat on the back of his head, his topcoat much too long. He was a thoughtful and polite producer. He was meticulous; nothing escaped him and he would require some minute part to be repeated endlessly, but always with gentleness and apologies to the players. When the time for Fielding's own part came, Ninian Fox took the producing in hand. With him the case was different. He showed that he could be harsh and nagging.

"I 'm afraid of him," said Molly, as she and Wakefield sat at lunch in the tiny basement restaurant round the corner.

"Don't you dare be afraid of anyone," said Wakefield. "I won't have it, as my grandmother used to say."

"You are the first boy I 've ever known to quote his grandmother!"

"We all of us do. She made an impression on us that we can't get over."

"It 's not natural to me to be afraid but there 's something in Mr. Fox — anyhow, I 'm terribly happy. Did you have a good time in Ireland?"

Wakefield frowned. "It was rotten."

"Do you mean the crossing? Did n't you like the horse?"

"The sea was rough enough. I still feel a bit liverish. The horse is simply grand. Johnny the Bird, his name is."

"What a lovely name! It sounds so devil-may-care and Irish."

"Something really did go wrong," said Wakefield, gravely. "I think I told you that the brother I live with was separated from his wife. It was right that he should be. But he met her in my cousin's house and they 've come together again. She 's come to live with Finch and me and I wish she had n't! That 's all."

"Then shan't I be able to go to tea with you and your brother, as you promised?" A candid disappointment clouded her eyes. "She 'll probably not want me."

"Sarah will be very nice to you. I 'm sure of that. I wonder what you will think of her. You must come soon. Let 's see — you can come to-morrow afternoon?"

She gave a little laugh. "I 'm open for engagements at any time. That 's not as pushing as it sounds. It just means that I 'm rather lonely and that —" She hesitated.

"That you rather like me?" Wakefield's dark eyes laughed into hers.

"I heard it said of you this morning that you are extremely likable."

The waitress appeared with her tray and set their chops before them.

"How lovely!" she said, staring at them hard, like a child.

She looked too well pleased, he thought, and after eating in silence for a space he said ingenuously: —

"You know, I was wondering if you 'd like to borrow

a few pounds from me, till our first salaries are paid. I 've just had a check from home."

A bright color came into her thin cheeks.

"Oh, no, I could n't borrow," she said quickly. "I never have and I 'm not going to begin."

"I 'm dying to do something for you — however small. I think you might let me. Do, please!"

She began to laugh.

"What are you laughing at?"

"The expression on your face. I can see just how you begged for things as a little boy — as though your life depended on getting them. I 'll bet you were spoilt."

"I was not," he answered huffily. "I was made to behave by a grandmother, an aunt, a sister, and two uncles of the Victorian school, as well as several hard-handed brothers."

"And you got the best of them all! I can just see you doing it."

"I did n't think you could be so unkind."

The laughter went out of her eyes. "I 'd no thought of unkindness. How could I? When you 're so perfectly lovely to me?" Her lip trembled. An exquisitely sensitive upper lip, he thought. He just touched her hand that lay on the table and asked: —

"Will you let me lend you some of my superfluous cash?"

She exclaimed angrily, "Am I going about wearing a cadaverous expression? What 's the matter with me, anyhow?"

"Nothing," he answered tranquilly. "And if you don't want me to lend you a fiver, I shan't. But as you have discovered I 'm a spoilt boy I confess that it makes me ill not to have my own way. It would be rather a pity if I were taken ill at the beginning of rehearsals, would n't it? Then that other chap who almost got my part will really get it, won't he? I saw him talking to Ninian Fox this morning."

"That boy! I should hate to act with him. He 's got horrid hands."

Wakefield pushed away his plate. As he did so she glanced at his shapely brown hand, then swiftly into his eyes.

"I can't make you out," she said.

"Neither can I make myself out. I 've never been this way before. I mean wanting so frightfully to do something for somebody. It is n't that you 're pathetic or appealing. On the contrary, you strike me as being extremely self-sufficient. It 's just some quality in myself that is released by your nearness."

"That 's all right then. You 'll get over it as soon as we part."

"I suppose I shall but it 's disintegrating while it lasts. I simply can't eat."

"That 's a pity because the food is so good." She helped herself to Worcester sauce.

He watched her eat with interest. He continued: —

"Perhaps, if you won't let me lend you a little money, there is something else I could do. Has anyone been rude to you? I 'd love to knock him down."

"Everyone is nice to me. If you won't eat I won't." She laid down her knife and fork. "*Please,* Mr. Whiteoak!"

"I 'll eat on one condition only. If you 'll call me Wakefield and come out to lunch with me every day for a fortnight."

"Very well. I agree!" She gave him a smile that was almost motherly. "I think you 're sweet."

With an air of triumph he took up his knife and fork. "That sweetness, my girl, conceals an iron will." He attacked a chop.

But, though they might talk of other things, the subject that held never-ending fascination was the play. They were so enthralled that they all but forgot the afternoon rehearsal.

They hurried on to the stage breathless, to find the others being amiably harried by Fielding, with the exception of the leading lady, Phyllis Rhys. She and Ninian Fox were enjoying a whiskey and soda in his office. The theatre was very cold.

Wakefield was impatient of the easy-going slackness of the actors, the way they mumbled their lines. His idea was to do the thing beautifully from the start. He was irritated by Fielding's tolerance and good humor. He and Molly threw themselves gayly into their first amusing brother-and-sister scene. Everyone smiled at them. When they were free they went to sit together on a coil of rope in the wings. They lighted cigarettes.

"Will you come to our place to tea to-morrow?" asked Wakefield.

"After having had lunch with you? Don't you think that's rather too much?"

"Not for me. I want you to meet my brother. I should like to know what you think of him and his wife. Do you generally stand by first impressions or do you sometimes reverse your judgment?"

"I think first impressions are always the truest."

"Now tell me what were your —"

"I shall do nothing of the sort."

The youth who was to understudy Wakefield put his head round the corner.

"You're wanted," he said, with a smile that showed small, widely spaced teeth, then vanished.

"I hate that fellow," said Wakefield. "I know he thinks he can do Frederick better than I can."

"Anyhow he's making himself generally useful."

"Will you come to tea, Molly?"

"Yes, Wakefield."

The rehearsal proceeded on its confused and muddling way.

Wakefield was anxious that the house in Gayfere Street should look its best the next afternoon. He had acknowledged Sarah's position there by asking her if he might bring Molly Griffith to tea. Sarah had agreed. She had even seemed pleased.

That morning he went down into the kitchen to prepare the way with Henriette. She was sitting at the kitchen table eating bread and margarine and drinking tea, her large weak eyes gazing upward through the window at the legs of the passers-by.

" Legs, legs, legs," she was saying to herself, as Wakefield came into the kitchen, " legs coming and going — God only knows where and why. I 'd give a good deal if they 'd stop."

" Oh, good morning, Henriette," said Wakefield, cheerfully. " I 've come to tell you that I 'm having a friend to tea and I 'd like it to be even nicer than usual. I 'll bring home some petits-fours."

While he spoke, Henriette had been slowly and painfully rearing herself to her feet. With each twinge in her joints she gave a groan. Now she towered above Wakefield.

" 'Ave n't the teas pleased you? " she asked, with a tremor in her voice.

" They 've been perfect. I said *even* better than usual, did n't I? "

" I did n't 'ear it that way. But then my 'ead buzzes so I don't 'ear half that 's said to me. As for bringing cakes 'ome, I 've shopped in London for forty years and my father was a French chef. I think I know a petite four when I see one."

" Sit down, Henriette, do sit down! I only wanted to buy them because it 's such fun."

She lowered herself into her chair with a groan. " *Fun,* did you say? *Fun?* I wish I found such things funny."

" Well, you see, Henriette, it 's new to me."

She looked at him disparagingly. " Yes," she said. " You 're very new."

" I 'll bring home some flowers for the table," he said.

" Yes," she agreed. " I like flowers, though they do make me think of funerals."

" I 'll bring such gay-colored ones they can't possibly do that."

" The gayer they are the more they make me think of funerals. I realize how short their little lives are and how our lives pass — mine in this 'ere kitchen."

He ran up the stairs two steps at a time. He was afraid he would be late for rehearsal. He and Sarah and Finch had been to a play the night before and he had slept late. He was extraordinarily happy. He had recovered from the shock of Finch's reunion with Sarah. He was beginning to think that it might not after all be so bad having her in the house. Finch certainly seemed to have a new confidence and had returned to his practising with fervor. But Wakefield realized that the greatest cause of his happiness was his friendship with Molly Griffith. He poured out himself to her in their leisure periods. She heard so much from him about Jalna and his family that she had dreamt of them the night before and in her mind she began to confuse them with the characters of the play she was acting in.

The rehearsals were becoming more serious. Robert Fielding was, Wakefield thought, too fussy about the grouping on the stage. He would stare at the actors in an agony of consideration, then try some other grouping. Not till the leading lady showed irritation and Ninian Fox impatience could he bear to let the acting proceed. When he was taking his own part things went better, for he played it with zest and Ninian Fox directed with a firm touch. Wakefield was angered by his attitude toward Molly. He treated her as a beginner with no experience. He intimated that, though she did the lighter scenes well, he had grave fears that she would never succeed in the more emotional ones.

Mr. Trimble, the sandy-haired author of the play, invited Wakefield and Molly to lunch with him. The three got on well and Wakefield learned more about his part than he had in rehearsals. " Now I feel that I 'm really getting inside Frederick," he said. " Don't you feel like that about Catherine ? " he asked Molly.

She shook her head. " Not yet. Mr. Fox has made me self-conscious."

" You 'll get over that, won't she, Mr. Trimble ? "

" I find Mr. Fox very irritating," he returned. " But I was prepared for that. I 'd been told a good deal about him."

In the afternoon things went better. Wakefield and Molly were in good spirits when they set out to walk to Gayfere Street. The day was clear and cold. They discovered that they walked well together. " I wish you could walk with me in the Welsh hills," she said.

" I shall ! " he exclaimed, above the traffic. " I 'm sure I shall."

He pictured her in the hills and himself striding beside her. His blood ran quickly in his veins and he had a swift sense of power. After all, this crowded street was glorious — almost as free as the hills. Perhaps it was that Molly brought the hills with her.

He stopped to buy flowers from a barrow.

" You choose," he said.

" What flowers suit your room ? "

" None. Anyway there is n't much choice. Do you like violets ? "

" I love them."

He bought six bunches.

" Goodness gracious ! " she said. " You 're reckless."

As they strode on he admired the way she carried herself, the long graceful sweep of her thigh, the strength and buoyancy of her step. He compared Sarah's short, gliding steps, her rigidly held torso, unfavorably to this easy and generous walk. And she could move beautifully across the stage, too. Ninian Fox had praised this in her.

"I 'm nervous," she said, as they turned into Smith Square.

"Of what?"

"Of meeting your people."

"You might well be, if you were to meet them en masse. But these two! Finch is very easy to know. And as for Sarah — well, she 's a queer, remote creature. A devil too, I assure you. I expect you 'll dislike her but it does n't matter. Be nice to Henriette. She hates visitors."

"I 'm more nervous than ever."

Henriette gave them a watery smile of welcome. Wakefield noted with humiliation the toast crumbs down her front. But she had put on a large brooch containing the plaited hair of her father, the chef.

"This is Henriette who does for Finch and me," said Wakefield. "Till you have tasted Henriette's soup you don't know what the joy of the palate can be."

Henriette's smile grew firmer and she murmured that she made the best soup she could with what few bones she could get hold of.

The sitting room was empty of people but seemed full of flowers. Roses, lilies, carnations, were everywhere. This is Sarah's doing, thought Wakefield, and how like her to overdo it! He said: —

"Our violets will be lost here. Leave them in the hall. You must take them with you when you go."

He was chagrined. He had pictured Molly and himself decking the room with violets.

"Oh, thank you," said Molly. "But it 's really too much." She put the violets in the hall, then went into the room and buried her nose among dark red carnations. As usual, music was scattered everywhere. Finch's spectacles, his pipe and tobacco pouch, were on the floor. Wakefield went about tidying and growling his disapproval.

" What an old scold you are!" she exclaimed. " You 'd never do for our house, which always looks as though it had been stirred up with a stick."

He looked at her, surprised. " Does it? I think of your house as beautifully kept."

She gave a little bitter laugh. " Come and see."

They heard a step and Finch came into the room.

" This is my brother," said Wakefield. Molly and Finch shook hands.

" How different you two are!" she exclaimed. She looked from one to the other, hesitated, then added, " But there 's a certain resemblance. I see it now."

" It 's our devotion to art," said Wakefield.

" Perhaps it 's our inability to make a living," said Finch. He added: —

" Sarah will be down in a moment." He moved rather nervously about the room. He asked: —

" How do you like the flowers?"

" Very much. But I wish there were n't so many of them. Why did Sarah do it?"

Finch flushed. " In honor of Miss Griffith, I think."

" It 's like the First Night of a star," said Molly. " I shan't know how to thank her."

Wakefield went to look at the tea table. Certainly Henriette had done well as to cakes and there was a bright fire in the grate. She came sighing into the room with the teapot and looked appealingly at Wakefield.

" Everything 's beautiful," he smiled.

" That 's a blessing," she returned, in a lugubrious whisper, " for if I 'ad anything more to do I 'd have dropped dead."

Sarah had come into the room. Molly and Finch had

been talking rather shyly when she appeared in the doorway. Finch said, in the same shy voice: —

" This is my wife, Sarah, Miss Griffith."

Molly had made no definite picture in her mind of the Sarah whose presence Wakefield so resented, yet she was startled and disconcerted by Sarah's appearance. Perhaps, after the profusion of roses, lilies, and carnations, she had expected someone rather opulent, with hair that might justifiably be called tresses. Sarah came with her gliding step, looking, as Finch had once sneeringly remarked in the days when he was struggling not to love her, as though she were on wheels. She wore a kind of peignoir, very narrow and straight, of steel-gray moiré, fastened down the front by cut-steel buttons. The black plaits of her hair lay flat against her head, and from her small pale ears drops of tourmaline hung like frozen sea water.

Finch said — " Miss Griffith admires your flowers, darling. I told her you had bought them for her and she said they made her feel like a First Night."

Sarah smiled, well pleased.

" I said," put in Molly Griffith, hastily, " they made me think of a *star's* First Night, not mine."

Sarah still smiled but said nothing.

" Tea is in," announced Wakefield.

" Oh, look, Finch!" cried Sarah. " The lovely cakes!"

She snatched one from the plate and began to eat it before she sat down.

Molly wondered whether she was going to like or hate her. She knew she was going to like Finch. There was an odd, hungry look in his eyes and his thin cheeks, but his laugh had a sudden hilarity and his mousy-fair hair was untidy like a small boy's. " He keeps looking at Sarah in a puzzled way," she thought, " as though he wondered why he loved her."

" Have you many friends in London?" Finch asked.

"Very few. I don't make friends easily."

"You 're like me," said Sarah. "I could travel over half Europe and never make a friend."

"You wear such unfriendly clothes," said Wakefield.

"But when I do make a friend, it is for always. I never change."

Finch's eyes were on her.

"What about enemies?" asked Wakefield.

She poured herself a second cup of tea. "I am always willing to turn an enemy into a friend." She turned to Molly. "After tea will you and Wake do one of your scenes together for us?"

"I 'm afraid not. We don't know our parts well enough."

Wakefield added, "We discovered to-day, with Mr. Fox's help, how little we do know."

"Not you," said Molly.

"He was after me too."

Sarah persisted. "Please do a scene. I love acting. Make them, Finch."

"If you want to see Wakefield make a monkey of himself, I don't," said Finch. "Have one of these nice scones."

"There goes the doorbell!" said Wakefield. "I 'll answer it and save poor old Henriette's legs."

But she was there before him and brought the cablegram into the room on a silver tray. The tray shook as she held it toward Wakefield.

"They always make me tremble," she said. "There 'd ought to be a law against them."

All eyes were on Wakefield as he read.

SAIL FOR IRELAND IN FORTNIGHT SEE YOU IN LONDON WRITING RENNY

"He 's coming!" shouted Wakefield. "Renny 's coming! I knew he would! God, I hope we 've done the right thing, Finch! How excited they must be at home! And how excited I am! Look, Molly, here he is." He tore open the desk and took out a newspaper cutting to show her.

"Is he coming to stay 'ere?" asked Henriette. "Not that I mind a crowd. It 's just me veins as goes back on me."

"Not he," said Wakefield. "He 'll stay at a comfortable hotel."

"Ah, I suppose so," mourned Henriette. "I can't make anyone comfortable, no matter 'ow I try."

Sarah, Finch, and Wakefield chorused that they were more comfortable than ever before in their lives and, only partially mollified, she drifted moaning from the room.

Molly took the picture from Wakefield and saw a tall lean horse mounted by a tall lean man. Underneath was printed, "R. C. Whiteoak, Esq., on Mrs. Spindles."

"There he is," repeated Wakefield. "What do you think of him?"

"I like him," she answered gravely. "And the horse too."

"He rode that mare in the New York Horse Show and won a big prize."

"Did he?" She held the picture from her as though she were long-sighted and added — "He brings the outdoors right into this room, does n't he?"

Sarah put out her hand. "Let me see the picture, please."

She examined it with a little smile, then said, "I 'm glad he 's coming."

Wakefield thought — "So you can flaunt your recapture of Finch in his face, my girl! That cruel little smile is n't for nothing."

Finch was twisting his fingers together under the table.

"Are n't you glad he 's coming, Finch?" asked Sarah.

"I 'm always glad to see Renny," he answered.

VIII

PREPARATIONS AND JOURNEY

ALAYNE had hoped that there would be no family discussion over the visit to Ireland but she was disappointed. Piers and his family, Meg and her family, Uncle Ernest and Aunt Harriet, came as usual to dinner on Sunday. Throughout the meal and for an hour afterward the controversy raged, threading its way in and out of the question of Johnny the Bird, into fields quite unconnected with horses and even into the remote past, when Nicholas and Ernest had words as to which of them actually owned a carriage and pair they had kept in London, in the early nineties.

Perhaps because Meg and Maurice had been told nothing of the project till it was two days old, perhaps because they honestly thought the idea of buying Johnny the Bird was ridiculous and harebrained, they were heart and soul against it. They won Piers to their side, which stirred Renny to anger. The three made a solid implacable wall against his going. On his side, Renny had only the two old uncles (Nicholas nowadays became very much flustered when he argued, lost his breath and his heart thumped), Pheasant, and Aunt Harriet. Maurice and Meg both felt that Aunt Harriet, as a comparative newcomer, had no right to be so aggressive, but because she was charming to them and more especially to their daughter, Patience, they bore with her.

She leaned forward in her chair, talking volubly and with great clearness, on Renny's behalf. She was thrilled and exhilarated by her part in such discussions. She was like a theatregoer who had long wished herself an actress and suddenly found herself one. She did not realize that what she said carried little weight with the family.

Even Ernest was glad when she stopped talking. Even Renny was faintly abashed by her partisanship, though he loved her for it. Alayne on her part sat silent, detached and amused. She knew that all the talk was futile. Renny had made up his mind to go. She had agreed. Nothing they said could stop him. Nothing they said could send him on his way. All was settled. Yet there he sat, when he did not in his excitement stride about the room, behaving as though all hung in the balance.

She was pleased with herself in this mood. It was one she did not often achieve. And Renny was so happy about going to Ireland. It was true that he needed a change, spiritually if not physically. She knew too that he yearned to see those two of "his boys" who were in London, especially Wakefield. Sometimes she thought that the desire to see him counted for more than his desire to inspect the horse, though it was the horse he talked of.

When the visitors were gone and Nicholas had heaved himself up the stairs to lie down for a bit, Renny and Alayne were left alone together. She had a feeling of tenderness for him. She had heard him attacked. She had heard him repeatedly justifying his actions. She had felt for the thousandth time that the family did not appreciate him or the generosity that was the very stuff of his being. He was going away from her, they would be separated for weeks, and the thought of the house without him was the thought of a hearth without fire. She went about the room putting it in order. Surely no other family could do so much to untidy a room. Maurice invariably left pipe ashes somewhere. Meg always managed, though no one saw her do it, to replace certain ornaments in the position they had occupied in her day. It was a constant struggle between her and Alayne as to where a certain china gentleman, with a three-cornered hat and a flute in his hands, should stand. Alayne now gave him an accusing look, took him from the mantelpiece and firmly replaced him in his obscure corner.

"Do you like him there?" asked Renny.

"I don't really like him at all."

Renny was astonished. "Why, I 've always admired him, ever since I was Archie's size."

"I quite understand," she said. "But, you see, I did not meet him till my taste was formed. I think he looks quite well on this table in the corner, don't you?"

"He might easily get knocked off. He was one of my mother's wedding presents."

Alayne returned the flute player to the mantelpiece. She bent over Renny's chair and kissed the top of his head. He caught her and set her on his knee.

"How long shall you be away?" she asked.

"Well, by one of the small ships, ten days each way. As the St. Lawrence is still frozen I shall have to sail from New York. Say three weeks coming and going. A week in Ireland. Another in London. Five weeks. Is that too long?"

"If not for you, I can bear it."

"Alayne, come with me!"

"And add to the expense!"

"Good God, we have n't had a voyage together since our honeymoon! Surely we can afford this!"

"You seem to think that as soon as you have a few thousand dollars ahead you can afford anything."

"Anything in reason!"

She outlined the widow's peak of hair on his forehead with her finger. "Is Johnny the Bird in reason?" she asked.

That look of flamboyant honesty which she deplored came into his eyes. She moved her finger from his forehead to his lips and pressed them together. "Don't say it!" she said. "I don't want you to be convincing and reasonable. I want you to go because you want so badly to go. Nothing you can say would make me believe in the wisdom of buying this horse."

His eyes were almost pitying now. "Of course not," he said. "Poor little girl! Do say you 'll come! We 'd have a lovely time!"

"I could not possibly face an ocean voyage in March. You would have a dreadful time with me. No — you must take your holiday alone. Make it six weeks or more, if you 're enjoying yourself. Dear knows when you will be able to go again. But, whenever it is, I will go with you."

"Me too!" cried a voice from the hall.

"Adeline," said Alayne, "you should not creep up on people like that. It makes them feel that you 've been listening. And you were!"

"I could n't help it. I just came down the stairs in an ordinary way. You were talking. Listen, Mummie! *Please* let me go with Daddy. I 've been talking to Uncle Nick. He thinks I *ought* to go. He says a war may come. Then goodness knows when I can. If I go I 'll not be a bit of trouble. Once, when I was little, I went on the train with Daddy and he often says how good I was."

Alayne interrupted — "There is no use of your talking about it. Your father would not want a child with him . . ."

"But I 'm not just a *child*. Daddy says himself that I 've a better head than lots of grown-up people."

"About managing a horse! I dare say. But this is quite a different matter."

"I 'd love to take her," put in Renny. Then added — "If I can't have you."

"I 'd never ask to go," said Adeline, "if she were going."

"You may have sense, Adeline," said Alayne, flushing, "but you certainly have not tact."

Adeline stared. "What is tact?"

"Being careful never to hurt other people's feelings."

"Are you?"

"I hope so." Sometimes she was aghast at Adeline's power of angering her. It struck her in two ways. First Adeline's intrepid air — not rude but intrepid, as though nothing could really subdue her. Then her physical vitality. She could never be said to be "bursting with health"; no — it was something much finer than that: the spring of the dark red waves from her forehead, the proud arch of her brows, her chest which seemed as though drawn by an invisible cord upward. Sometimes looking at it Alayne felt apprehension for the day when young breasts would swell there and a woman's eyes would look at her out of Adeline's face. She did want to be friends with her child and she did try, but how easily the anger flared!

Renny felt himself responsible in a fashion for those qualities in Adeline which were trying to Alayne. He slid from under the pressure of this by repeating that she was old Adeline over again, but he still felt himself responsible. He and Alayne had risen and separated. They stood looking down on their daughter, who, planted firmly on her shapely feet, stared up at them.

"I 'd be no trouble at all," she said. "I know all about dressing and washing. I 'm never ill. If I 'm sick it 's over with quickly — like the dogs. I have my new coat and hat and three pairs of shoes. And Uncle Nick has a scheme. You wait till you hear it. He 's coming down. He 's rested."

"Goodness," said Alayne. "I thought it would take him hours to rest, after all that talk."

"So did he," returned Adeline. "But when this idea came he forgot his tiredness. He 's coming now!"

They could hear Nicholas coming, with a shuffling haste, down the stairs. He appeared in flowered dressing gown and with gray hair upright on his head.

"I 've got an idea!" he said.

Adeline flew to him and clasped him tightly about the waist. Nicholas went on: —

"I want this child to go with you to Ireland, Renny. It was my mother's country and Adeline ought to see it. By gad, I 'd like Dermot Court to see *her!* It is n't as though you would be on a prolonged stay. Now, I am willing to pay half her expenses if Ernest will pay the other half. It would be an experience she would never forget and, as I said to her just now, if war comes dear knows what will be left of Ireland!"

"I 'm willing, if Alayne is," said Renny. "It 's mighty generous of you, Uncle Nick."

Adeline turned pale with excitement. "Now I can do it, if Uncle Ernest will toe the scratch!"

Nicholas broke into laughter. He turned to Renny. "Mamma will never be dead while Adeline lives," he said.

"That sounded very cold and calculating to me," said Alayne. "I 'm ashamed of you, Adeline."

"What should I have said?" asked Adeline.

Alayne hesitated, feeling helpless to explain. "If instinct does not tell you, I can't," she said.

"Ha, ha," laughed Nicholas, "instinct did tell her! Now I shall go straight to the telephone and ask Ernest what he thinks about it."

"I 'll go with you," said Adeline, "and if he does n't" — not wishing to use the offensive phrase again she substituted "seem agreeable, I 'll talk to him!"

They went off, linked together.

"No one," said Alayne, "could bring up children properly, with Uncle Nicholas in the house."

"Only too true," said Renny. "What do you think about it? Are you willing for her to go?"

In truth Alayne found herself more than willing. Six weeks of freedom from Adeline's vital activities would be a relief. Yet, even while she was conscious of this, she felt shame that it should be so and, when Adeline came back exultant, Alayne put both arms about her and held her close. Love for her child surged through all her being. Adeline's response to the embrace was to clasp Alayne's neck so hard that she feared for a moment it had cracked. She put her hand to it and turned her head from side to side.

"What a hug!" she exclaimed.

"Sorry," said Adeline. "My nature is boiling over. How can I live till the day!"

From then to the day of departure the time swept on. There were a thousand things to be bought for Adeline, or so it seemed to her. Alayne took her to town and they did their first shopping together as mother and daughter, and lunched happily in a restaurant. They sat smiling into each other's eyes, eating ice cream and cakes. The most exciting thing to Adeline was being given a cabin trunk that had been her great-grandmother's and bearing the same initials as her own. Each one of the family gave her a little present before she left. She was full of gratitude, but its richest flow was to her two great-uncles.

The day came, blustering, wild and sweet, with the first scents of earth on the wind and the first robin singing in the silver birch tree on the lawn. Renny and Adeline looked out of the car window at the assembled family gathered on the steps, and waved their hands. Piers and his boys cheered. Archer ran down the drive after the car and fell. The car turned into the road. The massed evergreens hid the house. They were off.

Adeline had made up her mind that her father must never regret having taken her with him, or her great-uncles that they had paid her passage. Everything Renny told her about washing, undressing, and sleeping in the train, she drank in with wide-open eyes and parted lips. She did exactly as she was bid, except to sleep soundly. She had always been a poor sleeper. At night her vivid imagination ran away with her. A part of her that was tranquil during the day drew a strange vitality from the night, so that she could do with far less sleep than the normal child and would have liked to dance and sing and shout in the extreme of her lively fancies; indeed she often had and this was one of Alayne's trials.

To-night she lay awake for hours, listening to the throb of the engine, feeling the vibration of it through all her being. The steady roaring, the scream of the whistle at a crossing, the jolts and gratings when the train stopped, jumbled the pictures she carried in her mind, like a pocketful of coins thrown on to a counter. Like faces engraved on coins, she saw her mother's face with its quick changes of expression: now serene, as she read a book aloud or arranged flowers in a bowl; now smiling, as she played with Archer; now suddenly exasperated or severe; now with the look she had for Renny which fascinated Adeline and filled her with a strange unease. Then the coin with Uncle Nick's face on it turned up — the thick gray hair and moustache, the big nose, the deep eyes that looked right into you, and the mouth with its smile that was both funny and sad. Then Uncle Ernest, looking as though he had just had a bath and his hair tidied, his lips shaped as they were when he was showing you how to pronounce a word properly — in the English way. Then Roma, with her hair like those things saints wore, or that look her face had when she was going to tell you something she was not supposed to know. Roma's face lasted a long while, sometimes almost fading away, blurred by those strange tears she often shed for nothing, then suddenly close again and shining like gold. Archer's little face came and went a dozen times, now contorted by rage, now stretched in some newly discovered grimace, now with that piercing look their mother called spiritual and their father said was caused by wind on the stomach. Piers's face, Mooey's face, Nook's face, the faces of all the fourteen relatives she had left behind, came to keep Adeline from sleep. Even the dogs and the horses came, and the house servants and the grooms and stableboys. She tried to imagine the houses she was going to. She pictured Cousin Malahide as gliding about like a snake; Cousin Dermot as living in a castle. Strange shapes came to torment her, wild music rose from the wheels of the train and hands reached out in the dark to touch her. She burst into tears. She filled her hands with her red hair and made herself rigid with anguish. She kicked the weight of the heavy blanket from her. She thought she saw the black hands of the Negro porter untying the tapes of her curtains. He would kill her!

"Daddy!" she cried, in spite of her teeth that she clenched against calling. "Daddy!"

He did not hear but in a moment she heard his voice. He was saying to the porter: —

"You may get my berth ready now."

"Yes, sah. Ah hope your li'l gal is comfortable, sah."

"I 'll find out."

Cautiously he put his head between the curtains.

"Sleeping, pet?"

"Yes, Daddy. Like a top."

She put up her arms and drew his head close.

"I 'll be just across the way," he said.

"Good."

Soon she was asleep.

She went on being no trouble, except for the responsibility of her, right through the brief stay in New York and on to the ship. When she found herself actually on the deck, with the glistening skyscrapers of New York retreating and the harbor a tumble of foam-flecked waves, she drew a deep breath, her nostrils dilated to smell the salt air. Her being was too small at that moment to support the spirit in her. She clenched her fist and struck it on the rail. "We 're off!" she exclaimed.

They stopped at Halifax to take on a cargo of apples. A dock hand loading them fell into the icy water. Adeline sent up a shriek for help.

"Save him!" she screamed. "You're letting him drown!"

But he was pulled out of the water and stood shaking with cold on the dock. He put up his hand and saluted her.

She was beside herself from excitement. Then she noticed that some of the barrels were from the orchard at Jalna. "R. C. Whiteoak" was painted on them. She flew to his side and clutched his arm.

"Look!" she cried. "Our own apples! On the ship with us!"

He was almost as pleased as she. They stood grinning down at the barrels. Adeline called out authoritatively to the men: —

"Don't you drop those! They're ours!"

She was so hot from excitement that she pulled off her hat and the icy wind played with her hair.

But toward the social life of the ship she was restrained and her behavior at table was decorous. Ernest had lectured her well before she left. She ate the food Renny ordered for her and, before eating it, bent her head with gravity and said grace. They two had a table to themselves.

She was standoffish toward the other children on board and reserved when questioned by grownups. Only once did she get into trouble with Renny. That was when he found her throwing the dice for the horse races. When she had finished he beckoned her from the door and, seeing the look in his eye, she went abashed.

Outside he said, "Don't ever again let me catch you making yourself cheap in a crowd. You ought to be ashamed of yourself. I've a mind to take a stick to your back. Throwing dice, with a lot of strange men about you! Don't do it again, do you hear?"

" Yes, Daddy." She was nine and it was hard to understand. In a small voice she asked: —

" May I go and look on? "

" Of course."

" And bet? "

" If you like. But I 'll take you after this."

" Thank you." She squeezed his hand. The blood that had rushed into her face retreated. She made up her mind she would be more careful as to what she did. When next day he asked her if she would like to go to the horse races with him, she said — " Not unless you want me to."

" I do," he said, smiling.

They sat close together and between them lost five shillings.

It was a rough voyage. Once, looking about the dining room at lunch, Adeline remarked: —

" I am the only woman who has survived. What a good thing Mummie did n't come! " She talked a good deal of those they had left behind, dwelling on their perfections. She exclaimed: —

" I guess there is n't a single person on this ship who has so many nice people at home as we have."

They landed at Cóbh, in a soft rain and a choppy sea. The tiny boat that took them ashore bounced on the frothy green waves. There was a monk aboard with a brown cassock and a rope about his middle. There were women wearing shawls and selling Irish lace. Out of her own money Adeline bought handkerchiefs with donkey carts embroidered in one corner and shamrocks in another to send to the children at home.

She stepped sturdily on to the soil which old Adeline had left as a young girl to go to India.

IX

DERMOT'S LONELINESS

DERMOT COURT and Renny Whiteoak sat on that first evening, over their wine and cigars, strengthening the friendship that had budded when Renny had come to Ireland after the Great War. Dermot's two sons were long dead and his only grandson had been killed in a hunting accident ten years ago. He had no near relatives left. The only one of those he had who was accessible was Malahide Court, and he thought little of him. He wished very much that Renny lived near, for he was a man after his own heart.

"No man," he said, "has a right to do what my grandfather did. He had nine sons and planted them over the countryside. Now they crop up in all sorts of unexpected places. The first and second generations of them have passed on but the other day I came across a Court who had a bicycle repair shop. I would have thought he had no right to use the name — till I saw the Court nose on him! It was one of the finest specimens I 've seen. I had to have some excuse for going into his shop, so I bought a bicycle bell and sounded it all the way home in my distress."

"I hear from my boys," said Renny, "that Paris Court is a nice young fellow."

"He is indeed, or seems so. I can't trust any son of Malahide's. I wish you were my son, Renny. You know, when I last saw you I was very hard-up indeed, and for many years after. But now, in my decline, at the last hurdle, my affairs have looked up. A brewery I own shares in has begun to make some new soft drink and, such is the degeneracy of the day, it 's selling like wildfire. I 've had the old house put in order, as you 've seen. Now what I lack is an heir."

Renny fixed his bright eyes eagerly on his kinsman and moved his chair a shade closer. Dermot Court went on: —

" I want to fool all these relatives of mine. Especially I want to fool Malahide, who, if he can get me to himself often enough, will somehow worm my money out of me. I feel a weakness coming over me when I 'm with him."

" Good God," said Renny, " you must keep away from him! "

Dermot dolefully shook his head. " Easier said than done. In a weak moment I told him about the brewery and since then he 's dogged my footsteps like a bailiff. Now what I want is a child in the house — a boy. I 've a good ten years more of life in me. I 'd like a boy with new blood — from the New World. Now your brother Piers has three boys. Do you think he 'd let me have one of them? "

For a moment Renny was too surprised to speak or even think. Then the faces of Piers's three boys flashed before his mental vision. What a chance for one of them! Particularly Mooey, with whom Piers did not get on any too well. He said, gravely: —

" I think it 's doubtful if Piers and his wife would consider parting with one of them. In any case, none of them are Courts, though the eldest sometimes has a look of the family. But he's a thoughtful boy and not very keen about horses."

" I like a thoughtful boy. I was too harum-scarum myself. How old is he? "

" Thirteen."

" Just the right age. I 'd last till he was twenty-one, — I 'm sure of it, — barring accidents. They would n't be giving him up entirely. He could visit them every year or so."

There was something pathetic in Dermot's desire for a boy. Renny looked at him consideringly, thinking how extremely nice it would be if he himself might be selected as heir. But to have anyone of the family chosen would be great good fortune.

Adeline came in to say good-night. She was in pale blue pyjamas with a little padded silk jacket. Dermot Court put an arm about her and scanned her face.

"It 's a sin," he said, "that you should n't grow up in Ireland."

"I 'm only one-eighth Irish," she said, rather defiantly.

"You are all your great-grandmother," he replied.

When the men were alone again, Dermot exclaimed: "What a woman she 'll make!"

"Yes," agreed Renny. He spoke absently. Once again he had taken up Johnny the Bird's record and was studying it.

"He has n't done much," said Dermot, "but that does n't signify. I tell you, he has it in him to win the Grand National. Unknown horses that were picked up for a song have done that. He 's got stamina and that 's what counts in that race. Just think of the course! Thirty jumps and each one as high as your chin! It tears the heart out of me every time I see them rushing in at the start. I 'd buy this horse myself, Renny, but I 'm too old."

"I 'll buy him," said Renny.

"No — you must n't say that. Not till you 've seen him. We 'll ride over first thing in the morning."

"It 's a pity," said Renny, "that you dare n't take the risk. I could wait. How many times have you entered for it?"

"Seven times — and never won it! But that 's nothing. I have a friend who has tried twenty-five times and had only one win. But any one of my horses might have done it. You must n't be discouraged."

Renny was not discouraged. He was tingling with his desire to have a fling at the great race.

" The first horse I entered," went on Dermot, " was a poor-looking fellow. But I knew he had stamina. He 'd have won if the blasted jockey had n't been sick after eating too much lunch and so held him up."

" Bad luck," groaned Renny.

" Well, I sold the horse and he won the race the following year."

" My God ! " said Renny.

" Another time I 'd have won if the jockey had n't ridden over someone's lunch paper and frightened the poor horse to death. Anything may happen but I insist that you have a good chance with this nag."

Renny could see that the old man was getting tired. They were to rise early the next morning. They said good-night and Renny was left alone with his pipe and a glass of whiskey and soda. An Irish staghound came and lay at his feet. For a while he thought of nothing but the race. The magic name of Aintree shone before his eyes. He felt that he could not sleep that night. He wondered if Adeline slept. He began to think of his family, particularly his brothers. One after another their faces passed before him. But he dwelt longest on Eden's. It was good that he was to see Finch and Wake so soon. He had had Wake's letter, telling that Sarah and Finch were together again, on the eve of his sailing. It had been a shock. He had felt deeply angry at Finch. But that had passed and something fatalistic in him had resigned him to this second trial of marriage for them. For his part the thought of Sarah, as a wife, was impossible. But Finch must know what he was about and if he found himself happier with her than away from her, let him take her on again ! Marriage was like the Grand National. Anything might happen. He thanked God that he had such a good wife, that they 'd somehow got over their hurdles and were now running pretty easily on the flat — and had lovely children, too! Adeline upstairs — how proud he was of her! And young Archie — there was a character! Renny gave a small, malicious grin as he remembered how, in Archer's babyhood, Alayne was continually remarking on his resemblance to her sainted father. She did n't remark that so often now. Somehow — he did n't know how he 'd managed it — but somehow he 'd got a little of the Whiteoak devil into his son. You could n't thank God for a thing like that. Still, he was glad of it. It would make Archie a better companion when he was older.

He liked this old house. It reminded him a little of Jalna only, of course, bigger. He saw the room peopled by the dim shapes of his ancestors, Courts with long bodies and long legs and big noses — and a look in their eyes of being all alive. He would n't have given his father for the whole bunch of them. That father with his broad shoulders and flat back, his bold blue eyes and fresh coloring. Still, he liked to think of the Courts. And while he was thinking of them his chin sank on his chest and he fell fast asleep.

X

A PURCHASE AND A HUNT

An interesting quartette rode to Madigan's the next morning. Side by side rode Renny and Dermot Court. Behind them Adeline and a young groom. All were well mounted, for Dermot would have none but good horses in his stables. In his heyday he had ridden to hounds with three grooms on three good hunters behind him, in case he needed an extra mount or to lead the way over gates. He was as happy this morning as an old man well can be. He had had a good night's rest. He had no more than a twinge of rheumatism. He had with him two of his own kin whom he liked and admired and he was going to look at a horse which might well bring honor to the family. He was an inveterate talker and he gave a running commentary on people and places they passed. Once he drew up and pointed with his whip to a splendid wall about a large park.

"D 'ye see that wall?" he demanded. "That represents five thousand pounds that by right belonged to me! My godmother, Lady Moynihan, promised to leave it me but somehow this fellow, Richards, got round her and she left it to him. And he put it all into a wall! It 's an insult to me every time I pass."

Adeline did not look at the wall but over it at the bright array of crocuses that blazed on a sunny slope. Only a little while ago she had left a land frozen and grim, leafless, with icy slush as the only promise of spring. And here were a misty blue sky, swelling buds, and a road soft beneath her horse's feet. Dermot Court had long ago forgotten such happiness existed as was hers this morning. If, for one blazing moment, it could have returned to him, he might well have dropped dead from its excitement. But the young groom had not forgotten. His freckled face wore a grin of admiration and fellowship.

Mr. Madigan met them with his same look of spurious intensity. He gripped Renny's fingers as though he would prove his own honesty by hurting him. They went straight to the stable, the owner leading the way with his rolling gait. Adeline had not smelled the inside of a stable for nearly a fortnight and she drew a deep breath.

Johnny the Bird stood waiting for them, his hazel eyes cool and speculative in his gray face. He had a habit of sitting on the edge of his manger and now, against its sharp edge, he rested, a straw dangling from the corner of his mouth. There was a devil-may-care look about him.

"Does he often sit like that?" Renny asked of Mr. Madigan.

"He does, and almost never lies down. I had a leather pad put on the edge of the manger to ease him but he ripped it off and threw it on the floor. He prefers it as it is, don't you, Johnny?"

Renny grinned delightedly. He put out his hand and touched the horse's shoulder. A tremor ran over his hide like a rippling wave over a granite shore.

Mr. Madigan began to extol his good points but Renny scarcely listened. He needed no man to tell him about a horse. This one certainly was not beautiful but muscles stood out all over him. Renny said: —

"I 'd like to see him jump."

Mr. Madigan mounted him himself. The paddock was in such a state of slush that he rode him on to the grass beside the house. He trotted him about, then put him into a gallop. Renny wondered what he was going to jump him over. It turned out to be a garden seat standing near. Johnny the Bird took it in a tremendous jump, half as high again as was necessary. Then he took him over a table, then a tall iron fence. Renny and Adeline watched this with fixed smiles on their faces. Her hand was held close in his.

In Mr. Madigan's parlor, over a glass of whiskey and water, the bargain was clinched. Renny wrote a check. Just as he signed it, Cousin Malahide was shown into the room. A beaming smile illumined his sallow face. In his soft voice, that the Whiteoaks had called oily, he greeted Renny like a loved brother. Obviously he was to get a commission on the sale of the horse.

The two had not met since Renny was twenty years old. Then there had been a feud between them. Renny could not have believed Malahide would look so familiar. The greatest change was the white hair, which gave him a look of benevolence contradicted by his cynical lips.

"Dear boy," said Malahide, "how glad I am to see you! What recollections you bring of my happy time at Jalna! Then your grandmother was alive. She was my idea of what a woman of noble breeding should be — the truth is, I loved her! Though she was eighty and I half that age!"

He exclaimed at Adeline's resemblance to her great-grandmother and bent and kissed her. A quiver ran through Adeline. She had heard too much against Cousin Malahide not to hate him at first sight. She rubbed her mouth with the back of her hand.

Malahide drew Dermot and Renny aside when there came an opportunity and smiled into their faces. Renny thought, "One would think we were conspirators, and in some dirty business too — instead of buying a horse in an ordinary and decent way."

Malahide lisped — "I think this is one of the best days' work we 've ever done. I 'm sure you have a winner there, Renny. You 'll make a lot of money out of that horse. All I ask for my trouble is your success. I do hope you and your daughter can come to lunch with us. And of course Cousin Dermot." He laid his arm about the old man's shoulders and drew him close. " A good talk with him is one of the few pleasures I have left."

A hangdog look came into Dermot's eyes. He raised them appealingly to Renny's. " Let 's get out of here," he said. " Do you want to have lunch with Malahide, Renny? "

Renny did n't, but he hated to go back to Jalna and say he had n't. The uncles would want to know all about Malahide's home life. He agreed to go. Dermot gave him a look of whimsical despair when he heard this but, when Malahide pressed him to come too, he accepted the invitation. Mr. Madigan and the groom helped him on to his horse.

Renny watched Johnny the Bird being led away with pride in the thought that he now owned him.

" Look," he said to Adeline, " how his hind legs stride past his forefeet as he walks. That 's a sure sign of stamina."

She stood with folded arms, forehead puckered into an imitation of the corrugations on her father's weatherbeaten brow, her mouth pursed into a firm red bud.

" If she were ten years older," said Malahide, " I should wish nothing better for my son than that he should marry her."

" Her father would have something to say to that," said Dermot.

Malahide flushed. " My son is good enough for any girl living," he said. " Indeed I might well hesitate to let my son marry one of the Whiteoak clan, for they are barbarians, if ever there were."

Mrs. Court evidently expected them. She had the air of being dressed for an occasion and she met them at the door. She looked at Renny with interest, for in all her married life she had heard him more abused and vilified than anyone else.

Adeline was the centre of interest and liked it. Her eyes swept Mrs. Court, and the room they were in, with a keener perception than Renny's. She saw that Mrs. Court's dress was "funny" and did not fit like her mother's clothes did. She saw her shabby shoes and her uncared-for hands. She saw the satin covers splitting from the cushions, the holes in the carpet, the wallpaper in patches of damp. She did not see these things with the cold disparaging gaze of the precocious child, but simply as a part of the scheme of life that was opening up before her. Some people and places were like this, some like that; all were, in a kind of way, right. There was a faded elegance in the house that pleased her.

But her poise was shaken when lunch was served. Never in her life had she seen so little food on a table and never had she been hungrier. Dermot Court had a small appetite and seemed satisfied. Malahide minced over his plate and never stopped talking. He was an entertaining talker. He had been everywhere and done everything but his conversation was of a sly, slanting sort that repelled a child's interest. Adeline could think only of how her stomach was struggling to clasp her backbone and how it clamored for more after each morsel she gave it. When the servant held the dish of green peas beside her (Mrs. Court had already refused them) Adeline calculated that, with three men to follow her, she must not take more than twelve peas. When the sweet appeared her spirits rose, for it looked a huge mound. But it turned out to be beaten white of egg flavored with fruit juice and there was no body to it. She raised her eyes to her father's and found his gleaming with amusement while he took a bit of froth daintily on the tip of his spoon.

Malahide was as good as his word, possibly for the first time in his life, concerning the portrait of the elder Adeline as a child. He might have found it convenient to forget the promise but he had truly had a great admiration for his kinswoman and here was her great-granddaughter, enough like the portrait to be its subject.

As they stood before it he said — " When Finch was here I told him I was going to give this to you and, now that I 've seen Adeline, I 'm not only resigned to parting with it, I 'm delighted." He placed Adeline beneath the portrait. Like a showman he gave a flourish of his hand.

" It might be she! " he exclaimed.

" By Judas," exclaimed Renny, " was that Gran? I 've never heard of the picture. Strange that my uncles never mentioned it to me."

" They did n't see it. I always hid it when any of your family were about. I was afraid they would ask for it and that I, being incurably generous, would give it. But now it 's little Adeline's by right and she shall have it." He removed the picture from the wall and placed it in Adeline's arms. " Take it, my dear, and may you have as long a life as your great-grandmother, with the same zest for it."

Mrs. Court saw that the back of the picture was draped in cobwebs. She opened a drawer, took out a duster, and possessed herself of the portrait. She began thoroughly to dust it. Its removal had left a damp, yellowish square on the wall, many shades lighter than the surrounding area.

Renny was strangely touched. Looking at the little face smiling from the tarnished frame, he felt tears behind his eyes.

" Thank Cousin Malahide, Adeline," he said.

Adeline embraced Malahide with all her strength. He had leant down to receive her embrace but was not prepared for its primitive onslaught.

" Easy on, old lady," cautioned Renny. He caught Malahide in time to keep him from toppling over and, at the same moment, gripped his hand. " Thank you," he said. " We deeply appreciate your doing this. My uncles will love having the portrait."

Malahide simpered in pleasure. He slipped his hand into

Renny's arm and leant on him as they returned to the drawing-room.

Mrs. Court remained in the hall, rubbing the back of the picture. Once she began to clean anything it was hard for her to stop, but the place was large and she was small so, with the best will in the world, she could not keep up with the cobwebs and the dirt.

The next day there was a meeting of the local Hunt. Dermot Court took his two guests with him. He was Master of the Hunt and, though because of his rheumatism he seldom attempted to jump a fence or even lasted beyond the first twenty minutes, he was very popular and exercised a shrewd control over hounds and men. He knew that he should have resigned years ago but he could not bring himself to do it, not only because he shrank from giving up the sport he loved but because his rival who had built a wall with the money which should have been his was panting to be Master.

It was a fair March morning with a sweet tang in the air when Adeline ran down the wide staircase in her riding things. Her hair was in two plaits and she wore a bowler hat well on the back of her head. Dermot Court and Renny were waiting in the hall below. They might have been father and son and, many a time in those days, Dermot wished they were.

He raised Adeline's hand to his lips.

"Here 's a picture I shall keep with me," he said. "Have you ever ridden to hounds before, my dear?"

"No, but I 'm not afraid."

"You had better stick by me. I 'll not do anything that will be dangerous for even a little filly like you."

Adeline nodded brightly but her mind was made up to follow her father.

"That 's good advice," he said. "Keep near Cousin Dermot."

He was a little uneasy about her for, though she could stick on a horse better than any child he knew, he was afraid the confusion and jostling might alarm her. As they went toward the dining room he gave her some good advice. She looked up into his eyes obediently but her mind was a wild turmoil.

She could not eat. A lot of people had come for breakfast. They were standing about with large sandwiches and cups of coffee or glasses of cherry brandy in their hands. They were an odd, mixed lot but she had a strange feeling of kinship with them for, in some way she could not have explained, they resembled her own family. She was an object of interest to them and Dermot was proud to show her off. She stood with a plate of potato chips and sausages which she could not eat, before her, talking to a horse-faced lady in a rusty black habit who turned out to be a marchioness, and a square thick-set man who made everybody laugh by saying there was going to be a war.

"You 'd better hurry home, little girl," said the lady, "or you may get caught in it."

The man added gravely — "That is indeed true, Lady Ryall."

Now they were in the cobbled yard where the horses were being held, their hoofs moving delicately in their eagerness to be off. The hounds were sunning themselves beside a wall, gentle and indolent-looking, dappled liver and white. Servants were moving about with trays of sandwiches and drinks. The air was a caress. Little birds were singing in the jasmine that covered the wall. A fox terrier ran here and there in a state bordering on lunacy, ignored by the hounds, shouted at by his master. Renny lifted Adeline to her saddle.

Like ladies swaying in a gentle dance the horses moved along the drive between the rows of linden trees. Adeline rode a little chestnut mare, cobby and reliable. She had ridden her but twice yet there was understanding between them. Adeline pressed her legs against the mare's sides and stroked her mane. Her fingers felt the delicious smoothness of the rein. All her life she had seen pictures of the Hunt. All her life she had heard reminiscences of it. She had been taken to meets in Canada but thought scornfully of them as drag hunts, having no real fox as their reason. Now she was in Ireland, out with an Irish Hunt, her old Cousin Dermot ambling at her side smiling down at her with a protective air. But she wanted no one's protection. She felt no fear. A fire was kindled inside her. She kept her eyes on her father's back, determined to be near him. A towheaded twelve-year-old boy was edging closer to her. Now they were out on the road.

She could see the hounds ahead splashing through small puddles, their tails waving as though the breeze blew them. In an orchard a host of daffodils were in bloom. In her nostrils was the scent of polished leather and well-groomed horse. They turned in at a gate where a group of ragged children, some old men, and girls with bicycles stood by to watch them. Now they were on a rise of ground and the countryside spread before them in hills and vales, in the misty green of springtime, threaded by silver streams and dotted by white cottages. The hounds were on the fringe of a wood trotting aimlessly, it seemed, in and out of the gorse. There were boulders on the hillside surrounded by gorse. An old white farm horse ambled close.

Renny looked about for his child, saw her safe with Cousin Dermot, and turned again to his companion, a beautiful young woman in immaculate riding habit with long skirt. Low white clouds moved across the sky. A tawny something moved out of the wood and flashed down the hillside. The horn wound sweetly on the breeze. The hounds raised their voices in wild clamor. The Hunt swept, with flashing pink and streaming tails, after the fox.

"Keep close to me," shouted Dermot.

Adeline laughed and nodded. Down the hill they swept. The boy was just ahead of her. He laughed at her over his shoulder, daring her. She could see the onlookers running through the mud of the field, keeping up as long as they could. The horses rose over a low wall at the end of the field. Beautifully the little mare jumped. Adeline felt all elastic muscle. She rose in the saddle. She was over the wall. Far ahead she could see the tawny streak enter a spinney. Forty waving tails pursued it. The thud of hoofs made a mystical music on the hillside.

Dermot stretched out a veined brown hand and caught her bridle. The horses relaxed into a walk.

"I promised to take care of you, young woman," he said. "Don't you go running away from me."

Adeline flashed a smile at him. "Don't worry about me," she said. She longed above all things to escape from him, to follow her father, to be near the towheaded boy. He approached her.

"Stick close to Granddaddy, baby," he jeered.

Adeline urged the mare close to his horse and, taking her foot from the stirrup, kicked it on the flank. It jumped aside, almost throwing the boy, who laughed good-humoredly.

"Spitfire!" he said and added — "Begad — they're on the scent again!"

The sweet clangor rose like threescore bells from the hounds' throats. Across the field, through a gate opened for them, into a lane muddy and full of holes and, at its end, a five-barred gate. Over the gate Adeline could see the huntsmen rise, hear them gallop away, saw some push through the bushes to find an easier way. Dermot was one of these and he beckoned to her. She pretended not to see. She would go over the gate! She would go over the gate!

Her heart was beating wildly. The joy that was in her seemed a thing apart from her. It sang and shouted like a living thing beside her. She patted the mare's shoulder. She gathered her close between her legs. She lifted her over the tall gate, the shouting going on inside her, herself and the mare seeming to float in mid-air. They passed two horsemen struggling in a ditch. They galloped on to smooth turf in a wide level stretch. She could see her father ahead and the flapping of his companion's skirt. Dermot was far behind. The towheaded boy was at her side.

"You 're a little rip!" he exclaimed. "You 're as good as any boy."

Renny came cantering back to her.

"What did I tell you?" he demanded.

"To stay with Cousin Dermot."

"Then why did n't you?"

"I could n't."

"You might have broken your neck."

Her face was radiant. "I did pretty well, did n't I? Oh, she 's a lovely mare, Daddy!"

For a space the hounds had lost the scent. Now their deep-throated baying sounded from a copse close to a stream. Horses and riders gathered themselves together in a jubilant rush toward the spot. The old fox dashed from the copse, with the pack in full pursuit after him. He ran through the mud at the edge of the stream, clambered over a wall, ran into a yard where a woman was hanging out clothes, hesitated, with his tongue lolling and his eyes starting, to look at her ducks waddling in terror from him. He ran through them. The woman screamed. Now he was through her gate on to the road. Now he had squeezed through an opening in a quick-set hedge to a ploughed field. His eager nostrils caught the scent of another fox. He crossed the scent. Keeping close to the hedge he labored up the hill toward the rear of the hunt. The baying was confused, less certain, not so close. He stopped to look and to ease his heart. The hounds were running hither and thither, confused by the mingled scents. There was silence except for the quacking of the ducks. Then a bitch sent up a whimper. The hounds, as though weaving a pattern, ran toward her. Then, in full cry on the new scent, they stretched their legs to the utmost and, like a dappled tide, retreated. The huntsman wound his horn. The towheaded boy gave a screech that went through Adeline's nerves like fire.

"Yoick! Yoick! Yoick!" he screeched, and she joined in.

The old fox trotted leisurely back toward the cottage. He thought he would hide in the near-by copse till the woman went indoors. He was ravenous and the thought of a plump duck made the saliva flow. He settled quietly in the undergrowth and began to lick a cut paw. There was silence except for the comfortable quacking of the ducks.

Going home in the late afternoon, through a fine misty rain, with missel thrushes singing in the hawthorns, Adeline had never been so tired in her life or quite so happy. They had hunted three foxes and not had a kill, but she did not mind. She had had the excitement of the chase and that was what mattered. She was not tenderhearted but something deep inside her was content that the foxes lived. She had had a fall, rolled over and over in the mud and been picked up by the towheaded boy. Renny had not known of the fall till he saw the mud on her back. She had said good-bye to the boy in the shelter of a wall where they had dismounted to take a stone from his horse's shoe. Or was the stone imaginary? At any rate she did not see it.

"I suppose I'll never see you again," said the boy, his towhead bent above his horse's foot.

"Oh, I'll be back sometime," said Adeline laconically.

He set down the hoof. "Will you kiss me good-bye?" he asked.

She looked surprised, then a dimple played in her cheek. "I warn you," she said.

"Why?"

"I 'm pretty strong. I almost knocked over Cousin Malahide when I kissed him."

The boy's gray eyes opened wide. "Did you? How old is he?"

"About seventy."

"I guess I can stand up to it."

Adeline dropped the mare's bridle and advanced on the boy. She threw her two arms about him and squeezed him with all her might. Deliberately she tried to throw him off his balance, but he was firmly planted. Then she kissed him on the mouth. The mare was beginning to crop the grass. The boy looked somewhat ruffled. His mother's voice came, peremptorily calling:—

"Pat! Wherever is that boy?"

The boy caught the mare's bridle and helped Adeline to her saddle.

"Gosh," she exclaimed, "I don't need any help!"

"You 're going to have mine," he said grimly. He remounted. Warm color suffused his cheeks. "Well — so long," he said. He waved his hand and trotted away.

Now going home through the rain she thought of the boy and wondered if ever she would see him again.

"What was that boy's other name?" she asked. "Pat was one."

"Which boy? There were several."

"The one with the white hair."

"I 've no idea. What a nice little mare that is!"

"Oh, she 's a darling! Daddy, I love hunting!"

"Good! So do I."

"When shall we come back?"

"Next year — for me. I don't know when for you."

"I expect that when Uncle Nick and Uncle Ernest hear how good I 've been, they 'll want me to come again."

"They 'll more probably think this will last you the rest of your life."

But she was not downcast. She moved in a happy dream. Between the little mare's pricked ears she watched the unfolding of the winding country road. She put her hand into her pocket and found a packet of ginger biscuits. She munched these as she rode.

Before dinner she had a hot bath. She was to be allowed to dine with the two men. The servant who had helped her dress stared at her in admiration.

"Ach," she exclaimed, "it 's lovely you are! With thim eyes and thim curls, that look all alive. I wish your dadda would leave you with us."

Adeline answered seriously — "Thank you, Kathleen, but I live in the best place in the world. I 'll always want to go back there."

She ran lightly down the wide staircase. She found herself alone in the drawing-room. A chandelier burned softly overhead and by its light she saw the portrait of her great-grandmother standing on the table.

It was lovely to think that the portrait was hers. She had a good look at it and then went to look at herself in a mirror. It had a wooden frame carved in a design of lilies and dimly gilded. She was wearing a little green velvet frock with rounded neck and short sleeves. The mirror seemed to reach out to her, to clasp her to it, in its gladness at her child beauty, after years of reflecting an old man and his friends. Not satisfied with reflecting her truly, it heightened her beauty, deepening the burnish of her hair, adding to the lustre of her skin and the depth of her eyes which were the color of a beechwood in autumn.

Adeline looked from her reflection to the child in the picture. That other child looked so real, so living, that her breast seemed to rise and fall with her breathing. Surely the little heart was beating fast in happiness. Surely her voice would break the silence of the room. But Adeline was not afraid. She waited, with parted lips, for a sign.

Renny and Dermot Court had come into the room. It was Renny's voice that broke the silence.

"To think," he said, "that she lived to be over a hundred!"

Adeline turned and faced them.

"Well, young woman," said Dermot, "and what have you to say for yourself?"

She put on her sweetest, most cajoling expression and came to him.

"I'm sorry," she said. "But I could not help it."

"I know, I know. But the next time you come I shall let your father take you in charge."

Ceremoniously he offered her his arm and led her to the dining room.

Across the table she asked, "Who is the white-headed boy named Pat?"

Dermot chuckled. "I saw the two of you racing and hallooing. That's young Pat Crawshay. Sir Patrick, to give him his title. His father was killed in a hunting accident when Pat was only three. He's a fine little fellow."

Adeline thought long about Patrick. She made up her mind that, when she returned to Canada, she would send him a picture postcard of Niagara Falls.

The next day they left for England.

It was a wild and stormy crossing. Adeline kept her legs under her but she was not herself. Her face was pale and there was a pessimistic look about her mouth as she stared at the tumbling gray waves. For the first time since leaving Jalna she felt homesick. When she thought of her mother a tightness came in her throat. Seeing her expression,

Renny put his arm about her and drew her into the chair with him. With a look of mingled misery and gratitude she snuggled close and fell fast asleep.

They had just a day to spare before the Grand National was run. And what a day it was! They went early to Aintree. It was cool, windy, and sunny. Renny knew several of the racing men there and had letters of introduction to others of them, from Dermot. Everywhere they went there were horsy-looking men and women.

They walked the four and a half miles round the course and inspected every one of the thirty jumps. They stood in rapt speculation by Becher's Brook. Would Johnny the Bird clear it? They both said they wished the race were to-morrow instead of in another year.

Adeline ate an enormous tea and developed hiccoughs. Neither sucking of sugar nor nine gulps of water, without taking breath, cured her. She sat facing Renny in the hotel bedroom, hiccoughing. Suddenly, with a look of horror, he pointed under the bed.

"A gorilla!" he gasped.

The fright completely cured her.

Next day they saw the Grand National run and, that night, in a train packed with people, set out for London.

XI
LONDON

It was morning, it was spring, there was a feeling of gayety in the air, even in the railway station. Wakefield had gone into the café and had a cup of coffee, for he had been told the train was late. Now he stood by a bookstall looking over the titles of magazines and weeklies: the *Illustrated London News,* the *Tatler,* the *Sketch, Punch,* the latest novels, the huge best-sellers. Should he buy something for Sarah to read? But she bought such masses of reading for herself it seemed quite unnecessary. No, he would buy chocolates for her. How her digestion stood all she ate puzzled him, but it did and she put on no extra weight. He moved to the sweet stall and bought a pound of chocolate creams. Then he remembered young Adeline. She would, of course, think the sweets were for her. Dash it, he thought, kids are a nuisance! He bought a *Sketch* and wrapped it round the telltale box. A train had just arrived. The people poured out of it on to the platform: businessmen strolling along, their bowler hats a little to one side, dropping a cigarette and feeling for their ticket; women leading children, women leading dogs, the dogs looking self-important, as though the train were theirs and they only tolerated human beings on it. One carriage was crammed with young fellows in the uniform of the Air Force. They were laughing and jolly. Wakefield stared at them and wondered if he would like to be a flier. A girl in a white overall pushed a tea wagon, the big urn glittering, the little glass case full of buns and sandwiches and plum cake. Wakefield was jostled first by one, then by another person. He was in everybody's way. He felt rather sorry for himself. He decided that, as he had bought sweets for Sarah, he should have some for Adeline. He went back to the stall and bought a box of chocolates with hard centres. He lingered by the imported fruits and dates. It would have been more wholesome if he had bought them instead of all that sweet stuff. He had a mind to exchange them. Then he heard another train arriving and ran out to the platform.

"Is that the train from Liverpool?" he asked a porter.

"Yes, sir. Number five platform."

Wakefield hurried through the crowd. He reached the iron gates of number five and looked right into his eldest brother's face.

It was so extraordinary to see him here, yet so natural to see him anywhere, that Wakefield stood smiling and saying nothing. Renny kissed him as naturally as though he were a little boy again.

"Hullo, Wake! Here 's Adeline."

Wake bent and kissed her.

"How she 's grown! What about your luggage?"

"That fellow over there."

They found a taxi. Renny looked his young brother over approvingly.

"You look fine, Wake. How 's Finch? Why did n't he come?"

"Practising. Lord, I get tired of it! But the recital is in a few days and our First Night is next week. So you 're in for an exciting time. I don't know whether or not Finch and I are glad to have you for those occasions."

"Well, it will put you on your mettle."

Wakefield gave his gay laugh. "Renny, you 're just the same! You never change. If ever you do, I shall feel that my world has come to an end."

"Lots of sailors and soldiers. A Colonel Somebody in Ireland says war is bound to come soon. What do they think here?"

" Everybody asks everybody else what they think. No one knows. But I don't believe we shall. I hope not. It would be too irritating with our play on."

Renny gave him an amused look. He put his hand on Wake's knee and squeezed it. " It 's good to see you looking so fit. How are Finch and Sarah getting on? "

" So far it 's a success. Finch is n't so nervously tired as he was. But he works too hard." He glanced toward Adeline. " I 'll tell you more later."

Adeline was staring out of the window of the taxi.

" Look, Daddy, is n't it splendid? Far better than Liverpool. What place is that? "

She asked questions so fast it was not possible to answer them. They went straight to Brown's Hotel where the family was well known. Wakefield would have liked to have a long talk with Renny. He wanted to tell him all about the play and, even more, about Molly Griffith.

" Could n't we stay here," he asked, " and send for Finch to come over? Then you need n't see Sarah at once."

" I may as well get that over with," returned Renny. " Anyhow I want to see what sort of place you 're in."

" But I think Adeline ought to rest."

Adeline declared she was not tired. In truth she could scarcely hold her eyes open but she was determined to see all that she could, and with no delay.

Renny sent her to the bathroom to wash.

" She 'd better come to us," said Wakefield. " You can't play nursemaid in London."

" That is what Alayne worried about." It had all seemed so easy in Ireland. Now he thought doubtfully of a small daughter on his hands. " Who would look after her? "

" Well, there 's Henriette. She 'd do anything for a little extra money. I think Sarah would take Adeline out and she could come to rehearsals with me sometimes."

" Good! " said Renny. " The very thing."

They set out for Gayfere Street.

Renny had managed it all with such expedition and authority that Wakefield, once again in a taxi with him and Adeline, felt no older than the little girl. He sat relaxed, smiling, expectant, sunning himself in the moment's recapture of the childhood he had so relished.

Henriette opened the door to them and achieved a wan smile, for she had been assured that the visitors were only temporary.

Finch was practising. They had had a glimpse of him from the window, bent above the piano, his hands chasing each other across the keys. When he turned on the seat at their entrance, his face was flushed. He had to make an effort to keep his lips from trembling. But Renny greeted him with reassuring warmth, then glanced about the room somewhat disparagingly.

"Rather a stuffy little place," he observed. "But I suppose you could n't do better."

"We love it," said Wakefield. "And Henriette too. She 's a treasure. I must go and tell her you 're staying for lunch. Come along, Adeline, and I 'll show you the kitchen."

Finch knew that Wake was giving him an opportunity for a word alone with Renny but he did not want to be alone with him. He had no words to justify what he had done, in Renny's eyes. Renny had gone through a great deal to free him from Sarah's hold and he had returned to her of his own will. It would take a lot of explaining. In truth he could not explain it to himself. There were moments when he still shrank from Sarah's nearness, when the clasp of her arms made him shiver and turn away his head. But there were other moments of a deeper ecstasy than he had ever before known with her. She was two women, he felt, the one whose very touch repelled him and the one who had so woven herself into the fabric of his life that to be separated from her was to be torn and bleeding. Or was it perhaps that he was two men, the artist who could not endure the violation of his own secret world and the sensualist who willingly sacrificed his flesh as fuel to passion? To have spoken to Renny of either of these states would have been to embarrass him. How lucky Renny is not to have such feelings, Finch thought in spiritual arrogance, knowing nothing of his brother's inner life or that his emotions might be equally piercing, though less complex.

He gave Renny a troubled smile. " I suppose you think I'm a fool," he said.

" Yes, I do, rather. But then I 've never understood your relations with Sarah. If you want to live with her again it 's your own affair. I hope it will turn out better than the first time, that is all."

" It will. I 'm sure it will. I 'm not like I was then. I 'm stronger. Don't you think I look stronger? "

" I think you look very well indeed." He smiled rather maliciously. " Can Sarah be civil to me, after the encounters we 've had? "

" She said only this morning that she was willing to forget."

" She may be willing but I 'll bet she does n't! "

Sarah had entered unheard.

She asked, " Is the *she* you 're talking about, me? "

" No — Henriette," answered Renny. He held out his hand.

She laid her soft cool one in his. She looked at him out of her eyes, which were set like jewels, with no white showing about the iris. She gave him a long, searching look, but found nothing to reward her search. He was invulnerable where she was concerned.

" I ought to hate you," she said, " but I don't, because keeping Finch and me apart has made us love each other all the more."

" That 's good news," he returned coolly.

A silence hung between them which none of them could break. Then Adeline and Wake returned to the room. Wakefield talked volubly, the strain passed. There was so much to talk about. The play, Finch's recital, the visit to Ireland. Adeline was encouraged to be forward by her uncles, then put in her place by her father. But nothing could keep her in her place. She overran boundaries as the wind.

Henriette was approached on the subject of Adeline's visit. The remuneration offered by Renny for her services seemed princely. Wakefield had never seen her so vivacious.

"She 's positively bouncing!" he exclaimed. "Whatever have you done to her?"

"Been just moderately generous. How does the poor old thing live down there?"

"Buys her own food and lives on buns and tea. She 's as honest as the sun. I love her."

"So do I!" cried Adeline. "When can I go to a rehearsal?"

Wakefield leaped to his feet. "Good God, I ought to be off now! Renny, when shall I see you again?"

"Are n't you having lunch here?"

"I have n't time. I had coffee and a sandwich at Euston while I waited."

He gave Renny a coaxing look and his elder followed him into the hall. While putting on his coat Wakefield said: —

"I 've made a friend, Renny. I want you to meet her. I think I 've spoken of her in letters. She 's an actress — Molly Griffith. When and where could I bring her to meet you?"

"To dinner at my hotel to-night, you blasted little fool."

"Why do you call me that?"

"Well, I can see that you 're gone on her."

"No, no — it 's just friendship, pure and simple. But

you 'll like her. She 's just the sort of girl you 'd like. She 's as different from Sarah as a mountain is different from . . ." he hesitated, then added — " a slug! "

" A neat comparison," said Renny. " If you feel like that about Sarah it must be hard living in the house with her."

" Oh, I 'm getting used to it."

Sarah appeared in the doorway.

" Talking about me again! " she exclaimed. " I knew how it would be, Renny. I knew as soon as you arrived there would be talk about me."

He was lighting a cigarette and looked at her across the flare of the match. " Wake was just comparing you with a girl he 's gone on."

" To my great disadvantage, I 'm sure."

" No — he was just saying that you are softer and more clinging."

She stood rigid, her head turning from one to the other, her mouth thin and small. " By George," thought Renny, " that girl's nose and chin will meet by the time she 's fifty! " She said: —

" I wish I could know what is in your heart."

He inhaled the smoke of his cigarette. Their eyes met in a swift encounter.

" You ought to find me easy to read," he said. " I 'm not complicated."

" Not complicated! " she echoed. " You're the deepest of all. I could feel with Eden. I can understand Piers and Wake. But you 're as deep as the sea."

" You read far too many stories," he said. " You should take a course in real life."

She had a beautiful speaking voice. Even when she raised it in anger, as she did now, it had a strange sweetness.

" Heavens, how I pity Alayne! " she cried.

" I 'm writing to her to-day. I 'll send her that message."

Finch had heard Sarah's raised voice. He came into the hall.

" Tell him how happy we are, Finch," she said. " Tell him not to torment me."

" Good God, girl!" interrupted Renny. " Have sense!"

Wakefield opened the door into the street.

" I must be off," he said.

" I 'll go to the corner with you." Renny followed him bareheaded.

In the street Wakefield exclaimed — " That woman drives me mad! It seems hard that I have n't had a moment yet when I could talk to you of Molly."

" Never mind. I shall meet her at dinner."

" But I wanted to tell you about her first."

" Tell me about her now."

Wake answered petulantly — " I can't set out to describe a girl, on a street corner, with just a few seconds to do it in. But it does n't matter. Nothing matters so long as Sarah and Finch have sufficient space to spread themselves in. Good-bye."

Renny watched him stride through Smith Square. He was half amused, half annoyed by Wake's petulance, yet he had a satisfaction in it. The boys still clung to him, were jealous for his attention. Neither of them was really changed by living in London. He stood pensive, the cigarette between his lips, the gray shape of St. Mary's Church rising before him. On the shining pavement lay the reflections of old houses. A tug on the river was making thick foggy noises, comfortable, rich-sounding noises, the very heart of London communing with itself. He heard steps scampering along the pavement. Adeline had run down the street after him. Now she stood with an arm about his waist.

" Is n't it funny, us being here together," she said, "so far from Jalna?"

Wakefield was late at the theatre. He had held up the rehearsal of his best scene with Molly. She was tense from waiting.

"Whatever kept you?" she asked. "Mr. Fox has been in a perfect stew. Miss Rhys is in a temper. We 're all at sixes and sevens."

"I 've been meeting my brother from Ireland. He wants us to have dinner with him to-night at his hotel. Will you come?"

"Did you ever know me to refuse an invitation?"

"But you will like coming. I can tell you, he 's a very nice fellow."

"The worst is that I have n't anything proper to wear. No — I can't go." She looked at him ruefully. "I have n't a decent dinner dress."

"Never mind. I 'll tell him we had to rehearse to the last moment and had no time to change. He 'll be glad."

"I 'm dying to meet him!"

They were called to take their place in the rehearsal.

It was an afternoon of hard work. Robert Fielding was in his most meticulous mood, making the actors repeat scenes again and again. In his own part with the leading lady they had an open quarrel as to how he should support her when she fainted. She fainted repeatedly — getting angrier all the while. At last it came to the point when she fell in one direction and he reached for her in the opposite. She would have fallen to the floor had not Ninian Fox caught her. She broke into a storm of weeping and left the stage. Wakefield went with her to her dressing room.

"Help me on with my coat," she sobbed.

"Please don't go, Miss Rhys," he pleaded. "You were doing so splendidly."

"What does that man Fielding think I am?" she demanded. "A dummy, to be thrown here and there! No, I can't stand it!" She wound a green chiffon scarf repeatedly about her neck as though to strangle herself in her despair.

Ninian Fox came to the door.

" Miss Rhys," he pleaded, " please don't upset everything by going."

" I 'm tired out," she said. " I 'm a complete wreck."

" I know, my dear — I know. But I 'm quite sure Mr. Fielding will let you faint as you please from now on."

" It 's too late," she said grimly. " I 'm going."

Fox came into the room and took her hand. " Come into my office and have a drink."

" You can write a letter to him," she said, " on my behalf, and tell him that if he does not show more consideration for me, I 'll throw up my part."

Fielding came into the room. He no longer wore the long topcoat but a natty gray suit and blue tie. His clever sallow face was deeply concerned, though how sincere the concern was, Wakefield could not guess. It might be simulated merely to pacify Miss Rhys.

" Phyllis," he began.

" There has been enough talk," she said, with a tragic wave of her hand. " I 'm going home."

" Phyllis — you can't do that! "

" I can and will." She jammed a becoming green toque on her head at a rakish angle and made for the door.

Ninian Fox intercepted her.

There was another door and she turned passionately toward it. There Fielding awaited her with outstretched arms and the selfsame expression he wore when she fainted in the play. It was too much. She struck at him. She faced both men like a tigress at bay. There was a moment's terrible tension. Then they advanced on her and put their arms about her. She laid her handsome head on Fielding's shoulder and sobbed — but suffered herself to be divested of her outer garments and led back to the stage.

The rehearsal began again.

One of the most emotional scenes was that in which Catherine accused her mother of having been a bad influence in her life. Molly could not do her part to please Ninian Fox. He listened to her with a smile of suffering on his ascetic mouth, then interrupted her with a staccato — " Miss Griffith ! " Each time the color fled from her face and she started like a sensitive child.

" Again, please," he would say. " Miss Rhys, will you please say that bit beginning — ' Cathie, you 're still a child to me.' "

" ' Cathie, you 're still a child to me. You 're still my own dear child. If you say such things, you 'll kill me.' " Miss Rhys's magnetic voice pierced Molly to the heart, yet her response never satisfied Mr. Fox. He would exclaim : —

" Miss Griffith, I wish you could hear yourself saying, ' But why did you bring Captain McArthur to the house, Mummie ? ' It 's just as though you were saying, ' But why can't I have jam with my blancmange, Mummie ? ' You must remember this is a moment of high emotion on your part. Now let us try it again."

In the taxi on the way to Brown's Hotel Molly said, in a small, controlled voice : —

" He hates me. I shall never do my part to please him. I 'm getting worse instead of better. I know Miss Rhys thinks so. If it were n't for you, I should wish I 'd never got the part."

Wakefield looked tenderly at the pale profile turned to him. " I 'd like to bash his head in," he said. " I think you say your lines beautifully and so does Trimble. So do Robert Fielding and the others. Keep your courage up. You 're going to be a success. Especially in the scenes with me. Look round, Molly."

She turned her face to him and smiled. She laid her thin hand impulsively on his.

"You 're so sweet to me," she said, then added — "I wish we were going to be alone. I 'm not in a mood to meet strangers. Your brother will think me stupid."

"Don't worry about meeting Renny. I 'm glad he 's married. Otherwise you 'd be casting me off for him."

He spoke teasingly. She laughed and with childlike swiftness she turned to a happier mood. She took out a vanity case and made a few swift dabs at her face.

"Is that better?" she asked.

There was nothing provocative about her.

"Yes, much better," he answered, matter-of-factly. "But you 're paler than I like to see you. I wish you could have a week in the country."

"I wish I could. I 'll not be happy till I 've shown you the Welsh mountains."

That remark drew them still closer. A feeling of adventure made the air in the taxi quiver with a new life. A flower seller's barrow at the corner overflowed and flowers followed them all the way to the hotel. Wakefield doubled his tip to the driver.

Renny was waiting for them in the lobby. Wakefield had forgotten to tell him that Molly would have no time to dress for dinner and he wore a dinner jacket. Molly drew back behind Wakefield.

"I can't go in," she said. "You did n't tell him!"

"Good Lord, I forgot! But it does n't matter." He took her arm and drew her in. Renny came to meet them.

"Sorry," said Wakefield. "We simply had no time to change. We 're straight from rehearsal."

"Wakefield promised to telephone," said Molly, when the introductions were over. "I know I look all wrong."

"You look very nice to me but, if you like, I 'll change."

"Goodness, no!" She gave him a look almost of wonder. Compared to the men she and Wakefield had just left he was a being from such a different world that she felt she could find nothing to say to him. She was indeed almost silent during the first course of dinner. Renny appeared to ignore her, perhaps to put her at her ease, more likely because he had spent the afternoon with some horsy acquaintances whose conversation he repeated almost word for word. This conversation had great import, in his eyes, because of his recent acquisition of Johnny the Bird.

But he was conscious of Molly. She was very different from what he had expected. She seemed not to belong to the theatre as he pictured it. There was a courage in her way of holding her slender body and in the tilt of her face that troubled him, he could not have told why. As he saw her constraint wearing off he drew her on to talk. He was not particularly interested in the play but she found he was interested in Wales. She could see that he loved country life and felt himself at home only there. He had a way of turning his head aside and looking out through the window as though escape were in his mind. Yet he was not restive. The three brothers, she thought, were strangely alike, with all their outward differences. She felt Renny's swift, penetrating glance in all her nerves. He seemed to be asking her some question for which she had no answer.

On his part he wondered at his interest in her. He was not a man who was attracted by young girls. He preferred the society of experienced women. But he was glad that the girl Wakefield had apparently fallen for was like this. There was something good and wholesome in Wake. He believed he would run straight. He asked the two of them if they would like to go to a play. They would, and instantly chose a Russian revival running at the Westminster.

His look of resigned boredom at such a prospect made Wakefield exclaim: —

"No, no — not that play! It 's too highbrow for Renny. Let 's see a musical comedy or a thriller."

Now Renny saw the girl's disappointed look. He forced his weatherbeaten features into an expression of purposeful asceticism. "I like Russian plays. I don't often have the chance to see them. We'll go to the Westminster."

Molly's face lightened. "Oh, I'm so glad!" she said. She gave him a grateful look.

Wakefield scarcely saw what was passing on the stage. He only knew that his eldest brother was deeply conscious of Molly, and she of him. Wakefield felt no resentment as yet for her interest in Renny. It was natural. Women felt like that about him. But what right had he to look at her the way he did? What was in the look? Wakefield could not tell. He felt himself suddenly terribly young and inexperienced. He felt bewildered and swept by moments of rage. He remembered remarks he had heard about Renny's love affairs. Yet he did not seem particularly keen about women. He seemed, in fact, a devoted husband. But when they went to the foyer between acts Wakefield saw that intense look in his eyes, that adroit look about the lips, as though they knew, without effort, just what to say and do. Renny went to get sherry for them, his narrow, hard-looking head with the pointed ears rising above the crowd. Wakefield asked: —

"Do you like him?"

"Very much."

Wakefield searched her face for embarrassment but found none.

"Is he what you expected?"

"No one ever is."

"Do you form such fantastic ideas in advance, then?"

"He is much more exciting than I had expected."

"Really?" Wakefield gave her an icy look.

Renny returned with the sherry.

"Do you like the play?" she asked him.

"Very much. But, upon my word, those people led an awful life."

"Don't you think that all of us are like that underneath — only we don't know it?"

He made a quick grimace of amusement.

"Do you want me to believe that you are?"

Again that look in his face. Wake felt a sudden dismay. Surely Renny could n't do such a thing to him! Not Renny, who had been like his father!

"Why are you so quiet?" asked Molly.

"Am I quiet? I did n't know."

As they moved along the aisle to their seats she whispered — "Are n't you enjoying yourself?"

"Of course I am," he answered irritably. "You don't expect me to be hilarious at this play, do you?"

She was hurt and showed it.

He recovered himself during the last act and at supper afterward was able to force some liveliness into his talk. Renny, returned from the Russian atmosphere, was exhilarated. He hoped he would never have to see such a play again but he was glad they had seen it, because the girl was so obviously delighted by the acting.

"I 'll wager you can do as well," he said.

She opened her eyes wide. "Me? You should hear the things Mr. Fox says of my acting."

"He 's an old brute," said Wakefield. He put unnecessary vehemence into the words. He wondered at himself. He scarcely knew what was wrong.

When they had dropped Renny at his hotel and stood outside her lodgings in Ebury Street, a new feeling for her welled from Wakefield's heart. Renny's disturbing presence was gone. They stood alone together in the cool dark night. He wanted to take her into his arms and press his lips to hers. He wanted to prove that love had really flowered that night in him. Yet he was too unhappy to have confidence in himself more than to touch her hand. It hurt him to think that his love should flower in anger and jealousy. It had all been so beautiful.

"Do tell me what is wrong," she urged, in a low voice.

"Nothing. I 'm tired. That 's all."

"I 'm so sorry." She pressed his fingers. "Your hands are cold," she said.

He wondered how she could touch him and know nothing of his emotions. Perhaps she was cold, self-centred. But no — she just did n't feel any love for him.

"Good night," he said huskily.

"Good night, Wake, and thank you for a lovely evening."

"Don't thank me," he said bitterly, "thank my brother."

"Why, it would have been nothing without you!"

He wheeled on her. "That 's not the truth," he said harshly, "and you know it!"

She drew back from him. "I don't know what you want me to do or say to-night. Perhaps what I said was not perfectly true, but your being there made all the difference. Why, all the good times I have come from you!"

In the light of the street lamp he could see tears glistening in her eyes. He stood hesitating, bewildered by his own confused thoughts and emotions. The arms of his spirit reached out to her in compassion but he heard himself saying — "I 'm unreasonable, I suppose. Good night, Molly. See you to-morrow."

He walked to Gayfere Street. Sarah had gone to bed. Finch was reading alone in the sitting room. Wakefield went in and sat down without speaking. Finch looked up from his book as though just conscious of his presence.

"I did n't hear you come in. Have a good time?"

"Very. We saw *A Month in the Country.*"

"Was it good?"

"Molly said it was beautifully acted. I did n't notice."

Finch laid down his book. " Did n't notice? "

Wakefield broke out, " I did n't notice anything except the way Renny looked at Molly Griffith and how interested she was in him. You know, Finch, I love Molly. You don't think — you don't think — " He could not go on.

Finch's eyes were filled with pity. This poor young beggar was very unhappy! " You mean do I think Renny would be so heartless as to play with your girl's affections? If that 's what you mean — no, I don't."

Wakefield walked up and down the room. " I tell you, Finch, she had no eyes for me when he was there. And he looked at her as though she was the one girl on earth. As though he wanted to find out all about her. As though he were playing a game of skill and was the hell of a champion at it."

Finch's voice, which in moments of emotion he could not control, broke out loud and trembling: —

" He can't do that to you, Wake! You must n't let him."

" How can I prevent it? "

Finch spoke more quietly. " Why, Renny would n't do anything to hurt you. He 's too fond of you. All you need to do is to let him see that you love the girl — "

Wakefield interrupted — " He knows I 'm terribly keen about her. No — he 's off on a holiday. He's going to have a little fun and he does n't care who suffers for it."

" Wake, I won't believe that Renny would consciously make you miserable. Shall I speak to him? "

" No," Wakefield answered bitterly. " If I am such a weakling that I can't hang on to my own girl — "

" Rot! "

" It is n't rot. . . . If my girl thinks so little of me — "

" Wake, you 've been engaged. You know something about women — "

" I was engaged to Pauline Lebraux. She would n't have looked at another man as Molly looked at him to-night."

" But you 're not engaged to Molly."

" No. And probably never shall be! " He sat down and buried his face in his hands.

Renny's presence was in the room with them, heady and strong; easy and ruthless, they felt, where women were concerned.

" And I looked forward to his coming! " exclaimed Wakefield. " I wanted him to meet Molly! "

Finch spoke comfortingly. " Now look here, Wake, you 're overwrought and perhaps you 're making a mountain out of a molehill. God knows, I do the same thing myself. After all, they need never meet again if you don't want them to."

" I 've seen them meet to-night. Things can't be the same again."

" In a fortnight he 'll be on the ocean."

" He 's done something that will remain."

" Why don't you have it out with Molly? A talk with her would clear the air."

" Perhaps I shall. Anyhow I 'm going to bed now. . . . I wish I knew what is in his mind."

" Probably he 's fast asleep and dreaming of Johnny the Bird."

In spite of himself, Wakefield laughed.

XII
PLAY AND RECITAL

MOLLY was so natural when Wakefield met her at the rehearsal next day that he felt a momentary ease of mind but it did not last. A note from Renny was handed to him. It read: —

DEAR WAKE,

I 've got to take young Adeline about a bit. A friend who owns a launch has asked us to Marlow this afternoon for tea on the river. She 'd like to have you, and Miss Griffith too, if you 'll come. The boy will wait for an answer.

R.

Wakefield knit his brow into furrows that gave him an odd resemblance to Nicholas. He did not know what to do. He could, as Finch had said, keep Renny and Molly from meeting. On the other hand, if he watched them together, he might find that his jealousy had no substance in fact. But if he threw them together, he might bitterly regret it. Still, Renny was a married man. Even if he did admire Molly, what could come of it? This way and that, Wake's mind was torn by indecision.

The bell rang for the rehearsal to continue. He went to where Molly stood alone and asked abruptly, "Would you like to go up the river this afternoon? My brother has asked us."

She answered at once, "I 'd love to, if we can get away in time."

"We can. It 's Wednesday. There 's a matinee. All right, I 'll accept."

He scribbled — "Thanks. We 'd like to come," on the back of Renny's note, and gave it to the boy.

The bell rang again.

They were rehearsing in the bar of the theatre. The little tables were pushed against the wall. Ninian Fox was producing. He sat on the edge of a table, gently swinging his leg and smiling at Miss Rhys, Fielding, and the leading man, who had begun one of their comedy scenes. Miss Rhys was indeed inimitable. She played with such zest that Wakefield was no longer conscious of the rattle of dishes in the adjoining kitchen and stared at her, as her son Frederick, in mingled tenderness and rage. His cue came and he threw himself impetuously into the scene. Things went well. He was better than usual. Ninian Fox was so pleased that he allowed Molly to say most of her lines in peace. They had not before had such a satisfactory rehearsal.

They had tea and sandwiches from the bar. Shafts of thin sunlight came in at the windows. Molly had a lovely color in her cheeks. Wakefield thought — "She looks radiant, all because she 's going up the river. Or is it because she 'll be near Renny? Whichever it is, I have no part in it." He said coldly: —

"It 's been a good rehearsal, has n't it?"

She gave him a swift glance.

"Yes. Splendid. I 'm so happy about it I wish we could go on all the afternoon."

"What about the river?"

"Oh, I 'd forgotten that."

He saw that she spoke the truth. He could not doubt her. Happiness flowed back into him.

"I 'd like to go on too," he said. His eyes caressed her. But he did not see her. He was half blinded by the love that struggled to engulf him.

The principals were loudly talking, oblivious of the looks given them by the waitresses who were rearranging the tables. The theatre was beginning to fill. One of the actresses of the current play looked into the room.

"Is Mr. Fox here?" she asked.

He went to her, keyed up for trouble of some sort. She kissed him and they hurried off together. Miss Rhys was arguing with Fielding, but amiably. The leading man offered his cigarette case to Wake and Molly.

"The last act is going to be a flop," he said, cheerfully.

"Oh, I think it's lovely," said Molly.

Wakefield looked judicial.

"I think it's impossible to say till we all know our lines better."

"You mean me?" laughed the leading man. "Oh, I'll know them, when the night comes. But I can tell you the end's all wrong."

The waitresses almost pushed them from the room. They glimpsed a scattered audience in the house.

"*Is n't* it a lovely life!" cried Molly, as they ran into the street. "I would n't be anyone but an actress, in the whole world!"

They stopped to look at the poster advertising their play. They riveted their eyes on the space where their two names appeared.

"Some day yours will be in large letters," said Wakefield.

"Yours too."

"I'm not so sure about that. I'm too intelligent, if you know what I mean. I'm always thinking of different ways to do my part. I can't settle down to any one way. While you settle down and go right ahead."

Renny was waiting for them round the corner in his friend's car. Adeline was there too. Though it was barely the first of April the air had summer's warmth and in the parks the flowers showed an exquisite forwardness. London sprawled in the sunshine, peaceful and friendly, like an overgrown village.

Molly and Adeline immediately made friends. Renny was sitting in the front seat with his friend Mrs. Blake.

She wore mannish clothes but had added to them long green earrings. Though she was of masculine tastes and thought of little else but fox-hunting and racing, the feminine strain in her was very up and doing. After an appraising glance and a brief welcome to Wake and Molly she devoted herself wholly to what, from the back seat, appeared to be a flirtatious attack on Renny.

Adeline sat upright between Wakefield and Molly. She was eager to miss nothing of what she saw. "I must remember to tell Archie about that," she would say, or — "How I wish Mooey were here!" When they reached Richmond she was the first to enter the launch. She established herself close to the man at the helm, then, remembering her manners, she turned and asked Mrs. Blake's permission to do so.

"Delighted," said Mrs. Blake absently. She was choosing the best chairs for herself and Renny. The two young people sat together in the stern.

Molly was in a state of dreamlike happiness. She was one of those people who are never content in towns yet by their ambition are driven to live in them. This was her first outing on the river. Wakefield was at her side. The background of care, of her family life, was dissolved like a troubling mist. She wore a new, bright-colored scarf. New spring clothes were impossible to her. This gauzy scarf kept fluttering against Wakefield's ear. It made delicate fluttering noises, like words uttered in confidence. It flicked his cheek. It wound itself about his neck, binding him and Molly together, yet she knew nothing of its vagaries. She sat gazing blissfully at the riverbanks, her hands relaxed in her lap. They were ringless, thin, capable-looking.

One riverbank lay in sunlight, the other in olive-green shadow. They passed barges and small river craft, but after Windsor, with its Castle ethereal against the sky, they had the river almost to themselves.

Adeline had captivated the man at the helm. She had it in her mind to steer the launch herself but was just biding her time. She had taken off her hat, and her hair, in waving russet vitality, curled itself on the breeze. Her black-lashed brown eyes were raised in sweet blandishment to the helmsman's face.

"What hair!" exclaimed Molly. "And what eyes! It 's easy, of course, to see where she gets them."

Wakefield gave her a searching look.

"What do you think of my brother?" he asked.

"You asked me that before."

"Did I? And what was your answer?"

"I said I liked him very much."

"What an answer! It 's worse than none."

"If you want the truth, I find him hard to talk to. I can't explain why. It 's as though he and I had known each other before but could not reach a state of friendship again."

Wakefield considered this, frowning. He said — "I think that is probably a girl's way of expressing a great attraction toward him."

"Goodness, he 's a married man! I 'm not that sort of girl."

Wakefield said, with a disapproving glance at Mrs. Blake, "Marriage does n't seem to be an obstacle to that lady. I don't know what the world 's coming to!"

"You talk like a grandfather rather than a young actor. Just the same, I think it 's adorable in you." Then she added, after a moment's thought — "Anyhow, I don't think your brother's wife need worry. He strikes me as pretty reliable."

"*Does* he? Tell the truth, Molly. Does he strike you as reliable where women are concerned?"

She laughed but would not answer. She trailed her hand in the cool green water, caught at a water weed and drew it along.

Wakefield felt a helpless rage toward her. She had no right to be teasing when he was so deeply in earnest. Her scarf fluttered against his cheek. He took it and caught it in the front of her jacket. She saw that he was angry.

"Do you expect me to be serious on a day like this?" she asked.

"I don't expect you to lie just for the fun of it."

"I did n't lie. When I spoke I believed what I said. Then quite suddenly I seemed to see him in a different light. I can't explain why."

"And it made you just laugh and laugh!"

"Well, I suppose I might have cried and cried."

"I can tell you that, at this moment, I wish he were back in Canada."

"Then we should n't be here — on the river."

"And I should n't have this beastly sensation inside me."

She gave him a suddenly tender look, as though he were a precocious child. The object of their argument looked back at them over his shoulder and asked — "Having a good time?"

Mrs. Blake also looked back but rather as though she resented their being there.

"Perfect!" answered Molly.

"Yes," agreed Wakefield, "I 've never seen the river lovelier."

Adeline was giving exclamations of delight. They were entering a lock. The great gates swung to. The lock keeper came to greet them. Mrs. Blake showed her license and tipped him. Up and up the launch rose against the cool dank walls. At last they were at the top. The gates opened and the launch slid out on the river.

"Oh, how I wish Mooey and Nook were here!" cried Adeline. There was a spirit of generosity in her that could not wholly enjoy without sharing with those she loved.

" And, of course, Archie and Roma and Mummie and the uncles ! "

Wakefield cursed himself for his unease of spirit. " I have no cause for it," he thought. " She 's just as free and gay as the scarf she wears. But, because Renny 's in the boat, I can't be happy. What has come over me ? "

In a wooded reach of the river they drew in to shore and a tea basket was produced. Renny and Mrs. Blake set out the tea things. With a solicitous air, Adeline waited on the helmsman, her inner eye always on the guiding of the launch downstream. She sat munching a sandwich, watchful lest he should lack anything.

Mrs. Blake talked to Renny, of things the others knew nothing about. But now and again she gave them a flashing smile and an invitation to partake of more cake.

When tea was over a group of swans came alongside, arching their necks and pouting their snowy bosoms on the river. Renny moved from his place by Mrs. Blake and began to feed the swans with scraps.

" We used to have swans," he said, " on our stream at home. But they flew away and did n't come back."

Molly wanted to feed them too. She held a piece of bread in her hand and looked at Wakefield.

" Go on," he said testily, " for heaven's sake go and feed them ! "

She cast him a reproachful look. " Is thy servant a dog ? " she asked.

He caught her hand and squeezed it. " What a beast I am, Molly ! I don't know what 's the matter with me to-day."

She went to Renny's side and they leaned together over the gunwale. She glanced back at Wakefield. He was smiling at her. " Why should he smile and at the same moment be so jealous ? " she wondered. She had no jealousy in her nature. She could not understand. She saw

Renny hold the bread within reach of the male swan, then, just as he was about to snatch it, jerk it away. The female swans were each possessed of a scrap and in elegant greed were devouring it. The male, greatly agitated, wheeled, bowed, and returned to the side of the launch with open beak. Renny offered him the bread. Gracefully his head shot out to snatch it but it was gone. Again he described a circle in the water, his great wings trembling.

"There 's something cruel in them," thought Molly, "something teasing and cruel." She said — "Please give it to him! He 's getting *so* upset."

"It 's good for him to worry a little," he returned. "Life 's been too easy. See how plump and sleek he is." Again he held out the bread.

The swan fairly lifted himself out of the water. He trod it as though it were a marble floor and reared his white wings in fury. Renny was laughing.

"Come on! Come on!" he urged. "Why, you 're the weakling of the flock — come on!"

Molly snatched the bread from his hand and threw it to the bird who sailed majestically away, leaving a silken wake in the green water.

"I 'm sorry," she said, "but I had to do it. I could n't bear to see the swan so furious."

He stared at her surprised. "Could n't you? But they 're really bad-tempered things. One of ours attacked a cousin of mine and might have killed him if I had n't arrived in time."

"I 'm sorry," she repeated.

"It 's all right." Then abruptly he asked: —

"How old are you?"

"Going on nineteen."

"I wonder at your father — allowing you to live alone in London."

"I 'm quite able to look after myself."

His brows went up incredulously.

"If you were *my* daughter I 'd not let you. The stage too — that 's a precarious life for a girl, is n't it?"

"Oh, yes."

"Can you ride?"

"No."

"Never been on a horse?"

"Never."

"What a pity! Come to Jalna and I 'll teach you."

"I 'd love to. Perhaps, if our play is a success, we 'll go to America."

Wakefield strained his ears to hear what they were saying, while he made an attempt at conversation with Mrs. Blake. The launch was moving down the river now. The sun was lower and the shallows golden.

Adeline had got her wish and was steering the launch. Her hands grasping the helm, her hair blowing back from her face, that face bold and confident as an infant figurehead for a Norse ship, she kept the boat in midstream through all its windings.

Wakefield went back with Renny to his hotel. He had a desire to be with him, not to let him out of his sight, as though continued watchfulness might clear the situation. He stared so hard at Renny during dinner that the latter exclaimed: —

"What the dickens are you staring at?"

Wakefield colored. "Was I staring? Well, you 're leaving soon and I guess I wanted to impress your image on my mind."

That would have been unconvincing to anyone but Renny. He beamed at his junior.

"God, I wish you were coming home with me," he said.

Wakefield's heart melted. This was his old Renny, his protector, his wall against the world. Renny could not have it in his heart to hurt him. If he did hurt him, it was unknowingly. It was his instinct. Perhaps not even that but just something in him that drew women to him. Wakefield knew every inch of the face smiling at him, the sharp curve of the nostrils, the arch of the brows, the lines of arrogance and anxiety. But what a mystery he truly was! For a moment he had it in his mind to tell Renny of his jealousy, then the fear of being laughed at, the fear that his jealousy had a just cause, kept him silent. But it was hard luck, he thought, that Renny's visit should be marked by such feelings, for the first time in their lives. "They 're all on *my* side," he thought. "Renny is as natural as Johnny the Bird."

But he made a good dinner. He had a feeling of chagrin when Renny exclaimed: —

"Well, there 's nothing wrong with you! You 've an appetite like a horse."

"I had no lunch," answered Wakefield glumly.

"You used to be such a finicking little chap about food. Do you remember when Meggie had to take all the fat from your plate to hers? Finch was the boy with the appetite. I wish he were here with us. But there 's always Sarah. If only I 'd got here in time I 'd have put the lid on that reunion!"

"I shall be glad when his recital is over. I 'm sick to death of the sound of the piano. He 'll be off on his tour then and I 'll have the house to myself. Henriette and I."

"Will Sarah go with him?"

"Will she ever let him out of her sight? She follows him up and down the stairs, in and out of the rooms. He can't have a bath in peace! The one good thing is that she lies in bed all morning — reading magazine stories and eating sweets. She eats tons of crême-de-menthe jellies."

A boy came with a cablegram for Renny. He looked startled, then concerned. He stared with suspicion at it. "I wonder if anything has happened at Jalna," he said.

Half-a-dozen dire possibilities shot through Wakefield's mind. Renny opened the cablegram with a frown. Then his brow cleared. He read aloud: —

MUCH PERTURBED BY EUROPEAN SITUATION FEAR WAR IMMINENT FEEL YOU SHOULD RETURN AT ONCE ALAYNE

"I wonder why she 's got the wind up," said Renny. "People here are n't worrying about war."

"Sometimes I think we don't worry enough," said Wakefield. "If it comes, I shall join the Air Force."

Renny regarded him proudly. "Good man! And I shall rejoin my regiment here."

Wake's emotional life paled into the background. He talked easily and naturally to Renny now. He felt strangely exhilarated. He wished they could part at this moment so he might keep this evening's impression of his brother.

Renny cabled to Alayne that he and Adeline would sail in ten days. He was far from ready to go home. He would have enjoyed another month in London. He thought of Finch and Wakefield as his boys and he wanted to be with them as much as possible. Then too he was deluged with invitations from army and racing friends. Another month! He would have relished a six-month. Still, Alayne must not be worried. She might even be right about war coming. It was remarkable how often she was right about international affairs. He was proud of her powers of penetration and he loved her so dearly that the thought of returning to her sent a heart-warming glow through him. He set out to enjoy his last ten days to the full. He kept late hours and rose early in the morning. Yet he never felt tired.

With the Victorian simplicity in which he had been reared, he did not consider the addition of Adeline to the house in Gayfere Street as something to be reckoned with every hour of the day. He temporarily washed his hands of her. He was giving Henriette a tidy sum each week for helping with her and he thought that, with Henriette's help, Sarah and the boys ought to be able to look after her. She 'd been little or no trouble to him.

As he contributed, more generously than he could afford, to the upkeep of the house, his brothers felt that they were bound to take a bit of trouble for his child. Finch's share was to take her on long walks and they both looked back on these as one of the pleasantest parts of the visit. Finch was proud to take her to the parks. In a city of beautiful children, people turned to look at Adeline. Perhaps her hair first attracted them but something in her face held them. And when she had passed, her eager prideful walk drew many a glance. Once Finch hired horses and they rode in the Row. Adeline could have shouted with joy to feel a horse under her again. She gave an exhibition of riding that was almost too good. A crowd gathered. When this was told to Renny he forbade her riding again.

She was so disappointed that Finch was sorry for her. To ease the blow he told her that, in any case, he could not have afforded a second such treat. Adeline had been good for him. He looked forward to his recital with less apprehension than usual. That was, until the last two days. Then the accustomed tremor in his stomach began and he could eat nothing. He envied Wake his temerity over the First Night of his play. Sarah was deeply concerned for him and showed it at every turn. The way she looked at him made him feel like a sick man. When he dressed to go to the concert hall she looked at him in horror. He had had a fresh haircut and looked gaunt and flattened.

"You look horrible!" she cried. "Oh, how could you!" She ran at him to rumple what hair he had left.

He backed away. "Sarah," he said loudly, "if you do anything to my hair I 'll do the same to yours, so look out!"

Wakefield had a rehearsal that night. Renny took Sarah

to the concert hall. There was a good audience. Seated side by side, marooned on an island as it were by the sea of unknown faces about them, linked by their memories of mutual hate and distrust, made one by their desire for Finch's success, their fears for his failure, they sat shoulder to shoulder, their eyes fixed on the door where he would enter.

"He is feeling terrible," whispered Sarah, as Finch crossed the platform. "I can tell by the way he holds his hands."

"He 'll be all right," reassured Renny.

Finch bowed with gravity and that look he had, somewhere between distinction and awkwardness. He sat down and began to play. The first half of his programme was classical. In the Bach "Prelude" his nervousness was evident. They could see him trembling as he rose and bowed. But he overcame this. His playing was fluent and firm. It was hard to believe in his suffering before the concert. Renny and Sarah strained their ears to hear the comments of approval about them. It was his playing of Chopin that brought most of these.

Renny faintly remembered some of these pieces. One of them was played by Nicholas, though somehow his playing made it seem different. Two others he had often heard Finch play at Jalna in the old days. They were the best, he thought. Some of the others made him feel pretty restive. He was glad he had been firm and refused to bring Adeline. She would never have sat still. Strange, this ear for music — that is, difficult music. Martial music he himself liked, and church music — in the right place. Passionate Spanish music, gypsy dances, were not without their effect on him. His eyes slid toward Sarah's profile. Nothing there. Face of a statue. And not a nice statue, either. And Finch, poor devil, would have to go home and sleep with her!

She turned to him smiling, clapping her hands with all her might.

"Clap!" she urged. "The first half is over."

He made sharp, explosive clappings. People turned their heads toward him. He felt chagrin, folded his arms, and tried to look like a musical critic.

The second half of the programme was modern music. Finch was no longer nervous but he faltered strangely. He seemed strangely moved by his own playing. Once in a Ravel number he stopped and stared straight ahead of him. Sarah clasped her hands against her heart to still its thudding. Was he going to break down? No — he was going on, and with such swiftness and passion that a ripple as of wind across a field of grain passed over the audience. That brought his best applause of the evening. On the whole the recital was a success.

He joined Renny and Sarah outside his dressing room. Two newspaper reporters and some girls with autograph albums had been with him. As they got into the taxi a hilarious grin spread across Finch's face. He threw his arms about Renny and Sarah.

"Thank God, that 's over!" he exclaimed. "How did I do?"

"You 're the greatest living pianist!" cried Sarah.

That was nonsense, he knew, but he was in the mood to accept all praise. Indeed he had at one moment believed in his own greatness and the flush of that moment still burned on his brow.

"I 'm glad it 's over, too," said Renny. "I find that sort of thing quite a strain. Shall we go and have something to eat?"

"I was never hungrier in my life," said Finch.

Their cousin, Paris Court, overtook them. He had been sitting in the gallery and had heard there what Finch thought of as true criticism. It had been almost entirely favorable. Paris was enthusiastic.

"I wish you could have heard them! One said, 'His

technique is far from perfect but he more than makes up for it by his feeling. He makes you see pictures. We shall hear a great deal more from him.' Was n't I proud? I put my head over his shoulder and whispered — 'I 'm his cousin.' And he answered, 'Well, tell him from me that I had rather hear him play than any pianist I know — except the French fellow.'"

"Good," said Renny. "Come along and have supper with us." He liked Paris as much as he disliked Malahide.

Finch was in a state of such relief that he had a feeling of incredulous bliss. Again and again he said to himself — "It 's over. I 've got through. To-night has gone into the past with all the other nights. It 's melted and gone and even the sound of the piano will never be heard again. It 's staggering to think how I worked and worked to be able to make those sounds on the piano, and they passed into nothing, just as quickly as the sound of that motor horn."

He stood in the middle of the road, thinking. He might have been knocked down but Paris caught him by the arm and pulled him along.

"Upon my word you 're not fit to be out alone," he chaffed affectionately.

In the glowing heart of the restaurant they found a table for four. Renny ordered champagne. They sat looking about them, happy and relieved. They felt as though all the other people had been in the concert hall and recognized Finch. But not one of them had.

"I know that the woman with the red dress and the man with the eyeglass were there," said Sarah. "I saw them."

She knew that she lied but she had to do it. She had to draw those two people into the circle of ripples emanating from Finch. She held his fingers under the edge of the tablecloth. It seemed to her that they two were flowing together like a single stream through the brightly lighted night. But behind the lights the darkness was waiting for them, and she smiled when she thought of its wild strangeness. She put the glass of champagne to her lips.

"It's wonderful to me," said Paris, "to be here with you three. Just think—I might never have met you! Renny, I wish you were n't leaving so soon but I envy you, going to Canada."

"Better come back with me," said Renny.

Parry's face lighted. "If only I could get a job out there!" he sighed.

"I think you could. I'm pretty sure of it. Anyhow, I could find plenty for you to do through the summer and autumn."

"I'll come—if my parents will help me! I can't think of anything I'd like better."

"Lucky dog," said Finch, "I envy you."

"There's nothing to prevent your coming too," said Renny.

"Nothing, except me," said Sarah. "I'd die rather than see him throw up the place he has made for himself here. What is there for him *there?*" She spoke with intentional scorn.

"The best in life, in my opinion. You'll see, he'll end by coming back."

Paris broke in to ask questions about the cost of the journey and what he should provide himself with. His face sparkled with animation. He was so eager and enthusiastic that he could always get a job, but he was so volatile and so ready for change that he seldom kept one. Only the week before he had been full of hope over his latest, his employers were the best yet. Now he gayly considered how short a notice he might give them.

"I'm sure my parents will let me go," he said.

"We shall be glad to have you at Jalna," said Renny. "I miss my own boys there."

Now that Finch's recital was over the attention of all

was focused on the First Night of Wakefield's play. They saw little of him for his time was taken up by rehearsals. Renny said he should like to see one of these and Wakefield readily agreed. Once more his relations with Renny were natural or he made himself believe they were. As the thought of Renny's care over him, his generosity and gentleness, came to him more and more often in these days before Renny's departure, Wakefield had an almost passionate desire to draw nearer to him, to erase from his own mind any feelings of bitterness he had had.

This was one of the last rehearsals and, as a matinee was in progress at the Preyde Theatre, it was held in the club-room of a Foreign Waiters' Association. Renny arrived rather late. The last act was being rehearsed.

In the lobby he had to push his way through a number of foreign-looking men, waiters out of work. Advertisements were pinned to the walls and they stared eagerly up at these. He made his way up a bare staircase and found the room to which Wake had directed him. It was a large one and many chairs stood in rows or were piled in corners. Framed certificates of chefs hung on the walls. At one end there was a sort of dais with a red plush chair standing on it. This was not used as a stage but merely stood as a reminder of the room's real use. Skylights let in a cold light and the whole effect was shabby and down-at-heel. The scene however, which was being acted in the open space, was dramatic enough to make one forget surroundings.

It was between Phyllis Rhys, her lover of the play, and her son, played by Wakefield. Renny sat down in a chair rather far back and tried, at first unsuccessfully, to find out what it was all about. Then he discovered that Wakefield was giving the two older people his unvarnished opinion of their behavior. And how well he did it!

"By God," thought Renny, "how the boy can act!" Amazing how these half-brothers of his were so talented.

Of course they had got it from their mother. It was curious that Piers was the only true Whiteoak among his brothers. Yet, sitting there, Renny suddenly marveled to think that it was to these artistic, temperamental brothers that his heart went out most strongly. Perhaps it was because they required more looking after, called more often on his protective instinct.

He was annoyed when Wakefield was interrupted by Robert Fielding.

"It won't do! It won't do at all!" objected Fielding. "I 'm so very sorry."

Wakefield turned to him excitedly but submissively.

"Could you do it more like this?" said Fielding. "Not quite so big, you know, but — shall I say — more poignant?"

He looked and sounded extraordinarily foolish, Renny thought, doing Wakefield's part, but he watched him with intensity and, when Wakefield repeated the words, Fielding ejaculated, "Good! Much better!"

The rehearsal proceeded toward the curtain. Frederick and Catherine, their mother having left them for her lover, were alone. Catherine had given up the man she loved, for Frederick's sake. Inexperienced, terribly vulnerable, inarticulate in their emotion, the two talked of commonplaces as the play ended.

Ninian Fox had come and introduced himself to Renny. He annoyed him by making noises of disapproval whenever Molly was saying her lines. At the end he groaned.

"That girl," he declared, "will ruin everything!"

"Why?" asked Renny coldly.

"She has no fire. She has no feeling. Only Miss Rhys can save the play from annihilation. Hmph, well, I might have known it."

"I don't agree with you," said Renny. "I think she 's good."

"Do you? That 's comforting." But he did not look comforted. He rose.

"Will you two young people please do that last bit again?"

Molly Griffith, her young face drawn with anxiety, returned to the charge. Wakefield, tense and determined, exclaimed: —

"'It 's as though we were children again, Cathie.'"

"Come, come," interrupted Ninian Fox. "That 's not the way you said that line before."

"I know."

"Then what 's the matter?"

"I feel that this last scene needs something done to it. It 's really hard to put across."

The sandy-haired author, sitting in a distant corner, jumped to his feet.

"I agree," he declared.

"But what can be done?" asked Mr. Fox.

"I 'll try to think of something."

Every eye was on him as, with his large, pale eyes fixed on the ceiling, he meditated.

"This play," offered Ninian Fox, "is going to be a failure."

"Oh, no, it is n't," said Robert Fielding, "but I do think something ought to be done about this last scene."

"Can you think of anything, Phyllis?" Ninian Fox turned pathetically to the leading lady.

She was playing with her Pomeranian.

"I might come on again," she said.

He looked dubious.

"If we just had some stronger lines at the end, it would be fine," said Wakefield.

The author stared helplessly at the ceiling.

The Pom began to run in circles about his mistress, barking.

"Darling, be good!" she exclaimed.

The leading man offered — "I might come back, just for a moment, and say something ironic — if Mr. Trimble could think of anything."

Mr. Trimble grasped a handful of his hair.

"I had an idea," he said, "but it 's gone."

"No one can think in a noise like this," said Fielding. He bent and picked up the Pom. It bit him and he put it down.

"Bobby, how could you!" cried Miss Rhys. "I 've warned you about touching him."

"It 's nothing!" But he reddened and sucked his knuckle.

"I lost three thousand pounds on my last play," said Ninian Fox. "I 'm a fool to tackle plays by unknown authors."

Mr. Trimble also reddened and turned a vindictive look on the manager.

Wakefield's eyes filled with tears.

"Poor boy," said Miss Rhys, and patted him on the shoulder.

"Well," said Robert Fielding, "the play opens on Monday. We can't go on like this. We 've got to do something."

The various members of the company stood about in melancholy groups.

"I was thinking," said Renny, "that the boy might say something spirited at the last, such as — 'Oh hell — let 's go for a ride!'"

They gathered about him, friendly and companionable, eager for any suggestion.

"That 's an idea," said Fielding. "Perhaps not those very words but something of the sort. Perhaps you could do something with it, Mr. Trimble."

Trimble took out a notebook and retired to a distant corner. The company proceeded to rehearse the play from the beginning.

Renny ceased to listen to it. He saw only the slender figure of Molly Griffith, moving in and out of the scenes. Each time she spoke her voice stirred some memory in him which he could not recapture. It was a memory of mingled tenderness and pain and an indefinite something. A perilous state of recollection went through him — of what he did not know.

Wakefield was not in this first scene. Renny found him at his side, staring at him. Wakefield's eyes seemed to accuse him of treachery. Perhaps not quite that, but there was accusation in them.

Wakefield asked — "Well, what do you think of it all?"

Renny answered, with a calculated exaggeration of his own manner — "An awful life! I should hate to live it."

Wakefield laughed rather bitterly. "All life is awful, I guess."

"That sounds like the things Eden used to say."

"Perhaps I am like Eden — bound for unhappiness."

"No, you 're not. You 're not in the least like Eden." He put his hand on Wakefield's arm. "Is this thing nearly over? Will you come to dinner with me?"

"Shall I bring Molly Griffith too?" Wakefield looked him straight in the eyes.

"No, no. I shall soon be leaving for home. I want to see all I can of you — with no others about."

He did not see Molly Griffith again till the night of the play.

In the house in Gayfere Street the tension was almost as great as, and had a wider scope than, before Finch's recital, because now Adeline and Henriette had their share in it. Renny came to the house at least once every day. He,

Finch, Sarah, Adeline, and Henriette were one in their admiration of Phyllis Rhys, their disparagement of the rather phlegmatic leading man, their anger at Ninian Fox's nagging of Molly Griffith. They knew all about it, but possibly Henriette's feelings were deepest of them all.

As she arrived with Sarah's breakfast tray the morning before the First Night her expression was woebegone almost beyond belief. She was out of breath with the long ascent but she did not set down the tray. She stood with it poised against her stomach, towering above Sarah. " If that there play," she said, " is a failure, there is only one person to blame and that is Mr. Fox 'isself. In the first place, he don't pay a decent wage to any but the leading lady. In the second, e 's always predicting failure. In the third, 'e won't let that lovely young lady alone. Wot 's the matter with 'im is, e 's jealous of her and Mr. Wakefield. I 've seen every sort of person under the sun and I know 'is sort well. E 's biological — that 's what 'e is."

Sarah, in her delicately carven beauty, lay on the lacy pillow looking up at her.

" You 're quite right," she said. " I 've been so annoyed by the whole affair that I wrote a very strong letter to Mr. Fox but Mr. Wake would n't let me send it."

" 'E was right. 'T would only have made matters worse. No — we 've got to go through with it. Though 'ow I shall live through the first performance, I can't imagine."

" Well, you have a good seat, Henriette."

" Yes, and I thank you for it, but I 'd 'ave been better suited to the gallery with my clothes and all."

" Nonsense. People will take you for a dowager duchess."

" I 'm going to have me hair done at the hairdresser's this afternoon. I fancy a few little curls about the back of the neck. Dear, oh dear, I wish it was all over ! "

" You 'll enjoy it when the time comes."

"I suppose I shall but just now it seems more like something weighing down on me than something lifting up. Well, you 'll want your breakfast before it 's cold."

She set down the tray in front of Sarah. As she raised herself, one of the many pins and needles stuck in her front caught the topmost piece of toast and held it fast. Quite oblivious of this she departed, sighing heavily.

Finch found Sarah sunk in the pillows weak with laughter.

"My toast, my toast," was all she could say. "It 's gone."

"But where?"

"With Henriette! Don't ask me."

Sarah was very happy in these days. She was living in the midst of excitement with no exertion on her part. She was constantly with Finch. Renny's presence, his antagonism, gave spice to their reunion. Their connection, through Wakefield, with the theatrical world gave color.

Renny had wanted to give a supper party, after the play, at his hotel. But Sarah would not hear of this. It would look strange, she said, for him to give a party in a hotel when she and Finch had a roof over their heads. Renny might provide the supper but she wanted the party in the house in Gayfere Street. When Renny objected to the smallness of the rooms she insisted that a crush was jolly and that Henriette would be brokenhearted if they went elsewhere. He gave in.

Wakefield came back from the theatre to change and snatch a bite of dinner. He was in a state of nervous depression. They all, he said, had struggled with the last act till they were in tears. Molly Griffith had all but fainted.

Henriette took a bus to the theatre. Renny called for Sarah, Finch, and Adeline. They arrived early and, with avid interest, watched the theatre fill. Between seats sold, seats given away, and the press, the house was full. No other play was opening in London that night. The Preyde Theatre was of the old-fashioned type that pleased both Sarah and Renny. The gilded, curved fronts of the boxes, the florid curtain, gave that sense of opulence and mystery which they thought fitting in a theatre. In truth, they had never been so much in accord in their lives as at this moment when they sat listening to the orchestra and waiting for the curtain to rise.

Finch had just taken his seat when an attendant handed him a note from Wakefield. It read: —

Come behind as soon as you get this. We 're in a terrible fix. — WAKE

Finch handed the note to Sarah, then followed the attendant along the aisle and through a door concealed by a curtain.

Wakefield met him under a glaring white light beside two men on a stepladder.

"Don't fall over that rope," he warned, then went on breathlessly — "you know, in the second act, Phyllis Rhys plays the piano. It 's a very important scene. She can't play and the fellow who was faking it for her has just slipped on the stairs and broken his wrist. You must take his place. She 's worried almost to death. Here she is! Oh, here 's my brother, Miss Rhys!"

"You 'll do it?" she breathed. She was wearing the costume for a winter cruise and wearing it superbly.

"Why — I don't know — what do you want me to play?"

"That waltz by Mozart — you 'll find it on the piano! You 'll do it! Thank God, you 're here!" She threw both arms about his neck.

Finch clasped her to him while waves of apprehension ran along his spine. But he said comfortingly — "Don't worry, Miss Rhys, we 'll get through it somehow."

Wakefield led him across the stage, which was furnished

as a charming, very modern lounge, to where a piano stood in the opposite wing. The players were already arranged for the rise of the curtain.

"I don't go on for ten minutes," said Wakefield, "so I'll have time to put you on to the ropes. Here is the music. It will be easy for you. Now, when this light over the piano comes on, you must begin to play — at first softly, then getting louder till the music is lively. You play to where that cross is, then break off suddenly. Do you understand? Begin to play the instant the light comes on."

Ninian Fox put his head round the corner. He looked old and haggard.

"Is it all right?" he whispered.

"Yes, sir — perfectly all right."

"Sh!"

The playing of the orchestra ceased. The curtain rose tremblingly. The leading man's resonant voice was heard. "'Tell that story again,'" he said. "'It's the best I've heard in months.'"

The play had begun.

Finch watched enthralled. There had been a time when he had had a success in amateur theatricals, had even thought of becoming an actor. All that came back to him now. He threw himself into the scene, now in the person of one of the players, now another. It was a moving play. The first scene between Frederick and Cathie was amusing. Wake and Molly did it so well that Finch laughed out loud. Fortunately the audience did the same. Finch was in despair with himself. "Shall I never grow up?" he thought. Yet he again forgot his self-restraint and, at the fall of the curtain, applauded loudly.

"Good!" he exclaimed when Wakefield came to him

"Do you think it's going well? Was I all right?"

"You were splendid. So was Molly."

"Now, for heaven's sake, don't make any mistake in

the piano business. The instant the light comes on begin to play. It 's one of Miss Rhys's best scenes."

Wakefield had sent a note to Sarah explaining Finch's absence. She and Renny sat watching the stage, feeling in themselves a stern responsibility for the success of this act. Phyllis Rhys carried all before her. Though the audience deplored her behavior they could not help sympathizing with her. That was what she strove for. She sat down at the piano. Cathie was standing tense in the centre of the stage. The mother spoke in a caressing voice.

"'Do you know, I was in this room just a few hours before you were born. It was a very different-looking room then. Old-fashioned — almost Victorian. But the piano was the same. I sat down at it, feeling rather strange. I almost asked you just now if you remembered. Fancy! I began to play. I remember the very piece. A little waltz by Mozart that I 've always loved. Listen.'"

As she pressed the pedal the electric bulb over Finch's piano lighted. She dropped her hands to the keys and began to play but no sound came. Her back was to the audience so there was no need for her to conceal the consternation in her face.

Sarah gripped Renny's fingers.

"He 's not playing! Oh . . ." she said, in an agonized whisper.

"What 's the matter?" asked Adeline.

"Sh!"

They had a glimpse of the author, three seats ahead, tense and despairing. A ripple of laughter ran through the audience.

Finch began to play.

The little waltz stole exquisitely, hesitatingly, apparently from under Miss Rhys's fingers. She turned her face with a tender smile to her daughter. Never had the young man with the injured wrist played like this. Indeed his playing had been a source of irritation to Miss Rhys. When the curtain fell she went to Finch and once more threw her arms about him.

He gave her a shamefaced look.

"I wonder," he said, "that you don't hit me. But the truth is, I was so interested in the play that I forgot all about my part."

"It did n't matter! Will you — dare I hope you 'll help me again?"

"I 'd love to. And I promise I 'll not make such an ass of myself another time."

The play gained impetus, the actors confidence in it and themselves. The last act, over which there had been such heartburnings, turned out to be the best of all. The first had shown the skillful interplay of the company. The second had been a triumph for Phyllis Rhys. The third brought rounds of applause for Wakefield and Molly Griffith. Ninian Fox might have misgivings about her emotional power. The audience had not. Her beauty and her unconsciousness of it, her evident absorption in her part, had roused their interest in her at the start. Now, in the final scene, she had her first taste of a storm of handclapping.

At the fall of the curtain, the entire company had two calls. Then, holding hands, Miss Rhys and her leading man bowed their thanks. Then Miss Rhys with Wake and Molly in either hand. Then Wake and Molly together, radiant with happiness. Last, Miss Rhys alone and a few contralto words from her.

"Author! Author!"

Mr. Trimble rose reluctantly from his seat and bowed.

"Speech! Speech!"

With still more reluctance he made his way down the aisle and on to the stage. An expectant silence fell. Mr. Trimble, in rather crumpled evening clothes, made a really brilliant speech but he spoke so low that only the members of the orchestra heard it. He was once more applauded and the orchestra began to play the National Anthem.

Adeline could scarcely contain herself for pride. There she was, wearing her best dress, the only child in a theatre full of people. She was traveled, an experienced person, a woman almost. She had crossed the ocean. She had visited Ireland, been in an Irish Hunt, seen the Grand National run. Soon she would be at a grown-up party, treated as an equal by grown-up people. Her eyes on a level with the shoulderblades of those in front, she could see almost nothing. Nevertheless her eyes flashed, her lips curved, and she drew a deep breath of pride. Music and crowds — she was in the thick of things!

Somehow the little house in Gayfere Street was almost able to contain the people who poured into it. The night was warm and there was an overflow on to the pavement. Somehow Henriette and the waiters assisting her were able to provide each of the guests with refreshment. In fact a great deal was drunk. The actors, the producer, the author, felt that the play was going to be a great success. Only Ninian Fox and some of the critics were doubtful.

XIII

END OF A VISIT

ADELINE and Henriette were out early the next morning to buy the newspapers. Hastening along the damply sunlit street they were a great contrast to each other: Henriette with her large unwieldy body, her large flat feet and bulky skirts; Adeline, small, light-footed and barelegged. But the look in their eyes was equally expectant. In Marsham Street they bought the papers and hurried home. Adeline insisted on carrying them all.

Wakefield, sitting up in bed, with Finch and Sarah, Adeline and Henriette, crowded into the room, read aloud the notices. When they were good, which all but two were, and only one of them really bad, he read in an impressive, almost clerical manner. The two unfavorable ones he read in a staccato voice, with pauses for scathing comments on the critics. But nothing he could say equaled what was said by Sarah, Henriette, and Adeline. They scarcely had words for the expression of their contempt.

"It 's the very limit of idiocy," exclaimed Sarah.

"'E 's jealous, that 's what 'e is," said Henriette. "Jealous and miserable in 'is mind. I can say this truthfully that there 's never been a better play nor better acted since the time of Shakespeare and that 's a long time."

Adeline kept repeating — "What things to say! They deserve to have a stick to their backs!"

When the notices had been read, Wakefield chose the best comments on his own and Molly's acting and read them aloud again, to everyone's great satisfaction. Then he had breakfast. Then he spent half an hour at the telephone. Then he dressed and went out to meet Molly.

There was so much to do. Quite suddenly he was deluged by invitations. Renny gave him a check and he bought himself a spring suit in Bond Street. Photographs of the company were taken at the theatre. Their pictures were in the papers. Finch's recital was almost forgotten. But he was soon to start on a tour. Rumors of war persisted but people had become so used to these that they were less disturbed by them. At a dinner party, Renny had an opportunity to ask the opinion of a member of the Cabinet, but before he could speak the gentleman turned to him and said: —

"Do you think there 'll be war, Mr. Whiteoak?"

"Yes," he answered. "My wife, who is a very clever woman, has cabled me to that effect."

The last days of the visit sped so swiftly that the morning of departure was on them unbelievably soon. Renny took Adeline shopping and they bought presents for the family at home. Their trunks were packed. Only the good-byes were to be said. Paris Court was returning with them and his delight at the prospect made the good-byes cheerful.

Henriette came down the narrow stairs bent under the weight of Adeline's trunk.

"Good heavens, woman," cried Renny, springing up the stairs to meet her, "you should n't do that alone!"

Still retaining one end of the trunk, Henriette answered, "I 'm used to being overworked. I 've been overworked since I was ten. But it 's bound to tell on me some day. 'Uman flesh can stand so much and no more. I don't suppose you 'd be needing any extra 'elp at Jalna?"

Renny looked at her doubtfully. "I 'm afraid not, Henriette." He put a ten-shilling note into her hand. "Thanks for looking after Adeline so well."

She pushed the money from her. "You 've paid me too well as it is. Money is n't everything. Many a rich person 'as a broken 'eart. You and your family 'ave given me kindness."

Henriette was tearful when she said good-bye to Adeline, who was as eager to be off as she had been to arrive.

Paris shook hands with Wake. " When next we meet, I shall be a millionaire," he said.

" Probably they 'll not let you into the country," said Wakefield, slapping him on the back.

Paris turned to Sarah. " If you get tired of Finch come out to me, darling."

Renny kissed his brothers in turn.

" This is n't good-bye for me," said Wakefield. " I 'm going to the station with you." His suspicions of Renny had vanished. He felt that he could not do enough to make up to his brother for having harbored them.

Renny saluted Sarah on the cheek. " Good-bye, my dear," he said, " and don't take your love too seriously."

" It is like you," she said, " to leave behind some remark which rankles."

" That 's as sound a piece of advice as ever I gave," he retorted.

One taxicab heavily laden had started on its way. Paris called out that they would miss the train. He and Adeline were already in the other cab. Renny and Wakefield clambered in after them, laden with packages. Finch and Sarah were left on the doorstep.

XIV
RETURN TO JALNA

Everything was ready for their reception and Alayne had gone to the porch and looked down the drive half-a-dozen times. It seemed a very long while since Renny and Adeline had left home. Yet in some ways the time had flown. Her days had been uneventful. She had had time for reading and making notes on what she had read. The roads were better and Alma Patch, the nursemaid, had taken the children for long walks. Without his sister's stimulating presence, Archer had been more amenable. No child could be less trouble than Roma. Alayne felt rested and young. She wore a new French wool dress, blue, the shade that best suited her.

The children had brought in some catkins which she had put in a green vase. She had grown daffodils in pots. Rags had washed and groomed the dogs and they sat shivering in anticipation in the hall. Nicholas wore his velvet smoking jacket. He was restless and could not be still for a moment.

"How many times," he exclaimed, "I have waited in this room for some of the family returning from England!"

"Yes, I suppose so," answered Alayne absently.

"How well I remember, when I was just Archer's age, my parents coming home! It was shortly before Christmas and suddenly the snow came pouring down. Papa's shoulders were white with it and he was laden with packages. Mamma wore a new sealskin dolman and enormous hoops. I can't imagine how she got in and out of the railway carriage. I hope Renny has remembered to bring me a new pipe from

Dunhill's. It was a great misfortune my breaking my favorite old one. Why, Alayne, I 'd had that pipe since — let me see — What was that? Was that the car?"

"No, it 's only Archer on his tricycle. Dearest, I wish you would n't ride it in the house."

Archer looked in from the hall.

"I 'm lonely out on the drive."

"That 's nonsense."

"I want you always to see me." He stared at her from under his pure high forehead and her heart melted. She could deny him nothing.

"Well — don't run into things."

He pedaled into the sitting room, humping himself over the handlebars. He showed no interest in the preparations for his father and sister. His own activities engrossed him.

"Look," he said, "I 'm a monkey."

"I don't want to see," answered Alayne, firmly.

"Look! Look, Uncle Nick!" He twisted his infant features into a wry monkey face and made his hands into claws.

"Gr-r-r," he growled.

"Stop it, this instant," said Alayne.

"I can't. It 's me."

She went to him and lifted him from the tricycle. She carried it from the room and put it in the far end of the hall. When she returned he was lying on his face on the floor.

"Get up, Archer, at once," she said sternly.

"I can't," he whined. "I 'm a baby! Lift me. I can't walk."

"Smack him behind," said Nicholas. "It 's a good chance."

Alayne stood her son on his feet. He collapsed again. He had no sooner done so than he rose with agility, for he heard the car on the drive.

"Somebody 's coming!" he exclaimed. "Who is it?"

"Why, Archer, it 's Daddy," Alayne reminded him reproachfully. "Daddy and Adeline."

"I thought they were in Ireland."

The dogs had heard the car. Blind old Merlin rose stiffly and uttered a stentorian bark. The others joined in. Nicholas was stuck in his chair.

"Alayne," he called, as she reached the hall, "come back and help me! I 'm stuck here!"

She flew back and somehow he was got to his feet. But Rags had forestalled her at the door.

"Welcome 'ome, sir. Welcome 'ome, miss. My word, 'ow you 've grown! 'Ere are the dogs waiting. Wot a time I 've 'ad, getting them ready!"

Through the barking dogs Alayne pushed her way to Renny's side. He clasped her to him. Their lips met. For an instant she felt faint in the bliss of his return. Then Adeline embraced her. There was a confusion of hugs among the children. Nicholas gripped Renny by the hand.

"It 's good to have you back," he said. "I had n't realized how I missed you."

Renny had put off writing of Paris's coming till too late. In one of his fits of economy he considered the sending of a cablegram a waste of money. In any case it was a pleasant surprise for the family. He introduced him first to Alayne.

"This is our cousin, Parry Court," he said. "You 've heard of him. He 's come to pay us a little visit."

The word *little* was reassuring. Alayne gave the attractive young man a welcoming smile.

"Who is he?" asked Nicholas, in what he believed was an aside.

"Paris Court, Malahide's son."

"Whose son? I did n't hear!" He took Renny by his coat lapel and drew him closer.

"Malahide's son."

" That snake *Malahide's* son!"

" Be careful. Yes. He 's come for a little visit. He 's a fine young fellow, Uncle Nick. Quite different from his father."

" He 'd better be," growled Nicholas. He gave a sardonic smile and held out his hand to Paris.

" I never thought," he said, " to meet your father's son."

" I 've heard so much of you from my father," returned Paris easily. " He 's often talked of his visit to Jalna."

Piers had met the trio at the station. He whispered to Alayne: —

" Prepare for a long visit. Once one of that breed gets into the house it 's impossible to move them."

Merlin could scarcely bear his joy. He whimpered. He nibbled Renny's legs and hands. He sought to climb up into his arms.

" Dear old boy," said Renny, stroking him. " You 're looking pretty fit, too."

" His rheumatism is bad," said Piers.

Archer had retired to the end of the hall. He now appeared riding his tricycle.

" Hullo!" said Renny. " That 's something new."

" The uncles gave it to him," said Alayne. " So far it 's been rather a trial."

" I 'm a monkey," said Archer, " so watch out." Humping himself worse than before, pulling an even worse face, he pedaled toward his father, clawing the air with his hands.

Flushed by anger, Alayne went toward him.

" Gr-r-r!" he growled and made a pass at her.

Adeline did what he wanted her to — shrieked with laughter. Renny snatched him from the tricycle and kissed his distorted face.

" Well," he laughed, " you *are* a little monkey!"

Archer sat beaming on his father's arm.

" I'm glad you 're back. I 'm tired of everybody else."

" Oh, Archer, how can you say that! " said Alayne, reproachfully. She thought of the hours she had spent amusing him.

" Well, naturally," said Renny, " he 's glad to see his daddy."

" I'm a baby," whined Archer, " don't put me down." He drew his lips over his teeth. " Me has n't any teeth. Me tan't talk."

" I 'm in despair with him," said Alayne. " He 's never his real self for more than five minutes at a time."

" Did you bring me the pipe I sent for? " asked Nicholas.

" When can we open the trunks? " cried Adeline. " You 've never seen such lovely presents."

The dogs set up a barking. The front door opened and Ernest and Harriet came in. She ran with short light steps to embrace Renny. Ernest bent to kiss Adeline. Paris was presented to them and made such a favorable impression that Ernest wiped out all evil recollections of his father. In spite of himself Piers also took to his young Irish cousin. He could scarcely wait to carry him and Renny off to the stables.

Ernest said — " We were delighted that Finch's recital was such a success. *What* good notices he had! I 'm afraid he 'll never come back to us."

" How we envied you being there to see it," added Harriet.

" And Wake too," added Nicholas. " That must have been a great night."

" Yes, it was," said Renny. He was on his knees before a trunk. He had got the lid only a few inches open when small hands were thrust into the aperture.

"Wait, children! Don't! " cried Alayne. But they could not be restrained.

Nicholas bent forward, breathing heavily.

"Is that my pipe?" he asked.

Archer began to climb into the trunk. His father lifted him out and he rode away on his tricycle.

"Here 's your pipe, Uncle Nick! Aunt Harriet, this is for you. Roma, hold out your arms. Now then, Piers, don't say I 've never given you a nice present. Alayne, shut your eyes and put out the third finger of your right hand."

Alayne thought — "He might have kept my present till we were alone!" She tried to tell him so with a look but he saw nothing but the circle about him and fancied her look spoke of eagerness. He stood up smiling. "Now this is important," he said.

Obediently she held out her finger and shut her eyes. She felt the cool caress of the ring. She felt his hand encircling hers. Her mind flew back to their wedding day.

Maurice, Meg, and Patience had entered unseen. Meg came close behind Renny and put her arms about his waist.

"Guess who 's here," she asked.

Alayne opened her eyes. She saw the sapphire on her finger and gave an exclamation of mingled reproach and pleasure.

"Oh," she said, "you should not have done that!"

"Do you like it?"

"It 's perfectly lovely."

"Have n't you a word to say to your sister?" asked Meg. He turned round in her arms and kissed her.

"How well you look," he said. "Look here, I 've something for you, too!"

Alayne thought — "How like Meg to arrive just at this moment! And ready to give an envious look, too! Oh, why did n't he keep the ring till we were alone?"

"You might kiss Daddy for it!" said Adeline. "He took hours and hours to choose it."

"I 'm sure he did." But Alayne felt angry with the

child. She drew down Renny's head and kissed him on the cheek.

Everyone was opening packages. Nicholas was blowing through his new pipe. Meg's present could not be found. Renny and Adeline turned the trunk topsy-turvy, searching for it. They unearthed all the presents but hers.

" Never mind," she cried, with a slight tremor in her voice, " I don't want a present. It 's quite enough to have you both back."

" Nonsense," said Maurice. " Of course you want a present. You have n't looked in that compartment yet, Renny."

" Those are the things for Piers's boys."

" Please, please don't mind me! What a heavenly ring, Alayne! "

Pheasant and her three boys arrived. Between dogs, people, and trunks, the hall was indeed crowded. Archer rode through the crowd on his tricycle, his eyes fixed blankly in front of him. He had tied the packet containing his present behind the tricycle but had not opened it. It bumped along precariously.

Renny suddenly remembered that Meg's present, a brooch, was in his waistcoat pocket. He straightened himself, red in the face, and produced it.

Two hours later he was walking alone through the path in the orchard. It was strange to have left spring in flowery abundance in England and to find only its first tentative budding here. He remembered orchards gay with daffodils, lawns in velvet grass where the crocuses threw their petals wide to receive the gentle sunlight. He remembered thorn trees that were boughs of pink bloom. Why, there in that hollow, there was a skein of snow! But pushing up through dead leaves near it was the fragile blossom of bloodroot. The air played about him in quick flights as though it possessed wings. All about him was quivering life, scarcely born but already vigorous.

Suddenly he stopped as though a voice had spoken to him. Some recollection from the past gathered itself together from the trees, from the wind, from the worn path itself, to trouble him. At first it had no shape. Then, with great clarity, it took the shape of a tall slender girl, in riding clothes. It was Chris Cummings, the girl who had schooled horses for him after the War. She was only a girl in appearance, though she was the mother of a sturdy baby boy.

He moved on among the budding trees. Merlin was close at his heels. Strange, what had brought her so vividly to his mind at that moment. Why, she 'd been so clear to him he 'd not have been surprised if she 'd spoken, put out her hand and touched him. Kit, he 'd called her. She 'd been very dear to him, too. And how she could ride! What hands — what courage! She 'd gone back to England. Gran had had her finger in that pie.

Now he emerged from the orchard into the open. The six hundred acres of his own land were spread about him in the promise of springtime. It was good to be home again. No matter where you went or how you enjoyed yourself, it was good to be home again.

XV
YOUNG MAURICE

THEY had arrived home on a Saturday. When Renny woke the next morning he had a moment's puzzlement as to where he was. Was he at Cousin Dermot's? In his London hotel? On board ship? Yes, it must be the last, for his bed was heaving. Then he opened his eyes and saw that Merlin had got on the bed with him and was walking heavily about. He could have laughed for pleasure. He put out his arms and drew the old fellow to him.

"Merlin — glad to have me home again?"

The spaniel snuffled against his face and made noises of pleasure. Merlin came as near to talking as any dog. Now he said: —

"Glad! Am I glad? I'll show you!"

Old as he was, stout as he was, blind as he was, he gamboled over his master, leaving him and the bedclothes in a state of demoralization.

"Enough — enough!" gasped Renny. "You're killing me, old man!" He caught him by the scruff and held him still.

Suddenly he remembered that it was Sunday. He had been to church only once in England. That was the day he had taken Adeline to Westminster Abbey. Now that he was home he must begin again. He turned his eyes to his father's large gold watch that stood in a leather frame on the table beside the bed. It was eight o'clock. He could hear the children laughing upstairs. What a pretty laugh Roma had! He wondered if Alayne were awake. How pleased she'd been with the ring! For once he'd made a good choice in a present for her.

He went across the passage to her door and tapped. "May I come in?" he asked.

"Yes."

He went in and sat on the side of the bed. He saw that she was wearing the new ring. He took her hand in his.

"I 'm so glad you like it," he said.

"I 'd be a strange woman if I did n't. Darling, you should not have bought anything so expensive."

"Well, I treated myself to a horse, did n't I?"

"I do love sapphires."

"Alayne, did you miss me?"

Her fingers closed about his. She held his hand to her lips. "Terribly."

"But you had a nice rest — I mean, with Adeline away. You 're looking lovely. I 'd forgotten what beautiful pigtails you have." He took one in either hand. "Long and shiny! Are you coming to church?"

"Oh, don't let 's go to church this morning!"

"Very well." But he looked disappointed.

"Of course, if you want to go . . ."

"Well, old Fennel will expect me. You know, we 've always gone to church the first morning we were home after a journey."

She gave him a smile of mingled irritation and tenderness.

"If all men were like you," she said, "the world would n't be rocking."

"Is it rocking? I had n't noticed."

"What do they say in England about war?"

"A good many people think it 's coming. But you 'll find that Britain and France can handle the Germans."

"I hope so, with all my heart."

"Will you come with me to church?"

"Yes, I 'll go. We might go alone — just we two. Uncle Nick is tired. I don't believe he 'll feel like going."

"Very well. I 'd like that. It 's a lovely morning. Shall we walk across the fields?"

"What a good thought! Renny, I don't know when we 've had a walk together." He laid his face on the pillow beside hers. He whispered endearments in her ear.

It was lovely walking across the fields in the freshness of early May. The land looked proud in its promise, the earth of a rich golden brown. Tiny short-stemmed wild flowers had come into bloom almost as soon as their buds had pushed up from the earth. It was a late spring. There was no time to waste. So thought the robins and song sparrows hastening by with streamers of straw and horsehair. So thought the frogs at the edge of the stream, croaking to their loved ones to come out into the sun. Even the church bell had a note of hurry in its ring. Or perhaps old Noah Binns, having heard that the master of Jalna was returned, was giving him a special summons to worship.

As Renny and Alayne entered the door they saw him beneath the tower, bent double in the effort of pulling the rope. He gave a toothless grin at Renny.

"Dang him," he thought, "he 'd better come!"

Renny had gone round to the vestry to get into his surplice. It was the first time in Alayne's life that she had walked down that aisle alone. Surely the old grandmother was at her side! Or Aunt Augusta, or Eden! But why should she think of the dead rather than the living? Her answer to her own question was — "I have a naturally unhappy disposition. No matter how gay I am — as I was gay with Renny a moment ago — I 'm far too ready to turn to introspection and melancholy."

She saw Piers look over his shoulder and stare in surprise at her. Then Pheasant looked and stared in surprise. Then the three round faces of the little boys showed their surprise over the back of the pew. She went into the pew behind them and knelt down.

Miss Pink began to play softly on the organ. The Vaughans were just coming in. Alayne saw Meg's eyes sweep the family already assembled. She saw her whisper the news of *her* presence to Maurice. He looked decorously across the aisle at her and smiled. Patience was plainly conscious of the new hat with long ribbons that Renny had brought her from London. Alayne now felt the approach of Ernest and her Aunt Harriet. Ernest's clearing of his throat was scarcely audible yet so characteristic. There was a faint odor of Hoyt's cologne emanating from Aunt Harriet. Yes — she was right — they were coming into the seat with her.

Ernest whispered, "Is anything wrong with Nicholas?"

"He's just rather tired."

She saw the shadow on Ernest's face. She knew he worried about his brother. He could not tolerate the thought that Nick might be failing. Aunt Harriet leaned across him to say: —

"How nice it is to see you at church, dear!"

Alayne smiled in return but her smile was a little wry. She could not help remembering how earnest a Unitarian her aunt had been and how she had always held a gentle contempt for what she thought of as the less intellectual denominations. But Aunt Harriet had considered it a wifely duty to accept her husband's religious faith. She could not expect, at his time of life, to change his views, but the gusto with which she accepted that faith was highly irritating to her niece. Aunt Harriet had in fact taken the little church, its Rector, and the Book of Common Prayer under her wing. She was President of the Women's Auxiliary.

Alayne remembered intellectual religious discussions between her father and Aunt Harriet. She wondered what her father would think if he could see his sister to-day.

She heard Noah Binns's boots squeak as he made his way

to a back seat. Miss Pink began to play the Processional hymn. The voices of the choir rose. The chirping of the little birds outside the window near her was silenced. The round heads of the choirboys reached her side. But it was Ernest, Piers, Maurice, Meg, and Renny who led the singing. It was their nature to sing fast. It was Miss Pink's nature to play slowly. Year in, year out, the duel between Miss Pink and the Whiteoaks went on, without either side losing the sense of their own entire rightness. The heavy notes of the organ clung like millstones round the necks of the family but without avail. The last syllable of the Amen came roundly from their throats before she had tackled the first. Midway between these opposing forces the helpless choir wavered, now hastening with the Whiteoaks, now dragging behind with Miss Pink. Mr. Fennel, the Rector, had long ago solved the problem for himself. He gave no heed to the organist, the choir, or the family, but sang to suit his own mood, in a particularly fine baritone. Now, with his open hymnal before him, his beard spread on his breast, he came at the end of the procession. Renny walked ahead of him, his eyes fixed on the stained-glass windows of the chancel which were dedicated to the memory of Captain Philip Whiteoak and his wife, Adeline.

As Renny's surplice touched Alayne's shoulder she glanced swiftly into his face. How many billions of faces in the world, she thought, yet only one that had the power of making heaven or hell for her. Deeply as she loved her son he could never take his father's place. Sexual love was stronger than maternity. Yet, knowing herself, she felt that this should not have been so. If she had not been uprooted from her own sphere, she thought, it would not have been so. But she would not have had her life otherwise.

In the vestry, his head just having emerged through his surplice, Renny had been greeted by Mr. Fennel.

" It 's good to have you back," he had said. " I 've heard that the trip was a great success."

" Yes, yes — I bought a grand horse."

" In Ireland, eh? "

" Yes. In Ireland."

" How are Finch and Wakefield? "

" Fine."

" You know what the Lessons are? "

" Yes. Uncle Nicholas found them for me."

" Good. There goes the organ. Are you ready, boys? "

The choirboys shuffled their feet and made their soap-shiny faces solemn. Renny poked one of them with his hymnbook.

" You 're out of line," he said.

They passed through the door and began to move decorously down the aisle.

Kneeling in the chancel, the smell of his freshly ironed surplice in his nostrils, the worn leather book in his hand, he thought how good it was to be at home again. Wherever he went, no matter how long he stayed, it was good to be home again. This was his place. He had a pity for men who had no fixed or definite place in life. In varying degrees he knew every soul under this roof. A stranger seldom came in at the door. From Noah Binns, whom he had always disliked, to Alayne whom he loved with passion, each one fitted into the scheme of things as the pieces of stained glass fitted into the windows. Each was needed to complete the design. He was conscious of his own dire deficiencies but felt, without humility, that he was needed too. Somehow he was the receptacle of what had once lived in his forefathers. He was tough-fibred and strong. That something he would guard and pass on to his son.

He went to the lectern to read the first Lesson. He saw Alayne's eyes on him. He knew she did not enjoy coming to church. She had come to be near him. They would walk back through the fields together. He cleared his throat and read: —

" But be ye doers of the word, and not hearers only, deceiving your own selves. For if any be a hearer of the word, and not a doer, he is like unto a man beholding his natural face in a glass: For he beholdeth himself, and goeth his way, and straightway forgetteth what manner of man he was. But whoso looketh into the perfect law of liberty, and continueth therein, he being not a forgetful hearer, but a doer of the work, this man shall be blessed in his deed."

Alayne thought — " What grand words! I wish they might be shouted from the housetops in these days. I wonder what Renny thinks of them. Or does he think about the Lessons? He read better than usual. To-day he seems almost perfect to me. If only I could go on feeling like this!" She gave her little ironic smile. One thing she liked about church. It was a good place for thinking in.

The service was over before she realized it, she was so deep in thought. She had made no attempt to listen to the sermon. In a dream she rose at the end with the others, passed down the aisle and waited outside the door for Renny. She lifted her face to the sweetness of the breeze. The air inside the church had grown close. Not feeling unfriendly but merely aloof, she moved away from the family and walked slowly down the steep path toward the gate. She knew they would not be pleased at her doing this but she did not care. They all would be at Jalna for lunch. She was entitled to this privacy. She wanted to make sure that Renny and she would have the walk home together. She clung, with almost pathetic tenderness, to these first moments of isolation with him. In a strange way the feeling of her first love for him came back to her, its troubled and perilous straining toward their moments alone. She shunned every face she knew and walked out of the gate and down the road alone.

He came running after her.

"You are in a hurry!" he said.

He gave her a swift look, conscious of some emotion in her deeper than she would reveal. He smiled down into her face.

"I had to shake hands with everybody," he said, "and they all seemed to know I'd bought Johnny the Bird."

"Darling," she said, and caught his fingers in hers.

They dallied on the way home, following the stream, looking for the first hepaticas. The sun came out hot. Alayne's shoes were muddy. It was a long while since she had been so carefree and happy. She was glad that she had not stood in the way of his going to Ireland. "If anything happens to him," she thought, "I can say that I did not stand in the way of his doing the things he most wanted to."

It was the first time she had ever thought of anything happening to him. He had seemed immune to illness and danger. Since their marriage he had had many accidents but had come through them so well that she had a sudden feeling of shame to remember how calmly she had taken the news of a bone broken in polo, cuts and bruises in his other activities. Suddenly, moving among the trees, he looked strangely vulnerable in his quickness and leanness. Why, a bullet, a splinter of shell, would kill or blind him as easily as any man. She knew that, if war came, he would join his old regiment. What if she should lose him or have him returned to her arms maimed?

When they reached Jalna the family was there in full possession. Returning and finding them everywhere Alayne felt how slight was her hold on the place, compared to theirs. In truth she never had had any feeling of possession toward the old house. Like an alloy, which it could not absorb into its metal, it rejected her. Yet young Philip Whiteoak, who had not slept half a dozen nights under its roof, seemed as much a part of the place as Piers.

Nicholas was rested, freshly shaved and eager for company. He and Paris had had a long talk and Nicholas had decided that the young man was as unlike his father as possible and a very lively companion. Everyone asked questions about Johnny the Bird, the Grand National, the house in Gayfere Street and the doings of Finch and Wakefield. Maurice and Meg both said they thought it was a good thing that Finch and Sarah had come together again. It did seem a pity that her fortune should be lost to the family.

Paris Court had heard Jalna and its occupants so often described by his father, yet described as they were thirty years ago, that he had a strange dreamlike feeling, as though he had slept and woken to find figures in some familiar tale grown up or aged in the interval. What a letter he would write home! He pictured his father and mother laughing over it for weeks. The well-stocked stables, the crowded table, the abundant food, the sense of plenty, gave Paris the feeling that the Whiteoaks were indeed relatives to be cherished, to say nothing of the fact that he liked them for their own sakes. The portrait his father had given Renny was a delight to the family. Adeline, the child, was hung beside Adeline the young woman, and the living Adeline was stood beneath them for comparison and a deep satisfaction.

If anything were needed to spoil her further, thought Alayne, the visit abroad and the acquiring of the picture were enough. Adeline's head was carried more overbearingly, if possible, her glance was more daring than before. Yet she was overflowing with love and her gentleness toward Archer was charming. He, coming downstairs in his Sunday best and finding the house full of people, walked among them as though the weight of the world were on his brow.

"Upon my word," said Meg, "the look of him would turn sweet milk sour."

"It does n't mean anything," said Nicholas. "He really is a good old scout, are n't you, Archie?"

Archer gave a wry smile, stared past them and marched on about his business.

The afternoon was well on its way before Renny was able to have Piers to himself. He took him to his own room further to inspect the photographs and record of Johnny the Bird. While Piers was still examining these Renny said: —

"It strikes me that Mooey is n't coming along very well."

Piers frowned and answered impatiently — "You 're right. He 's a problem, that boy. He 's growing fast yet he does n't eat as he should. He 's lackadaisical about riding. He gets in a blue funk if a horse begins to cut up. If I reprimand him he 's on the point of tears. I 'd think he was like those artistic brothers of ours but he does n't show any talent for anything — not for anything."

"I 've always been fond of Mooey," said Renny.

"Good Lord, so have I! If I had n't I 'd have skinned him alive. Now I understand Nook — more or less. But I don't understand Mooey and never shall."

Renny took a pipe from the rack and began to fill it. He said, "I was telling Cousin Dermot about Mooey."

Piers looked vague and said, "Oh, were you?"

"He was very much interested in him. His own sons are dead and his only grandson was killed in the hunting field some years ago. He has a nice fortune and he has no heir. He liked what I told him about Mooey."

Piers opened his eyes wide. What was coming? Now he was completely alert.

"The upshot of our talk was," Renny went on, "that Cousin Dermot would like to have Mooey visit him. If they got on well together — and I 'm sure they would — he would want to keep Mooey as his own son — make him his heir. It would be a grand thing for the boy."

"How long do you think the old man will live?" asked Piers.

"Do you ask that from a mercenary point of view?" asked Renny sharply.

"You are asking me to part with my eldest son!"

"Well — Cousin Dermot says he's good for another ten years, and I'm inclined to believe him. Mooey would then be twenty-three."

"Pheasant would never agree."

"We should tell her that it would be just a visit but that it might lead to Cousin Dermot making the boy his heir. Pheasant's too sensible not to realize what that would mean to Mooey. It would change his whole life, without a doubt."

"When does he want him to go? How would he get there?"

"I am thinking of sending Wright over to help with the training of the horse. I want someone of my own on the spot. Wright would look after Mooey very well. He's known him all his life."

A glow of fatherly feeling welled up in Piers's heart. It was one thing to find your son a problem, quite another to give him up. He tied his forehead into a knot and bit his thumb. "You'd better tell Pheasant about it yourself."

Renny did. He returned with Piers and his family that evening and laid the plan before Pheasant after the younger boys were in bed and young Maurice was undressing. She listened with a startled, wary look in her brown eyes.

"For heaven's sake," exclaimed Renny, "don't look like that! I thought I'd something pleasant to tell you."

Pheasant wrung her hands together. "I've felt this coming," she said.

"Did you ever see such a girl?" said Piers. "That's the way she takes things."

Pheasant laid her arms on the table and her head on her

arms. "If I give him up now, I 'll never get him back," she said.

"Now that 's all nonsense," said Renny. "He can come back whenever you say the word or if he does n't like living in Ireland. But I do think you ought to consider his future."

"Would you give up your boy?" she cried.

For a moment he was disconcerted. Then he said, "If I had three sons I should certainly think I was lacking in foresight if I refused an offer like this."

"Then you 'd be willing to sell your boy!" She raised her streaming eyes to their two faces.

"You need n't do it," said Piers, "if you don't want to."

"Of course not," said Renny. "We 'll not talk of it any more. But, just before we close the subject, I want to tell you that Cousin Dermot is a very kind old fellow. He has an understanding way with him. I think perhaps he 'd understand Mooey better than his own father does."

Piers said nothing.

"Are you sure," asked Pheasant, in a shaking voice, "that it 's just for a visit?"

"Positive. Unless you wish otherwise. I 'll tell you what. Let 's have the boy down and ask what he thinks about it."

Piers went to the foot of the staircase and called up: —

"Mooey!"

"Yes, Daddy," came from above.

"Come down here."

Piers waited at the bottom step for him. Mooey descended slowly, his eyes, darkened by apprehension, on his father's face. He was in his pyjamas and his fine brown hair was tumbled. What had he done, he wondered. Was there trouble in store for him?

But as he reached Piers's side, Piers put an arm about him and, holding him so, led him into the sitting room. Then he went and sat down beside Pheasant. She had dried her eyes but she shaded them with her hand and forced a smile to her lips.

"Uncle Renny has something to tell you," she said.

Mooey stood, slim and straight, facing them. A load had rolled from his mind. He had done nothing wrong. His father had even given him a caress. But why did his mother's face look so strained? Why was her hand before her eyes? Why had Uncle Renny that smile which was not a smile?

Renny said, as though speaking to another grownup:—

"I hope you don't mind being brought down here at this hour."

He answered politely, "I don't mind, Uncle Renny."

"Good. Now, look here, I 've got a nice surprise for you."

If it was a nice surprise, why did his mother look like that? He answered:—

"What is it, Uncle Renny?"

Renny stretched out a long arm and drew Mooey on to his knee. Now his smile was truly a smile. Mooey relaxed. I hope it has nothing to do with horses, he thought.

Renny came straight to the point. "You heard me tell about Cousin Dermot and what a fine place he has in Ireland. Very well. He lives alone and he likes boys. He has invited you to visit him. You 'd have a grand time. What do you say?"

He could say nothing. He could not take it in. He had never been away from home in his life. His mother—his eyes flew to her face. Her lips were parted as though she had been running but her eyes looked brightly into his.

"Wake up," said his father, "and tell us how you like the idea. Mind, you don't have to go unless you really want to."

"How could I get there?"

"Wright is going over," answered Renny. "He 'd take you."

"And bring me back?"

"Good Lord!" exclaimed Piers. "Boys of six have crossed the ocean alone. I 'll bet Philip would think nothing of it."

"Wright will bring you back too, if you like," said Renny.

"How long should I stay?"

"As long or as short a time as you want. I think you 'd enjoy it immensely. You don't want Adeline to be so far ahead of you, do you? She loved it. There 's a nice boy near by about your age named Pat Crawshay. It would be fun for you to be the only child in the house and have everything your own way. Cousin Dermot is very keen to have you and to give you a good time. He told me so."

Mooey rose and went to the other end of the room. He stood rigid, his arms at his sides. Bewildering pictures passed through his mind. Himself, on a hill in Ireland, free from all things that troubled him. Himself and Cousin Dermot shaking hands, and neither understanding a word the other said. Himself free from the journeys to a school he did not like — free from the constant strain of pretending that he liked to ride, pretending he was not afraid. Himself separated from Nook — torn from his mother's arms! He wanted to ask if he would have to ride to hounds or at the horse show but he could not find words in which to conceal his reason for asking. He was silent so long that Pheasant exclaimed: —

"You don't want to go, do you, Mooey?"

"Give him time," said Renny. With a sudden swift intuition he went to the boy and put his arm about him.

"Come with me," he said. "I want to talk with you alone for a bit."

He took him into the dining room and closed the door.

"Now," he said, "what is it you want to ask me?"

Mooey twisted his fingers together. He put one bare foot on top of the other.

"Uncle Renny, will you please not tell Daddy what I 'm going to ask?"

"May I drop dead if I do."

"Well — I want to know — I want to know, if I 'll ride to hounds like Adeline did. And if I 'll have to school polo ponies."

"Neither. I promise you. Not unless you really want to. I told Cousin Dermot that you did n't like horses and that your father could n't understand and he said that did n't matter. He said you were to do as you pleased. That 's the way when you 're visiting, you know — you 're not forced to do things you don't like."

Mooey drew a breath from the very bottom of his being. He went to the door. Then he said over his shoulder: —

"I 'll do it. I 'll go. Tell Daddy."

He tore up the stairs.

When Piers and Pheasant were again alone, Piers said: —

"I don't want you to think for a moment that I 'm urging this. I don't want to part with Mooey — except for a visit. But you look as though you were giving him up forever." He spoke almost angrily.

They were standing in the hall, the dark spring night framed in the doorway between them.

"I am," she answered in a choking voice, "I know I am. And another thing — " She was going to say something she 'd never intended to say but now she could not help herself. The bitterness of years made the words burn her lips: —

"You don't love Mooey! You never have!"

Piers was aghast. He stared at her in silence for a moment. Then he shouted: —

"That 's a lie! I 'll not let him go! I 'll go right upstairs and tell him he 's not to go!"

He began to run up the stairs but she ran after him and held him. She burst into tears.

"I did n't mean it, Piers! I don't know what made me say such a thing. I want him to go to Cousin Dermot. I know he 'll have a lovely time — poor little boy!"

XVI

THE PLAY'S PROGRESS

THE audiences at the Preyde Theatre grew more and more scattered. More complimentary tickets were given away. Every day Ninian Fox became more irritable. Phyllis Rhys was considering a new offer. The leading man more frequently visited the bar round the corner. Molly was afraid to send money home and Wakefield called at a theatrical agency to see what were the prospects for a new part. He was more disappointed than ever before in his life. He had been so sure that the play would be a success. He knew it was a good play. Everyone said it was beautifully acted, yet, for some reason, the public did not like it. Ninian Fox tried several newspaper stunts to rouse interest in it but without avail. One afternoon he announced that the run would come to an end in a fortnight. He was putting on a new play.

Wakefield and Molly left the theatre in silence. They turned their eyes from the pink posters in the street. There was heaviness in the air, heaviness pressing down on their spirits. Wakefield no longer used taxis. They went to a near-by basement restaurant for tea. No others of the company were there. They were glad of that. They wanted nothing to remind them of the play.

They ordered crumpets and tea. The waitress knew them well by now and asked sympathetically: —

"How 's things? Any better?"

"No," answered Wakefield. "We 're closing. They 're putting on a new play."

"My goodness, what a pity! I do hope you 'll be in it."

"No such luck."

He gloomily pressed the melting butter into the holes in his crumpet. The way his hair grew on his forehead, and the bend of his lips, touched the waitress. She wished she could do something to help the play.

When she had gone Molly said — "I wonder if ever we shall act together again."

"Probably not."

"I wonder if it will be very hard to get new parts."

"Very hard indeed, I should say."

"Well, I shall have to get a job of some sort."

"Do you think you 're fitted for anything else?"

"Not particularly."

"I sometimes wish I 'd stayed in the monastery."

"I suppose they 'd take you back."

"And I suppose you 'd be quite willing," he returned bitterly.

"Well, you just said you wished you were back."

"I said I wish I 'd *stayed* there. Surely you can see the difference."

She was silent. After a little he said — "Perhaps war will come. Then I need n't worry. I shall join the Air Force."

"Phyllis Rhys says there 'll be no war. Her husband has just come back from Paris and he says the Germans will never dare to attack France. He says France has a magnificent army."

Wakefield laid his hand on hers.

"Don't look so serious, Molly. You look like you did when we first met. Let 's not care what happens. Let 's try to be happy."

She smiled. "All right. I 'll try."

How plucky she was, he thought. She had a way of bracing her slender shoulders that touched him. He said: —

"If it 's humanly possible, we 'll get parts in the same

play. Let 's go to the Agency in the morning. If we can't do anything else we can go into summer repertory."

" It 's late for that. It 's June."

They took turns in despondency and in cheering each other. They had two crumpets apiece.

Henriette was in a state of black disapproval of the populace of London.

" They don't do anything to improve their minds," she said. " All they ask is tea at Lyons and the flicks. Why don't they improve theirselves while there 's time! Since my own association with the theatre my friends marvel at me. I 've told them straight — I never want to see another flick."

That very night she waited up late to see Wakefield on his return from the theatre. She stood under the ceiling light in the hall, strange shadows etched on her large face, her pendulous underlip trembling in excitement.

" I 've been to a crystal gazer," she said. " I 'd made up my mind to find out the truth about the play even if it did cost five shillings. This man has told things to my friends that 'as made their 'air rise and 'e 's never wrong. I said to 'im, says I, ' I 'm connected with a play in a London theatre.' Says I, ' Is this play going to be a success or a failure? I may tell you, I 'm worried about it,' I says. He stared into the crystal for a long while with a dismal look, then 'e smiled. ' The play is about to come off,' 'e said, ' but don't you worry. That play is just gathering speed. It will move fast. It will move to a larger theatre.' "

Wakefield smiled tolerantly. " Thanks, Henriette. It 's sweet of you to have done this for me. I 'll try to believe it but, if you 'd seen the theatre to-night, you 'd have wept."

She patted him on the shoulder. " Don't you worry. The crowds will come yet."

The two following nights were just as dispiriting, but at the Saturday matinee there was quite a good house. That night the theatre was more than half-full. A thrill of hope went through the company. They strained toward what the following week might bring.

It brought better and better houses. It was one of those mysteries of the theatre which no one can solve. On Saturday night the house was sold out. The actors were in good heart. Ninian Fox was at his wit's end to know what to do with the two plays on his hands. The improvement held and even gained in the next week. It was announced that the play would be moved to a larger theatre. That night Wakefield carried a dozen roses and a box of chocolates to Gayfere Street for Henriette. She felt as much justified in her triumph as the playwright himself.

Ninian Fox announced that there would be a week's holiday with pay during the transfer. Molly Griffith invited Wakefield to spend the week at her father's house in Wales. At last they were to walk among the Welsh hills together.

They made their preparations in a state of almost complete happiness. A whole precious week beckoned them. Everything was propitious. Sarah had lately acquired a car and, in one of her moments of erratic generosity, she offered to lend it to them. She liked Molly and she was tired of Wakefield as a single man about the house. She would like to see them marry.

June was presented to them like a bouquet in a crystal vase, as they sped northward. Little gardens overflowing in flowers, rivers tracing their silver way through opulent meadows, flocks of grazing sheep fringed by capering, woolly-legged lambs. No extravagance could flatter the beauty of the day.

They drove through Oxford, its spires pricking the green roundness of its groves, its streets lively with young cyclists. They turned westward through the Vale of Evesham. They saw the Severn winding its pleasant way and had a glimpse of the stark Malverns humped against the sky, their sides purple in the shadow, the ancient British Camp guarding their crown.

They had left London at seven in the morning. It was midafternoon when they entered the Valley of the Wye. The deep-bosomed beauty of Herefordshire enfolded them. They got out of the car and lay on the grass high above the river to rest. Before them, wooded as thick as trees can stand, rose Symond's Yat.

" Some of the names begin to be funny," said Wakefield. " Are we getting near Wales? "

" Pretty near."

She plucked nervously at the grass in silence for a space, then she said — " I think I ought to tell you something about my family."

" You have mentioned your brother but scarcely spoken of the rest. I expect I talk so much of mine that I have n't given you a chance. I wish you 'd tell me what they 're like. How Welsh are you? "

" Christopher and I are n't Welsh at all. We 're English. You see, my mother made a second marriage. My stepfather had three children, all girls. He was an engineer. He built bridges and things. But he drank and he made mistakes. We lived near London for years. Then we could n't afford that and Mother thought it might be good for Father to go far into the country. He 'd inherited a house and some land in Wales, so he agreed and we went there. Christopher loves farming and animals. He was very happy. Things went better for a while. Then Mother died." Her voice began to shake. Wake put his hand on hers but she drew away.

" Don't sympathize with me," she said. " It always makes me cry. I shall be all right in a minute."

After a little she went on steadily. " After that Father seemed not to care how things went. It 's Christopher who keeps the family together. He 's a lovely brother — and stepbrother, too. He 's just as good to the others as he is to me."

"Molly," asked Wake, "are you fond of your stepfather?"

She nodded. "Yes. I am. He 's very kind — in his own way — especially when he 's not been drinking."

"It 's all different from what I 've pictured."

"My sisters are shy. You 'll probably find them odd at first, especially Gemmel. She 's crippled and rather spoilt."

"Which of them paints?"

"Althea, the eldest of all of us, and the shyest too. You must n't ask about her pictures unless she suggests it."

"Which is the youngest?"

"Garda. She 's only sixteen. She 's a fat little thing and sensible. She and Christopher hold the place together. If it were n't for them, I don't know what would happen."

Wakefield considered all this, then looked at his watch.

"I say, how much longer will it take us?"

"About two hours. Are you tired?"

"Just pleasantly. Do you know what I 've been thinking?"

"What?"

"That I wish we could spend the night somewhere about here and take our time to-morrow."

"I wish we could," she answered simply.

There was nothing flirtatious about her, he thought. It was one of her charms that she was so straightforward.

"I wonder what we shall be saying when we drive back this way," he said.

"I never look forward more than I can help."

"How strange! I 'm always looking forward."

"You 've nothing to fear."

He was startled. "Have you?"

"Well, it 's like this. Father has a small annuity. When

he dies that dies too. Whether Christopher and I could make enough between us to keep the home together is what worries me. The girls simply are n't capable of looking after themselves."

"Good Lord! Are you to have them on your hands for the rest of your days?"

"Don't look so upset, Wake. I may be famous and make masses of money."

"Perhaps your sisters will marry."

"Maybe Garda. Not the others. Come, let 's go on." She sprang up and brushed the grass spears from her dress.

As he slid under the wheel he asked — "Why have n't you told me this before, Molly?"

"Why should I worry you?"

"You know very well why. That 's what I 'm for."

"You are sweet to me, Wake. Let 's not think about my troubles. I daresay Father will live to be ninety. . . . He would if he 'd behave himself," she added, bitterly.

They drove in silence for a while, each content in the thought that the intimate space within the car was shared by the other. Clouds came up from the west and the breeze freshened to a wind. They turned into a narrow road, with low irregular stone walls on either side. The face of the country changed. From opulent curves it changed to a hard boniness. The land was open and sparsely treed. There were scattered farms but no large houses. The air had a sharpness in it. Molly threw back her head and took deep breaths. She laughed.

"I 've got you here at last," she said. "We 've a whole week ahead of us."

"If you think," said Wakefield, "that I can drive straight when you say things like that, you 're mistaken."

He turned swiftly and kissed her on the cheek. The car swerved. Her cheeks were a bright pink.

"Be careful!"

"Of what?" he asked.

"Of our precious tires. This is a rough road."

It grew wilder and rougher as they penetrated deeper into the heart of Wales. They were among barren hills that seemed to have upheaved themselves from the bowels of the earth. Beyond and beyond they reared their rocky heads, their shoulders shaggy with bracken. Beyond and beyond they crouched and sank like retreating waves. There was endless variety, and endless monotony. The motorcar was like a gray beetle making its way along the rough road. Wakefield exclaimed: —

"If Sarah had known what her car would go through she 'd have thought twice before lending it."

Molly was concerned. "I should have told you. I do hope the car won't be hurt. Anyhow we shall soon be there. . . . Is it as wild as I said?"

Wakefield put on the tone of his Uncle Ernest. "My child, I 've never known such an example of understatement. It 's as though you said you were going to present me to a gazelle and produced a dinosaur."

She was delighted. "I thought you 'd like it. . . . Look, there 's the Abbey, and away below — our house!"

He stopped the car on a level green plateau. On a rocky hilltop before them stood the ruin of an Abbey. A broken arch of stone and a crumbling tower, dark against the fragile blueness of the June sky. A flock of sheep were grazing on the rich grass surrounding the ruin. The white lambs sported in and out like mischievous choirboys. Below in the valley a gray stone house had spread a flower garden about it as though in passing challenge to the hills.

Wakefield stared in silence, trying to fit Molly Griffith into this picture. Then he said: —

"I can't do it. I can't believe in your living here. Perhaps I shall later, but just at this first glimpse it seems incredible."

She laughed. "When you see Christopher you 'll think he fits in. And so do my sisters. Do you like the Abbey? It was built in the thirteenth century. Christopher says the monks had a garden and that a richness is still in the soil. That 's why it 's such good pasture. Those sheep are his."

"I see a girl," said Wakefield, "going down the mountain-side beyond the valley."

Molly exclaimed, "It 's Althea! She 's been sketching. Remember, you must n't ask to see her pictures. We 'd better go. They 'll be expecting us. I 'm tired and hungry. Are you?"

"I scarcely know what I am. I 'm in a dream."

Slowly the car bumped down the steep road into the valley. It lay in the purple shadow of the mountain. In that light the colors of the garden flowers took on a strange intensity. The house looked incredibly remote. An old thorn tree, distorted by gales, grew by the door. A great boulder, half hidden in flowering gorse, lay near the tree. The girl descending the mountain path had evidently seen them and was hurrying to the house.

Molly seemed tense, Wakefield thought, almost as though she were uncertain of their welcome as they stood in the stone porch. An iron boot-scraper was by the door, flakes of mud beneath it.

"We 'll go straight in," said Molly. But she opened the door softly and stood as though irresolutely in the hall.

It was square and furnished only with an old oak table and settle where a yellow cat lay sleeping. He rose, arched his back, and blinked a half-welcome at Molly.

She bent to stroke his back. "Hullo, Owen! Where is everybody?" She pushed open a door and disclosed an old-fashioned parlor, small and unused, with a faint smell of must.

"Wait here a moment," she said. "I can't think what 's become of everybody."

Wakefield waited, thinking how different this was to Jalna, where no one could arrive without a warning from the dogs that brought the family on the scene. These people were odd and he pitied Molly. He had a sudden desire to protect her from her own family. He had a feeling that he would dislike them on sight. The cat had followed her and he was alone. There was nothing in the room that gave him a clue to the tastes of the younger generation, for it had obviously been furnished at least fifty years before.

Wakefield was both tired and restless. He could not sit down. He looked out of one window and saw the mountain-side in deepening purple, flame-etched clouds moving westward above it. Up there, there must be a strong wind. Here, everything was still.

A voice spoke suddenly behind him.

" How do you do? " The voice was clear, young, and self-assured.

Wakefield started and looked sharply round. He discovered no one. Then came a teasing laugh with a note of triumph in it. It came from under a table over which lay an old-fashioned embroidered cover. But the voice was not a child's voice. He drew away to the other side of the room.

A corner of the tablecover was drawn aside. A girl's face, pale and pointed, with dense dark hair and greenish-blue eyes, smiled up at him.

" Oh, how do you do," he answered. " I did n't see you before." He tried to speak naturally. If this was the way they welcomed guests in Wales he must play up to it.

She came from under the table on her hands and seat, moving quickly, as though accustomed to this means of getting about. Though she was pale it was not the pallor of ill-health. She looked strong and her hands were extraordinarily supple and capable-looking.

Now she folded them in her lap and sat looking up at him.

He saw that her back was somewhat curved, though not deformed. She asked: —

"Did Molly tell you about me?"

"She said . . ." He hesitated.

"Then she did! I wanted to be the first to meet you. We 've all been so curious. We never have visitors, you know. You 're the first in years and years." She looked up at him admiringly. "Goodness, you 're handsome! No wonder Molly raved about you!"

He was recovering himself. "How nice of her! Well, I 'll tell you what she told me about you. She said her sisters were shy."

She answered seriously — "I am when I want to be. It saves me trouble. But I 'm not going to be shy with you. You 're our first visitor and I want to do all I can to make your visit happy." Was there malice in her smile?

He heard Molly's quick step. She came into the room.

"Oh, Gemmel," she exclaimed — "you 're here!" She bent to kiss the girl, who was about her own age. She put up strong arms and pulled Molly to the floor beside her.

"Sit down here," she said, "where I can look at you."

They sat on the floor, side by side.

How extraordinary all this was! For a moment Wakefield did not know what to do with himself. Then he dropped to the floor beside them.

"Good," said Gemmel. "Now I can see you better too." She gave him a long look, then turned to her stepsister. "He 's just like you said, Molly. I could n't have believed it."

Molly gave a little apologetic smile at Wakefield.

"Did n't I tell you she is spoilt?" she asked.

"No," declared Gemmel. "You told him I was shy. But, as I said to him, I can't afford to be shy with our only visitor in years. I 've got to make the most of him."

"Here comes Christopher," said Molly. "He will take you to your room. Then we 'll have some food."

Both sisters turned eagerly to the door where the one brother entered.

Christopher was lightly built and of a fairness that takes on a warm golden tan. It was easy to see that he and Molly were brother and sister, but while her young face showed her awareness of the threatenings and pitfalls of life, his wore an expression of serene confidence in the good intentions of the world. Wake thought he had never seen a sweeter smile. The two shook hands.

Wake and Molly had got to their feet. Gemmel had moved herself so as to be the centre of the group, turning up her face to peer inquisitively into theirs. From this continual upgazing her neck had become extraordinarily supple. She turned her face from side to side with a graceful movement, as of a windflower on its stem.

Christopher smiled down at her good-humoredly. She struck at him with petulance.

"I should think you 'd be ashamed," she said, "to come in here wearing those old clothes. Why did n't you change?"

"I had n't time."

"Where is the honey in the comb you promised to get for me?"

"By George, I forgot."

"There 's a brother for you!" she cried, scornfully. "He promises one thing, and does another. I 'll bet you did n't forget the things Althea ordered!"

"They were for the evening meal, Gemmel."

"And the honey was for my breakfast. I won't eat any breakfast. Do you hear?"

She looked furious, but Wake had the feeling that she was showing off. Where Finch would have been embarrassed by the situation, Wake was amused. Her voice pursued them into the hall. She propelled herself swiftly to the door and raised her face to their retreating figures.

At the top of the stairs Christopher turned to Wakefield with a smile. " She 's often like that to me," he said. " It really does n't mean anything. She 's very fond of me."

" That 's easily to be seen," answered Wake, adding grimly to himself, " Sadistic little devil! "

It was a low room under the eaves to which Molly's brother led Wakefield. The casement was half hidden by a climbing rose and through its greenness he could see the hill, topped by the ruin of the Abbey, now ruby-tinted in the sunset. The fleece of the sheep was ruddy too and the young lambs bleated as they sought the ewes' udders for the good, night feed.

" And Molly belongs here! " thought Wake, as he put on his tie. " Instead of bringing her closer, it 's made her seem almost like a stranger. I 'm meeting her for the first time. Of course, I can believe in Christopher. He 's like Molly. But those sisters! "

Yet he was pleasurably excited as he went down the stairs. Christopher was waiting for him. They went straight to the dining room. Its ceiling was so low that Wakefield could have put up his hand and touched it. He liked this room as much as he disliked the parlor. It belonged to a much earlier period, with its oak refectory table and Welsh dresser and dark blue and red Mason stoneware. The flagged floor was bare, so were the oak walls; there were no curtains to the small-paned casements that stood open to the pure air from the mountains.

He could see Molly in this and her smile drew him closer as he sat down by her side.

Gemmel was already sitting at the table in a high-backed leather chair. Her peculiar characteristics were for the moment obliterated. " She looks," thought Wakefield, " like any other girl, till she moves her head and her eyes slant up at you." At her side the youngest sister seated herself. Molly had briefly introduced her as Garda. She was sixteen, shy and too plump. She looked sturdy and wholesome. Christopher sat in an armchair at one end of the table.

"This is Father's place," he said, "but I 'm sitting here to-night. He 's feeling seedy."

At the same moment there was a heavy thud in the room above. The brother and sisters gave each other a startled look, then Molly began to talk eagerly of what she meant to do on her holiday. Every time she looked at Christopher their eyes smiled. The place at the other end of the table was still vacant. A middle-aged servant brought in the soup. Molly gave Wakefield a thick square of bread.

"It 's homemade," she said. "I used to dream about it in London."

"Delidgious!" he agreed. The word was a joke between them. An Italian waiter in a restaurant they went to in Soho always said it that way.

"Delidgious!" repeated Gemmel. "How lovely!"

Garda began to laugh and could scarcely stop herself. Her color became rosy in her cheeks.

Wakefield was startled to see that the seat at the end of the table facing Christopher was now occupied by Althea. She was fair and slender but not in the way Molly was fair and slender. Althea's fairness was pale, almost wan; her slenderness that of extremely small bones. Yet she was rather tall. She sat with eyes downcast, like a nun, her long narrow hands moving nervously.

Molly looked at her anxiously. "Althea, this is Wakefield Whiteoak," she said.

"How do you do." Althea's voice was scarcely audible. She did not raise her eyes.

"It 's so kind of you to have me," said Wake, his brilliant gaze trying to force a return glance.

She neither looked up nor answered. She did not speak

again during the meal. But her silence was not a chill or damping one. Indeed a smile played once about her mouth when some nonsense passed between Wakefield and Molly.

Wakefield found Molly's family, with the exception of Althea, easy to get on with. Christopher was always ready to laugh at other people's jokes. The accounts of theatrical life filled him with an amused wonder. Wake thought he had never met a young fellow of twenty-one so unsophisticated, so naïf. He felt like a grandfather beside him and, being the youngest of a large family, enjoyed the feeling.

After dinner the two young men sat on the bench in the porch smoking. Before them the dark humps of the mountains rose and fell till they melted into the hyacinth horizon. There were other small farms tucked away in the valleys but none in sight. In this light the mountains no longer seemed granite-hard but malleable and changeful, as though they took on new postures, moving like ponderous bedfellows to curl closer for the night. The sheep huddled by the Abbey, becoming one with its paleness. Sometimes out of this pale fleecy bulk came the plaintive bleat of a young lamb.

"How peaceful it is here," said Wake. "You know, in some ways, I envy you living in such a prehistoric sort of place. You may read of upheavals and war but you can't believe in them."

"I like it here," said Christopher, puffing at his pipe. "It just suits me. I don't think I shall ever want to live anywhere else."

"What would you feel if war came?"

"Oh, I'd join up at once, but I should hate it," he answered simply, and added — "Do you think there's going to be war?"

Always the same question, wherever you went! Always that look in the eyes, as though the questioner had a vain hope of reassurance.

"Yes," Wakefield said. "I think it's coming but perhaps

not very soon. I hope not soon." He laughed and added, "I don't want you to leave your lambs, or Molly and me our play."

"I don't think it will come," said Christopher tranquilly.

Wakefield had a glimpse of Garda, laboring up the stairs, carrying a large tray. "Dinner for Papa," he thought. He discovered that Gemmel's room was off the parlor.

Christopher said: "I expect she 'd like to be with us." He went into the house and returned carrying Gemmel on his back. She smiled mischievously over his shoulder at Wakefield. Christopher deposited her on the seat beside him. Soon they were joined by Molly and Garda. A slip of a moon had risen above the Abbey. Its gray stones looked ethereal now. It might float away at any moment like a cloud. The breeze was light and playful as though it mocked the austerity of the mountains. The boys and girls sat talking together like old friends. But Gemmel could not leave Christopher in peace. She teased him. She got his pipe from him and hid it behind her and seemed to expect admiration from Wake for these tricks. Molly spoke to her as though she were a child.

After a while Christopher said — "Let 's sing, shall we?"

"All right," said Molly, "if Wake does n't mind."

"I 'd love to hear you," he said.

"You must sing too."

Wake saw that Althea had come into the porch. She sat in the corner beside Christopher, half hidden by his broad shoulder.

How they could sing! Their young voices filled the night air with silvery strength and sweetness. It was like the moonlight turned into song, Wake thought. He added his own good tenor to their voices. Molly exclaimed: —

"It 's just what we needed! Is n't it, Christopher?"

"It 's splendid," he said with satisfaction. "There 's nothing I like in the evening so well as singing."

They sang for an hour. Wakefield strained his ears to catch the separate sound of Althea's voice. He did, and thought it was the best of all. He turned to smile at her. She put up her hand as though to shield her face and, after a moment, went into the house.

A casement upstairs was thrown open and a man's voice called out: —

"If you 're going to keep up that row any longer, I wish you 'd go into the mountains."

Dead silence fell in the porch. The casement closed.

"Father is not very well to-day," said Christopher. "Perhaps we 'd better go to bed."

Wakefield realized that he was very tired. The little group dissolved but he had a moment alone with Molly.

"I love your family," he said.

"I 'm so glad. I never hoped you 'd fit in so well. But then, you 're so adaptable — you 'd fit in anywhere. You must n't mind Father's speaking like that. He 'll be all right to-morrow. Probably very glad to see you."

"Shall we walk together on the mountain to-morrow?"

"Yes. Good night, Wake." She swayed almost imperceptibly toward him. He put his arm about her and laid his cheek against hers. He would not kiss her. No — that precious moment was to be kept for the mountaintop.

Mr. Griffith's voice came from above. "If they 've stopped that row down there you may open my window."

"Don't mind," said Molly. "He is n't really like that. He loves singing himself. He has a fine bass voice."

"Has he?" said Wakefield lamely.

Christopher reappeared in the doorway.

"I 've been listening to the news," he said. "I don't at all like the sound of it."

Molly and Wake gave each other an anxious, yet shamefaced, look. They were thinking about their play. They could n't help it.

XVII

IN THE RUINED ABBEY

ALL the beauty of the night sky foretold nothing. The next day the rain came down relentlessly. It drummed on the roof like an advancing army. It ran down the mountain-sides in rivulets and drew a curtain between the house and the ruin of the Abbey. Christopher and the shepherd, attending a sick sheep, came in dripping. Molly was bitter in her disappointment.

"It will do this for a week, you 'll see!" she said, in despair. "We might as well have stayed in London."

"It will clear," said her brother. "This can't last more than a day or two."

"You 're always so horribly optimistic, you don't cheer me at all. You make me feel worse."

He looked at her ruefully. "Anyhow," he said, "you will have seen us."

"I know, and that is worth everything to me, but here is Wake longing to explore the mountain."

"Here am I," said Wake, "completely happy."

But he wondered when he would have Molly to himself. Garda brought out her collection of butterflies to show him. Christopher rarely had another young man to talk to and he wanted Wakefield's views on a number of subjects. When Wake slipped into the chill parlor, hoping Molly would follow, he found Gemmel peering up at him from beside the hearth. She was knitting.

"I 'm beginning a pullover for your birthday," she said. "Molly tells me it is this month. Come here, please, and let me see how the color suits you."

He went and sat down beside her. She held the golden-brown wool next his cheek.

"Lovely!" she exclaimed.

"It 's frightfully kind of you."

"Do you like me?"

"How can I help — when you 're so kind?"

"I mean do you like me for myself?"

"Of course."

"How much?"

"As much as that." He held up his hands.

She pushed her head between them. Her hair was thick and lively and there was a look in her eyes.

"Well — are you going to?" she asked.

He kissed her lightly, quickly.

"I 've won!" she exclaimed, laughing.

"What?"

"Garda and I had a bet as to which of us could get you to kiss her first. She 'd no luck with the butterflies. She told me so."

Wake laughed. "She did n't give me time."

"Neither did I."

She heard her father's heavy step on the stair. She began to talk fast about her knitting.

Mr. Griffith came into the room slowly. He held out his hand with a genial smile.

"I 'm so sorry I was laid up yesterday," he said. "I hope the children are making you comfortable."

"I 'm teaching him to knit," said Gemmel.

Her father smiled down at her indulgently. He was very different from what Wake had expected. He had pictured him as somewhat battered and disgruntled but here was a man well-groomed, well pleased, apparently, with himself and his situation. He was blond, stoutish, and tall. He had a smile that took one into his confidence, a voice that made his most trivial remark telling. No wonder his family stood a good deal from him. He added pleasantly: —

"I heard your singing last night and wished I could take part in it. I 'm very fond of a good song."

It was as though a middle-aged London man-about-town had remarked how much he enjoyed a good game of croquet.

He asked a number of questions about Canada and said he had often considered taking his family out there. The morning passed in talk. In the afternoon it was the same. Mr. Griffith dominated the scene. They were like children beside him. He arranged amusements like a bachelor uncle entertaining a rather awkward lot of nieces and nephews. He made Christopher sing. He made Garda, who twice broke down doing it, play a piece on the piano. He made Gemmel recite Wordsworth's "I wandered lonely as a cloud," which she did so well that Wake felt a new pang at her helplessness. That girl, he thought, might have somehow made a name for herself. Then Mr. Griffith himself recited and you could see where Gemmel had her talent. Obviously he was proud of his children and seldom had a chance for showing them off. He tried to persuade Althea to display her sketches but she fled from the room. She never spoke.

The rain came pouring down till evening. The rivulets swelled to rushing streams down the mountainside. The sheep, with the lambs trotting beside them, went into the Abbey and took possession there. The sky rested, in solid grayness, on the mountaintops. But at evening it broke into swinging purple clouds as a strong wind whistled inland from the West. The rain lessened, blew slantwise, then ceased. A clear greenish blue fringed the rims of the clouds. Molly and Wake put on windbreakers and went out. For the first time they were really alone together.

The air lay like a cool hand on their hot cheeks. They

wanted to run up the steep stony path. They were aimlessly wild like birds suddenly set free. They ran here and there, picking up odd stones, finding mountain flowers that, for all their fragility, had captured the wonder of the mountains in their tiny staring faces.

The Abbey rose pale and rain-washed before them. The sunlight, piercing the purple of the clouds, flickered over the delicately wrought pillars. The stone groinings supported little more than the stormy sky. Here one of the bosses had fallen from a column and lay like a broken lily, there a pilaster was topped by a bird's nest built of mountain grass. The sheep had discovered that the rain had ceased and they came shouldering each other through the Abbot's own door, all but one who lay with her lamb beside her on the fallen altar. She lay chewing her cud and blinking coldly at Wake and Molly through her white eyelashes.

"It 's too overwhelmingly picturesque," thought Wake. "I can't say what I want to here. I wish I 'd said it in London."

Molly looked the sheep over with an appraising eye. "They 're a nice lot," she said. "Christopher is pleased with them."

"Yes. They 're a lovely flock. It 's all lovely and strange and quite unbelievable. Shall we really be back with Ninian Fox next week? I can't imagine it. I almost wish we could stay here forever."

"You 'd tire of it."

"You forget that I lived in a monastery for a year."

"So you did! But I had sooner be working in London."

"Well — I want to be wherever you are."

Something in his voice made her suddenly aware of herself physically. She moved, as though for more space, to one of the windows and leaned out. He followed her.

"Look," she said, "it 's going to be a lovely evening."

Mountains and valleys unrolled themselves in a luminous

scroll. Some, not before seen, showed themselves in the golden distance. The clouds had gathered themselves into purple immensity and were sweeping toward England. In the clear pale sky above, a skylark was pouring down his song unseen.

Wakefield's arm touched Molly's and a fire passed through them. He felt his breast swell. He felt that he could draw the mountains, the valleys, the very blades of grass into his heart and enfold them there. He felt a constriction in his throat. Moments passed before he could speak, but the skylark spoke for him, pouring out his love.

Then he drew her toward him. All he had meant to say was suddenly worthless. The simplest words were enough.

"Molly — I love you — will you marry me?"

"Yes," she answered, almost in a whisper. "Yes, Wake, I will."

XVIII

BACK IN TOWN

THE play had reopened with a gala night in its new theatre. The press notices had been even better than at the first. It was established. It was the thing to see. It became fashionable. The younger members of the company began to gather their courage to ask for a rise in salary. Molly, who had always been free to accept any invitation, now had more than she could cope with even by going to two or three parties each night. Wakefield seldom rose before noon and often did not come back to Gayfere Street till dawn. Finch and Sarah saw little of him. But they were very proud of him and took some acquaintance to see the play each week. Henriette carried his breakfast to him in almost trembling eagerness for the latest gossip of play or players. She treasured every newspaper cutting connected with them and pasted them in an exercise book. Photographs from scenes in the play were revered almost as sacred pictures in her room.

Wakefield was deeply happy in his engagement. He did not buy a ring for Molly. He wanted her to wear the ring left him by his grandmother for his intended wife. He wrote letters to each separate member of the family to tell of his engagement and in return received their congratulations, advice, and warnings. Piers wrote — " I hope you 'll be happy in your engagement while it lasts."

Now the visit to Wales seemed like a dream except for that moment when he had told Molly he loved her. It stood out like a torch against a misty background. Even when Molly read him letters from home, the members of her family were blurred in his mind like figures in a dream.

But he wanted to see them again. He felt tender toward them. They seemed remote yet curiously vulnerable. After his introduction to Althea she had not once spoken to him. Yet he had seen that she wanted to. He had found her book of sketches on a table in the parlor and he was sure she had left them there for him to see. They were curious, wild and harsh, utterly alien, it seemed to him, to the delicate, elusive girl. He had tried to talk to her of her pictures but she had almost run from the room and the sketchbook had disappeared. One day Molly said to him: —

"You made a great hit with my family. They all like you — especially Althea. I wish you could have heard the things she said about you. I really became jealous." She laughed and put her arm about his shoulders.

Wakefield did not tell her that he had kissed Gemmel.

One hot July day, at the end of a matinee, Ninian Fox overtook Molly and Wake as they were leaving the theatre. He was very excited.

"There's a New York manager here," he said. "He has seen the play and likes it tremendously. He likes you two very much and wants to meet you. Would n't it be splendid if he'd buy it for New York?" He slipped his arm into theirs and walked between them, with a secret air, beaming at them like an old friend.

Molly felt rigid at his touch. It was like him to be decent to her now, when someone else had discovered her value!

He propelled them back to his office. They were introduced to Mr. Elias, who was short and smiling and had fleshy aquiline features.

"I do like this play," he said, when they were seated. "And I'm going to write to New York about it at once. I like you young people very much. Mr. Fox says he thinks he could replace you if I took you over there. Would you like to come?"

They would like it so much that they were almost speechless but they showed proper caution in considering the suggestion. Mr. Elias also wanted Phyllis Rhys and the leading man. The other parts could be filled by actors in New York. Mr. Elias seemed to love to make plans. He talked as though the play had already made a fortune in New York. He had Ninian Fox completely baffled, for he had been prepared to handle Mr. Elias with great shrewdness. It seemed unnecessary. Mr. Elias was ready to pour himself out and, with his good will, the gold of the New World. But when it came to the contract he was more than a match for them all put together. The salaries were not so large as the actors had expected. Ninian Fox, after struggling violently, had to take a smaller percentage than he considered his due. The author came out worst of all.

But things were settled before long and, early in August, they sailed from Southampton. Wakefield and Molly were gloriously happy. They had not a wish unfulfilled. The very sea was kind to them. The voyage was all too short. The morning came when the skyscrapers of New York towered before them in torrid heat. Their foundations seemed to have dissolved in heat, left them suspended in burning sunlight. The ship, through which the salt wind had raced for a week, was sultry and swarming with people. The four members of the company collected in the lounge where aliens were gathered. They waited perspiring, passports in hand.

Mr. Elias came to meet them. He was in a state of heat that surpassed even their own, but it did not trouble him at all. He was cheery and helpful. He gave each one an oily handshake. After his arrival everything seemed miraculously speeded-up. Their passports were examined; they were on the docks. Their luggage was examined; they were in the taxicabs. Through shabby streets, where newspapers were blown about and dirty children played on the frying-pan pavements, they emerged on to clean streets with soaring skyscrapers to shade them. People in light-colored clothes thronged the pavements. Wake and Molly looked on each as a potential part of an audience.

Their hotel was cool but breathless, yet, when they opened their windows, the heat and dust poured in.

Phyllis Rhys had a sitting room. She was known in New York and already it was filled with bouquets of flowers from her friends and from Mr. Elias. He also had sent a dozen roses for Molly. Wakefield ordered iced drinks for everyone but when he saw the bill he was chilled without the ice. The leading man had got newspapers. There was one apiece. They stood staring at the huge headlines. War, which had receded in the salt spaces of the ocean, now pressed in on them.

"Is the threat worse," asked Wake, "or is it just these papers?"

Phyllis Rhys was determined there should not be war. "It 's the papers," she said. "If they don't have scarifying headlines no one will read them."

"It all depends on Poland," said the leading man.

"I wonder what things will be like here," said Molly, in a small voice, "if there 's a war."

"It would n't make any difference," said Phyllis Rhys. "But there 'll not be one."

"I 'd not be here to know," said Wake. "I 'd be back in England."

"You could n't go off like that." Phyllis Rhys's voice was sharp. "You 're under contract."

"I'm willing to bet," said her leading man, "that it will come this year."

"Well," cried Wake, gayly, "let 's make the most of peace while it lasts! Come on, Molly, we 'll explore."

They put on their thinnest clothes, which were not nearly thin enough, and went into the streets.

"Gosh," said Wake, "to think that I 'm on the same land

as Jalna! If I ran fast enough and far enough I should be there!" He was in wild spirits. Everything was fun. All he saw delighted him — the hard bright finish of the shops, the cosmopolitan crowds in the streets, the "tough" taxi drivers, the Negresses dressed in the latest style. What a contrast to London!

"Oh, I wish we were married and on our honeymoon!" he exclaimed. "It would be even better fun."

"I could n't be happier than I am," she said. His eyes challenged her. "Wait and see."

Rehearsals began as soon as the cast could be finally selected. Robert Fielding had followed the others on the next ship and was to produce the play and act the comedy part as he had in London. The weeks flew by. The play was to open in mid-September. Mingled with their excitement over the opening, the strain of preparation, was the mounting apprehension of war. Then one morning Wake tapped on Molly's door. He said through it: —

"It 's come, Molly! War is declared."

XIX

YOUNG MAURICE AND DERMOT COURT

DERMOT COURT had not felt so nervous in many a year. He was waiting for the return of the car which had gone to meet Wright and young Maurice. The train must be late. That was usual in Ireland. But the continued watching and waiting had begun to tire Dermot. He began to feel a little depressed and to have misgivings as to his wisdom in bringing a child into the house. It was so many years since he had had a child of his own that he felt he had forgotten their language. To be sure, he had got on easily with little Adeline, but she was an exceptional child and her father had been with her. Now this boy was to be on his hands without help from anyone. Of course, he could send him home if it came to the worst, but he did not want to send him home.

He saw the maid, Kathleen, passing through the hall. He called out to her: —

"Is the boy's room prepared?"

He had asked this question every time he had seen her that day but she answered patiently — "Indeed and it is, sir, and a lovely comfortable room that ought to make him settle down if anything will."

"Good. Patsy should be back from the train by now. I hope the car has not broken down."

"The car could n't break down, sir, not after the way Patsy overhauled it yesterday. There he comes down the drive now!" She hurried to the door.

A stab of excitement passed through Dermot, making him weak. What if he should hate the boy on sight! What if the boy should hate him! If he had it to do over he never would have risked such an undertaking.

"Keep him with you, Kathleen," he said, nervously, "while I have a word with the man. Send the man in to me." He sat down in a deep chair and waited.

He heard movements, voices in the hall. Then the door opened and a stocky man, obviously dressed in his best and quite self-possessed, came into the room.

"You 're the man who has come to help school the horse?"

"Well, I guess so, sir," answered Wright, laconically.

"And you 've brought the young gentleman safely to me?"

"I 've done my best, sir."

Dermot thought that if he disliked the boy as much as he disliked the man all would be up. He said: —

"I hope you had a good voyage."

"I guess it was all-right, sir. We were both pretty sick for a day."

Dermot looked at him coldly. "You may send Master Maurice in to me," he said.

Wright left the room. He was thinking: —

"If Mooey don't like that old man any better than I do, I pity him, living with him."

Dermot sat waiting, his eyes on the door. He felt amused at himself when he remembered that he had dressed with unusual care that day. He hoped he did not look so old as to frighten the boy.

Mooey came slowly into the room. He wore dark blue shorts and blazer and a white flannel shirt. He looked smaller than Dermot had expected, smaller and paler. But Mooey was nervous too. However, he advanced steadily and held out his hand.

"How do you do," said Dermot, clasping it in his strong old fingers.

"Quite well, thank you, sir."

"I hear you were seasick coming across."

" A little. After that it was fine."

He spoke clearly but with a slight tremor in his voice. He looked searchingly at Dermot. Something he saw reassured him. He smiled up at Dermot, who asked: —

" Do you think you can bear to visit me for a while? "

" Yes. I 'm sure I can."

" Remember — if you don't like me you may go home whenever you choose."

" Mummie told me that."

" But I 'll say this for myself — I 'm not hard to get on with. Some of the Courts were, you know."

" So I 've been told."

Dermot laughed. " Your great-grandmother among 'em. Do you remember her? No — of course you don't."

" I was only a baby when she died, sir. But I've heard a lot about her."

" I 'll wager you have! " Dermot took Mooey into the next room, where tea was laid. Pheasant would have trembled for her child if she could have seen the battalion of sandwiches, cake, and macaroons. They sat facing each other across the round oak table. Through the open window came the song of a blackbird and the whir of a machine cutting hay. Now Mooey was the more possessed of the two. Dermot's tongue seemed paralyzed. He could find nothing to say. The stupendousness of undertaking to live with a small boy overwhelmed him. An ocean of experience that no ship could cross lay between them.

" I was an old fool," thought Dermot. " I should have let well enough alone. The worry of this will probably shorten my life."

He ate little but sat sipping his weak tea. He saw how a chicken sandwich could disappear in three bites, and how extraordinarily attractive a mouth could look when chewing — no wrinkles, just elastic muscles and red lips in action, with a glimpse of white teeth.

If he could have seen into Mooey's mind he might have felt fewer forebodings. Mooey was thinking: —

"I guess this is the best tea I shall ever have here. He could n't live like this every day. It would cost millions. He 's nice and kind-looking. He 's something like Uncle Nick. Funny how his hand shakes. When he begins to talk about horses I must n't let him know I 'm afraid of them. I 'll just say I don't much like riding."

"Have a piece of chocolate cake," said Dermot.

"Thank you." Mooey took a piece.

"When you 've finished we 'll have a little walk about the place. I suppose you 're keen to see Johnny the Bird?"

"Oh, yes, sir. But —" Mooey's face became tense — "somehow . . . it 's funny . . . I don't like riding very spirited horses."

He looked anxiously at Dermot to see the effect of this confession on him. Dermot looked unperturbed.

"You 've ridden a good deal?"

"Ever since I can remember."

"Had a good many falls?"

Mooey nodded.

"It hurts, does n't it?"

"You bet. Especially falls from polo ponies. I 've helped school them a lot. But I don't think it 's the hurt I mind. It 's not knowing what the horse will do next."

"Yes," agreed Dermot gravely. "It 's the feeling of uncertainty. I ride nothing but a steady old cob myself nowadays and I 've another I 'll give to you if you like him. You can try him anyhow. You may ride or not, just as you like."

"Thank you, Cousin Dermot." If his mother could hear she would be pleased with his manners, he thought.

They went into the garden after tea, Mooey walking carefully and slowly by Dermot's side. It was strange to him to be alone with an old person after living with his young parents and his two small brothers. Dermot laid his hand on his shoulder as they walked and Mooey braced himself to be a support to him. They passed through the arbor over which the ancient pear trees were trained, into the formal gardens lately put in order again after years of neglect. How different it all was from Jalna! The flowers looked tender and full of moisture and their stalks green and juicy. The very smell of the hay in the near-by field was different. The birds' voices had a strange note in them as though of an old mysterious tale they told. From a knoll where a gnarled beech tree sent its tapering roots across the grass and deep below they could see the gently rolling countryside with white cottages dotted on its greenness, and the flash of a stream. It came to young Maurice as a place he had long dreamed of and now discovered.

As he lay in bed that night he thought over all the happenings of the day — the confusion of the landing at Cóbh in a choppy sea, the long railway journey, the discussing with Wright of everything they saw, the meeting with Cousin Dermot. His home seemed so far away that he felt it was in another world. He was too newly arrived in this world to know its ways. He felt suspended, as it were, in mid-air between two worlds. He looked back at his home across immeasurable space and saw the familiar objects of his short life. He saw his brothers, as he had last seen them, waving him good-bye. He saw his father, fresh-colored and stalwart, his blue eyes prominent with that look that made one tremble. He saw his mother's face.

No — no, he must n't think of her! He could n't bear it. Not in this large quiet room, in this tall four-poster. It had been different on board ship. There he could lie, a part of all the strange movement of ship and sea, giving himself up to imaginings. He was a part of nothing here. But so long as he kept his thoughts from his mother he was not afraid. Yet there was nothing to take her place when he thrust her out of his mind in self-defense. Just a black void was left. Then bits of her would appear. The smooth creamy-brown back of her neck and the lock of brown hair that nestled there. Her left forefinger on which there was a scar where a dog had once bitten her. Her mouth when she smiled. No — he must n't think of that! He dived down under the bedclothes and pulled them over his head. He began to cry.

After a while a hand was laid on him. He started in fear, then thought it was Wright. He drew down the sheet a little way and said huskily: —

"I 'm all right. What do you want?"

But it was Cousin Dermot. He sat down on the side of the bed and laid his hand on Mooey's hot head.

"Do you mind if I stay with you for a little?" he said. "I get rather lonely at night."

"Yes, please stay," said Mooey eagerly. "I get a little lonely too."

Dermot stayed a long while and, when he left, Mooey was fast asleep.

XX

THE NEWS IN GAYFERE STREET

At the end of June Sarah told Finch that she was going to have a child. He was little short of astounded. He had never expected this. It had seemed to him that parenthood was against the nature of each of them. He could not picture himself as a father, even though he was more interested in children and tenderer toward them than Piers was. Yet Piers seemed the inevitable and perfect father. He could not picture Sarah as a mother. Sarah simply could n't be a mother. She had n't the body for it or the instinct. She was a cold crystal receptacle for passion. Anything more would shatter her. He walked about their room, confused and almost horrified.

"Are you positive?" he asked.

"Positive. The doctor says so — definitely."

"When will it . . . happen?"

"In December."

"December!" he exclaimed, as though it were a month of doom.

She laughed gayly. "It will be my Christmas present to you."

"Good God!"

"Are n't you glad?"

"Are you?"

"I don't realize it yet. It 's been fun having this secret to myself for a whole week."

"Why did n't you tell me before?"

"I wanted to think it over."

"And still you say you don't realize it!"

"Well — I feel a new person."

"Have you made any plans?" His tone was almost impersonal.

"I'm leaving that for you." There was a malicious gleam in her narrow greenish eyes.

He had a sudden feeling of anger, as though she had played a trick on him, yet this was a moment that should have brought out his tenderness and his nobility — if he had these qualities! So he thought and turned to look into the street that she might not read his thoughts.

A woman was passing pushing a pram. He pictured a pram standing in the narrow hall below. He pictured Sarah pushing one. Pictured Henriette pushing one. He pictured himself pushing one and laughed.

"Why are you laughing?" she asked.

"Trying to think of myself as a father."

"You'll be a perfect father! Oh, Finch, I hope it's a boy and like you! What do you hope?"

"I hope it's a girl and . . ." in an insane moment he almost said — "like Henriette." He caught himself in time and said — "like you."

She threw her arms about him from behind. "There can never be another like me!"

"You can't have it here, can you?" asked Finch.

"With Henriette as midwife! No — I'll find a proper place." She spoke with confidence. He had a rush of tenderness, picturing as a dreadful upheaval all she would have to go through.

He had to be away for several weeks on a tour. It was a success. He came back feeling well and happy. But he found a changed Sarah. She had been suffering from ills peculiar to her condition. She was pale and despondent. She threw herself into his arms and wept. She said she must have sea air and wanted to go to the Cornish coast.

Finch wondered why she should choose the place where she had spent the honeymoon of her first marriage, but he said: —

"Very well. We'll go there, if we can find a house. It's pretty difficult at this late hour."

"Henriette knows of one through a friend of hers. She is cook in a family who find they can't go. There's nothing I want to do so much."

The thought of being by the sea drew Finch almost equally. He had been too long among crowds. His dismay at the thought of the coming child was calmed by the picture of a lonely cottage on a Cornish cliff, of lonely wanderings over the rocks when the tide was ebbing.

The place turned out to be neither a cottage nor remote. But the white house, one of a group of half a dozen, was airy, open to the west wind and furnished with just the sort of things Finch liked. They had brought Henriette with them. There was a gale and lashing rain the day they arrived. It was always so wherever they went. It rained and it blew all the first day. Henriette was in a mood of deep despondency. It was her belief that nature should be kept under control as it was in the London parks. When she saw the ragged cliffs, the momentous boulders, the raging sea and the great slate quarry — now overgrown by grass and flowers — in the hillside behind the house, she shook her head and her pendulous underlip trembled.

"It was never meant to be," she said.

But Sarah was happy to settle down here for a month. She ran from room to room placing things to her taste. Every time she and Finch met she threw both arms about him and pressed herself close to his breast.

"I'm so blissfully happy," she said. "I scarcely think of the baby. It's just you and I together by the sea. Do you think it will be fine to-morrow?"

"I'm sure of it," he answered, laying his cheek against the glossy convolutions of her plaits.

But there was an unreality about her to him. She was a new, a dual being, the one he knew and the one unseen and unborn. And both these were bound up in each other and antagonistic to him. He had no sense of having begotten the child. As he saw Sarah's form enlarge with its growth he felt a shrinking from her and a distaste for all that was to come. Her greed and her erratic appetite set him on edge. He thought with horror — "Am I going to turn against her again? I must n't! I must n't! I 'll not let myself. Every time I feel one of these sensations, I 'll go straight to her and kiss her." But this brought no relief.

The sun came out warm and bright. Finch took Sarah for walks on the smooth grassy downs along the cliff. She delighted to go as far as the nearest resort and sit in a sheltered spot watching the bright-colored surf bathers riding through the foam. But when Finch spoke of joining them himself she was horrified.

"And see you drown before my eyes! Never! My father was drowned, my first husband was drowned. Once I was almost drowned. Do you remember how you and Arthur saved me? The sea is my enemy!"

"Then why do you want to be beside it?" he asked coldly.

"To watch it," she answered, with a sly smile. "One needs to watch one's enemies."

The morning walk was all she could do in a day. That left him free to wander on the shore in the afternoon. He would lie on the sands in the bay where the green waves scampered in like playful children trailing seaweed. He would loiter on the rocky headland when the waves had retreated, leaving their toys behind them. He would peer fascinated into pools where miniature forests and grottoes had been arranged by the salty fingers of the sea. Then he made himself no more than a receptacle for the mysteries of the shore.

A strange communion existed in these days between himself and Henriette. He had a feeling that Henriette knew a good deal about him. She too wandered on the shore, leaving large flat footprints on the sand. Once he espied her in a solitary orgy of paddling, her heavy black skirt drawn up to her knees, disclosing enormous white legs that took dancing steps in the foam. The kitchen was briny with the treasures she had collected, shells of all sorts, starfish and limpets. Once she came trailing seaweed as long and limp as herself.

"It goes *pop* when you squeeze it," she said. "I 've popped it till I 'm worn-out."

Another day she brought home a jellyfish. "You can see its innards," she mourned. "It was never meant to be."

She and Finch made a bargain that they would not speak of war in front of Sarah. She should have this time in peace. They kept the newspapers from her and she never asked to see them. She was satisfied with her magazines and library books. She became more and more engrossed in herself. She would send Finch across the downs to the distant village to buy some pastry or cheese she fancied. He marveled at the amount of Cornish cream she could eat.

He went in the early morning to bathe, his towel about his shoulders. He grew tanned and the hollows in his cheeks filled out.

They motored back to London on the last day of August. Three days later he ran down the basement stairs to Henriette.

"War is declared," he said. "How shall I tell my wife?"

"I 'll tell her," said Henriette. "I 'm a good bearer of bad news."

"I 'm afraid it will be a great shock."

"Yes, it will be enough to bring on a premature birth."

"Had I better fetch a doctor before we tell her?"

"No. Just 'old yourself ready." She plodded up the two flights of stairs.

She loomed dejectedly in Sarah's doorway.

"The worst 'as 'appened," she said.

Sarah sat up in bed.

"What's wrong?" she asked wildly.

"War. It's declared — in all its 'orrer."

"War! Why — I thought that scare was over!"

"We kept it from you as long as we could. Now you must face it like the rest of us."

It was strange, but this way of breaking the news suited Sarah. She took it quietly. She asked Finch: —

"Do you think we shall be bombed?"

He was sitting on the side of the bed with her in his arms.

"You must go into the country where you'll be safe."

"You too! I'll not leave you!"

"There'll probably be work here for me." He knew that neither his eyesight nor his nerves would pass an army test.

"I shall die if we're separated."

"We'll not talk of that yet."

Her arms tightened about him.

"You've something in your mind! Something against me! I can feel it."

"My one thought," he said, "is to do what is best for you and — the child."

"You're as cold as ice!" she cried. "You don't love me any longer. You hate the thought of the baby. If you loved it you'd call it our baby, not the child!"

"Give me time," he said. "You can't expect me to love something unborn."

"You hate our baby," she kept repeating.

He could not tell her that it was not a baby to him but one of those embryo creatures he had seen in pictures. Yet, he calculated, by now it must have features and hands.

"I'll wager anything," she went on, "that Renny loved Adeline before she was born."

"If you compare me to him it must always be to my disadvantage."

She dragged herself away from him and, crouching on the bed, made her pale face into a mask of hostility.

"Now you are deliberately tormenting me. You know that I hate Renny more than anyone on earth. Yet you accuse me — what are you accusing me of?"

"My God!" he cried, in exasperation. "I 'm not accusing you of anything. I merely said that in my opinion . . ."

"You did n't say in *your* opinion! You said in *my* opinion."

"I said neither thing. I only said . . ."

"I don't want to hear it repeated!"

"You 're absolutely unreasonable."

"What can you expect? You 've known all along that war was coming. Now you let it burst on me in one flash and expect me to be reasonable. But you 'll not have me with you much longer. This is going to kill me!"

"Sarah!"

"Don't put your hand on me!"

He flung out of the room.

"Come back!" she shrieked. "Would you leave me alone at such a time?"

He came back and stood at the foot of the bed.

"What do you want me to do?"

"I want you to remember that I 'm a pregnant woman and that this is your child."

"Have I ever forgotten it?"

"You 're utterly self-centred. God pity the woman who marries an artist!"

"You said to me not a week ago that you pitied Alayne and Pheasant from the bottom of your heart."

"I pity them because they don't know anything about love as I know it."

"Perhaps Renny and Piers are the happier for that."

"Never mind — I shall die!"

"You must be mad to say such things, Sarah."

"If I am, you have driven me to it." She threw herself violently on the bed and rolled in her bulk on it.

He tried to take her in his arms but she fought him.

"I shall die!" she moaned.

"Sarah . . ." He began to shake with sobs.

She lay still, feeling the reverberation of his sobbing through her body. The child leaped inside her.

Suddenly she was almost tranquil. She laid her hands on his head and drew it to her breast.

XXI
IN THE KITCHEN GARDEN

NICHOLAS WHITEOAK was taking advantage of the warm sunshine and having a little exercise in the kitchen garden. There would not be many more days like this. It was as though October, with her apron full of fruit, had picked out the most symmetrical and gayest-colored peach and presented it to her child. He was eighty-eight years old that month.

He wore a brown and buff check jacket, an old favorite of his, and a brown silk tie with yellow flecks that Alayne had given him on his birthday. His iron-gray hair was still thick and would last him the rest of his life. He was freer of gout than he had been in years. Yet it was obvious to those who knew him that the last twelvemonth had aged him greatly. His broad shoulders were more bent; his mouth, under his gray moustache, was gentler and less humorous; his brown eyes sometimes looked vague and even confused. He continually said, "My memory is going," but he always straightened his shoulders as he said it and would have been hurt if anyone had agreed.

The kitchen garden was a perfect place for walking in the fall. There was no grass to hold the heavy dew and the narrow paths were dry as pavement. Already they were strewn with little yellow leaves from the row of Lombardy poplars that edged one side of the garden. Between the poplars he had a view of the stables and the paddock where a show horse was being taken over some hurdles by Piers. It was very companionable. Companionable too was the sight of Mrs. Wragge, taking armfuls of billowing white sheets from the line, and the pigeons walking on their pink feet among the raspberry canes picking up late raspberries. There were quite a few of these and he tried one himself but found it disappointingly sour.

He examined the cucumbers, abundant and roundly curved, still clinging to their leafless vines. He tapped a marrow with his stick and it gave a faintly hollow sound. The cabbages were a fine crop, their centres smooth and hard, their outer leaves crisply crinkled. He knocked a fat green worm from one of them and trod on it. The parsley was of an amazing strength and greenness. It looked as though no frost could kill it. The mint was up to his knees and covered with tiny purple flowers. It was curious, he thought, how he took more and more pleasure in these trivial things. They somehow gave him a feeling of reassurance. He picked a leaf of mint and crushing it between finger and thumb sniffed its herby sweetness.

The war had been a shock to him. Well, Mr. Chamberlain had said there 'd be peace for all our time — and it had n't lasted even his short time! Why, the entire House had been deeply moved by the Four Power Conference and its agreement. Small wonder if an old man, away out here in Canada, had been taken in!

He moved slowly along the path, his feet scuffling through the dead leaves. A yellow caterpillar was coming in furry waves toward him and he wondered whether or not it would get out of his way. Evidently he was too colossal for its notice. He just managed to avoid it. The asparagus bed was the prettiest thing in the garden. When he had looked out of the bathroom window that morning he had seen it silver-gray with dew. There must have been a ground frost, too. Even now the feathery plumes bent under the weight of moisture. A fine monarch butterfly hovered above them for a space, then darted to the nasturtiums that covered the low picket fence surrounding the garden.

The gate at the farther end opened and his brother Ernest

came through it. He moved briskly toward Nicholas, greeting him with: —

"Good morning, Nick. Getting the sunshine? That 's right. Lovely morning, is n't it?"

Nicholas gave an affirmative grunt and smiled at his brother. Ernest said: —

"I 've just had the London *Times.* I brought it over so we could read the leader together."

"I hope there 's no more bad news," said Nicholas.

"No, no. If there were, we should have heard it over the radio."

"Of course." But he looked unconvinced.

"The loss of the *Royal Oak* was a terrible thing," he said.

Ernest turned to walk beside him. "We 'll have to face things as they come, Nick. What I dread is our nephews' joining up."

"I was thinking of Wakefield," said Nicholas, "as I was walking here. You know, I miss him greatly. I can't believe he 's grown up and gone away. He always liked to walk with me here and this morning I could just feel his little thin hand resting in mine."

"That 's because you 've been worrying a bit about him, Nick. But you must n't worry. It 's bad for you. That 's what I tell Harriet. She worries herself ill over the news. I tell her not to listen to it but she 's always at the radio. This morning I made her stay in bed."

"Quite right. . . . There 's a fine lot of carrots, is n't there?"

"Fine. Harriet has bought a little squeezer thing and we each drink a glass every day. She has great faith in vegetable juices. I may say that she has revolutionized my diet."

Nicholas grunted and stared at a hummingbird whose beak was probing a flame-colored nasturtium.

"Look," said Nicholas, nudging Ernest in the side. "Look!"

"Pretty thing. Mamma always admired them. Do you remember? She used to say — 'I like small, wicked things and there's something wicked in a hummingbird.'"

Nicholas grunted again. He held Ernest stock-still so they might not disturb the bird. But he was put to flight by the approach of Meg, who came hurrying into the garden. It was not often that she hurried, so they turned to her expectantly.

"Hullo, Uncles!" she cried. "How are you both?"

Both said they were well and waited for her to go on.

"I've had such an exciting cable from Finch!" she said. "Sarah is going to have a baby and he wants her to be out of England. He cabled to ask if we would take her into Vaughanlands and, of course, I cabled back that we'd be delighted. But, upon my word, I tremble to think of having Sarah Court, in that condition, on my hands. It seems quite unnecessary that she should have a child. Still, it's wartime and babies seem to come along then. And we also must be tolerant. Sarah has plenty of money so, if Finch's earnings cease, he need n't worry. Nor need we. I must say Maurice and I will be grateful for the extra money now. I think she ought to pay well — considering everything, don't you? She's bringing a maid with her."

Her uncles agreed that Sarah should pay well for the accommodation. It was lucky for her that her money was invested in Canada. They were glad that the new Whiteoak was to be born so near home but it was difficult to think of Sarah as a mother.

Meg slipped her arms through her uncles' and so linked, they strolled up and down the sunny path. For a woman of her age her skin was unusually clear and elastic but she had a slight double chin. She was not at all sensitive about it. She considered that the time had come when a double chin was becoming to her and, if she had been asked to part with it, it is doubtful whether she would. She discovered a little clump of French marigolds in a corner behind the Brussels sprouts and she stuck one in each of the old men's coat lapels. The three were deliberately gay, as though they would ignore the black cloud arching above the horizon. The warm contact of their bodies reassured them. As a family it was noticeable how often they touched each other. Old Adeline had always wanted her descendants close about her. She had liked to sit with one on either side, holding their hands. The uncles leant on the shoulders of their nephews. Meg stroked her brothers' heads and never, unless in a state of indignation, met them without a kiss. The younger boys had clung to Renny's sleeve or his fingers. They alone knew how many times he had smacked, cuffed, or hugged them. Young Adeline was lavish of her kisses. At times Renny might have been seen stroking the walnut newelpost of the stairs which was carved in a design of bunches of grapes and their leaves. His thin muscular hands seemed curved to fit the flank of a horse. There were times when Finch caressed the keys of the piano in soundless communion. So, in common with the world of nature which is ever reaching out toward the pleasure of touch, the Whiteoaks drew strength from that sense.

Ernest and Meg did their best to keep Nicholas's mind off the war but it was not easy.

"What I can't understand," he said, "is why we let them pull the wool over our eyes a year ago. Something should have been done."

Meg answered — "Maurice says that if the Germans had made war on us a year ago they 'd have got an easy victory. We were n't ready."

"We have Mr. Chamberlain to thank," said Ernest, "for saving us from the greatest disaster in our history."

" Hm, well, perhaps so. The last time we were over, a Colonel Rivers said to me . . ."

Meg interrupted, " Here comes Piers. I must tell him the news. I wonder what he 'll say."

" Hullo," said Piers, coming up. He was in riding breeches and a sweater and he was eating an apple he had picked from the old tree beside the paddock. His cheeks were ruddy from exercise. The sweater rose and fell quickly above his breast.

Meg kissed him. " What do you suppose has happened? Sarah is going to have a baby and Finch is sending her to us. A maid too. I suppose they 'll stay for the duration of the war. What do you think of Sarah as a mother? "

" I think it will be damned good for her."

" It will be a great responsibility for me."

" Send her to us then. We should like a little extra income."

" In that little house! "

" It 's warmer in winter than yours."

" I 'm afraid Sarah would not be comfortable there. As for the financial side of it, I would never ask her a penny more than it costs me."

" Oh, yeah! "

" I don't know what you mean by your horrid slang."

Childish voices were heard and Adeline and Archer came running from the house toward them.

" I 've a letter! " cried Adeline. " A letter from Mooey! " She was waving it in her hand.

Meg sighed deeply. " Poor little Mooey."

" Why do you say that? " asked Piers.

She opened her eyes wide. " Well, I should n't like my child to be in Ireland with a war on."

" He 's as safe there as here."

" I can't help feeling sorry for him."

"Well, it 's very irritating to me. Especially when I 've done what I consider best for him."

"Three thousand miles away — in that lonely house."

Adeline flew toward them along the path. The letter fluttered in her hand.

"Read it to us," said Meg. "How nicely it 's written!"

Adeline read glibly, because this was the third time: —

DEAR ADELINE,

How are you? How is everybody at home? Tell Nook to write to me. I am getting along fine. I have dinner with Cousin Dermot every night. I call him Granddad now. He has wonderful stories to tell and lots of books. I share lessons with a boy who lives near by. He has a tutor. We have great fun together. His name is Pat Crawshay and he told me to remember him to you. I often think of the old days at Jalna. Love from MOOEY.

Archer, far behind Adeline, reached the group as she was reading the letter. They might have been trees for all the notice he took of them. He stalked through their midst looking straight ahead of him. In one hand he carried the body of a dead crow he had found, in the other a trowel.

"What a nice letter!" said Meg. "Poor little man! Fancy his saying he often thinks of the old days at Jalna!"

"It would be funny if he did n't," said Piers.

"But it sounds so touching."

"I remember Pat Crawshay," said Adeline. "He was a nice boy. I want to see him again."

"Heaven only knows when you will, since this war is on."

"Look at Archer," chuckled Ernest. "I do wonder what that boy will be!"

"An undertaker," said Piers, "by the look of him."

The weather continued fair. Life at Jalna moved on, accompanied by the various reactions of the family to the war. Wakefield wrote from New York saying that, as soon as they were free, he and Molly would come to Canada and he would join the Air Force. This news brought mingled pleasure and foreboding. They were proud that their delicate stripling had grown to a strong young man ready to fight for his country, but the thought of his dying for it was terrible. Renny was already in touch with the headquarters of his old regiment in England and expected to join it before spring. Secretly he intended that this should take place before the running of the Grand National. He was in constant communication with those who were training Johnny the Bird. The possibility that Johnny would win the race, the thought that he himself would again live a soldier's life, help to win the war, gave color to every hour of his day. His stablemen had never known him so good-humored. His family had never known him easier to get on with. Piers took advantage of this by getting whatever he wanted for the farm and an increase in the share of profits for himself. This was well-deserved, for Piers was heart and soul in his work. He also had had a physical examination for military service and had come out in Class A.

Toward the end of October, Sarah arrived, accompanied by her French maid whom she had dismissed some time before her reunion with Finch. Mathilde was glad to return to her and to go far from scenes of war.

With her maid, her mountain of luggage, and her arresting looks, Sarah came to Vaughanlands as a being exotic and troubling. Nothing so brought out the best in Meg as preparing her house for those who needed her care and lavishing that care on them when they had arrived. But Sarah was undoubtedly a trial. She made no pretense of staying in the rooms allotted to her as bedroom and sitting room but strewed her belongings all over the house. Magazines, shawls, empty chocolate boxes, even hats and shoes, marked her path. She dropped ash and cigarette ends wherever she smoked. Rings from glasses of sherry or milk marred the table tops. When she used the telephone she invariably left off the receiver. She outdid Meg in wanting food at odd hours. She and Mathilde were always talking volubly in French together. As for the maid, she was no help at all, only a hindrance. Yet, when Meg complained as she certainly had a right to do, Piers only laughed and said: —

"Send them along to us. We 'll be delighted to have them."

But financially Sarah was a substantial help. She was careless in money matters, so long as the expenditure had to do with her own comfort or pleasure. She would send Mathilde into the town to shop for her and appear to care nothing about what was spent or whether or not the change was correct.

"But it 's terrible, Sarah!" cried Meg. "You must let me do your shopping for you. I should never trust that Frenchwoman."

Sarah gave her an enigmatic smile. "How kind you are!"

Meg did the shopping to the great annoyance of Mathilde, who had found these excursions a compensation for the Canadian climate.

Meg knitted countless tiny garments for the coming child. She kept them in a drawer in her room, scented with lavender. When she showed them to Renny, he frowned.

"What has she done?" he asked.

"She tried to knit a little jacket but got the stitches in such a mess I took it from her."

"She ought to make these things herself. She imposes on you."

Meg beamed. "I do it for Finch rather than for her. Remember, it 's his child."

"Let 's hope it resembles him."

The antagonism between Renny and Sarah had indeed not lessened. He disliked her secretive air, her small-mouthed, curved-nosed, pointed-chinned face. He hated her exotic perfumes, the heavy scent of her Russian cigarettes. She always seemed to be smiling slyly at him, gloating over having bested him, recaptured Finch. In truth she never met him without this inward triumph. She disliked him. He had no physical attraction for her. She feared him. His air of hardihood, his remoteness, the feeling that, at the first opportunity, he would again come between her and Finch, kept her resentment smouldering. When he came to Vaughanlands, as he often did, he wished she would keep out of his way. But there she always was, talking . . . talking of Finch, what they had done in London, what he would make of his talent. She wore brilliantly colored tea-gowns, a contrast to the austere colors she had chosen for London, which well concealed her bulk. She showed no apprehension of the ordeal ahead of her.

In November something happened which thrust Sarah into the background. Aunt Harriet died after only a short illness. Ernest was convinced that the war had preyed on her mind, undermining her health. Certainly in her last days she had seemed capable of thinking of little else. She strove with all her fragile power to make over the world, as she had striven to make over herself into a Whiteoak. Doubtless this last had been a considerable strain for, from the day of her coming to Jalna, she had scarcely performed an act which was not self-conscious. Surrounded as she was by the Whiteoaks, their strong personalities had pressed in on the more rarefied atmosphere of the life that was natural to her.

Her loss came as a great shock to Ernest. He had thought of her as merely ailing, and for a time he was dazed. After the funeral, he wandered vaguely through the house which she had made into such a happy home, not knowing what to do with himself. He looked bereft and ill.

Then Nicholas took things in hand. Ernest must close

the house, he said, and return at once to Jalna. He could not live alone and his own place was waiting for him. Nicholas had secretly resented Ernest's marriage. It had broken in on the companionship of a lifetime. Such companionship was no longer possible with an active, gently domineering wife, always at Ernest's side. It would be nice to have the old fellow back at Jalna, to bicker with, to confide in, to share his last days with. When he saw Ernest once more established in the room next his, Nicholas felt a profound satisfaction. The old oak which had been uprooted was miraculously restored to the side of its brother, their branches again intermingling.

And, after the first sharpness of sorrow, a new peace descended on Ernest. There was a dignity in his relations with Nicholas that had been lacking in the old days. Then Nicholas had sometimes made his brother feel his inexperience in one aspect of life. Nicholas had been married and divorced. Ernest was only a bachelor. Now Ernest could talk of matrimony. He had the dignity of a widower. His marriage had been happy.

There was another and secret side to his peace. With Harriet's active and analytical New England mind no longer prodding him on, he could sink into comfortable old age. He had no longer to be on his guard lest he should disappoint her. He could read what was light and amusing. He could talk or be silent as he chose. If he slept all the afternoon, that was his own business and no one worried about him. The pleasant ways of bachelorhood opened again to receive him.

To Alayne, her aunt's death brought back the loss of her loved father and mother. As long as Aunt Harriet had lived, there was someone to whom she could talk intimately of them, someone who would mourn for them with her. Now there was no one. She had not a near relative in the world. At the same time, Alayne's affection for Harriet had altered since Harriet's coming to Jalna. Alayne had watched her making herself into a new person, and the sight had given her both amusement and irritation. Harriet's new personality had not been convincing to Alayne. She had been so admirable as she was. Why had she wished to change? Another source of irritation was that, if any disagreement rose between herself and Renny, Aunt Harriet was certain to take his side. She could see no fault in him.

Of all the family, it was Renny who grieved most sincerely for her. He had loved the little woman from the time of his stay in her house on the Hudson. In his view she had never changed in the least. It was simply that her life at Jalna had brought out certain latent qualities in her which only added to her excellence. And perhaps in this he was right. She had been motherly toward him as no other woman had, and he could not even remember his own mother.

XXII

WREATHS OF HOLLY

THE play had a three months' run. Wakefield and Molly had made a distinctive place for themselves in the hearts of New York theatregoers. They admired Molly's look of fragility and breeding combined with vitality. When she wore riding clothes she looked capable of hard work with a horse. They liked her freshness and lack of self-consciousness. Now that she was away from Ninian Fox, her acting showed more freedom and initiative than before. No young actor in years had so captivated New York as Wakefield. The management wanted them to go on tour with the play. They had offers from Hollywood. But what they wanted and what they had done was to come to Canada. Wakefield was to enter the Air Force and Molly to find some sort of war work. They wanted to be married in the New Year.

They arrived at Jalna the night before Christmas Eve. There had been no snow in New York but here the ground was white and the stars trembled blue and low above the treetops. The spruces crowded the driveway in their black bulk but the old silver birch cast a fine tracery of its branches on the snowy lawn. The steps were shoveled clean, the snow mounded high at the sides in glistening peaks and pale blue shadows. All the windows were alight and, in those on the first floor, holly wreaths hung.

None of the family had come to meet them. There had been much to do in preparation for Christmas and that morning Sarah had given birth to a son. If anything were needed to give Wakefield's homecoming a glittering sense of the Season it was the news that a new Whiteoak had chosen Christmas for the time of his arrival.

Wakefield felt almost unbearably excited as they got out of the car and he helped the man carry their bags to the door. When he had left them, Wakefield took Molly by the shoulders and placed her in front of the door facing him.

"I want to see you in your new setting!" he exclaimed. "I want to see how you become Jalna. For it is our home whether we live here or not."

A smile illumined his face. His eyes were shining. He kissed her on each cold cheek, then on her warm lips. He opened the door.

"You become it very well," he said.

He stood in the hall and looked about him, drinking in the familiar scene, the heavy scrolled wallpaper which had been there since the house was built, the slender grace of the banister, the hatstand with the carved head of a fox grinning down at them. Renny's hat, weatherbeaten to a soft mole color, hung there with children's caps and a dog's lead.

The dogs rose in a ferocious chorus from where they lay about the glowing stove. They almost knocked Wakefield over before they discovered who he was. Then they almost knocked him over in their joy. Meg came out of the drawing-room and closed the door behind her.

"I had to be the first to greet you," she said. She clasped Wakefield to her bosom in a moment's bliss before she turned to welcome Molly.

"We are so glad to have you, my dear," she said.

Well might Wake look on her as a mother, Molly thought. It was easy to see how she adored him.

Meg took them straight into the drawing-room where the uncles and Alayne were waiting. Alayne had faintly resented Meg's welcoming of their guest but it was Meg's way to be possessive. Alayne gave Molly her hand, smiling and critical. She thought — "An attractive girl but I don't believe I'm going to like her."

"What a charming child!" said Nicholas, aloud. "Do you mind if I kiss you, my dear?"

She held up her face like a child. Nicholas kissed her, so did Ernest.

"You see," said Ernest, "we 've been told of your engagement."

The boy and girl looked so young standing there that the elders felt a compassion for them, wondering what sort of life they would have together, what sort of world awaited them.

Nicholas drew Wakefield aside. "What are they saying of the war in New York?" he asked.

"They 're calling it a phony war," laughed Wakefield.

Nicholas blew through his gray moustache. "Phony? What 's that?"

"Well . . . it 's not very exciting to watch."

Nicholas turned to his brother. "Do you hear that, Ernie? They 've got a word for this war over there. They call it *phony*."

"Well, well," said Ernest.

Adeline and Roma had been allowed to stay up. They now came into the room. Roma, as always, stood as though sheltering behind Adeline.

Wakefield kissed them and exclaimed at their growth as he had heard returning elders exclaim at his when he was a child.

"Have you done any hunting since I saw you?" he asked Adeline.

"Lots, but not real foxes. And I sent a postcard of Niagara Falls to Pat Crawshay and he sent me one of Blarney Castle."

Meg put in — "Now I must take Wake and Miss Griffith to their rooms." It was as though she were mistress of the house.

"Call me Molly."

"May I? That will be nice."

"To-morrow night we hang up our stockings," said Adeline. "The Christmas Tree is in the sitting room. You can't go in there."

"I can smell it!" cried Wake. "I've been wondering all along what the lovely scent was." He went eagerly to the door of the sitting room and put his nose to the keyhole. The pungent spicy sweetness of the spruce tree came through to him. The mystery, the entrancing tremors of childish Christmas Eves, stirred him. He put out a hand to Molly.

"Come," he said, "come and smell."

She bent and sniffed.

"How lovely! What sort of tree is it?"

"Spruce."

"We don't have them so sweet in Wales."

He laughed. "They grow only at Jalna."

The children had followed them into the hall and crowded to the keyhole to sniff the tree.

"Children!" called Alayne. "You must go to bed!"

They giggled together, hiding behind Wakefield.

"I've never had a Christmas Tree," said Molly.

"How appalling!" said Wakefield in consternation. Then added — "But I'm glad you'll have your first one with us. And, unless I'm very much mistaken, you'll get a very nice present on it."

"Never had a Christmas Tree!" cried the children in unison. "But why? Did n't you like them?"

Wake answered — "She lived on a mountaintop where there were no trees."

Meg came and led all four upstairs. Wake ran his hand along the banister. "I used to get smacked for sliding down this," he said.

Archer called out from his mother's room where he slept. "Come and see me!"

They found him sitting up in his cot, his rather stiff tow hair standing upright, his eyes intense beneath his tall white brow.

"The future master of Jalna!" said Wake gayly.

Archer held out his hand. Molly took it and Wake kissed the top of his head. He deigned to smile.

"Sit down and we 'll talk," he said.

"Now Archie," said Meg, "you know we can't do that. It 's time you were fast asleep."

He dived under the bedclothes, making them into a tent. From beneath it he made terrifying noises.

"He 's a hyena," said Roma. "He 's been one all day."

Alayne came running up the stairs. She was deeply humiliated. She tried to draw down the covers but, knowing the touch of her hand, he made himself into several hyenas. The cot heaved and strained under his rollings and shriekings. Meg came to Alayne's assistance and together they managed to uncover him. He looked imperturbably up at them. His hair and his pyjamas were wet with sweat. Alayne took him into her arms. He languished against her.

"I 'm a ba-a-by," he said, and took the lobe of her ear into his mouth.

The little girls ran, shrieking with laughter, up the stairs to the third floor where Alma waited to put them to bed. A choir was singing Christmas carols over the radio.

In his own room Wake felt himself enfolded under the roof as a child on the breast. The smells, the sounds, the feel of the carpet beneath his feet, drew him back into the old life. It would always be the same. But now Molly would become a part of it. No matter where they went they would belong here. She was his and he was hers and they both belonged to Jalna.

XXIII

CHRISTMAS JOY

It was like a Christmas card, thought Molly, looking out of her window. One of those cards that glittered with a frosty powder and had a bow of red ribbon at the top. You might stand them on your mantelshelf or send them to your friends but you never believed in them. They were symbolic of a child's idea of Christmas.

Yet here she was, the centre of just such a Christmas-card scene. The land hushed beneath a blanket of downy snow, the sky of a hard polished blue, the boughs of the spruces and hemlocks bending beneath the weight of what looked so ethereal. There was a rabbit flying across the snow into the blue shadows of the trees, its white scut flashing! There came the dog yelping on its trail, in an anguish of desire! There was a man carrying a bucket toward the stables, a red scarf wound round his neck! There were icicles a foot long hanging from the eave! There came the children's voices from above, chattering and laughing over their stockings! Yes — "Merry Christmas" should be written beneath it in flowing gilt letters.

Molly found that she was shivering like a leaf. She leaped back into bed and drew the covers up to her chin. She lay looking about the room. It had once been Meg's. There were a flowered carpet, flowered wallpaper, and a pink chenille curtain at the door. There was a washing-stand with a pretty little ewer and basin. On the walls hung watercolors done by Ernest Whiteoak and a photograph of Renny, at the age of eighteen, in the uniform of a cadet of the Royal Military College.

She lay gazing at the photograph. She recognized at once who it was. How little he had changed except for the few sharp lines that were now cut into his experienced face. His hair was as thick, his eyelids as clearly cut, he was just as thin, though his thinness now had an enduring, weathered look. Certainly there was a resemblance between this picture and Wake, but Wake had a gentler and more intellectual look. She did not know whether or not she liked Renny. At one moment she felt happy and at ease with him. At the next, something came between them like a shadow, a threat, as though he held something in his mind against her.

She looked at her watch. It was half-past eight. Breakfast was at nine, so she had better dress. She would put on the hunter's-green dress that was piped with red. It looked Christmasy, she thought. She wondered what was the present Wake had for her.

Twelve people sat down to breakfast. Besides Wake and herself, there were the two uncles, Renny and his wife, Paris Court, the three children of the house, and Piers's boys, who had arrived soon after sunrise, carrying the contents of their stockings. Porridge, sausage and bacon, toast and marmalade, were the breakfast, and from the uncles down the family ate with gusto, with the exception of Alayne and Archer. She was occupied in keeping him in order and he was preoccupied with some little lead animals he had brought to the table. He made them jump back and forth over his porridge. Such behavior would never have been tolerated from Wake when he was Archer's age. He looked disapprovingly at his nephew.

" Archer," said Alayne, " you must eat your breakfast or leave the table."

" I want to leave," he answered, coolly.

Rags bent over him. " Give them to me and I 'll tike them to the kitchen and feed them."

"I want to come too." He began to climb from his chair.

"Darling," whispered Alayne, "eat your breakfast and we'll have a lovely time afterward."

"No. See this elephant jump!"

Nicholas stretched out a long arm and took possession of the elephant. Archer slid on to his backbone and down under the table.

"Leave him there," said Renny.

"I prefer to take him upstairs."

"Nonsense. I'll take him, if he must go. Archie, come here!"

Archer crept the length of the table and scrambled up between his father's knees. His tow head appeared above the edge of the table. He clasped his father round the neck. Renny offered him a piece of sausage on his fork. He ate it with relish.

"He'll eat for me," said Renny.

"It is better," said Ernest, "to persuade small children, rather than force them."

"Do you remember," said Nicholas, "how Mamma used to feed Wakefield biscuits soaked in sherry?"

"Don't believe it, Molly," said Wake.

"I am finished," said Alayne. "I will take Archer upstairs."

As she came toward him he burrowed into his father's breast. He had so much that was beautiful and good in him, she thought, it was humiliating to see him behave like this. Adeline was chuckling.

Archer scrambled from his father's knee and wobbled down the room. "I'm a jellyfish," he said.

Everybody laughed but Alayne. She followed him, humiliated.

"A jellyfish," he repeated, shaking from head to foot. "A wimbly wambly jellyfish."

Rags carried him from the room. He lay limp across

Rags's arms, staring impassively at the ceiling. Alayne followed with folded arms and bent head.

"Chief mourner," whispered Wake to Molly.

All that happened excited and amused her. She wondered if ever she could be unhappy again.

In all her life she had been to church just three times. She had attended the wedding of a maid in a Nonconformist village church in Wales. She had been to an Easter-morning service in Westminster Abbey. She had gone to Mass on Sunday in New York with Wakefield. When he spoke of his religious experiences to her she was embarrassed. They were beyond the bounds of her knowledge of him. Religion for her was an uncharted land. She knew little more of religion than a young heathen but she knew how to love, to forgive, and to put others before self. She knew she had to become a Catholic, outwardly at least, in order to marry Wake, but the little books he had given her to study were in the bottom of her trunk. She simply could not understand them, nor did she know how to go about the searching of her soul. She only knew that she loved Wake with every bit of her and she saw no reason why a God who was a complete stranger to her should enter into their scene. Yet, if Wake wanted her to be baptized in his faith, she was willing.

"I really should n't go to a Protestant church," he said to her that morning, "but I know old Renny would love to have me and I very much want you to see the church my grandfather built and — to see my family in action in it!"

"Had n't you rather go for a walk?"

"No. I want you to come to church."

She lightly stroked his cheek.

"Very well, but you must show me what to do."

"I 'm glad, Molly, that you 've never had any religious instruction. It will all come as a revelation."

"You 're revelation enough for me! Do you know, you 're the first actor I 've met with an atom of religion in him."

"I 'm much besides an actor," he answered, a little stiffly.

Renny was delighted when he found that Wakefield was coming to church. "I 'll tell you what," he said to Molly, "we 'll get him away from the papists between us. We can do it, if we work together."

"On the contrary," said Wake, "I 'll convert you two. I 've got Molly and, sooner or later, I 'll get you."

He had no hope of such an achievement but he liked to tease his elder.

The church was full of the scent of spruce and hemlock. The pillars were twined with them, the pews embowered. Flame-colored chrysanthemums burned on the altar. Smilax and holly twined about the pulpit and lectern. Surplices were white as snow and smelled of the frosty air. Some few must have worked very hard. Never did Noah Binns ring the bell more vigorously, never did his boots squeak louder. In spite of much scraping of soles outside the door, clots of snow were tracked up the aisle but soon melted in the warm air. There was a good deal of coughing, sneezing, and blowing, as people settled into the pews.

Wakefield crossed himself.

Molly, beside him, made a faint gesture with her hand just above her waistline, then looked apprehensively about her not knowing what to do next. The effect of Wakefield's act on those about him was electric. Noah Binns had been squeaking up the aisle to do something to a window and was at Wakefield's side at the moment of devotion. Noah stopped dumbfounded, his jaw dropped, staring at Wakefield's face. Across the aisle the three Vaughans bent their startled gaze on him. Piers nudged Pheasant and said something. There was a quirk beneath Nicholas's moustache. Ernest lost his place in his hymnbook. Mr. Fennel thrust his fingers in his beard and looked sternly at Wakefield. But it was Renny who put things into movement again. He raised his voice in the Christmas hymn with more than wonted vigor. The family joined in. Noah squeaked on his way. Wakefield looked at his hymnbook as though unconscious of the stir he had created. Molly looked at him.

She sat absorbing the strange new atmosphere. Mr. Fennel's voice went on and on. It was a good voice and she liked the way he read. She wondered what sort of actor he would have made. She began to choose parts for him and for all the family. What would they say, she thought, if they knew what was going on in her mind? What was going on in their minds? Were they as completely absorbed by this strange ritual as they appeared to be? Wake had said — "There is so much in me besides the actor." She must try to understand that other part of him. There must be nothing alien between them. Their understanding must be many-sided and complete. She remembered how he had opened his heart to her family. Now she must do the same by his. As she sat there unobserved, she was aware of a singleness of heart, a staunchness, that seemed a part of the very fabric of this little building. She felt it encircling the family, and her in the midst of them. The Rector had come there as a very young man. Now his beard was gray. How many times had he gone through the intricacies of the service? Why, surely he must be able to do it in his sleep! Yet there were freshness and good faith in his movements as he stepped up into the pulpit. He folded his hands and said a short prayer.

Mr. Fennel could scarcely keep his eyes from Molly's face as he repeated the story of the Birth. Her face was so rapt, she might be hearing it for the first time. He could only conclude that never before had she heard it so well told.

His heart glowed. His fingers sought his beard and his beaming hazel eyes dwelt on the Whiteoak pew.

Outside she caught Wakefield's arm.

"What an old pet the Rector is! He 'd have made a fine actor, would n't he?"

"He wanted to go on the stage when he was a young chap but something — I think it was his father — stopped him. He 's the happiest man I know. I 've told you that he taught me when I was a small fellow. He 'll be coming to supper to-night."

The Miss Laceys, very old and bent, came to make much of Wake. They cherished a playbill from the London Theatre, they said, with his and Molly's names on it. They congratulated the young pair. Other old friends crowded about. Merry Christmas was on every lip. The children ran in and out among the snowy gravestones. Wakefield led Molly to the family plot. Here the graves were obliterated. It was a smooth white coverlet under which the dead Whiteoaks rested. The stream that threw an arm about the graveyard was frozen. Here was complete immobility.

Molly stared at the names on the granite plinth.

"What a lot of you are buried here!"

"Yes. It looks forbidding now. But you should see it in summer, or when the maples are red in the fall. Now the crosses marking each grave are covered. But look."

He stepped over the low iron fence and with his hands brushed the snow away from one of them. It bore the name of Eden. "I 've told you about him."

"Yes. Poor Eden!"

Roma peered round the corner of the church at them. She was filled with curiosity because she knew they were engaged. She wore a little red hat, her cheeks and nose were pink from cold. Molly did not connect her with the cross marked "Eden." Roma was followed by Nook and Adeline, pelting each other with snow. Nook was a happy boy in these days for, as he was not old enough to take the journey to school without Mooey's protection, he now again had lessons with the children at Jalna.

The children were followed by Piers and Pheasant. He said: —

"We're going to Vaughanlands to see the new baby. Pheasant thought you two might like to come."

"I'd love to," Wakefield agreed at once.

"Oh, yes," said Molly, "it's a perfect thing to do on Christmas Day."

They sent the two boys on to Jalna and made their way over the snowy road to Vaughanlands.

Meg was already there to welcome them. The living room was homelike in bright chintz and a dancing fire. Patience, now a boarding-school girl home for the holidays, was possessive toward the baby.

"I'll bring him down," she said. "No one can make him so comfortable as me."

They waited expectantly. She returned with the infant, carrying him deftly. An odor of warm flannel came with him, and a kind of sanctity, because he was newborn and it was Christmas to-day.

"Oh, the darling!" cried Pheasant, clasping her hands.

"My goodness," said Wake, "he looks a hundred!"

Piers blew out his cheeks. He said: —

"I've never seen an uglier one. He's got the worst points of both parents."

"He's sweet," said Molly. "What are they going to call him?"

"Dennis — after Sarah's father."

"May I hold him?" asked Pheasant. She took him tenderly into her arms.

"Be careful," warned Patience. "He must be held just so."

"How is Sarah?" Piers asked Meg.

"I 've never seen such an ecstatic mother. You 'd think no one had ever had a baby before. She 'd love to see you for a moment, Pheasant."

Sarah looked statue-white and still, as her sisters-in-law went into the room. But when she opened her eyes they were bright with bliss. She gave her small, secret smile.

"Is n't he beautiful?" she asked.

"Perfectly sweet," answered Pheasant.

"And to think he came at Christmas time! We 're calling him Holly for a pet name. Oh, if only Finch could see him! He must come! I 've made Maurice cable him. He must see the baby in his first exquisiteness. Did you ever see such skin — such eyes? I always knew he 'd be beautiful but I never dreamed of anything like this. I shall live for him. How thankful I am I got him safely out of England! Tell Patience to bring him, Meg. I can't bear him out of my sight."

Patience brought him and Sarah curved her body about him like, as Pheasant said on the way to Jalna, a cat about its kitten.

"I always knew she 'd be like that," said Piers. "Three cheers for Finch! He 's freed himself. He 'll never be of any importance to Sarah again, mark my words."

Wakefield exclaimed: —

"If the baby has accomplished that he 's my favorite nephew!"

"'My name is joy!'" quoted Molly. "'I am but two days old!'"

"I wish we all were," said Piers. "The four of us. On our way to the Christmas Tree with a comforter in each of our mouths. Instead of which I 'm Santa Claus."

"Are you really?" said Molly.

"Wait till you see him. He 's grand."

Piers looked modestly pleased. "I do my best. Having

the ruddy countenance and the portly form necessary, I 'm not so bad."

Molly found herself enfolded in an atmosphere of Christmas bustle such as she had never before known. The Dinner rose, like a succulent mountain to be demolished, before the climax of the Tree was reached. The sitting room, a sweet-smelling fortress, was still unstormed. Through the other rooms and up and down the stairs children and dogs circled, raced, shouted and barked. The baritone and tenor voices of seven men made a rich masculine background for the voices of women and children. Rags flew here and there with trays of sherry and biscuits. The children were eating the sweets from their stockings in spite of their mothers' warnings.

Parry Court had known but meagre celebrations in his home, though he had invariably traveled from wherever he was to be with his parents at that season. Here he was gayest of them all. Piers and he kept the children in a gale of excitement. He was more congenial to Piers than any brother he had. Parry, as a good rider and a lover of good farm stock, had been of real help in the past months at Jalna. By skillfully playing Renny against Piers he had made both believe he had worked much harder than actually was the case. Everybody liked him. To the old men he seemed atrociously modern, yet sympathetic and with the high spirits of the young men of their day. In the past two months Ernest had found him a real comfort. Of all those under the roof, Pheasant was the least happy, for she was always thinking of Mooey.

Archer's usually pale face showed a bright pink cheek. He was drunk with half-mad expectancy and present hilarity. He had shouted till he was hoarse. He did not even hear his mother's warnings. He stalked, a tiny and ruthless bandit, through the forest of the grownups. He did not care what he did. He would as lief hurl his drumstick at the head of Santa Claus as not. He could not eat his dinner and its most savory smell was nothing compared to the smell filtering through the keyhole of the sitting room.

Old Merlin had not felt so well in months as he did to-day. Again and again he raised his rich voice and declared that this was so. He had had an injury to a toenail and one forepaw was bandaged. This he held up to each new arrival for sympathy, then told how well he felt. He was the only one of the dogs which Alayne allowed in the dining room. Proudly, with waving tail, he walked past the other dogs, scenting their envy, and took his place by Renny's chair.

It was a tribute to the carving powers of the master of Jalna that each one of the seventeen people about the table had been served with a suitable portion of the glistening brown turkey and that he himself had swallowed two bites of his own portion before the seventh served (who was Piers) applied for a fresh helping. Rags came tottering in pretended exhaustion under the weight of a second turkey and Renny, desperately filling his mouth and with a flourish of the carving knife, attacked it.

After the dark succulence of the pudding — which was the one part of the dinner Archer craved, refusing to eat the jelly and cream provided by Alayne — came the crackers. Finch had sent these from London and, to show their appreciation, everyone said he had never heard crackers crack so loudly before or seen such splendid headdresses come out of them.

Ernest put on a pink frilled bonnet for a moment, then, out of deference to Harriet's memory, took it off. There was delight when a jockey's cap came out of Renny's cracker. It became him just a little too well, Alayne thought, and wished he were not so excessively pleased with it. Wonder of wonders, Archer drew a judge's wig and sat glowering at the company from under it as though for two pins he would pronounce a drastic sentence on each one.

Piers disappeared.

What a jostling there was in the hall! Rags had built too great a fire in the stove, so that it was unbearably hot. Then someone had flung open the front door and the icy air, bright with fine snow particles, came flying in.

Ernest was roasting on one side and freezing on the other. He demanded: —

" Who opened that door? "

Paris answered, " I 'm afraid I did, sir. Shall I close it? "

" Yes, do, or I shall be in bed to-morrow."

Someone stepped on the sheep dog's toe and he yelped in agony.

" Who did that? " shouted Renny.

" It was Uncle Nick."

Nicholas glowered. " It was not. I 'm miles from the dog."

Young Philip at the keyhole cried — " The candles on the Tree are lighted! "

Meg swept him from the keyhole and blocked it with her plump person.

" What are we waiting for? " asked Archer.

" Santa Claus, you little silly," answered Roma.

" I thought he came last night."

" He did, but he 's coming again."

" Why? "

Renny swung him to his shoulder. " Wait and see."

Wake said to Molly — " I wonder if you 'll like your present."

She asked — " Is it large, small, square, round, soft, or hard? "

" It 's small, round, and hard."

" Is it something lasting? "

" It will last forever."

Maurice exclaimed, " What the dickens is the matter in there? Thump on the door, Meggie."

Meg began a steady thumping.

" We want Santa Claus! " everybody sang out in unison.

" Where is Daddy? " asked Nook.

Archer, from Renny's shoulder, whined: —

" I 'm hungry. I want my tea."

" My goodness," cried Patience. " You 've just had a Christmas dinner."

" I don't remember."

Alayne came to Renny's side.

" I think I 'd better take him back to the dining room and give him something to eat," she said. " He can come to the Tree later."

" He won't go."

" I think he will. Will you come with Mother, Archer? "

" I don't know. Try me."

She attempted to lift him down but the moment she touched him he screamed. She desisted.

" Now I know," he said, with puckered brow. " I don't want to go."

" The door is open! " cried Adeline. She was first to enter the room.

There was the Tree, its spicy boughs bending beneath the weight of many bright packets. Frost powder gleamed in the light of a hundred little wax candles. Gay-colored fish, birds and cornucopias, trembled on the tips of the branches, and on the topmost twig hovered a pink cherub that had delighted Renny and Meg when they were small. From behind the Tree a burly blue-eyed Santa Claus appeared and demanded of the children whether or not they had been good.

Roma, Nook, and Philip had no doubts of Santa Claus. Patience and Adeline knew he was Uncle Piers but the glamour of his costume, the authentic gleam in his eyes, his jovial laugh, swept them along to willing acceptance of him. The Tree was half stripped of presents when Archer exclaimed, in a piercing whisper: —

"Why, Santa Claus has got on Uncle Piers's new boots."

He was swept up by Rags and carried to the basement, where, on his old tricycle, he pedaled round and round the kitchen, into the larder and down the brick-paved passage to the coal cellar, relieved to be rid of the burden of so much merrymaking.

Molly could scarcely believe in her present from Wakefield, it was so beautiful. Old Adeline had, in her will, left an article of jewelry to each of her grandsons for his wife or his prospective wife. None of the family would ever forget the scene between Meg and Piers when this clause was read, for Pheasant was already the possessor of a ruby ring given to Adeline by an Indian Rajah.

Renny had kept one of the most valuable of the rings for Wakefield. It was a cluster of five diamonds exquisitely placed in the old-fashioned low setting. Wakefield had had the stones polished and the family had scarcely realized their beauty till they saw the ring gleaming on Molly's thin young hand.

"The stones would be still more brilliant," said Wakefield, "if they were cut in the modern way."

"They 're perfect," she answered, laying her left hand on her right as though it did not belong to her but now had a separate and superior life of its own.

The excitement of the Tree was over and in the dimness of the hall, among the dogs, they kissed for the third time that day.

"Let 's go out for some air," he said. "The children are making snowballs. Will you come?"

"How lovely! I 've never made a snowball in my life." She ran upstairs to get her things.

"Wrap yourself up!" he called after her. "It 's turning very cold."

In the cupboard under the stairs he found his old windbreaker and cap with ear muffs, his goloshes. He felt as though he had never been away from home as he rummaged through the miscellaneous collection there.

Outside this cupboard was the door that led into his grandmother's room. He had not been inside the room since his return. Now he opened the door and stepped in. It was lighted by a red shaft of light from the lowering sun. He looked about him almost timidly. He could remember everything in this room since his first consciousness. Nothing was changed except that the tall old figure stretched on the richly colored leather bed, or seated in the wing chair, was missing and the gay-plumaged parrot on the perch was the stuffed figure of Boney who had died two years before. It was all so real yet so unreal. Wakefield said, in a low voice: —

"My Grandmother, I 've just given your ring to Molly and she loves it."

He heard Molly coming down the stairs and went to meet her.

"Oh, how quaint you look!" she exclaimed. "Wherever did you get the cap?"

"I 've had it for ages. What do you suppose I 've been doing?"

"What?"

"I 've been telling Gran that I 've given you her ring. Her room 's back there."

Molly looked a little startled. "Wake, you do say odd things!"

He laid his head on her shoulder. "Molly," he said, "you must always love me. I suddenly feel afraid to look ahead. There 's so much can happen."

"I 'll always love you, Wake," she promised.

Renny, Piers, Pheasant, Paris, and all the children were romping in the snow. The dogs went tumbling through the door to take their part, none more eager than Merlin. When Wakefield appeared, Pheasant threw a snowball at him.

"Here comes the matinee idol!" she cried.

"He 's getting quite above himself," said Piers. "Let 's roll him over, Renny!"

The two elder brothers made for Wake. He was helpless. Molly was positively alarmed for him but Pheasant and the children laughed. When at last he was freed he was white from head to foot. His cheeks were scarlet.

"Thank God for ear muffs!" he said.

Piers sprang up and caught a snow-weighted branch of hemlock in his hands and hung there. The snow came down in a miniature storm, enveloping Molly. The children surrounded her, bearing her down. Adeline leaped on to Parry's back and he galloped with her, her hair bright as a flame.

Molly felt that never before had she met with really high spirits. There was something reckless in their gayety. It was as though they realized more than others the shortness of life and would live it to its full.

They found the path to the stream and scrambled down its bank. They swept the stream with pine boughs and made a slide. Everyone slid but none compared to the long, swift, eagle slide of Renny. Molly's eyes were always following him.

"You 're always watching Renny," said Wake, his eyes narrowing. "Is he so fascinating then?"

"No. I don't know. I think it 's just that he 's so different from anyone I 've known."

Once more the stab of jealousy pierced Wake's heart.

"Renny 's old enough," he said coldly, "to be your father."

She stared. "Well, what of that?"

"Nothing!" he answered. "Nothing — of course — nothing!"

But he was happy again when, in the drawing-room, Rags, with a pontifical air, carried a tray of raisins, blazing in brandy, up and down the room. The children danced about him, striving to snatch a handful of the fruit but terrified of the blaze. The grownups joined in. It was Alayne who coolly thrust her hand into the flame and divided the spoils among the children.

Nicholas sat puffing at his pipe, his eyes shining. A good Christmas, he thought, and wondered what would have happened by next Christmas.

XXIV

TAKING DOWN THE WREATHS

As always the Christmas greens were taken down on Twelfth Night. As long as they remained there seemed a kind of spiritual barrier between Jalna and the war. Though they dried and their needles were scattered on the floor and holly berries lay withered on the sills, even Alayne said — "Let us leave them till the last moment."

But after Twelfth Night it would be unlucky to preserve them, so down came the wreaths and the Christmas Tree, in all its majesty, was borne from the house. All were mounded in the little field between the kitchen garden and orchard. There was a great crackling blaze as the wreaths subsided to ash and a smell like incense was given off.

It had been a time of pure happiness to Molly. There had been dinners and dances in the town but it was at Jalna that her happiness was keenest. This was a new life to her. There was skiing, there was skating, there was that feeling of permanence which brought an inward satisfaction to the heart.

It was the morning after Twelfth Night when Renny said to Molly, finding her alone with a book: —

"You have never properly seen my stables. Should n't you like to come with me now, if you 've nothing better to do?"

"Yes, I 'd love to." She rose eagerly. "I 'll fetch a coat and hat."

"Where 's Wake?"

"With his Uncle Ernest. I think they enjoy a talk together."

There had been one of those fairy snowfalls that leave a

fragile and ethereal world behind them. Every twig bore its pretty burden, light as air. A puff of wind would send a fine spray from the trees, turning them into fountains. The air was colder than Molly had ever experienced but she did not mind. She could have flown.

As she strode by Renny's side she wished the way to the stables was longer. It was a pity to go indoors out of this. She said so.

He stood stock-still and looked at her. "You need n't come if you don't want to," he said, "but I must."

"Oh, I do want to! I often wish I were two people here, there 's so much to do and see!"

"It 's probably just as well that there are not two of you," he returned. "It might cause trouble. But you have enjoyed yourself at Jalna, have n't you?"

"I 've never been so happy in my life."

He opened the stable door, the latch of which was meticulously decorated with snow. Inside it was warm. Shafts of sunlight touched clean straw, well-groomed flanks, and vigorous manes. A rich content permeated the stables, as though the occupants were assured that their world was secure, their god good. The aged mare Cora was as happy as the youngest colt. The stable cat, who had just caught a mouse, was purring on a beam above the stallion's stall. A stableman came along the passage carrying a bucket of water in either hand. Through the open door of the harness room another could be seen polishing leather. Renny led Molly from stall to stall, giving her a brief account of each horse. The horses reached out to nuzzle him or to nibble his sleeve. They were jealous of his attention.

But he scarcely knew what he was saying. From the moment he had entered the stable with the girl at his side he had been bewildered by his own sensations. His mind was groping into the past. He was in the past. It was as though he were in a dream from which he could not wake. She spoke but the voice was not hers. It belonged to another girl. A girl who had once stood beside him in that same loose box, looking at another horse.

What was Molly saying?

Something about the Grand National.

"Yes," he answered. "Yes. Of course."

It was not the answer she had expected. She looked surprised.

He said abruptly — "You tell me your mother is dead."

She drew back a little from his abruptness.

"Yes."

"Is it long? — Since she died, I mean."

"Eight years."

"Your stepfather's name is Griffith." He looked at her almost accusingly.

"Yes. We — Christopher and I — took his name when Mummie married him, but our name is really Dayborn."

His face was inscrutable. He kept running his fingers through the mare's mane. After a moment he asked: —

"Was your mother ever in Canada?"

"She never mentioned Canada to me."

"I ask," he said, "because I once knew a Mrs. Dayborn." He stopped himself. He must be careful. He twisted his fingers in the mare's mane.

"Was your mother fond of horses?" he asked gently.

Molly's face lighted. "She loved them! She knew all about them. She 'd schooled show horses at one time in her life." For her the barriers were down. Trembling, she asked, "Do you think my mother was ever in Canada?"

"Was her name Chris?"

"Then you did know her!"

They stared at each other, she on guard to protect her mother's secret, if secret there was, he living again the moments when he had held that other girl in his arms in this very spot — all those years ago. But he must be careful — terribly careful. He must say nothing to imperil Wake's happiness.

"You are nineteen?" he said.

"Yes."

Then almost angrily she broke out — "What are you trying to tell me or — keep from me?"

"I think your mother was here but she probably had a reasonable motive for not telling you. Perhaps you'd better not speak of it to Wake. She was a lovely young woman. Do you remember her clearly?"

"Oh, yes. It was terrible for us when she died. She was going to have a child. She was n't well. She thought perhaps she'd had too many falls from horses. She almost died when I was born."

He winced. He turned away his face from her. Then he turned to her again and took her arm. "Let's go into my office," he said, "where we can talk without interruption."

He led her into the small room that was warmed by a stove. She sat down in the chair facing the desk and he sat behind the desk. His hands moved mechanically among the papers on it. After a moment he said: —

"I think there is no doubt that your mother came to Jalna with her husband, Jim Dayborn, to school horses for me. It was directly after the Great War. I'd only just come home. I think she'd been through a pretty hard time. Evidently she thought it better that you should n't know about it."

"Renny," — she had been calling him that since coming to Jalna, — "I want to tell you something rather strange. Just before I left England I was going over some things of my mother's. Things in a writing folio. There was a newspaper print of you on horseback. I recognized it as the same picture your brothers showed me in Gayfere Street. The name was cut off. I thought it was a coincidence. But she 'd never mentioned Canada to me so I did n't speak of it to Wake."

"Thank God!"

She was startled. The color heightened in his weather-beaten face. He gave a short laugh. He said: —

"Well, perhaps it 's not so important as all that but if your mother wanted her stay here kept secret, I think we should do it, don't you?"

"Oh, yes. I wonder what Christopher would say."

"Was he called Tod, as a baby?"

"Yes. Mother always called him Tod."

"To think of it!" he ejaculated.

She saw how his hand trembled as again he moved the papers about. She laid her own two hands on the desk as though for support. His eyes rested first on her hands, then on his own. He saw the well-articulated lines of his repeated in her girl's hands. He saw the thumb, with the clear half-moon on its nail, the curve of the little finger, the very shape of the bones. He raised his eyes to her face and searched it in vain for any resemblance to himself. Then he noticed how her fair hair grew in a point on the forehead, as did his, her ears that were pointed and lay close to the head. The icy finger that had just touched his heart now stretched out to cling about it.

He rose and went to the window and looked out into the dazzling day. . . . It could n't be! He was mistaken. This dreadful thing could n't have happened to him . . . could n't be waiting to ruin Wake's happiness! He must get rid of the girl. He must be alone to think. He almost hated her, sitting there, as though some trick of fate had brought her and Wake together!

He pulled himself up. She was speaking.

"It 's all so confusing."

He turned to her. "Yes. I expect the best thing we can do is to put it out of our minds."

"And not tell Wake?"

"I should n't tell him, if I were you."

"I find it hard to keep things from him. He 's so sympathetic."

"Yes, he is. You 're nineteen, you say. When is your birthday?"

She told him. He stood motionless with knit brows. The icy hand of foreboding was pressed on his heart. He had never felt like this before.

"Your mother's first husband, James Dayborn," he said, "when did he die?"

"My own father? He died of lung trouble when I was three."

"Lung trouble! Tuberculosis! God, that 's an awful thing! I had a brother die of it. You 're strong, are you?"

"Oh, yes. I 'm perfectly healthy."

"Good. You 're thin, though."

"It 's natural to me. My mother was thin. Do you remember?"

"Yes. And strong as steel. I 've never known a woman to ride as she could. Well — we must have another talk later. Remember, don't mention this to Wake." He spoke peremptorily.

"No." She answered in the tone of an obedient child.

He went to the outer door with her and stood watching her as she went toward the house. The walk — the fair hair showing beneath the little hat — she might be Chris! He bit his lip to keep back a groan. The dazzling, fairy scene was dark for him. Talk of feeling confused — he scarcely knew what he was doing!

A groom came to him and asked if he had seen a certain bottle of liniment. He stared uncomprehending.

"Liniment?"

"Yes, sir. The bottle the vet left this morning."

Renny wheeled and walked blindly into the office. He picked up the bottle and handed it to the man, who went off, thinking, "It 's not like him to have had too much to drink at this hour in the day. Gosh, he looked queer!"

It was hot in the little room. He threw up the window and the bright snow came sifting in. He sat down at his desk, resting his head on his hand.

He thought — "She 's mine. She 's my child. Mine and Chris's. . . . There 's no doubt about it. . . . Her hands. The way her hair grows. The time of her birth. She 's mine . . . mine and Chris's. . . . Oh, Chris, how could we do this to young Wake!" He twisted his fingers in his strong red hair. He could have torn it, in the bitterness of his anger at himself.

"Talk of pigeons coming home to roost! If ever any man paid for his sins, I have. God, I 've always been found out — from that first time — the gypsy woman when I was nineteen! Perhaps she did something to me — put a curse on me! She was clever enough. But Chris — that sweet girl! I loved her. I 'd have married her if I 'd had the chance. She was n't a wife to Dayborn. He was a cantankerous devil. She never loved him but how she slaved for him and his child!" He remembered how she used to come in the early morning, along the path through the orchard, Dayborn carrying the baby Tod on his shoulder. She was better than Dayborn at schooling the horses. She was afraid of nothing. What hands she had for a horse! And for a man . . . he could feel them on his hair, on his face. And she was dead! In childbed. . . . Too much hard work . . . too many falls . . . poor little Chris! He had thought she was buried in his past but now pity for her pierced his breast. Had he been to blame? He supposed he had. Nature had made him into one of those men who are always to blame. But if only their love had not produced this dreadful crisis — this girl whom Wake loved!

For a space his mind ceased to work. It was a confusion of images — of instincts — of a blind struggle to protect Wakefield. The icy air rushed in on him. The papers swirled on the desk, fell to the floor. He rose and shut the window.

A knock came on the door.

" Go away," he shouted. " I 'm busy."

He locked the door. He walked up and down the narrow space of the room, trying to think. He lighted a cigarette and sat down on the edge of the desk, forcing himself to be calm. One thing was certain. He must be hard — ruthless — he must put an end to this connection between Wake and Molly. Well — they were young. They would get over it. But how could he tell Wake the truth? Yet there was no other way out.

The stable clock struck one. Lunch would be already on the table. He could n't go in. He could n't face Wake. When had he better tell him? This afternoon? No — no, he could n't tell him to-day! He 'd give him another day — a few days more — to be happy in! What if Wake were killed in the war? There would always be that thought — the knowledge that he had spoiled Wake's last months. If only some miracle might happen! If the two would quarrel — break off their engagement of their own free will! But they 'd never do that. You only need see them together to know how deeply they were in love. He went into the stable and sent a boy to the house to ask for lunch to be brought to the office.

" Tell Mrs. Whiteoak that I 'm very busy."

Mrs. Whiteoak! Alayne! She must never know of this. It would be dreadful to her. He 'd got to practise a lot of self-control in the coming days!

The lunch was brought and he burned the food in the

stove. He drank a little whiskey and water. He thought he would like to get roaring drunk — drown his troubles in the flowing bowl — that was the way poets put it!

The fire went out. He sat a long while in the cold office. Then he went to his horses, talked to his men. He had a few hot words with Piers over an item in the vet's bill. That somehow calmed him, gave him courage. Piers looked at him curiously and he turned away.

He joined the others at tea. He drank a good deal of tea and managed to eat something. He talked and joked with Paris, who was easy to talk to, but kept his back turned to Wakefield. After tea he played with the children. He made them quite unmanageable, so that Alayne had to be very stern to get them to bed. She was annoyed at him and he had a hangdog feeling. In the evening they played bridge. He played so badly that Nicholas lost three dollars and was disgruntled with him.

When he went to his room that night he shook some aspirin tablets from the bottle without counting them, crunched them in his strong teeth, and washed them down with a glass of water. He slept. He was awake for some minutes next morning before he remembered what was wrong. He rolled over with a groan and pressed his face into the pillow. He would tell Wake that morning — get it over with!

Perhaps the boy would never be the same again. Perhaps the last affectionate words had passed between them. But it had to be. He had to tell Wake who Molly was. Better anything than this weight of apprehension in his chest. Still he could not bring himself to get up.

He heard the familiar morning sounds. The dogs' noisy rush outdoors to chase away imaginary trespassers. The shaking down of the coals in the hall stove. Uncle Nick's morning cough. Alayne's reasoning with Archer. The snow being shoveled from the paths. He 'd got to get up. There was no escape. He 'd got to send Wake's world crashing, the young brother whom he 'd protected all his life. There was no help for it!

Suddenly he sprang up and began to dress. He and Ernest were at the breakfast table together but Ernest was absorbed in the morning paper and did not notice that Renny ate nothing. He asked Rags for coffee and drank three cups.

He could hear Wake and Molly coming down the stairs. He escaped from the room into the back of the hall and out through the side door. It was not so cold as it had been. Already the icicles on the eave were dripping. One fell and splintered on the flags.

When he decided that Wake and Molly were in the dining room he went back into the hall and got his hat and leather jacket. He heard Alayne coming down the stairs and again fled.

He spent an hour in the stables, then, looking through a window, he saw Wakefield going toward the garage. He went out and waylaid him.

" Where are you off to? " he asked.

" I 'm going to the Rectory."

" Oh." He stood staring speculatively at Wake.

" Anything I can do for you? " asked Wake.

" No thanks."

" It 's not so cold, is it? "

" No. We 'll be having the January thaw." Wake opened the door of the garage.

" Wait a minute."

" Yes? "

" There 's something I want to say to you."

" Yes? "

" We 'll walk along the path for a bit."

" Molly 's waiting."

" It won't take long."

" Very well."

They walked along the snowy path.

Renny threw Wake a quick glance. He saw the warm color in his cheeks and remembered what a large-eyed sallow little boy he had been. Wake was looking interested, expecting something pleasant.

" I suppose you 're full of plans for the future," said Renny.

" Yes, rather."

" Life 's an uncertain business. You can't tell what will happen."

" I 'm not looking any further ahead than my marriage."

" That 's what I 'm going to speak about. I 'm afraid it can't take place."

Wake halted and looked inquiringly at Renny. He thought he had not heard him rightly, or that Renny was joking.

" It will be a terrible disappointment to you, I know."

" A disappointment? "

" Yes. You can't marry Molly."

Wakefield shouted — " What do you mean? "

" Hang on to yourself, Wake, and I 'll tell you. Let 's walk on."

They strode on.

" Is this a joke? " asked Wakefield.

" I wish to God it were."

" Then what 's the matter? "

" Molly is too closely related to you for marriage."

" She related to me? Are you out of your mind? "

" She 's my daughter, Wake. You can't marry your brother's daughter."

" What the hell are you driving at? " Wake's color was gone. His lips were white.

" I have found out that her mother was a young woman

who schooled horses for me after the last war. Both she and her husband worked for me. They were estranged, but she loved me. . . . I wish she had n't."

"Are you telling me that Molly is that woman's daughter and that *you* 're her father?"

"Yes."

"I don't care!" shouted Wake. "I don't care whose daughter she is! I 'll marry her!"

"But you can't. She 's your *niece!*"

"You 're my half-brother. She 's my half-niece. She was born and brought up three thousand miles away. There 's no resemblance between us. What can it matter?"

"Would you marry Patience?"

"That 's different."

"There 's no difference."

"No one need know about this. Not even Molly."

"It 's against the law."

"No one will ever know."

"It 's against the laws of nature."

"Half that happens in the world to-day is against the laws of nature! I tell you, Renny, nothing can stop me." His lips were white and set. His voice harsh. He asked: —

"How did you find this out?"

"She kept reminding me of someone —"

"Is that why you looked at her — the way you did — in London?"

"Looked at her? I don't know. I suppose it was."

"God!" broke out Wakefield. "I suffered then — from jealousy. I little knew what was coming!"

"Wake — I 'm horribly sorry."

Wakefield's face was set. His eyes granite.

"I 'd give my right hand," said Renny, "to have spared you this."

"It 's not going to stop our marriage."

"It must. You can't go on with it."

"Who 's going to stop us! Not you, I hope. You 've done about enough."

"I can't let it go on."

"Do you mean you 'll tell Molly?"

"*You* must do that."

"I 'll never do it! Does she suspect anything? Have you said anything to her?"

"She only knows that her mother was once at Jalna. She feels something mysterious in it. She found a picture of me among her mother's things."

Wakefield looked at him with hate. He said — "You 've caused a lot of trouble in your life, have n't you?"

Renny's color rose. "I suppose I have," he answered. "But Chris loved me, as I loved her. We met on an equal footing. I 'd have been glad to marry her. Gran suspected this and she stepped in and paid their way back to England. I never saw Chris again. I did n't know her husband had died and she 'd remarried."

"Why did n't she come back here and marry you?"

"I don't know. I suppose she loved this Griffith."

"I don't believe it. I think she knew you did n't really want to marry her."

"That 's all in the past. It 's the present we 've got to think of. I want you to get through all this with — "

"I 'm going to marry Molly!" said Wake, hoarsely.

"You must tell her who she is."

"I will tell her." He wheeled to go back to the house. "She shall be judge."

Renny caught him by the arm. "It 's not a matter for Molly's judgment. You must tell her who she is and that you can't marry her. Either that or tell her that you 've changed your mind and don't want to marry anyone yet." He gave Wakefield an almost beseeching look. "Perhaps that would be best. You need not even do it at once. It could be broken off by degrees and she would suffer less."

Wakefield's face was contorted. " What about me? What about my suffering? I suppose it does n't matter. I can tear my heart out — because you once had an hour's pleasure! "

" Wake, I shall tell Molly myself — if you want me to."

He spoke quietly. They were in the pinewood. The pine trees towered in their silvered majesty above them. There was a sudden harsh outcry and a dozen pheasants rose to the treetops. Once there, their bright plumage caught the sun.

Renny spoke still more quietly. " Whatever your feelings are, Wake, whatever Molly's are or mine, we can do nothing to change this situation. If you don't believe me go to your priest and ask him."

" I will go to him. I 'll go now."

" Good. I 'll take you in the car."

Wakefield looked dazed. His color had come back and lay in blotches of red on his ravaged young face. They strode back the way they had come. They got into the car and in almost complete silence drove to the priest's house.

Renny sat outside in the car waiting for his brother. He nursed his chin in his hand. His sombre eyes saw nothing of what passed.

Noah Binns came trudging down the road. He stopped when he saw Renny and came to the side of the car. He looked in with his toothless grin.

" Marnin'," he said. " Chimney 's smokin'."

" What chimney? "

" Church chimney. Flues need cleanin'."

" Why don't you clean them, then? "

" They need expert cleanin'. I ain't expert, am I? "

" Tell Jimpson to clean them."

Noah trudged on, his footsteps screeching on the snowy road.

Renny still kept his face averted when Wakefield returned to the car but, out of the corner of his eye, he saw that the priest had come to the door with him. He was a small thin man with an ascetic face.

They drove back toward Jalna in silence for a space. Then Renny saw that Wakefield was crying. He took his hand from the wheel and laid it on the boy's.

"You'll have to tell her," said Wakefield. "I can't."

XXV

RENNY AND MOLLY

THEY crossed the little bridge that spanned the silent stream and went up the steep on the other side of the ravine. The children ran behind them drawing their sleighs. Archer's was a Christmas one, painted scarlet and gold, and he had tied on it a sleighbell from an old cutter. The bell filled the air with its clear sharp jingle.

"How lovely it is!" said Molly. "I wish Wake were with us."

"Yes. But the fact is I wanted to talk to you alone for a bit and I thought this would be a good place."

"Oh." She looked thoughtful, wondering what the talk was to be about.

They passed through the oakwood and across a field. Then the house where Ernest and Harriet had lived stood before them. A thin spiral of smoke was rising from the chimney.

"We keep a fire here in the coldest weather," said Renny, "because of the furniture. Later on we shall try to let the house furnished."

"It looks very cozy."

"It is. Aunt Harriet had very good taste. She brought quite a lot of her own furniture from the States. One of us comes over twice a day to the furnace. Will you wait here while I go down to the cellar?"

He unlocked the front door and showed her into the living room. There he left her and she could hear him descend into the cellar and shake down the ashes in the furnace. She was puzzled, but not really troubled, by his air of mystery. Perhaps he had brought her here to tell her something of her mother's life in Canada. The air of the room was lifeless and she put up a window a little way. She could hear him putting on coals. He seemed a long while down there.

Presently he returned to her. There was a smudge of ash on his forehead. He smiled at her, as though reassuringly.

"Fire nearly out," he said. "Do you find it cold here?"

"Oh, no. I opened the window."

"It 's a pretty room — don't you think so?"

"Very. It must have been frightfully hard on your uncle to — give it all up."

"Yes, indeed. I wish you could have met Aunt Harriet. She was a sweet woman. She and I were great friends. She made that drawing of Rheims Cathedral when she was quite young. And the one of the Greek Theatre at Taormina. She 'd traveled all over France and Italy. She was very intellectual." He sighed.

The sound of Archer's sleighbell came tinkling through the open window. Renny went to it and looked out. The children were running toward the house.

"You can't come in here," he said. "You 'd better run home."

She heard their receding laughter, detached and half-defiant. They felt independent and daring.

He turned again to Molly.

"You 're sure you 're not cold?"

"Perfectly."

But he put down the window.

She looked inquiringly at him.

"I have something to tell you," he said, "which I 'm afraid will upset you terribly."

She stood looking into his eyes, waiting. She had a sudden feeling of trust in him, as though it would not be possible to him really to hurt her. He said: —

"I suppose you have thought a good deal about your mother since our talk yesterday."

"Yes, I have." So it *was* about her mother! She had expected that. A thought illuminated her mind. He was going to tell her that he had loved her mother!

"Perhaps you know," he went on, "that your mother was not happily married."

She hesitated, then said — "I — yes, I knew."

"You 'll think I have no right to talk to you like this but I want you to believe that I only do it because I must."

"I do believe that, but — why must you?"

"I 'll tell you in a moment. But first I must tell you that I loved your mother and that she loved me. She was estranged from Dayborn. They did n't live together as man and wife. It was a great surprise to me when I discovered through you that she had had a daughter after her return to England. Then I began to calculate. I asked you the date of your birth, do you remember?"

"Yes, I remember." She looked straight into his eyes, not flinching.

"It came to me like a bolt out of the blue — that you were not Dayborn's daughter, but mine."

In his self-control he spoke in an almost matter-of-fact tone.

Her mouth was unbearably dry. She swallowed before she could answer.

"Perhaps you 're right. There was that picture of you I found in her things. I found a letter from — my father — oh, I have to call him my father! It was an unkind, angry letter. There was a hint I could n't understand but — I understand now!"

She had said she understood but he could see that she was using all her strength to steady herself, that she had not grasped the import of what he had told her. He came and sat down beside her on the sofa. She had dropped to it as though weak, had grasped its arm in her hand so that the knuckles stood out white and tense.

"We loved each other," he said. "We did n't think we were harming anyone. She 'd been a better wife to Dayborn than he deserved. She was so courageous. She seemed never to think of herself. I suppose that 's why —"

He could not go on.

"Yes?"

"I suppose that was why you were born. She never thought of herself."

She turned to look into his face. Her eyes were feverishly bright. She exclaimed: —

"But you can't be positive of this! After all, you 're just guessing, are n't you? My mother never wrote to you to tell you I was coming, did she?"

"No, she did n't tell me, though we exchanged letters for a time. Then she stopped writing. Evidently she did n't want me to know. There was a kind of deep reserve in her that makes me understand her doing this. I think you have it in you, too."

"Then you 're only guessing really!"

"I have no written proof but I am positive. You do believe in instinct, don't you? And there 's more than that. Look."

He took her hand and held it in front of her. He put his own right hand beside it.

"I have a very individual hand," he said. "I want you to look at it and then at your own."

Obediently she examined his lean, muscular, man's hand, then her own thin, girl's hand.

"They don't look alike to me," she said.

"Not look alike! Do you see the bend of the little finger — the length of the thumb and the way it 's joined to the hand — the shape of the nails! Why, the two hands are identical."

"That might be chance."

"But it is n't chance. And look here, —" he led her to the mirror above the mantel, — "I want you to examine our foreheads and the way the hair grows. Do you see? Look at my ears — then at your own! You are marked, Molly, as my daughter. There 's no getting away from it. At first I kept thinking — 'How like her mother she is!' But now I can see only your resemblance to me. Don't you see it?"

"Yes," she answered, half reluctantly. "I do. And there was that letter. The one I found among my mother's things. He —" she stumbled over the word, not knowing what to call Dayborn — "he said in it — 'You 've never been able to get that red-haired fellow out of your mind. I 'll swear there are n't many husbands as forgiving as I am.'"

"Brute!"

"He went on to ask her how much money she had and to send him as much as she could. That letter turned me against him."

"No wonder. But, if you had known him, you 'd have forgiven him a good deal. . . . The question is — can you forgive me?"

Old Adeline, propitiatory, challenging, wary, looked out of his eyes. He forgot, for the moment, his harassment of the past twenty-four hours.

She turned to him swiftly and laid her cheek against his shoulder. She said: —

"I 'm glad . . . in a strange sort of way. I can't explain."

He put his arm about her.

"Do you realize what it 's going to mean to you and Wake?" he asked.

She looked trustfully into his face. "What had I better do? Tell him or keep it secret?"

He answered, almost irritably, "I've had it out with Wake. He realizes that you can't marry now."

His arm tightened about her. He waited for the impact of the blow. He felt her go rigid. Then she began to cry wildly and loudly. She beat on his shoulder with her hands.

"We can't marry!" she cried. "We can't marry!"

She would have fallen to the floor but he took her in his arms trying to quiet her.

At last she said — "I must go away."

"Yes. That will be best. . . . Molly, I'd have given anything I possess to have prevented this. It's been one of the worst days in my life."

"It has broken my heart," she sobbed.

"Poor little girl!" He stroked her hair.

"I'll go back to England."

"You and Wake must settle what is best to do."

"When can I see him?"

"Whenever you like. Shall I send him here?"

"Yes. Tell him not to be long, will you?"

"I'll send him as soon as I can find him. Molly — you'll have to be strong. It's going to be awful for Wake to give you up."

"What did he say — when you told him?"

"He was terribly upset."

She began once more to cry, wildly.

He found some brandy in the sideboard and gave her a little. He chafed her hands, which were icy cold. As he looked down at their hands, his warm and strong, bringing the life back to hers, the resemblance between them seemed suddenly to typify the whole heartbreaking business to her. She closed her fingers round his and held them to her breast.

XXVI

RENNY AND ALAYNE

ARCHER WHITEOAK went down through the ravine and over the bridge, drawing his new sleigh behind him. The bell on it jingled merrily but he did not feel merry. Somewhere he had lost his cap. He could not remember when but he now realized that the cold wind was whistling in his ears and over his crown. The sleigh felt heavy, much heavier than on the way over. The two girls and Nook had disappeared long ago. He had been left to find his way home alone. He would tell his mother.

Though it was still early afternoon the sun was slanting through the trees, etching a pattern of great beauty on the snow. Diminutive snow clouds were sometimes blown across its crust. Archer saw no beauty in the scene about him. It existed for him as an immense icy basin across which he had a long way to traverse. In the illimitable distance was the circular shape of a cookie or a sweet biscuit or a snow apple. This was all that kept him alive crossing the ravine.

He passed through the little wicket gate on the lawn. The gate was propped wide open by a snowdrift. He discovered that he had a sore spot somewhere. He had coughed and it had hurt.

He pondered on this hurt with gathering gloom as he trudged toward the porch. The sheep dog was sitting in the porch, a bundle of snowy gray hair, and ran joyfully to greet him. He gave it a shout of warning but that was of no avail. It knocked him down as he knew it would. The sore spot hurt again!

He made no attempt to pick up the rope of his sleigh but went howling straight into the house.

Alayne came down the stairs, her mind balanced between annoyance and sympathy.

"Whatever is the matter?" she asked.

He threw himself on the bottom step and lay there, filling the house with his woe. She picked him up and began to divest him of his outer garments.

"Darling, are you hurt? Where is your cap?"

"My feet are cold! They went and left me!"

"What a shame! Where were you?"

"At Uncle Ernest's . . . Oh — my feet! Oh — my sore spot!"

Rags came and she gave him the small snow suit to shake and hang up.

"Come upstairs with Mummie," she said.

"I can't wa-alk!"

His face looked fragile but he had a sturdy body. She found him heavy and was glad to set him down in her room. She undressed his feet and held them in her warm lap. She looked anxiously into his face.

"Where is the sore spot?"

"It 's where somebody hit me."

"Hit you! Who was it?"

"I forget." Deliberately he gave his rare smile that always stirred her heart. "I 'm hungry," he said. "Can I have a cookie?"

"Archer, I cannot let you eat between meals."

There was silence for a moment while he watched her ministrations to him. Then he said: —

"I don't feel well."

"Then why do you want to eat?"

"To make me feel better." He put his hand to his side. "There 's the spot! I hurt it when I fell off my sleigh. Daddy was kissing the girl and I fell off my sleigh. It was his fault."

Alayne looked at him, unable to speak for a moment in her astonishment. Then she demanded: —

" What do you mean, Archer? You must tell Mummie just what you mean."

He laid his hand on her head as though he were blessing her. " If I had something to eat I could talk."

She rose and went to a cabinet. She took barley sugar from it and gave him a piece.

" Where was Daddy? " she asked, trying to speak without concern.

" In Uncle Ernest's house." His cheek was distended by the sweet. " I stood on my sleigh and looked through the window. The girl was on the sofa — "

" What girl? "

" Molly. You know Molly, don't you? Tickle my feet and see if I can keep from laughing."

" In a moment. Did Daddy and Molly see you? "

" No. They were on the sofa. She was being naughty and he kissed her. Now tickle me! "

Gently Alayne caressed his pink sole with the tips of her fingers. She looked compellingly into his eyes.

" Tell me, why did you leave the window? "

" Molly frightened me. I fell off my sleigh and came home."

" Did n't they see you? "

" No. Tickle me harder! "

" Tell me right from the beginning what happened and you shall have another sweet."

" Well, they looked in the glass and she put her head on his shoulder and cried and he carried her to the sofa and held her like you do me and gave her something to drink in a glass and kissed her. And she kissed him. The spot is right here." He laid his hand on it. " It does n't hurt so badly when you tickle me and I have a sweet."

Alayne heard Renny's step on the stair. He came into the room. A cold rage toward him possessed her. She could have screamed in her rage at him. She felt rage, like a living thing, turn in her breast, but she pressed it down and spoke in a controlled voice.

"Tell Daddy how you hurt yourself, Archer."

He began eagerly — "It was your fault, Daddy, was n't it? Because if you had n't been on the sofa with Molly I 'd not have looked through the window and — "

Renny interrupted — "What are you saying? I don't know what you mean."

"Why, yes, Daddy. You closed the window and I looked in and you — "

"Shut up!" exclaimed Renny sharply. "You 're talking nonsense and you know it."

Alayne smiled. "You should choose a more secluded spot for your rendezvous," she said.

"I don't know what either of you mean."

Archer turned his bare feet together till the soles met. He clasped his hands and his brow became accusing. "I fell off my sleigh," he said, "because I tried to see what Daddy and Molly were doing."

"You may be willing to encourage the boy to be a spy and a liar," broke in Renny. "I can't agree."

Alayne began to draw on the little boy's socks.

"I don't want to go!" he whined.

"I hear Adeline in the passage. She 'll take you up with her. It 's almost your teatime."

He stiffened himself to a poker. "I won't go!"

If he was a poker Renny's grasp was iron. He carried him into the passage and closed the door behind. Adeline was standing with her back against the opposite wall, very straight, as though her height were to be measured.

"Adeline," he said, "I want you to take Archie up to the nursery! He 's got some nonsense in his head. Make him forget it. It 's damned silly."

Her eyes searched his face.

"Yes, Daddy."

She took her brother by the hand and he walked stiffly toward the stairs. He began, in a dictatorial tone: —

"Daddy should n't have made Molly cry and then — "

Adeline interrupted him with a gay laugh. "I know and I 'd have cried too but I laughed and laughed and what do you suppose I laughed at? An owl and a squirrel fighting in the ravine! The feathers and the fur flew. Come and I 'll tell you."

Renny gave a wry smile and went back to Alayne.

She was standing, waiting.

"Our children are getting an early training in deception," she said.

He tried to touch her but she drew sharply away.

"Alayne," he said, "I ask you, in all truth and sincerity, to believe me. I — "

She interrupted — "Believe you! When there 's another woman in question!" She put her hands on the foot-board of the bed and gripped it to steady herself. "Never! I know you too well."

"How dare you say that to me!" he exclaimed roughly. "You talk as though our life was a succession of affairs on my part and endurance on yours. It 's unjust."

"You 'll be telling me next that you 've always been faithful to me and that Archer saw nothing."

"I was unfaithful — if you want that word — *once! Once,* I tell you, in all our married life! I thought that was over — forgiven — forgotten — it was the only time. There was something to be said on my side. I 'll swear there was! As to what Archie saw — I was comforting Molly because she is in trouble."

"Yes — yes — I know that sort of trouble! She wants you! That 's her only trouble."

"My God! She *adores* Wake."

"I 've seen looks pass between you. I could n't understand. Now I do. There 's no use in talking to me.

Archer saw something in that room that shocked him."

"He saw Molly crying."

"Why were you kissing her?"

"I was n't!"

"You were!"

"You take that mere baby's word against mine?"

"Your own face gives you the lie! The moment you stepped inside the door and heard Archer talking you looked excited and defensive. What was she crying about?"

"Her father. She worries about him. He 's drinking hard."

"My God, why need you and she go to an empty house to talk about her family affairs? Where was Wakefield? Why did n't she tell her troubles to him?"

"She thought I could help her." He stared steadily into Alayne's eyes.

"And I don't doubt that you did," she sneered. "You helped her by kissing her! Well, you are not the first middle-aged man to want affairs with young girls."

He still looked steadily into her eyes. "Alayne," he said, "anyone who heard you say that might wonder if you have an atom of love left for me."

There was a moment of quivering silence, then she began to cry bitterly. "You can't imagine what it is," she sobbed, "to be a woman who sees her looks going and her husband . . ." She could not speak. She covered her face with her hands.

"Now listen to me," he said. "You know that I have never been interested in girls. The one woman who came into my life after our marriage was a woman of my own age. If I kissed Molly Griffith — and I don't think I did — "

"You acknowledge it then!"

"I stick only to one thing and that is that you are the only woman I love and that — "

"Please don't try to explain!"

"Let me speak!"

"It's too painful, I can't bear it."

"But you can bear to say things to me that cut me to the heart!"

"Can you wonder at anything I say?"

"What has happened? Just tell me!"

She answered, in a shaking voice, "You have made love to a girl visiting in the house."

"Whose word have you for it?"

"Your own! You can't deny it."

"Alayne, you might have heard every word that passed between us —"

"Why were the two of you on the sofa?"

He laughed. "Have I so little finesse that I would forget to draw down the blind if it were expedient?"

"The house was empty. You thought you were far from everyone."

"I knew the children were outside."

She put her hands to her forehead and pushed back her thick hair. She said: —

"I can't talk about it any more. It exhausts me. I have lost my looks. I have lost your love. That's enough, is n't it?"

"You have lost neither."

"Are you going to tell Wake of your meeting with — that girl?"

"He already knows."

She broke out wildly, "Oh, you're too much for me! You're too clever. Too experienced. But you've done something to-day that I'll never forget. You've broken down something I've been for years building up. You'll go away to the war leaving me with this feeling!"

He looked at her contemplatively, as a surgeon might look at a patient, wondering if she were strong enough to bear the operation he had in his mind.

After a space of silence, he said — " I think I had better tell you the whole truth about this."

" Are you going to tell me you want a divorce? " she asked, in a voice not her own.

" Alayne, don't make it harder for us! Just listen to me quietly. Something terrible has happened. That is, terrible for Wake and Molly. You must remember that they are deeply in love. They expected to marry in a few weeks. Now they find that they can never marry. They can never marry because — " How could he go on? What would be the effect of such a disclosure? Well — she 'd asked for it. Let her have it!

" Can't marry! " she repeated, her eyes still hard with suspicion.

" They can't marry because — Molly is my daughter." He spoke in a matter-of-fact tone in his effort to calm her. " You can imagine what it means to me to tell you this but I feel it 's better than that you should think what you do."

" But — " she spoke in a hoarse whisper — " how can that be? "

" Have you ever heard the family speak of a girl named Chris who came to Jalna, after the last war, to help train horses? "

" Yes. She and her husband were both here. They were English people."

" They were a very unhappy pair. There was no love between them. She and I . . . that summer . . . Do you understand? "

" Only too well," she breathed, wringing her fingers together.

" Well, from things Molly said, I began to suspect. Then I became certain. This morning I told Wake. This afternoon I had to tell Molly." He smiled grimly. " A nice sort of day, eh? "

He stood waiting for her to speak. She sat shielding

her eyes with her hand but he could see her mouth. He looked at it a moment, then, as though its expression hurt him unbearably, he dropped his eyes to the floor and stood waiting.

Alayne tried to think clearly but there was a buzzing in her ears that distracted her. He stood there waiting. She must say something. That girl, his daughter — he had just come home from the War! Now he was about to go to fight in another war. What a stirring life! The courage, the masculinity, the unscrupulousness of it! A slow deep joy welled up in her, spreading from her breast to her very hair and finger tips as sap through a tree. It felt like life itself welling up in her. She had not lost him! Her mind revolved in burning eagerness round her relief, her love. She could not think of the boy and girl torn apart. Not yet. Not while she was still quivering under the reverberation of her relief.

She took her hand from her eyes and looked up at him.

"Can you forgive me?" he asked.

"That is all in the past," she answered.

She was sitting and he came and knelt beside her. He put his forehead in her lap. A wave of possessive tenderness, all the more passionate because he must so soon go away, swept over her. She put her arms about him and held him close.

XXVII
THE SEVERING

Molly was sitting with her hands clasped between her knees when Wakefield came into the room. She raised her eyes, heavy from weeping, to his. She was shocked by his pallor, his drawn look. She said:—

"Oh, Wake, what has Renny done to us?"

He answered hoarsely, "He 's ruined our lives." Then he added—"But Renny did n't know. It 's a blow to him too."

They felt as though a gulf had opened between them. He stood just inside the door, looking at her. She might have been a stranger whose features he was trying to impress on his mind. After a little he said:—

"Do you believe it, Molly?"

She nodded, wringing her fingers together.

"Have you just what he thinks to go on or do you know of anything else?"

"Now that he 's told me, other things come to my mind. A picture. A letter. Then our hands. It 's as though they were cast out of the same mould."

"Yes. I see it now. . . . I 've been to my priest. I thought something might be done. But it can't. There 's nothing to do, Molly."

She sprang up and went to him. She remembered how Renny had said she must be strong. She laid her hands on his shoulders but he drew away.

"Don't touch me! I can't bear it."

"Am I a different person, then? Since you 've found out this about me?"

He controlled himself with a painful effort.

"I don't know," he answered. "I don't know. I can't think. It 's just as though a blight had fallen on us. Our love is poisoned. It 's no longer in flower. It 's — "

"You must n't say such things! Nothing can ever change my love for you. I 'll love you to my dying day. Yes — to the last breath I draw."

A feverish light came into his eyes. Suddenly he put both arms about her and drew her close. "Molly, darling, my precious one! There is no need for us to be separated. We can love to — the last breath we draw — just as you said!"

For a moment of ecstasy she gave herself to his embrace. The room receded. They were alone, clinging together, in dizzy space. A flame shot through their bodies. Their lips met in a burning kiss. Whatever fate had taken from them it had given them this moment.

As clearness of mind came back to her she thought — "Our love would have been like this."

He would not let her go. He clung tightly to her.

"No, no, Wake," she breathed.

"But, Molly, don't you understand? We need n't part! Till our last breath. Even then — even after that — we 'd cling together. Don't you understand?"

Frightened she whispered — "No."

"There 's death — as well as love, Molly. . . . Now do you know what I mean? We could die, darling. It would be so easy. Lovers have often done it. Why not we? I 've thought of a way. Will you, Molly?"

She understood him. Blissful and terrible visions floated before her eyes. No parting. A continuance of their love till the end. A last, exquisite, dreamlike embrace. . . . No more wondering what to do next. . . . No dark uncertain future to face. . . . Just the end creeping gently on them till they slept. Perhaps not creeping gently but coming as an extinguishing flame. . . . Then she tore herself from him — with fierceness, as though she would have torn her heart out.

" How dare you suggest such a thing, Wake! You don't mean it! You know you don't. You love life too well. You love Renny too well. It would kill him — break his heart! And you a Catholic! Does your religion mean so little to you, then? "

He stood with folded arms and downcast eyes. He said: —

" Nothing seems to matter to me now."

" But it will — your religion, I mean. Everything will come back to you."

" Everything but you."

" I have n't left you, Wake. Only it 's got to be different. Oh, can't you help me bear it? If you don't help me I just can't bear it. Renny said I was to be strong and I 'm trying to."

" It does n't mean so much to you as it does to me."

" It means just as much. I think it means even more. You loved another girl once. But I 've never loved anyone but you. The way I am trying to look at it is this. I was trying hard — all the while I waited for you. Our country is at war. We 'll all have to work desperately to win. A lot of people are going to be killed. Perhaps you and I among them. But that would be an honorable death. Think how proud your family are of you, Wake! Almost every one of them has said to me how proud they are of you. You would n't want to let them down in such an appalling way, would you? "

He raised his sombre eyes to her face. He tried to speak but could not. But she read submission on his lips.

He turned from her and laid his arm against the side of the door, then hid his face on his arm. She dared not go to him but she spoke in a firm voice.

" We 're going to be all right, are n't we, darling? "

" Don't call me darling! " he cried hoarsely.

" Wake, then. Wake — my friend." She could not go on. She held her hand against her trembling lips.

A clear sweet whistling came to them through the window. The whistle was drawn and sweet as a blackbird's. Piers was coming along the path. He was bareheaded and wore a leather windbreaker. He called out: —

" Hullo, are you in there, Wake? "

He came to the window and looked in. He thought — " A quarrel, eh? A pretty bad one too, by the looks of them."

He held up a yellow envelope.

" A cable for you, Molly. I 'll bet it 's an offer from some London manager." But he looked a little anxious for her, as though he feared bad news.

She tore open the envelope and read. She looked dazed. She handed it to Wakefield. He too read it.

" It 's from her brother," he said. " Their father has died. Christopher wants to join the R. A. F. He asks Molly if she can arrange for their sisters to come out here."

Piers came in at the window. He put his arm about Molly and patted her on the back.

" Bad luck," he said, " but we 'll look after you. Everything will be all right."

His presence came into the room bringing life itself. Life, full of vigor and hope, radiated from him. Strange visions could not live in the room with him. He came like life, willing to lay itself down if necessary, but not in defeat.

XXVIII
THE SHUTTLE

THE tie that bound the Whiteoak family to the Old Land had been strong but since the war that tie had, as in the case of countless other Canadian families, so strengthened, toughened, and tautened that they now felt as one. The Atlantic crossing, which had once been safe, was now perilous, but a bridge of courage and loyalty had been flung from shore to shore.

Nicholas and Ernest would sit on either side of the radio, waiting for the news. Nicholas would hold his watch in his hand. When the news came they would impressively impart it to the rest of the household. Rags wasted much of his time in recalling incidents of the last war. He was in a state of ferment lest he should not be able to rejoin the Buffs in Renny's service. He got out their uniforms, aired and pressed them. He put more elbow grease on the buttons than ever he gave to the table silver. He all but shed tears of joy when he found that Renny's still fitted him to perfection. As for himself, he had considerably shrunken but he was as proud of his figure as though he were an Adonis.

" Broad in the shoulder, narrow in the 'ip, that 's wot I am," he would declare, never having noticed that his neck was too long, his legs too short, and that he stuck out behind. He paraded the kitchen, fairly bristling to have another fling at the Germans. His wife regarded him pessimistically.

" You 'd think," she said, " that it was just a picnic to go to war and leave your wife behind."

" In times like these 'ere, wives recede to the background."

" Aye, and sweethearts comes to the fore," she returned grimly.

He gave her a tantalizing look. " Let that be as it may, I 'ave a man's work to do and, if a little fun is thrown in, you need n't worry."

" Well, you 're not away yet. Like as not you 'll never get away."

He looked a trifle crestfallen at this and she added: —

" Dear knows who they 'll get in to do your work. With my allowance from the government I 'll have enough to live on. I think I 'll quit and take it easy for a spell."

" Now just put that idea out of your 'ead," he said angrily. " Wot you 've got to do is to 'old down this 'ere plice till I return. I 'd look well, should n't I, going round with me 'at in me 'and looking for a job when I come back! There goes the bell! Blast those old fellers — wot do they want now? I 've been up them ruddy stairs forty times to-day! "

" You can't go up with that there uniform on."

" Well, I 'd like to 'ear 'em object to the King's uniform in *my* presence! I 'd 'ave somethink to say."

In a few minutes he came rattling down the stairs again.

" Wot was it? " asked his wife, who was singeing a goose over the flame of the kitchen range.

" Mr. Ernest wanting a glass of 'ot water and bicarbonate of soder. Is there any 'ot water? Upon my word I sometimes think it would 'ave been better for 'im if 'e 'd never married, wot with all the 'ot water and soder and the fruit juice and the bran flakes 'e 's took to. W'y the 'ell don't you 'ave 'ot water always on the stove? " He banged the stove lids about.

Mrs. Wragge held the blazing goose precariously near him while her little eyes shot him a malevolent look. He sprang aside.

" Look out wot you 're doing! Do you know that you could be fined for willfully damaging the King's uniform? "

"Get out o' my way then!"

"Oh, I'll get out of your way! Don't you worry. I'll get out and probably be blown to bits by a bomb."

"A bad penny always turns up."

"Oh, does it then! I like that! Maybe it will turn up with the Victoria Cross on it!"

"More likely with a 'ole bored through it."

"Ow. I like that! Making fun of a dying soldier's wounds! Well, let me tell you, my lidy, this 'ere is going to be a civilian's war. You may yet see the day when you'll be bombed or gassed."

"I've often thought of stickin' me 'ead in the oven after a jaw from you!"

"Oh, you 'ave, 'ave you? Get out of my way with that goose or I'll do you a injury."

"You done me the worst injury possible when you married me."

As she uttered these words the master of the house came down the stairs. It was he who, twenty years before, had led Mrs. Wragge down the aisle of the church and given her to her bridegroom. Now he stood looking at the pair with an ironic grin.

"I had a hand in that, Mrs. Wragge," he said. "I hope you're not blaming me."

She colored, which is saying a good deal, for she was already crimson from full-bloodedness and the heat of the fire. "No, sir, but he does irritate me at times. 'Ere, take your 'ot water and get along with you."

Rags turned himself round in front of Renny.

"Wot do you think of the fit, sir?"

"Fine! I only hope you get a chance to wear it."

"I'll be 'eartbroken, if I don't."

"Rags, I've just come down to tell you that I can take you along!"

"Thank Gawd for that, sir! I could n't 'ave borne to

stay at Jalna and you at the Front! Now let 'Itler look out! Now let Goring and Gubbles 'ave a mind to themselves! *We're* after 'em! *You* and *me!* Same as we were after the old Kaiser. We'll do 'em in!"

He did a few hornpipe steps, with the cup of hot water in his hand, then hastened up the stairs to tell the good news to Ernest and Nicholas.

The news that Rags was to depart made the two elderly men feel drawn still closer to the war. The pattern of their world was changing so fast as to be bewildering. They had known from the first that Renny would go. Paris Court and Wakefield had been eager to follow suit. Harriet had died. Sarah's son had been born. Now Rags was to go. For nearly twenty-one years he had irritated and served them. Sometimes the irritation was uppermost. Sometimes the service. But they were always there. Sometimes the irritation acted as a counterirritant, as when, for instance, Nicholas and Ernest had had words with each other. Then one of Rags's misdeeds would bring them together again in hearty censure of his ways. He would leave traces of polishing powder in the crevices of heavily chased trays or jugs but he would rub thin old Georgian teaspoons so hard that they would bend double. When an important English army man on a lecture tour was entertained at dinner Rags brought coffee in everyday cups, but when the Rector and Mrs. Fennel came, as they did once a week, he would bring out the rare old Worcestershire china. It was impossible to teach him discrimination. It was his idea of taste to have every piece of furniture, every ornament, set cornerwise and a constant struggle was waged, with him on one side, Ernest and Alayne on the other. Rags always won. No matter how he might neglect to sweep up the crumbs from under the breakfast table, no matter how he continued to ignore windows that needed cleaning, or children's finger marks on doors, he had only to pass through a room and every chair and ornament stood cornerwise in his wake.

But how comforting his presence was at times! No one could tuck a hot-water bottle at an old gentleman's feet and cover him with an eiderdown with an air of greater solicitude. He would bring a glass of hot water and whiskey or a cup of hot water and bicarbonate of soda with equal expressions of the good he was certain it would do you.

Of course he had a nasty way of whispering to Renny at table when he sensed any family disturbance and wanted to show that he was on the side of the master of the house. On the other hand, he showed endless patience in searching for mislaid spectacles and never forgot the hours at which Ernest's medicine should be taken. It had been a shock to see him in his uniform.

Now Renny came into the room and once more they realized how soon they must part with his heartening presence. This war was quite different from the last. They had been twenty years younger then and their mother was living. While she lived there had been that feeling of stability and changelessness at Jalna but now all was changed. Nicholas gave a deep sigh and raised his heavy eyes to Renny's face. He noticed Renny's look of anxiety, the corrugations on his forehead, but he sniffed, with an odd sense of comfort, the smell of the stable that came with him.

Renny sat down near the fire and held a hand toward the blaze.

"Cold?" asked Nicholas.

"No. I just like the warmth."

"You 're like Mamma. She always liked the warmth of the open fire. Where are the young people this morning? I have n't seen them."

Renny looked at him thoughtfully. He wondered what the uncles would say if he told them all. For a moment he had a mind to. There would be a certain comfort in telling them. But no — they had enough to worry about without hearing of poor young Wake's heartache.

" Molly 's gone to town," he said. " She and Wake had to go to arrange for her sisters' passage from Wales to Canada. . . . Poor girl, she has a great responsibility. I 've been thinking that it would be a very decent thing for us to offer your house, Uncle Ernest, to those girls — if you agree. They would be safe here and under our protection. It would be a load off Molly's mind."

" Are they able to pay rent? " asked Nicholas. " I gather they are pretty hard-up. Molly said something about their income ceasing if their father died."

" We can't very well ask rent from refugees."

" Of course not! I 'd forgotten."

" By all means, let them come," said Ernest. " It would be a relief to me to see the house occupied by nice young women. Harriet would have wished it."

" After all," put in Nicholas, somewhat grumpily, " the house belongs to Renny."

" I have n't said it does n't, have I? However, the furniture is mine and Harriet's."

" Upon my word, Ernest, you take a lofty tone about family belongings. The furniture in that house — I mean the portion of it that came from Jalna — is as much mine as yours. Not that it matters. I 'm perfectly willing to lend it."

" Then what are you grousing about? " said Ernest.

" I 'm not grousing. But that card table in the living room was one Mamma gave me years ago. She also gave me that bedroom furniture and the rugs."

" But you never took them to England! "

" How could I? It would have been ridiculous."

" Then why claim the things now? "

" I 'm not. It 's you who are claiming them."

Ernest's color rose. He tried to speak but he could only stammer incoherently. Renny's voice broke in.

"I'm awfully glad you both agree to lending the house. I'll cable Christopher Griffith to-day."

He rose and moved toward the door.

"What's the matter?" asked Nicholas, eyeing him shrewdly. "Is something worrying you?"

"Well, I have a good deal on my mind."

"You look as though you had n't slept."

"I'm all right."

A shadow fell across the window. Wakefield passed. As he passed he glanced into the room. That glimpse of him was sufficient to discover his haggard eyes, his drawn mouth. He looked ill.

"Why," exclaimed Ernest, "did you see Wakefield? The boy's ghastly!"

"What's wrong?" Nicholas heaved himself about in his chair that he might face Renny squarely. "Tell us what's wrong, Renny."

Renny stood looking down on the experienced gray heads of his uncles. Again he had a mind to tell them the truth. A perverse curiosity made him wonder how they would take it.

"Surely," said Ernest, "the death of Molly's father would n't make him look like that."

Old Adeline's love of the dramatic flared in her grandson. The sardonic light that had on occasion gleamed in her eyes appeared in his.

"Molly's father is very near to Wake," he said.

"Why," said Nicholas, "that's impossible. Wake scarcely knew the man."

"Wake *knows* the man," returned Renny, driven by an impulse he could not resist. "He knows the man — to his sorrow."

"I do wish you would not be so enigmatic," exclaimed Ernest peevishly.

"I will tell you the truth then. I think it will be better." Renny walked the length of the room and back again. He put his hands in his pockets and touched a penknife that had belonged to his father. He himself had carried it for the past twenty years. Its worn ivory handle lay slim and cool in his fingers. In a strange way this small cool object brought back to him the warmth and vigor of his father's presence. He thought — "I wonder what he would be like if he were living now. I wonder what he would say to this."

The eyes of his uncles, one pair blue and questioning, the other pair dark and puzzled, were fixed on him. He said: —

"I suppose you remember the Dayborns who worked with me after the last war."

"Yes," said Ernest. "I never liked the fellow. There was something shady about him."

"Of course I remember them," added Nicholas. "Mamma paid their passage back to England. I forget why."

"I don't," said Renny. "She did it to separate Chris Dayborn and me because she had found out that we were in love with each other."

"Well, really," exclaimed Ernest, "that 's strange! Only yesterday I was thinking of that girl! She came into my head, I can't tell why, and I kept thinking and thinking of her."

"She came into your head," said Renny, "because Molly reminded you of her. And she well might, for she is Chris Dayborn's daughter."

Nicholas struggled in his chair. "Help me up out of here!" he demanded.

Renny went behind him and heaved him to his feet. Very lame from gout, he stumped about the room, a gray lock falling over his forehead.

"Well, well," he said. "Hmph, well. I see it all. What a fix! What a fix to be in!"

Ernest was chagrined. Usually it was he who had to explain things to Nick.

"I don't understand," he said. "What has all this to do with Mr. Griffith's death?"

"That 's just the point," said Renny. "It has nothing at all to do with it."

"You silly old fool," said Nicholas to his brother, "don't you realize that this child, Molly, is Renny's daughter? And that consequently she and Wake can't marry?"

Ernest sat bewildered, biting his thumb. Then his brow cleared. Then it darkened, and he exclaimed: —

"Those poor children! Those poor children!"

"Yes," said Renny. "That 's why Wake and I look — as we do. It 's been a blow."

"How did you find it out?"

"Just one thing after another. I was suspicious. Then I made certain."

"You must never let Alayne know this," said Ernest.

"She does know it."

"Good God!" said Nicholas. "How did she find out?"

"I had to tell her."

"You were a fool to do that."

"No. It was necessary. She was splendid." The color deepened in his weatherbeaten face. "I 've done nothing to deserve such a wife."

Nicholas blew out his cheeks. "It 's unfortunate. But after all, your affair with Mrs. Dayborn took place five years before you met Alayne. There 's no reason why Alayne should feel herself deeply injured."

"God, if ever a man's pigeons came home to roost, mine have!"

"It 's a blow for Wakefield," said Ernest.

Nicholas returned — "He 'll get over it. He 'll go to

the war and forget her. And, after all, he ought to make a far better match, with his looks and talents."

"He's deeply in love. I've been impressed by that from the first. Dear me, it was strange how that Dayborn girl came into my mind yesterday! I could n't forget her."

"And she's just died, has she?" asked Nicholas, suddenly confused.

"Good heavens, Nick! She died years ago. It is Molly's stepfather who has just died."

"Of course, of course, I know that. . . . Shall you tell Piers and Meg of this, Renny?"

"Never! But I thought you ought to know. I thought you might have a talk with Wake, Uncle Ernie. You might say something to cheer him up. And Uncle Nick might have a little talk with Alayne."

"I will. I will."

Renny looked at his wrist watch. "I'm meeting a man in the stables. I'm late."

Rags, in the hall, swiftly removed his ear from the keyhole and straightened himself. He felt a sharp pain in the small of the back.

"Cripes," he thought, in consternation, "am I getting some bloomin' kidney disorder? Maybe I shall never get to the Front with the boss!"

But his face was composed as Renny passed him and went out by the side door. What he had overheard was no great surprise to him. He had been in that house for twenty years and he was an adept in the art of human relationships. He had known that Renny and Chris Dayborn were lovers.

He thought he would go to the kitchen and make himself a pot of tea. That would buck him up. Probably there was n't much wrong with him. He'd had a crick in the back from bending forward so long. Overburdened as his mind was, he paused on his way to the basement stairs to set a Benares brass casket that old Adeline had brought from India cornerwise on the chest where it stood.

On the way to the stables Renny felt a small mittened hand pushed into his. He looked down into Adeline's face. She said rather breathlessly: —

"You know that nonsense Archer had got into his head, Daddy! Well, I think I've made him forget it. Every time he begins I put him on his back and tickle him. Now it's a game. Archer begins — 'Do you know what I saw through the window?' Then he stares at me and waits for a romp."

She laughed a little but her eyes were grave as she looked up into his face. She seemed to be trying to say — "Whatever you've done, I'm always on your side."

"Good," he said. "Archie's at a funny stage but you understand him, don't you?"

She held his hand for an instant against her cheek. High overhead, in the crystal air, an aeroplane was passing like a silver dragonfly.

"I used to like to look at the planes," Adeline said, "but now they make me think of war and you going away. I wish you were n't, or that I could go with you."

XXIX

NEW TENANTS FOR THE FOX FARM

WAKEFIELD and Molly stood at the barrier watching the arrivals from the New York train. They were waiting for her three stepsisters, whose passage had been arranged for by a succession of cablegrams. Finch was accompanying them. He was to give a series of recitals in America and it had seemed expedient that they should travel under his protection.

Wakefield and Molly stood shoulder to shoulder, so accustomed to each other, so intimate in the quick interchange of feeling, yet separated by a barrier that made them as strangers. They were like two ships sailing side by side yet glimpsing each other through the distortions of an iceberg that had risen from the deep to separate them. Every now and again a tremor ran over her.

" Are you cold? " he asked, not looking at her.

" No. Just excited."

" The train is late."

" Yes, it seems to be."

This was their third meeting since their relationship had been disclosed to them. The first had been in the living room of Ernest's house. At the second he had taken her to the small apartment in town where she had found temporary war work. In that meeting they had been bewildered, not daring to look in each other's eyes for fear of breaking down. Alone for a moment they had broken down and wept in each other's arms. Then he had hurried from the apartment and left her alone.

In the weeks that followed they had gained an uncertain self-control, the balance to be kept only by calculated coldness. But each had receded from the other. The charm and spontaneity of speech was gone from them. The warmth and candor of glance was no more. Love was turned to bitter and hopeless longing. They stood shoulder to shoulder waiting for the train with nothing to say but commonplaces.

She should not have let him come with her, she thought. Why had he offered to come? His presence was a torture. She looked sidewise at his stern, dark profile, the bitter bend of his lips, and wondered if this were indeed her young lover.

Sarah's voice came to them from behind. She was gliding toward them, dressed in gray fur and followed by Meg.

"It 's a good thing the train is late," she said, "or we should have kept them waiting. Meg was so annoyed. But then I 'm always late."

She looked sharply into their faces. "How wan you two are! But stations always make people look dreadful. I believe I 'll go out and wait in the car. I don't want Finch to think I 've lost all my looks."

"You look all right," said Wakefield, shortly. He made room for her between him and Molly.

Meg came to his other side and squeezed his arm. "Is n't it lovely to think Finch is coming?" she exclaimed, and added in a whisper, "But I suppose we shall scarcely have a word with him. Sarah is so possessive. Still, we can look at him!"

"There they come!" said Wakefield.

They were among the last of the passengers to appear and they made an arresting group. Even to Molly, who was accustomed to the oddities of her stepsisters, they looked strange in this new setting. To Meg they were strange and touching. To Sarah they were bizarre and a little ridiculous. She gave them an amused smile, then flew to Finch's arms. He clasped her to him, in her scented fur, and felt a dizzy joy mingled with foreboding.

"Darling!" she breathed. "What I 've gone through, with you on the sea! Every night I 've woken, picturing your ship sunk by a submarine! How well you look! Not a bit as though you 'd been worried. Yet think what I've been through since we parted! It 's a wonder I 'm here to meet you."

She clung to his arm, deliberately placing herself between him and his brother and sister.

Meg had almost forgotten Finch in her interest in the three sisters. Finch had led the way with Garda at his side. She was wearing a black bonnet-like cap tied under her chin and beneath it her thick dark hair hung down to her shoulders. She wore a heavy black coat and was weighted with bags and parcels. Out of this sombre attire her round child's face stared, rosy as an apple. She looked surprised at everything and held her mouth as though about to whistle. When she saw Molly, tears began to run out of her eyes.

Gemmel was being carried by a Negro train porter and a red-capped station porter. She too was in black but a feather hung from the brim of her velvet hat. She clung to the men's necks and her pointed features were still more sharpened by anxiety. She too began to cry when Molly appeared.

Althea came last, wearing an old-fashioned fur-trimmed cloak that had been her mother's. Her fairness was so accentuated as to be ethereal and the expression of her face was as remote as when Wakefield had first seen her on the mountainside in Wales. She too carried a number of parcels and a traveling rug for Gemmel.

To Molly their coming signified the breaking up of her old life. So long as she had been able to picture her family in Wales she had felt a certain solidity in her background. The fact that they had been uprooted had added to the distress of the past weeks. But even while they were tossing on the dangerous waves of the ocean she had not quite brought herself to believe in the upheaval. The picture in her mind, that picture of the dark Welsh hills, was still firm. She saw Christopher walking near the ruined Abbey with his sheep, Althea painting her strange harsh pictures and hiding from the outside world, Gemmel and Garda always about the house.

But now she saw them in this new land and she felt in truth that her world was shattered.

She sat with Althea and Garda in the rear seat of the car. Gemmel sat beside Wakefield, who drove. Molly could find no words. Her throat might have been paralyzed. She sat rigid, holding the hand of a stepsister on either side, her eyes fixed on Wakefield. How he had changed! He did not look like the same boy, she thought. Just that glimpse of the cheek, the compressed lips, the eyes fixed straight ahead, was enough to prove how he too was suffering. It was wrong of him to come! He should have sent someone else to drive the car, not subjected the two of them to this torture of hopeless nearness. The car skidded a little and she thought — "I wish we might have an accident and I be thrown into his arms and die there. It would be over and done with and I should be glad."

She thought of Renny with sudden fierce anger. It was his fault. He had done this to them. If he had kept his secret to himself what would it have mattered! Time and again she had remarked his paternal attitude toward his brothers. That fatherliness was one of his strongest characteristics, she thought. Yet she had seen not a sign of it toward herself and he had roused no feeling of a daughter from her. They were man and woman, connected by a tragic bond. That was all.

Blindly she saw the town left behind, saw the gray foam-flecked lake, the winter woods, the frozen fields. She heard Gemmel raining questions on Wakefield. She was thankful that the two beside her did not want to talk. Blindly she helped to carry the parcels into the house. She and Wakefield gripped hands and carried Gemmel up the slippery steps and put her down in the warm living room.

"How lovely!" cried Gemmel.

"Oh, I 'm so glad to be here!" cried Garda.

"Anything more you want?" asked Wakefield.

"Nothing more. . . . You 've been so kind. . . . Thank you. . . . Good-bye . . . good-bye."

An hour later, in their bedroom, Gemmel said to Garda: —

"I knew Molly would feel badly about Father but I 'd no idea how badly. Did you ever see anyone cry so? I thought she 'd die of her grief."

XXX

FINCH AT HOME AGAIN

THE scene in the car which carried Meg, Sarah, and Finch was very different. Maurice too was there, in the driver's seat. During most of the drive he played the part of listener but the two women talked ceaselessly, pouring out the news to Finch and asking him a thousand questions. Finch too was eager and excited, glad to be home again after a considerable absence. Everything his eye rested on came to him with the brightness of familiarity. The scene seemed to offer itself for inspection and approval. The country seemed to say — "War has not really touched me yet. I 'm young and unhurt." His eyes rested on lake, on fields; now on Sarah's face, now on Meg's.

When they passed the gates of Jalna he wished he might have alighted from the car and gone into the house alone. He craned his neck to have a good view of it. There was not a soul in sight, not even horse or dog or circling pigeons. The house looked very quiet and a little remote.

When they reached Vaughanlands, Sarah almost dragged him out of the car.

"Hurry! Hurry!" she exclaimed. "Baby is dying to meet his papa!"

Baby's papa felt suddenly shy. He was afraid he would not be enthusiastic enough to please Sarah. He stood with Maurice, inspecting a new collie.

"You think more of that dog than you do of your own son!" cried Sarah angrily.

Finch laughed. "Very well, show me the prodigy." He followed her into the house.

Meg had already hurried upstairs as fast as her increasing

weight would allow. She appeared on the landing, the infant in her arms. Sarah had him dressed in old-fashioned long robes, a mass of frills and fine tucks. He was pink-faced and fair.

"There!" cried Sarah delightedly. "Did n't I tell you? He 's the image of you!"

"Poor little devil," said Finch. Gingerly he bent and kissed the tiny face. He sniffed the scent of talcum and warm flannel.

"He 's nice," he said. "What did you say his name is?"

Meg gave him a warning look. He would have the girl in hysterics. "You 're impossible, Finch. You know quite well what his name is. Dennis Finch."

Finch's sensitive ear was afflicted. "The two don't go well together," he said, and he pronounced the name grievously, dwelling on the hissing sounds.

"I know," said Sarah, "but he had to have both names. Names of the only two men I 've loved."

The only two! Finch thought of his dead friend, Arthur Leigh, her first husband, and of how he had loved Sarah. How could she be so cold to his memory! She read his thoughts.

"I don't care," she said. "It 's true. It 's true. It 's true."

"Well, I loved him, anyway," said Finch, "and I shall never forget him. I 'd like to call the baby Dennis Arthur. Is he christened yet?"

"My God, no!" cried Sarah. "Do you think I would have him christened before you came? Everything is waiting for you and you spoil it all!"

"Now, you two must n't quarrel," said Meg. "It 's disgraceful at a moment like this. Sarah is quite right about the names. Arthur would n't be at all appropriate."

"I want it," said Finch stubbornly.

" Have it then! Have everything your own way. Oh, I have lived for this day! I have planned for it — dreamed of it! " She almost screamed these words, then went to her room and slammed the door behind her.

" Now you 've upset her," said Meg, patting the baby's back. " She 's a terribly difficult girl."

Finch fingered his son's finery. " I 'll bet I was never decked out like this," he said.

" No. You wore Piers's old baby-clothes. Now go and make it up with Sarah."

" I don't want to. I want to stay with you." Like a boy he rubbed his cheek against her shoulder. The baby stared up at them out of opaque eyes.

This was just what Meg liked — to have one of her brothers clinging to her, in spite of his wife. Now that she came to think of it, she believed she hated all their wives. She cast Dennis Finch, or Dennis Arthur, or whatever his name was, on to the bed in the spare room and clasped Finch to her deep bosom.

" You are a naughty boy! " she said.

An infantile love for Meg welled up in him. He wanted to lie on her bosom, as the baby had done. He wanted to toddle by her side holding to her skirt. He wanted her to pay no attention to anyone but him. He stood rubbing his cheek against her shoulder while she brooded over him.

At last she pushed him away. " Now go and make it up with Sarah. I must take baby back to his cot and then see about lunch. I have a Swedish maid and I smell something burning."

" I 'll look after the baby. I 'll carry him to Sarah."

" That 's a good idea. Oh, how nice it is to have you back! All four brothers at home. If only Eden were here! Do you know, Finch, I can sometimes see him as he was at the last, leaning over the banister in that light blue dressing gown, watching me bring an eggnog up to him. He was so weak he 'd lean hard on the banister — and that look in his eyes! But he 'd smile." Tears choked her.

"I remember."

Why should she recall Eden at this moment! Finch pushed the thought of Eden from him when Meg left him. He refused to let the thought of death touch him. He stood motionless in the passage between his wife and his son, undecided what to do. Obscure physical feelings pressed in on him from both directions. What should he do next? Go to Sarah and try to reëstablish their old relations or make them over, if possible, into something new? Go to that mysterious being in the spare room who seemed to be lying there sardonically viewing the parents that had given him life? It was settled for him by the sound of Sarah's footsteps coming toward the door. He darted into the room with the child and knelt by the bed.

She came and looked in. She was one of those rare women who can make a scene, weep or scream, and immediately afterward look as smooth as a cat.

Full of self-protective duplicity, Finch knelt by the baby, gazing into its pink face.

"He 's a miracle," he said.

"Then you really love him?"

"He 's yours and mine. Is n't that enough?"

"Then why were you so detached when you first saw him? You asked his name and if he were christened, as though he were a stranger's child."

"Everything went out of my head. I felt bewildered. It was all so new and strange."

He thought — "I 'm acting. I 'm insincere. But I can't help it. Something new has got to come out of this."

She knelt beside him. She was radiant. He saw how easy it was for her to forgive him — if only he would worship at her new shrine.

"You adore him, don't you, Sarah?"

"I 'm like a tigress with her young." She laughed but she was in earnest.

"And I am nothing but the poor old tiger now, eh, Sarah?"

She gave him an absent-minded caress. "See his hands. He 'll play the piano too, with such hands. Do you really want to add Arthur to his names?"

"Not if you don't."

"I agree. Dennis Arthur Finch. I really believe it 's more euphonious."

Lunch was over before Finch set out for Jalna. It had snowed all the night before and that morning the wind blew, heaping the snow in drifts. The walk would be too much for Sarah. A cap on his head and a muffler round his neck, Finch ran through the drifts across the lawn, leaped the fence, and found the path to Jalna.

He saw smoke rising from the chimney of the fox farm. The girls were settling in. He thought of the four of them, each so different from the others! He had got to know Gemmel and Garda very well on the voyage but Althea remained a mystery. He had not exchanged a dozen remarks with her. She had so openly avoided him that he might well have taken offense, but she was like that with everyone, outside the family, her sisters said. He liked the thought of them in that house. He would go to see them with Wakefield or by himself.

Boyhood reached out to him from the snowy wood where pine needles lay scattered on the drifts. He felt almost miraculously isolated and free. In a sense he was more bound than ever, being the father of a child, yet he had a perverse, wild sense of freedom. Something had happened to him, had given a fresh glow to his day. The air through the pine trees was vibrant with this something. What had the child given him? Somehow it had given him freedom, he was persuaded of that. Sarah's eyes had not that possessive look in them. Her attention was riveted on the child — a tigress with her young! Journeying toward her he had been filled with the same desolate fancies which her approaching nearness always brought, a sense of frightening loneliness. But now her emotions were focused on the child! Freedom ran through his thoughts like a wind through shocks of ruffled wheat. He hugged it to him like a fairy bride.

The snow was deep in the ravine and, as Renny one day had done, he struggled through it and up the other side. He found Wakefield waiting for him.

"I saw you coming," he said.

Finch glanced at him sharply. Wake looked like a stranger, he thought. He had always envied Wakefield the light heart he carried but now he saw him as a man with bitterness in his breast. And a pale stoicism was in his face as though he had made up his mind to suffer no more.

"Why —" stammered Finch — "what 's the matter, Wake? You 've something bad to tell me!"

"Bad enough. I can't marry Molly."

After he had spoken he stood with downcast eyes, looking at the snow. The wind swung round to the north and blew a cloud of powdery snow over them. The sun, which had been but well on its way up the heavens, was already beginning to decline. Finch put his arm about his brother's shoulders and drew him along the path.

"What happened?" he asked.

Wakefield gave a harsh laugh.

"You ask me as though I could tell it all in a sentence! Well, I guess I have told it all. We can't marry. That 's enough for me."

"But why? For God's sake, tell me why, Wake."

Wakefield raised his eyes to Finch's face. "I ought n't to tell you this, I suppose. But I can't help it. Remember, it 's to go no further."

"No need to tell me that."

"We can't marry because Renny is Molly's father. Her mother was an Englishwoman — a Mrs. Dayborn — who helped school the horses at Jalna after the last war."

Finch stood facing the wind, unable for a moment to realize the import of this statement. As Wakefield's face was cold and set, Finch's broke up into compassion and dismay. It was like touching something that had no feeling, to tighten his hand on Wake's arm.

"Are you sure?" he asked.

"Yes. We 're all sure — those of us who know of it. There 's no use in your getting upset, Finch. The marriage is off. We 've got to make a new life for ourselves. But at this moment the thing I most want to do is to go overseas and be killed."

It was characteristic of Finch and a certain comfort to Wakefield that he asked no questions. He accepted the tragic truth about Molly's parentage as something from the passionate past of their eldest brother which neither of them could make clear or change by a thousand questions and answers. He recalled certain remarks of Eden's concerning an attachment between Renny and a girl who could do anything with a horse. He recalled how, on the night of his recital, when they were seated at a table in the restaurant, he had suddenly thought — "Why, Molly Griffith carries her head as Renny does, and her hair grows in a point like his!" He had been going to remark this but something had interrupted him. Now he said: —

"This is awful for you, Wake. . . . I wondered what was wrong but I never dreamed of anything so . . . so devastating. I don't know what to say . . . I wish I could help you. I can see what it 's done to you. What does Renny feel?"

"Oh, he 's sorry."

"Sorry! I should think you 'd almost hate him."

"I do."

"There's one thing, Wake. You have your belief. Your religion. You're not like a fellow who has nothing spiritual for ballast."

"I have nothing spiritual for ballast."

Finch broke out excitedly, "But, look here, you can't do that! You can't throw aside your faith just when you need it more than you ever have! Now is your priest's chance to help you. Go to him."

"I have been and it's no use. He was kind. He could n't have been kinder. But something inside me has gone hard and cold."

"That will change."

"I hope so."

"Can you depend on him to keep it quiet?"

Wake opened his eyes and stared at Finch. "He is less likely to tell it than I."

"How many know of it? At Jalna, I mean."

"Besides we three principals" — Wake gave a short laugh — "only Alayne and the uncles. They've been very kind. Especially Uncle Ernest. . . . Oh, I shall get over it, I suppose, but — just now — I want — what I said."

They turned at the sharp crunch of footsteps in the snow and saw Renny approaching, followed by Merlin. The blind spaniel recognized Finch and jumped joyously about him but he was stiff from rheumatism.

Renny's weatherbeaten face now showed little sign of the stress and strain he had been through. Its decisive aquiline contours, its high coloring, gave it a kind of invincible sanguineness. He kissed Finch and exclaimed: —

"Hello! Back again! Well, it's good to see you. You look well."

He cast a quick glance from one brother to the other, obviously wondering what Finch thought of Wakefield's changed looks and whether Wakefield had told him of the broken engagement.

Finch colored under the glance but Wakefield was impassive. His eyes were fixed on a gap in the evergreens where, beyond the stables, he could see the snowy fields, fold upon fold, in white drifts. Renny put a hand on an arm of each and drew them toward the house.

"Come along in," he urged, "the uncles are wanting to see you."

Wakefield frowned and turned himself away. A strange antagonism filled him at the touch of Renny's hand but Finch moved obediently at his elder's side. They heard a shout and Piers came running toward them.

"Hi!" he shouted. "Wait for me!"

When he saw that they waited he slackened his steps and marched toward them with a military step. Finch was startled to see that he was in uniform. "He looks more than ever like Grandfather," he thought. After shaking hands he said: —

"I did n't know you were in training, Piers."

"I have been, all the fall and winter."

"Home Guard," put in Renny tersely.

"Home Guard be damned!" said Piers. "I 'm leaving for England in a fortnight."

Renny could scarcely have looked more astonished if one of the pines in the ravine had lifted its roots and declared its intention of going to the war.

"But you can't!" he exclaimed.

Piers opened his eyes wide. "I should like to know why!"

"Who will look after Jalna?"

Piers's eyes became still more prominent. "Why should I be the one?"

"You always have stayed at home."

"I know I have. I 've stayed at home while the rest of you have gone out and done things. But — there 's a war on now! And I 'm going to be first on the scene! Of course, it would have been a very nice arrangement for you to go off like a conqueror with Rags at your heels — Wake and Paris to get their wings and drop bombs on Berlin — Finch to do some sort of war work in London — and I wait here till I fight the Germans on the doorstep of Jalna! Thanks for nothing! I 'm leaving with the next contingent!"

Renny's face changed. He stood speechless, grinning at Piers's pugnacity. Piers wheeled, turned, tramped up and down in the snow. He looked fine in his uniform. The window of the sitting room was thrown up and Ernest called out: —

"What 's all the excitement about? Come, Piers, and show yourself! Finch, my boy, your Uncle Nick and I are waiting to see you."

XXXI

LEAVE-TAKINGS

It was a time of such upheaval at Jalna that Piers's going overseas was not such a shock to the household as might have been feared. It was not till he had actually departed that the full force of the blow was felt. Then it really was a blow. His going was so sudden, so inexorable, that nothing that might follow seemed impossible. Sometimes in the minds of the old uncles and Meg and Pheasant and Alayne, one disaster after another loomed as probable.

There had been so much to do before Piers sailed that there was little time for reflection. He was here, there, and everywhere, talking over the care of orchards and farmlands with his men, arranging for the future of his wife and sons in the event of his not returning, making his will — though he had little enough to leave. A family dinner party was given for him, the night before he left, at which he got drunk and made a very good speech.

Then suddenly he was gone! It was as though the sound of a bugle had died. It was as though there were a palpable rent in the fabric of Jalna. Whoever came or went, Piers had always been there. With his complexion as fresh as a spring morning, his eyes as blue as June skies, with the hardness of winter in his back and sinews, he had strode over the land throughout the seasons.

His uncles had placed him, in his uniform, beneath the portrait of his grandfather in *his* uniform. Piers's health had been drunk, he had been wished Godspeed and been full of pride. Whiteoaks had gone out to fight for England throughout the centuries and why not he?

But Pheasant walked the little empty house alone, wringing her hands, when he had gone. Mooey had been taken to Ireland. Piers had gone to the war. Would she ever again see either of them? The two sons left to her seemed small and weak and remote. Three times she had been brought to bed with Piers's sons. Now he was gone!

She folded his civilian clothes and laid them away. What a pity he had bought that last suit! He could well have done without it and she had been against buying it, but he would have it. Now here it was, still retaining the roundness of his body. And he was gone! She knelt beside the drawer where she had laid it, shaken by sobs.

The next to leave were Renny and Rags. It was now the first of March. Renny had so recently been in England that it seemed as though he were merely making another visit. The name of Johnny the Bird once more appeared in conversation. The Vaughans and Pheasant and her boys spent much of their time at Jalna. Like their mother, the uncles wanted the young people about them. Alayne lived in a kind of dream. She had felt strangely moved in the parting with Piers. Now in this leave-taking with her heart of hearts she felt dreamlike and almost detached. She did not think "He will come back" or "He will not come back." Her mind was not capable of such surmise. She only noticed the little things about him she had always loved. She could scarcely take her eyes off him. The passion of her earliest love for him tormented her, yet it was the passion of a dream.

On his part he felt a constant gratitude toward her for the way she had borne the news of Molly's parentage. Things might have been so bad between them but they were in truth happier than ever. He would sit beside her, holding her hand in his strong fingers, giving her directions as to what should be done in the stables about this or that, in certain eventualities — just as though she understood.

It was the first time he had ever talked to her of his horses in that earnest familiar way, as though he were confident of her understanding and sympathizing. She knew that, in doing this, he was showing his gratitude to her, throwing open that door of his other life. She was touched. But then — everything he did in these days touched her. There seemed a pathos and finality in all his acts, as though they were last rites before a sacrifice. Sometimes she felt like crying out that he ought not to leave her. He had fought in one war. His brothers were to fight in this. Let that be enough. Sometimes she was almost angered by the loyalty of this young country to the Motherland. Why should all these men be in training for a war in Europe? It might be better, she thought, if there were more hardheaded materialism and less idealism of a bygone generation. But there were other times when she too was carried on the tide and felt herself heart and soul in the struggle.

She talked to him of the children and, for the first time, confessed that she was disappointed in Archer. He had been such a wonderful baby with that noble forehead and that profound look in his eyes which so reminded her of her father. He had been so gentle, showed a thoughtful mind and a touching dignity. But now at five he showed neither ordinary common sense nor dignity. Nothing she could say *shamed* him. He was utterly absorbed in his own ignoble activities and had no real love for anyone. Tears filled her eyes.

Renny threw back his head and laughed.

"Ashamed of Archie! That 's nonsense. He 's a queer egg, but he 'll come through. He 'll go into business and retrieve the family fortunes. I promise you."

Before he left he gave Archer his first pony and the little fellow bestrode it with no more fear and no more pleasure than he showed toward his tricycle. He just sat there while the groom led the pony about the paddock looking as though the weight of the world lay on his brow, but Renny noted with pride that he had good hands on the reins and a good leg in the stirrup.

Renny had not seen Molly since she and her sisters had moved into the fox farm. She was taking the train to the town each day to her war work and on her return kept to the house for fear of meeting either him or Wakefield. But he felt that he must speak to her once again before leaving. He wanted to make sure that the girls were comfortably settled in.

On his last Saturday afternoon he went to the fox farm, thinking on this day he would find her in. But he went reluctantly, for he dreaded meeting her. He drank in the pure air and filled his eyes with the sight of the trees, ice-sheathed after a wild storm. He thought he would like to carry this picture away with him.

It was the first week in March but the countryside was ice-bound. There was a feeling of brittle restraint in the air. He had that same feeling in himself and his spirit strained to the time when he would break through and enter what lay ahead of him. A deep sensuous urge to see Johnny the Bird welled up in him. He wanted to win the Grand National with that horse. Perhaps the great race might not again be run for years but it was to be run this spring and Johnny the Bird must win it! He was not going into this war as he had gone into the last — fired by the spirit of careless adventure. Then he had gone, leaving his father as master of Jalna, with no special responsibilities of his own. Now he had wife and children, the uncles were old and depended on him. The thought of the race rose like a bright beacon above the sea of uncertainty and turmoil.

The girls heard the ring at the door. There were just three of them in the house for Molly had had to do extra work that afternoon and was not yet home. They had heard no step and were in a panic.

"Peep out between the curtains, Garda," whispered Gemmel, "and see who it is."

Garda tiptoed into the sitting room and back again.

"It 's the eldest Whiteoak," she whispered. "It 's Renny."

"Go and let him in. Talk to him. Find out what he is like. I 'd love to know. I can see that Molly hates him. I believe he has something to do with her engagement being broken."

Garda flushed crimson. "I 'd not dare."

"Then you go, Althea."

"Nothing would tempt me. He may knock all day, as far as I 'm concerned. Draw the curtains, Garda. He might walk round the house."

The curtains were drawn. Instead of the bell, there now came a knock on the door.

Garda began to laugh.

"Ssh!" ordered Althea sternly. "He must n't hear a sound."

"I have a mind to go to the door myself," whispered Gemmel. "If I were like you girls, I 'd go and talk to him. I think he 's wonderful."

"Oh, if only Molly would come!" said Althea. "Crouch down, he 's coming round the house!"

They heard his steps crunching the snow. They glimpsed him through the crack of the curtains. That house was so familiar to him, so full of the associations of his friendship with Clara Lebraux, that, even with strangers in it, he could scarcely feel an outsider.

Garda saw his brown eye peering through the chink in the curtains. She hid her face in her arm and shook with frightened laughter.

"Is the girl mad?" he thought. "And what sort of scene are they having in there?" He moved away from the window but he did not go.

"He heard you laughing! He saw us!" exclaimed Althea, in a voice of pain. "I must go to the door." She rose with dignity and went to the door. She could hear

Gemmel slyly following her on hands and thighs. That soft shuffle had followed her all her life. The agonizing shyness that cut her off from other people she now wore like a visible cloak as she faced Renny. He was struck by her ethereal beauty. He had not before been close to her.

"Good afternoon," he said. "I hope I have n't disturbed you. Is Molly at home?"

She shook her head.

"Do you expect her soon?"

Again she shook her head.

"Well, I 'm leaving on Monday for England. I wanted to say good-bye to her. And I wanted to know if you are quite comfortable here, and if there 's anything I can do for you before I go."

He looked at her inquiringly, with a puzzled, half-amused scrutiny. She knew she would have to speak but she could not. She heard Gemmel just inside the door of the sitting room. She fled to her, her hand to her mouth.

"Go to him," she said. "Tell him we want nothing."

Renny heard what she said. "Just as though I were a peddler," he thought, and his face was lit by a grim smile when Gemmel appeared. He looked down at her and said:—

"I 'm afraid I 've disturbed you but I 'd like to know if you 're quite comfortable before I go away."

She smiled up from under her tumbled dark hair. He saw her supple hands flat on the floor. She answered:—

"I don't know. I think we are. You 'll have to ask Molly."

"Shall I come in and wait for her?"

"Yes. Come right in."

She turned her body about and led the way. He could hear her sister's swift escape from the room.

"She 's shy," said Gemmel, looking after her.

"Yes, I have noticed that," he answered gravely.

"Garda is, too, but her shyness runs to giggles."

"It 's quite an affliction for a girl."

"Yes. I am afflicted but — not in that way." There was malice in her smile. Then she added — "I don't want you to think I 'd be other than — what I am."

"I admire you for that."

"My courage, you mean?"

"No. Your accepting of things as they are. Most people are dissatisfied if — they can't have everything. Do you like the house?"

"I love it. For my part I 'm glad there 's a war. Otherwise I 'd never have come out here. For one thing the floors are n't as cold here as they were at home. There they were mostly stone."

"Shall I lift you to the sofa?" He spoke with solicitude but no embarrassment.

At the same moment the front door opened.

"Yes, yes," said Gemmel, "lift me."

He took her in his arms and set her on the sofa.

"How strong you are!" She clung an instant to his shoulder, smiling at Molly, who now came into the room.

Molly looked very thin and pale. The freckles stood out beneath her eyes like golden flecks. She had the self-possession of the actress but the hand she put into his trembled. He repeated his anxiety for their well-being.

"Thanks," she answered. "It 's lovely here. We 've everything we need. Thanks for the baskets of apples and pears and all the vegetables. You all have been so kind."

"My wife," he said, "is coming to see you, when she gets me off her hands."

"Mrs. Vaughan and Mrs. Piers have been. They were very kind. Can you stay to tea?"

"Thanks, but I have a thousand things to do."

He asked her about her work, half absent-mindedly,

while his eyes took in the complications of her resemblance to Chris and to himself. Gemmel now sat silent like a child, her curious glance moving from one face to the other. When Renny left, Molly went with him to the verandah. They dropped their guarded looks then and he exclaimed: —

"Oh, my dear, I'd give my right hand not to have done what I have!"

She gave a little ironic smile. "If you had n't done — what you did — I suppose I should never have been born." Then she added, with a break in her voice — "I wish I had n't!"

"Don't say that! You have a good chance of a happy life ahead of you. You're just beginning."

"I think," she said slowly, "that I'm sorrier for Wake than I am for myself. It's been very hard on him."

"Yes, it has been hard on him. But he has the future ahead of him — just as you have. You know, when I was a boy — a few years younger than Wake — I wanted most terribly to marry a girl named Vera Lacey. But I could n't."

She gave him a disbelieving look. "Did you love her as much as Wake loves me, do you think?"

"No, I'm sure I did n't. This has been a heartbreaking affair for both of you. And it has for me, too."

"Christopher is my greatest hope now," she said. "If only he is spared! When the spring comes I want to go to England to be near him. My sisters will be quite happy here."

"That was an odd little one I was talking to."

"She's selfish and she's self-centred but I love her."

They stood silent, not knowing how to say good-bye. Neither was moved by paternal or filial emotion. They were just man and woman. He looked at his wrist watch and exclaimed: —

"I must be off! Good-bye, my dear." He hesitated,

then took her hand and raised it to his lips. "Try to forgive me!"

She returned to the room where her stepsisters were waiting. The three broke into a babel of talk. They told how they had kept him out, how they had been forced to let him in, their impressions of him. Althea's voice rose highest of all. She almost screamed in her excitement. Their voices beat about Molly. Althea had been so silly — Gemmel had been so bold — Garda had laughed till she cried. Just look at her wet eyes! How strong Renny Whiteoak was! Why, Gemmel's weight was nothing to him! He smelt of horses! Ugh — how he smelt of horses! He was handsome — far handsomer than Wakefield. He was n't handsome at all — only striking. Was there ever such an interesting family? What a pity Molly's engagement was broken off! But perhaps they would all find husbands out here. "Even me!" Gemmel covered her face with her hands and broke into peals of laughter. She had more charm than any of them, she declared.

Monday came and a gale of wind that made the shutters creak on their hinges and the mares' tails fly as they galloped about the paddock. All was bustle. The Vaughans were there. Pheasant and her boys were there. Finch, Sarah, and their child. It was his first day at Jalna. Rags wore himself out running up and down the basement stairs. Mrs. Wragge cried quarts, but still managed to cook a good lunch.

Nicholas drew Renny aside in the sitting room, Merlin close at their heels. Nicholas spoke with a great effort.

"I wanted to speak about the old dog," he said. "He 's rheumatic, you know. If he gets worse — so he can't enjoy his life — what had I better do, eh? Have him put out of the way?"

Renny took Merlin by his forepaws and stood him up.

"Merlin has promised me," he said, "to keep well till I come back."

Merlin lifted his lip in the sentimental, spaniel's smile.

"But," persisted Nicholas, "what if he does n't keep that promise! What shall I do?"

"He 'll keep it," said Renny shortly, and turned away.

The car was at the door. Alayne and Adeline were going to the station with him. Everyone was crowded into the hall. Renny shook hands with his brother-in-law.

"Lord," said Maurice, "I wish I were going with you!" But he had been disabled in the last war.

"Good-bye, Meggie!"

She burst into tears and clung to him.

"Well, I 'm ashamed of you, Meg! The Whiteoaks have always been soldiers. What would you have?"

One after the other he said good-bye to them, kissing the women and children, wringing his uncles' hands. Their voices were a bit quavering. But they told him they would carry on and not to stay away too long.

Wakefield stood in the background. Renny went to him swiftly. He took his hand and kissed him. Compassion and self-reproach were in his glance. But Wakefield kept his eyes downcast.

Archer was riding his tricycle round and round at the far end of the hall. The last moment had come. Alayne flew to him and dragged him from the saddle. She held him up in front of Renny.

"Daddy 's going now. Look at him hard. You must remember just what he 's like."

"I know just what he 's like," said Archer, wriggling so that his jersey came up round his ears.

"But he 's going to the war! You must say good-bye to him properly."

"Good-bye," said Archer, laconically. Then he made a hideous, snorting sound. "I 'm an armored tank," he said. "Put me down."

Renny snatched him from Alayne and covered his face with kisses. After several beginnings and withdrawings, Archer's rare smile overspread his face and he deigned to pat his father's cheek.

"Good-bye, Daddy," he said. "Don't get killed too soon."

Renny set him down on his tricycle and he pedaled off without looking back.

"Hurry up," shouted Finch. "You 'll miss your train!"

Renny, Alayne, and Adeline were in the back seat together. Rags sat in the front with Finch, who drove the car. Everyone came out into the snow to see them off. The western sky was glowing red. There was a softness to the snow, and a strange, flapping wildness to the wind. It was the flapping of the flag of spring. Renny craned his neck to see the group on the steps, to catch a last glimpse of the stables. Then he settled back in his seat and smiled into Alayne's face. She smiled back. They said little but they encouraged Adeline to talk — Alayne clung fiercely to every flying moment, wondered how she would face the moment of farewell. But when it came it was not so painful as she had expected. The station platform was crowded with men in uniform, their wives and sweethearts and sisters. There was a mother clinging to the hand of her son! There was a baby held in its father's arms, a press photographer taking a picture of them! Everyone's features looked sharpened and pale in the lights of the station. She smelled train oil, boot polish, and the queer woolly, harsh scent of the men's uniforms. Her man had become just one of the others. She was just another wife. Adeline another child. There was jostling, joking, the ringing of a bell.

There were things she wanted to say to Renny but she could not remember what they were. Another man in officer's uniform came up and spoke to him. He wore the uniform of the 48th Highlanders. He was tall and strong and looked fine in his bonnet and kilt. There was his wife, a dumpy little woman, and two half-grown boys. Renny was about to introduce them to Alayne when the train drew in. Then how quickly it was all over! There was more jostling, more laughing and shouting.

"Good-bye!"

"See you later!"

"Fire a shot for me, Bill!"

"Give Hitler a kick behind for me!"

She felt herself gripped in his arms, felt his lips pressed to hers, saw Adeline lifted up and kissed.

"Good-bye, ma'am," from Rags. "I 'ope all will go well at Jalna."

"Good-bye, Wragge."

"Good-bye, miss. Don't you forget old Rags."

Decorously Adeline gave him her hand. "Good-bye, Rags. And God bless you."

"Thank you, miss."

"Good-bye, Daddy. God bless you!"

"Good-bye, my darling."

Where was he? Had he gone? Was that his head above the others? No — he had gone! Finch was holding her by the arm. The train was moving out. A band struck up "The British Grenadiers." Oh, why did the band play? She could have so well borne it if the band had not played. The gay challenging voice of the horns pierced her soul. The drum beats were terrible to her.

Outside the station, Finch said — "Shall we go to a restaurant and have coffee?"

"No. I 'd like to go home."

She was glad she could speak so quietly.

Adeline would very much have liked to go to a restaurant but she hid her disappointment. She sat upright beside her mother in the car but did not look at her. After a little she laid her hand firmly on Alayne's knee and kept it there. She tried to make her hand feel like her father's. Indeed its firm pressure was a comfort to Alayne.

It was a relief to Wakefield to have Renny out of the house. Renny's look of concern whenever his eyes rested on him had been more of an irritation than a support to Wakefield. Renny could not come near him without touching him, as though to reassure himself that Wake was still his boy. But Wakefield did not want to be touched. He shied off like a nervous horse from all physical contacts. In the darkness of night he remembered the feel of Molly's arms, the caress of her lips, but in the daytime he wanted no one to touch him and, when once he had a glimpse of Molly in the road, he turned abruptly into the fields to avoid her. They had not met since the arrival of her stepsisters.

In these last days at home Paris Court was his most congenial companion. Since he had disclosed the secret of Molly's birth to Finch, he could not be with Finch without a desire to unburden himself further. Yet what he most wanted was to close the door of his past. Now he avoided what formerly had attracted him. He had always loved to talk but now he was silent for hours together. He had always, when at Jalna, spent much time with his uncles, delighting in their reminiscences of the past and their Old World atmosphere. Now he avoided them and they were hurt. He had always been a playfellow to the children but now they instinctively kept out of his way. He no longer knew whether he was Catholic or Protestant and did not care. But he did like Paris Court's carefree, worldly companionship. Paris was out for a good time in this life and did not much care how or where he got it or at whose expense. He had enjoyed his stay at Jalna but was quite willing to leave it. One winter in that climate was enough for him. He had come to Canada, not with the intention, but in the pleasant hope, of finding a rich wife. He had met only one rich young woman, Ada Leigh, the sister of Sarah's first husband. He talked of her incessantly to Wakefield, making graceless jokes concerning his hopes. When almost at the last he proposed and to his amazement was accepted, Wakefield felt the first pleasure he had experienced since the blow had fallen on him and Molly.

As for Sarah, Parry's distant cousin, it delighted her to think that two Courts were to possess the Leighs' wealth. She and Paris threw their arms about each other and danced triumphantly round the drawing-room at Jalna.

The marriage followed quickly and from then on Paris bore himself with the dignity of a married man, and a warm one at that!

The day before leaving, Wakefield wrote a short letter to Molly and posted it at the railway station.

Dear Molly —

I cannot leave without saying good-bye to you, yet I cannot bring myself to meet you. I dare not risk the comfort of a single touch from your hand or a word from your mouth. The ocean will part us but it is no wider than the gulf that has already come between us. I pray that you do not feel — no — I don't pray — I shall never pray again! But I hope from the depths of my heart that you don't feel as shipwrecked as I do. I think you are steadier and more sane than I. Perhaps some day you will find another man you can love but I do not believe you will find one to love you more deeply than I did — and do. Darling Molly!

Wakefield

When Wakefield and Paris were gone, Finch found himself the only one of the brothers at home. It was a strange sensation for him to go to Piers's house and see only Pheasant, Nook, and Philip. Surely at any moment the door would open and Piers would march in. But no, Piers had marched away to the war, in private's uniform. It was like him to choose that shortest way of having his fling at the enemy. It was strange to go to Jalna and find only the uncles and Alayne and the children, to know that those three strange girls, with whom he had crossed the ocean, were installed in the house where Uncle Ernest and Aunt Harriet, such a short while ago, had had their home. Perhaps strangest of all was the returning to Vaughanlands to find Sarah utterly engrossed by her son, watching the first dawning of his intelligence, his first reaching out to her breast, with a sensuous delight. At times when Finch saw her curl herself about the child like a supple Persian cat about her young, saw the concentrated gaze in her greenish eyes, where no white but only the iris showed, he felt a sardonic amusement. He had become, in the hour of her delivery, no more than the father of her child, the instrument by means of which she had reached her pinnacle of bliss. She had always been indolent but now she was satisfied to recline motionless and watch the child by the hour. She no longer wanted new clothes for herself. Everything was lavished on him. She embroidered his initials, surrounded by wreaths of flowers, on his cot coverings. She bought him a silver porringer lined with gold with his name engraved and the Court and Whiteoak crests emblazoned on either side. She looked on the other seven children of the family as nobodies and paupers compared to him. It was not long before she had offended Meg and Vaughanlands became too small to contain the two of them. Finch was puzzled as to where he should install her, for he was determined to go back to England and do his share of war work or whatever came his way. He had, since his return, given a number of recitals in the border cities of the United States and in Canada. He had given them with less nervous strain than ever before but his heart had never been so little in his work. He felt strangely free and light. He was filled with wonder when he saw Sarah with her child and remembered how she had enchained him in her passion. He had struggled in the chains of her desire, but now he was freed. She was as placid toward him as the waterlily toward the pool on which it floats. Except where the child was concerned.

"I pity you," Meg would exclaim, "when that boy of yours is older! He 's going to be the worst-spoilt child on the face of the earth!"

Alayne solved the difficulty by suggesting that Pheasant should come with her boys to stay at Jalna. She had always been fond of Pheasant and she loved little Nook. Then Sarah could take Pheasant's house till Piers's return. The rental would be a godsend to Pheasant.

Everyone fell in with this plan and it was made the easier because Miss Pink had lately opened a small school which Pheasant's boys, Alayne's children, and Roma could attend and be comfortably out of the way for the greater part of each day. Indeed it is probable that Miss Pink opened the school with the Whiteoak children in mind, for with these five and a few others from the neighborhood she would be able to carry on. She found these five quite a handful and there were usually several times a day when, with the exception of Nook, they were completely beyond her control. When this happened she simply opened the door and turned them out. Then they would squeeze their small bodies through an opening in the fence and run wildly about the graveyard or watch Noah Binns in awe as he drove his pick into the earth to excavate a new grave.

Archer attended school in two contrasting moods. Either he went with knitted brow and an avid determination to acquire knowledge, which he acquired at a rate that almost frightened Miss Pink (she and Alayne spent hours in discussing his mental endowments), or he declined to go at all. Then he would have to be carried to the car, lying stiff as a poker across the arms of the one who bore him, and that was a bad day for Miss Pink. In the car he would still extend himself stiffly, in whatever room he could make for himself, and at the school it was again necessary to carry him into the classroom. But Miss Pink was always patient with him for she felt that he had a great mind.

Finch had much time to himself in these days. He found pleasure in wandering about the countryside and in the woods, eagerly noting each fragile evidence of spring — the red leaf buds of the maples, the catkins in the ravine, and the joyful release of the stream. Scarcely a day passed when he did not go to the fox farm. He would spend hours with the sisters, finding their company oddly congenial. He was determined to break down Althea's shyness and counted it a triumph when she would laugh at some story of his boyhood or sit near the piano when he played. Sometimes he stayed to tea; then Molly would return from the town and join the group about the piano.

One day he found Molly there when he arrived. They were in terrible distress. A cablegram had come telling of Christopher's death. He had been killed in an aeroplane accident while training.

The four sisters did not seem able to take in the full meaning of the news. They were numbed and bewildered by it. But at the sight of Finch, they ran to him and clung about him, weeping. He put his arms about them, tears filling his own eyes, and tried to comfort them. But in the midst of his emotion he was startled by the electric thrill in his nerves when he felt Althea's slender body inside the circle of his arm. She lay against his breast, sobbing in complete forgetfulness of herself. He found himself pressing his lips to the silken fairness of her hair, calling her Althea, she calling him Finch. He felt shaken and strangely elated.

He had to be away for several days because of a recital and when he returned to the fox farm found Molly there, instead of at work as usual. She met him calmly. She said: —

"I 've had an offer from Hollywood."

"You have! But it 's not the first, is it?"

"No. Wake and I had offers when we were in New York. But we did n't want to go. Now I 'm sure it 's the best thing to do. You see, I must earn money and I should make quite a lot. Then too, the English actors out there give benefits for the British Red Cross. I can help England in that way. I want terribly to help. I want to go away from here and try to forget — all that has happened. I want to work hard and make money and forget — if I can." She held up her head and looked with proud sorrow into Finch's eyes. "I 've lost both Christopher and Wakefield. There 's nothing left but work."

"Will your sisters be all right without you?"

"Quite. Everything is new and wonderful to them here. I want to do the best I can with — my life — to be worthy of Christopher and Wake. They 're both gone but I have n't lost them. They still live in my heart."

Going home, Finch thought of Wakefield. There was something selfish, he thought, something self-centred and even cruel in the way Wakefield had behaved toward Molly. He tried to picture what he himself would have done in Wakefield's place. For one thing, he thought, he would have tried to do more to soften the blow for her. Wakefield had behaved, he began to feel, as though his own suffering were by far the greater. He had gone away without seeing her. He had behaved toward Renny as though Renny had done him a deliberate wrong. Perhaps he was being unjust to Wakefield. He knew in his heart that he had always been jealous of him, of Wake's position in the family as opposed to his own. "Little play-actor!" he had often said of him in the old days.

Suddenly Finch stood stock-still in the path. He had been struck by the remembrance of the nervous breakdown he had had a few years ago. He knew that he had made the household miserable because of his own wretchedness. Had he ever given a thought to the suffering of those about him? He could not remember having done so. Wake was not inflicting his unhappiness on the family. He was going forth to fight, perhaps to die. One thing was certain. He and Wake were not made of the stuff of Renny and Piers. Nor even of Eden. Even Eden! Why, Eden had borne one blow after another from fate and no one had heard him complain.

Thinking of Eden, he began to run, as though to escape. He ran through the twilight like a long lank ghost, past the lights of Jalna to Piers's house. Inside the door he hesitated and listened. Sarah was playing an Irish air on her violin. The smell of freshly baked bread came from the kitchen.

XXXII

LETTERS

SPRING was named on the calendar but no one could name her in the open. It was April, cold and wet. Four people sat about the fire in the sitting room. It was a shabby but comfortable room and its coziness recommended itself to them, especially in this backward spring. Birch logs burned on the hearth and Nicholas's favorite chair was drawn close to the blaze. He was cramming tobacco into the bowl of his pipe. Alayne and Ernest had divided the morning paper between them. She had just been reading aloud of the fall of Copenhagen. Pheasant was in the window seat knitting a pullover for Piers. The door opened and Mrs. Wragge brought in the post.

"Letters from England, 'm," she announced, handing them to Alayne. "I 've one too, from me 'usband. Now we 'll know all the detiles of the Grand National. It made me 'eart pound just to see the envelope." She breathed heavily as she left the room.

Ernest leant forward to peer at the addresses.

"Anything for me?"

"No, Uncle Ernest. There are just two. One for Pheasant, from Piers." She gave it to Pheasant. "And one for me, from Renny."

"To think," boomed Nicholas, "that he would win the race! What a triumph! I 'd have given a great deal to have been there to see it. Read out the letter, Alayne."

She opened it with a paperknife and four closely written sheets of notepaper from the Adelphi Hotel, Liverpool, were disclosed.

"By Jove," said Nicholas, "that 's a long letter for him."

"But what news!" exclaimed Ernest.

"Piers's letter is from Liverpool too," said Pheasant.

Renny's letter began "My own darling wife," but she read it as

Dear Alayne, —

I was delighted to get your united cablegram of congratulation. It was a good thought to send it because it made me feel how happy you all are about Johnny the Bird's victory. He is a grand horse and one of the youngest to win the great race. I got hold of Piers and managed to wangle a few days' leave for him. He 's writing by this same post to send his news. We came to Liverpool — Rags came too — by car, a few days before the race. So I was able to see Johnny the Bird in action before the great moment. I was very glad to see him and it almost seemed that he recognized me. To tell you the truth, I forgot all about the war for a few days, also other troubles. And even now I can't help being very happy. Johnny the Bird showed himself in fine fettle. I wished I might have ridden him myself but I 've nothing to complain of in my jockey. I 've heard these times called decadent by racing men but I never saw a better race or a horse more perfectly handled. I must tell you that in the Grand National the main thing is to get over the fences. No matter how fast a horse is on the level, he 's got to have any amount of stamina to undertake those thirty jumps. When I have more time I shall make you a map of the course with a full description of every jump. There are the thorn fences — five to eight feet high — the gorse hurdles and, of course, the water jumps. As you 've heard me say many times, Becher's Brook is the worst. This is a thick thorn fence four feet six inches high with a two-foot six-inch guard rail. On the landing side there is a natural brook nine feet six inches wide and six feet deep. Well, I can only say that Johnny the Bird went over these just like a bird. Once on the level something startled him and he ran suddenly to the left and my heart sank. But he gathered himself together and was rapidly among the leaders. He is an impetuous horse and he encouraged the other horses to cover the distance faster than usual. He did the four miles eight hundred and fifty-six yards in nine minutes fifteen seconds. This was wonderful because he was trained mostly on a soft muddy track and on this day the track was so dry the horses raised a dust. Oh, Alayne, I was terribly glad. It 's a funny thing but when I led him out after the race I suddenly thought of dear old Gran and how proud she would have been.

The prize money will certainly be acceptable. If it were peacetime nothing would satisfy me but to take Johnny the Bird home and clean up every steeplechase in America with him. As it is I think I shall close with an excellent offer made me by a New Yorker, a man I 've known for years. I 'll tell you all about that in my next.

Piers was simply hilarious and I never saw him —

Alayne stopped abruptly.

Pheasant leaned forward. "Yes?" she said. "Go on. He says he never saw Piers — "

"Gladder," finished Alayne, lamely.

"Drunker!" shouted Ernest. "And I don't blame him. I 'd have got drunk too."

Nicholas patted Pheasant's hand. "Read Piers's letter, my girl, and see what he had to say for himself."

"Perhaps Alayne has more to read."

"The rest of the letter is purely personal," said Alayne, glancing over the last page. "Do read Piers's letter."

Nicholas sat beaming through tobacco smoke. "What a triumph," he said. "What a triumph for the Jalna stables! And to think I was against his buying that horse!"

"I 'll never forget," said Ernest, "when the news came over the radio. I was sitting here alone, alone, mind you, listening to one of those horrible soap-flake advertisements, when the news came on. When I heard the words — Grand National — I leaped to my feet. When I heard that Renny had won the race I almost fell down again. I know I walked in a circle. I went into the hall and told the dogs. They were as excited as I, and — "

"Yes, yes," said his brother, "we 've heard all that before."

"Shall I read Piers's letter?" asked Pheasant.

"Yes, do."

She read aloud: —

DEAREST PHEASANT, —

I was very glad to get your letter with the nice little one from Nook enclosed. I think it is a splendid scheme for you and the boys to live at Jalna and let our house to Sarah. It will make quite a difference in our budget. Please thank Alayne for me. Well, at the moment, everything seems unimportant compared to the great victory at Aintree. Renny is giving Alayne details of that, so I shall only add that it was a grand race and that Johnny the Bird is the best buy Renny ever made. Old Redhead was in the seventh heaven after the race. I wish Alayne could have seen his face. There was a big dinner at the hotel but I was tired and went to bed early.

"Ho, ho, ho!" interrupted Nicholas.

"Don't interrupt, Nick," said Ernest.

Pheasant proceeded: —

I promised you that I would go to Ireland to see young Maurice at the first opportunity. Well, Cousin Dermot wrote that he was bringing him to Liverpool for the race. However, he was laid up with lumbago and could n't come. So I went to Ireland two days before the race, leaving Renny in Liverpool. It was a pity I had such a short time to stay for I enjoyed it thoroughly and so did Mooey enjoy having me. You would be very glad you let him go for this visit if you could see him. I 've never seen him look so well. He had a fine color in his cheeks and he 's grown much taller. It 's easy to see that he 's the apple of the old man's eye. It 's going to be a wonderful thing for Mooey. Cousin Dermot remarked my striking resemblance to my grandfather but he was shocked to see me in private's uniform. Well, my wish is to get a crack at the Huns. If all goes well I expect to leave for France in a few days. By the time you get this I 'll be in the thick of it.

My love to all at home and don't worry.

Your loving

PIERS

"I 'm so glad about Mooey," said Alayne.

"And so am I," said Nicholas.

"A very nice letter," added Ernest.

Pheasant drew a deep breath. "Yes. Very nice!" She rose with the letter pressed between her hands. "I 've things to do upstairs." She left the room, walking rather uncertainly.

"Poor little Pheasant," said Alayne. "It 's hard for her, parting with both Mooey and Piers. Not knowing when she 'll see either of them again."

"Yes, indeed," agreed Ernest. "Piers has probably been in France for a fortnight, in the thick of it."

Nicholas puffed silently at his pipe.

"I never can agree," said Ernest, "that Piers can compare with our father, though he is a fine-looking fellow."

"He has n't the distinction."

"Or the true elegance of proportion."

"Or the manner."

"Or the dignity."

The door opened and Mrs. Wragge appeared. She held a telegram in her hand. She looked anxious.

"It 's for Mrs. Piers," she said, in a whisper.

"Good God!" exclaimed Nicholas. "Something 's happened to Piers!"

"Who is to open the telegram?" asked Ernest, turning ashen.

"I will," said Alayne. She took the yellow paper from Mrs. Wragge and held it in tense fingers.

"Would it be about Johnny the Bird perhaps?" asked Nicholas. "Surely it 's not bad news."

Ernest rose and gripped the back of his chair in his hands. "We had better hear the worst," he said.

Alayne read — "REGRET TO INFORM YOU THAT PRIVATE PIERS WHITEOAK IS MISSING."

"Read it again," said Nicholas. "I don't take it in."

She read it again.

XXXIII
THE RESCUE

Six weeks later Finch and Wakefield were dining together in a small restaurant. Finch had arrived from Canada and Wakefield was on leave. Their meeting was a happier one than, at their last, Finch would have thought possible. He could not keep his eyes off Wakefield, wondering what was in his heart. He looked handsome in the R. A. F. uniform and he was full, even a little boastful, of the excitement and hazards of his training. Evidently he and Paris were better friends than ever and Finch judged that they had had some wild times together since returning to England. It was a relief yet, in a subtle sense, a disappointment to see Wakefield so master of himself. Finch thought, somewhat ironically, that no matter what Wakefield did or how he did it he himself was never quite pleased with him. It 's the same old jealousy, he thought. If he looks aloof and melancholy I think he 's posing. If he looks reckless and hard I think he has no real depth of feeling. I wish I could get over this stupid criticism of him and just enjoy being with him again.

They were a great contrast as they sat at table, their faces lighted by the amber glow from the table lamp. Finch's movements were hesitating, often awkward. He slumped in his chair or raised himself suddenly, straightened his shoulders, and turned his eyes toward the black-curtained window as though he longed to see the sky. He was obviously hungry and ate what was put before him without a discriminating glance. Yet there was something arresting about him that made people turn to give him a second look. Wakefield sat as though unconscious of his body. His movements were swift and sure, with the studied assurance of the actor. He ate less than Finch but ate it with more relish. His eyes saw everything that went on in the room. Taciturnity and melancholy seemed to have left him. He looked lively, hard, and reckless.

An orchestra was playing and there was some desultory dancing. There would be much more later. A strained excitement was in the air.

"There 's a very attractive girl over there," said Wakefield. "I 've met her. Would you like to dance?"

Finch shook his head. "Gosh, no! I 've no heart for anything like that. Not since we heard about Piers."

Wakefield's eyes darkened but he gave a little laugh. "Well — we may as well enjoy ourselves while we 're here. It probably won't be for long."

"Do you think there 's a chance that he 's living?"

"Not the slightest. As far as I can find out his unit was practically blown to pieces. Let 's have a liqueur. What would you like?"

"You choose. I like anything."

Wakefield ordered Benedictine with their coffee. He was really grown-up, Finch thought, with more poise than he himself would ever have. He sipped the liqueur and then said, in a low voice: —

"It was a terrible time at Jalna. Pheasant is heartbroken. The uncles took it very hard too."

Wakefield moved uneasily in his chair. "I know. I know. Let 's not talk about it."

Finch persisted — "Piers was always the strongest of us all. I just can't believe in this."

"I tell you I don't want to talk about it!" exclaimed Wake. "I 've got to keep my nerve for flying. I 've no time for worry about Piers. I worry more about Renny. God knows where he is! Somewhere — in that ghastly retreat! To think of four hundred thousand of them —

cut off over there — fighting for their lives! They 've no chance. They 'll be annihilated."

Finch raised his glass in a shaking hand and took a gulp of the liqueur. Wakefield's swift change from reckless liveliness to this passionate outburst of apprehension for Renny had made Finch almost lose his self-control. The lights in the room shook. The music became a frightening drone.

But the liqueur steadied him. He was able to answer quietly enough — "Perhaps something will happen. A miracle — "

Wakefield interrupted — "I 'm done with miracles. One happened to me. Was n't it a miracle that Molly and I should come together? A hell of a miracle! No — nothing can save them. They 'll be blown to pieces. We 've seen the last of Renny."

The girl Wakefield had pointed out rose from her seat and, passing through the dancers, came to their table. She was strongly made, with waving dark hair, wide-open hazel eyes, and a rich color in cheeks and lips. Her voice was deep and rather husky but agreeable.

The brothers rose and Wakefield introduced Finch to the girl.

"But I can remember only your Christian name," he said to her. "It 's Val, is n't it?"

"Yes and that 's enough for to-night. May I sit with you? I 've something terribly important in my mind."

They all sat down.

"Have a liqueur?" asked Wakefield.

"Thanks. Now you know this appalling retreat that 's going on in France. I 've an idea. I thought of it as soon as you came in and I 've been working it out in my mind ever since."

"Yes?" Wakefield's eager eyes were on her face.

"The Admiralty has sent out an order for every sort of

craft on the South Coast. They 're going to save these men. Not just a few thousand of them but as many as is humanly possible. My brother-in-law is over there. Well, he owns a yacht. It 's a motor yacht. It 's at his summer place near Ramsgate. What I want is to go on it myself and help with the rescue work. But I need a couple of men with me and I wondered if you —"

"I 'd like nothing better," said Wakefield. "What about you, Finch?"

"I 'm your man," said Finch. He rose, a little unsteadily, to his feet.

"But will they let a girl go into this?" asked Wakefield.

"I 'll put on some of my brother-in-law's things. I make a first-rate boy. What about you? How long is your leave?"

"Three days."

"Can we go now? I 've a car outside."

In ten minutes they were on their way.

It was dark in the cottage. Val went in and turned on the light in the living room.

"Wait here," she said, "and I 'll tell my sister." She ran upstairs.

"The miracle 's beginning," said Finch.

"God, I 'm glad to be able to do something!"

After a little Val came down with her sister, Mrs. Williams, who bore no resemblance to her but was small and delicate-looking. She carried a bundle of clothes.

"These are old yachting things of my husband's," she said. "You 'd better change into them and have some sleep and get an early start. I 'll have breakfast for you."

They changed and lay down in two small rooms next each other. They could smell the sea and hear its low murmur. The liqueur had had its effect on Finch and he dropped off quickly. But Wakefield lay thinking for a long while. He felt that he had had only a short sleep when a knocking on the door woke him. Val was there, wearing a pair of duck trousers and a dark blue jersey and tweed jacket. She had cropped the hair from about her face and pulled a soft hat low over her eyes.

"How do I look?" she asked.

"I'd never have guessed you were a girl," said Wake. Then he added — "But you should n't do this. It's going to be terribly dangerous. Do you understand that we'll be under fire? I think Finch and I — "

She interrupted — "What do you know about the yacht? Or the coast?"

"I'm afraid — nothing."

"Besides, I want to go. I want it more than anything on earth. Come down and have breakfast."

They collected Finch and went downstairs. Mrs. Williams had bacon and eggs waiting. She fluttered about them nervously and, when they left, followed them to the beach, a fragile but courageous little figure. They rode out to the launch in a dinghy and set about preparing it for the voyage down Channel. Finch had a strange feeling of hilarity, mingled with a sinking at the stomach. Val had a chart open in front of her. She was self-possessed, wasting no words. They found themselves joining craft of all sorts. Yachts, fishing boats, tugs, even canoes, all bound on the same mission.

There was a terse intimacy among the three as though every bit of their energy must be conserved for the work in hand.

There was almost a crush at Ramsgate. Owners of all manner of craft were crowding about, getting directions. They were given rifles and life belts, shrapnel helmets and first-aid outfit. They were told to go to La Panne, to arrive there the next day at daybreak if possible.

Across the Channel the motley flotilla set out. For a while it was peaceful and they had a strange holiday feeling, mingled with a piercing sense of great adventure and impending tragedy. Finch felt light and strong, as though he never could be tired again. Wakefield sat beside Val, learning how to handle the yacht. Suddenly she exclaimed: —

"Look!"

In the distance they saw planes fighting, two falling into the sea but too far away to make out their nationality. A little further on a British fighter streamed above them toward England, with smoke pouring from her, enveloping her. Then a German bomber flying toward France pursued by British planes unloaded her bombs. The bombs fell in front of the yacht. It rocked horribly. The three clung to their seats with frightened grins on their faces. Finch was tumbled to the deck.

"Gosh!" he got out as he picked himself up. "It 's really beginning."

All about them dead fish, big and little, rose and turned up their bellies. Millions of fish were on the surface of the sea, glistening in the pale sunlight. The planes disappeared and there was quiet again. Then they saw a launch overturned in the distance but they could not go to her help.

"Are you much frightened, Val?" asked Wakefield.

"Terribly. But I 'd not turn back for anything."

Mrs. Williams had well provided them with food and drink. The sea air was fresh. They were hungry.

"Did you say you had one brother over there, or two?" asked Val.

"Two. One missing. The other — in that hell!" answered Wake.

"I hope he knows we 're coming," said Finch.

The girl turned her wide-open eyes to him. "Do you believe in that sort of thing?"

"Yes. I think I do."

"I imagine you 're pretty fond of that brother."

"Yes. He 's older than we are. He 's been like a father to us. He was through the last war. Got the D.S.O."

"I do hope he 'll be saved!"

"And your brother-in-law, too."

"Yes. Jack 's a dear. He 's everything to my sister."

"What about you? I guess you mean a good deal to her."

"Well, this thing has drawn us together. We were n't very good friends. She disapproved of me."

Wake put up his hand. "Listen!" They could hear the deep thunder of the barrage from the French coast.

Finch thought of Jalna and the peace there. He could feel the peace as a physical thing, reaching up from the sun-warmed land. How far away and safe it seemed from war. What would the uncles say if they could see him and Wake at this moment?

On and on the strange raggle-taggle of the crusading flotilla moved. Another air attack came. A Messerschmitt fell into the sea not a mile away. When she hit the sea she exploded. Two small boats were overturned. Half their occupants were saved. The three felt that they were going through an initiation of horror for what lay ahead.

A slender new moon appeared on the horizon. The breeze fell and the sea was calm. In the distance they could see Dunkirk ablaze against the sky. Sometimes the blaze was low and sullen like smouldering hate. Sometimes it leaped upward in volcanic fury when a shell burst in its midst. As though to take part in some mad spectacle all the little craft hastened forward, little paddle steamers from the Thames, barges, wherries, lifeboats, motorboats. The moon, glancing between the clouds, revealed them to each other. The single purpose in the minds of those who manned them drew them onward like a compelling magnet.

Wakefield said — "You 'd better lie down and sleep, Val. Finch and I can get on all right."

"I 'm not sleepy."

"But you will be to-morrow — if you don't sleep to-night. There 's a hard day ahead."

"I could n't possibly sleep."

"Then curl up and rest."

She did, tucking a battered cretonne cushion beneath her head.

"Do you believe in dreams?" she asked.

"Yes. No matter how happy I have been my dreams were troubled. Now all my happiness is gone. When I left Canada, I hoped I 'd be killed over here."

"Oh, you come from Canada, do you?"

"Yes."

"But I 've seen you act in London."

"Yes. I 'm an actor."

"That was a lovely play. Where is the actress who took the part of Catherine?"

"She 's in Hollywood."

"It must be a wonderful life. Shall you go back to it after the war?"

"How can I tell?"

"What was her name? That actress, I mean?"

"Molly Griffith."

"Was she as lovely off the stage as on?"

"Quite."

Finch interrupted — "Talking of dreams! I 'd a queer one last night. I dreamed I had captured an enormous bird. It was shaped like a hawk but it was beautifully colored. Its plumage was like a rainbow. My brother Piers came along and took it by the neck. I was glad because I was afraid of it. He said he was going to strangle it. But before he could do anything it flew high into the sky, with Piers hanging on to it. It flew out of sight."

"Goodness, what a dream! Is it Piers who 's in France?"

"He is missing."

" Oh, I 'm sorry."

The night was full of the sound of the exhausts of engines. The pale fingers of searchlights discovered the small, low-lying clouds. There was a thunderous explosion at Dunkirk.

" That was a bad one."

" Yes. I suppose there are a lot of our soldiers right there."

" God, if only we can save them ! "

" Do you ever pray ? " she asked.

" Are you asking me ? " said Wake.

" Yes . . . Both of you."

" Well — I have prayed — a good deal — but not lately."

Finch did not answer. He sat staring at the blaze of Dunkirk. His face, at that moment, had a strange beauty.

" You look as though you were praying now," said the girl.

After that she was silent and, after a little, she slept.

" It was luck coming across her, was n't it ? " said Finch.

" Great luck."

" Who is she ? "

" I 've no idea."

" She makes a good boy."

" Now that she 's asleep she looks a girl."

" H-hm."

Dawn came slowly and in its misty light they saw the quiet water with its burden of little boats. Dead fishes slithered along the side of the yacht. A thick black pall of smoke, now and again shot with flame, drifted above Dunkirk. Val was steering, her hat drawn over her eyes. She was following a motorboat that was towing a string of eight wherries. She could see that the man in command was about seventy and delicate-looking. Several other elderly men were with him. Suddenly she cried out in horror : —

"Look! In the water!"

She pointed and they saw the bodies of men in uniform slithering alongside, just like the fishes.

"It's all right," said Wakefield. "It's all right, Val. Don't be frightened."

Finch's gaze was riveted on the bodies. He could not look away. When they had passed them he took a deep breath and pressed his fingers to his eyeballs as though to obliterate that image.

The East was growing pink. Now they could see what was going on. There was an air attack over Dunkirk, and shellfire. A black throng of men were on the beach. They could see enemy aeroplanes attacking them. They could see planes dropping bombs on ships which were loading troops alongside the jetty. Val steered the yacht in the wake of the motorboat, heading for a beach near Dunkirk.

All instinct for self-preservation, even all thought, was drained from them. They became mere empty vessels for the purpose of rescue. The girl felt mostly a dogged resolve to steer the yacht efficiently in these shallows, among the bodies of the men who had been machine-gunned while they were wading out into the water to safety. The bodies of the men looked strangely peaceful and remote. All their agony was over.

Finch had a desire to shout. He did not know why it was but he wanted to shout. He looked at the bodies in the water and felt an immense strength in himself as though there were nothing he could not do. A big hospital ship loomed near by. He saw a plane hovering above it, bombing it.

Wakefield's eyes were on the foreshore, which was alive with men. There were shell craters among the sand dunes and the men came running, stumbling from among these, toward the boats.

Wake kept the engine working. They were in four feet

of water. Soldiers were clambering into the wherries. Then, horribly, one of the wherries was struck by a shell. After the explosion, the moment's chaos, the three in the yacht steadied themselves, held themselves ready for the soldiers who came splashing toward them. Their faces showed what they had been through but they came splashing through the water, heaving each other on to the yacht, packing themselves in as though they would sink her by their weight.

Finch and Wakefield searched every face, looking for Renny. Then the yacht staggered with her load to the nearest ship and delivered the men into it. Then back to the shallows where more men came running to meet them, plunging through the water, pushing aside the floating bodies of their dead comrades, holding out their arms to grasp the side of the yacht, begging for a drink of water.

The sun came out hot. There was a glare on the water that made Finch's eyes ache. He was conscious of a pain in the back of his neck. But these did not matter. All that mattered was to load the little yacht, built to carry a dozen people, with fifty or sixty soldiers, till she was just able to stagger to the nearest ship. It filled him with a terrible rage to see that ship attacked by enemy planes. He could not understand Wake's cold resolute calm. He worked like a machine and the girl with him.

So the day passed.

It was miraculous how you could go on and on, when you felt completely played out, when you 'd given all the food to the soldiers, when your tongue felt like a dry sponge and your eyes like coals and you saw one horrible sight after another. Yet you could go on and on.

Wakefield now and again gave an anxious glance at Finch.

" Better try to sleep," he said. " It 's quieter now. To-morrow you 'll need all your strength."

" What about you and that girl? "

"We 're all right. You rest for a while."

"Very well." He fell, almost in a heap, in a corner of the cabin and slept.

"He looks awful," said Val.

"He's not very strong. He had a serious illness. Gosh, is there a drop in that teapot?"

She squeezed out half a cup of tea for him.

"Thanks. It tastes good. You ought to rest too. Please do."

"Don't worry about me. I 'm tough."

"You 're the bravest girl I 've ever seen."

"I could do anything with you beside me," she said. "I don't mean that I 'm in love with you. I only mean that you 're that sort of man."

He gave a short laugh and turned away.

Wakefield's year of hard work on the farm, his year of regular habits and healthy routine in the monastery, now stood him in good stead. He had a resistance that showed no sign of giving out.

They worked all night, in the illumination of Dunkirk, in the light of the young moon, in the chaos of bursting shells, in monotonous, deafening gunfire. The soldiers wading out to meet them seemed endless. Drenched with salt water, bloodstained, exhausted, they clambered over the sides of the yacht and begged for water. When daylight came the scene was revealed in all its dreadful activity. Many more small boats had arrived from England. They added their fresh vigor to the work. They were new targets for the planes. The launch and her train of wherries were hard at it, the old men and the young boys straining their loins side by side.

Finch had slept for four hours. Now he felt a new strength in him. He and Wakefield made the girl rest. She lay like a child, her head pillowed on her arm, and slept fitfully through the thunder of explosions, the roar of planes, and the shouts of men. It was as though some monstrous female were spawning them there, in endless monotony. The sun blazed out, hot and cruel, blistering their faces, bringing delirium to the wounded. The two opposing forces, the volunteers from England and the Germans, fought for the soldiers who had become passive objects of the struggle.

Wakefield seemed made of steel. Time ceased to exist for him. Once he wondered if his leave were up and what would be said to him when he went back. Val worked at his side, no one suspecting that she was a girl. Once, at some ghastly sight, she all but fainted. He steadied her in his arms.

"It 's all right," he whispered. "Shut your eyes."

In a few moments she was at work again.

They asked the soldiers for news of Renny or her brother-in-law. None had heard of them till, late in the day, one said he knew Captain Williams and had seen him killed.

"Jack 's dead," she said to Wakefield.

"I 'm sorry for that."

She answered, in an almost matter-of-fact voice:—

"Well, I shan't have to worry about him any more."

It was on the third day that they found Renny. They had almost ceased to think of him. Their senses were dulled by exhaustion. Then Wakefield saw an officer, supported by two soldiers, wading toward one of the wherries. One of the rowers was an old man whose face had become skull-like from fatigue. He looked like Charon at his task of rowing the dead across the River Styx.

Wakefield would not have specially noticed the wounded man but for the color of his hair. It was a peculiar dark red. He and the two who supported him were up to their armpits in water. One of them was Rags.

"Renny!" shouted Wakefield, and leaped overboard and waded toward him.

Renny looked at him, dazed.

" Renny, don't you know me? It 's Wake! Bring him to the yacht, men! "

Renny turned obediently and waded with difficulty to the yacht. They heaved him over the side and laid him on the deck. His bloodshot eyes looked inquiringly out of his sun-scorched face at his brothers.

" Hullo, kids," he said.

" I told you I 'd stick to 'im, did n't I? " said Rags, and fainted.

Wakefield pillowed Renny's head on his knee.

" Oh, Renny, are you much hurt? "

" I don't know. Not killed, anyhow. Have you any water? "

They gave him the last of the water.

They had taken him to the hospital ship and were on their way back when a bursting shell made several holes in the yacht. She was no longer fit for the work. They turned her homeward, toward England. They could reach England safely if the sea did not rise. If it rose they would be lost. But the miracle of the calm waters continued. The sky clouded and a gentle rain fell. The three, looking old and worn in their youth, left the hell of bombing and machine-gunning behind and turned back toward the island fortress. They turned their faces up to the rain and their ears drank in the silence broken only by the crying of gulls.

XXXIV
AUTUMN AGAIN

It was October once more and once more Nicholas was taking his morning exercise in the kitchen garden. He found this the most sheltered spot when autumn came and he had got one of the men to make a seat for him in the sunniest corner, for his gouty leg needed frequent rest. But he was not going to sit down on it yet. He would take three more turns round the garden. He put back his broad shoulders and raised his head to drink in the pungent sweetness of the air. Dead leaves were being burned somewhere near by and there was the pleasant scent of herbs and the tang of the tomato plants. They had yielded a poor crop this season. The tomatoes were small and sour. Now that he came to think of it, none of the fruit had been as good as usual. A nasty fungus growth had ruined the plums. There had been few damsons for his favorite jam. As for the apples, they were a disgrace to Jalna. What would Piers have said to them!

At the thought of Piers, a well of thanksgiving rose in his breast. It had been to-day week that the letter had come — that letter which had changed Jalna from a house of mourning to one of thanksgiving. The sight of his handwriting on the envelope had been a shock. It had been Nicholas himself who had carried it to Pheasant. "A letter for you, my dear. I 'm afraid it has been held up all these months." A letter from the dead, that 's what he had thought it was. With a frozen look on her little face she had torn it open, stared at it unbelievingly a space, then cried out, "Piers is alive, Uncle Nick!" and fainted.

Alive he was, in a prison camp somewhere in Austria. The letter had been brief, merely stating that he was well but a prisoner and sending his love to all at home. Of course he had n't been allowed to write any more. It had made Nicholas and Ernest feel ten years younger. Now they were better able to bear the anxiety over Renny and Wakefield. Renny was recovered from his wound and back with his regiment again. Little Wake had brought down God only knew how many German planes. It was a good thing that Finch had been sent home. He had done his share in rescuing air-raid victims in London, seen sights that had almost been more than he could bear. He 'd never quite recovered from that terrible time at Dunkirk. Well, he would regain his strength at home and it was grand to have him come in every day for a talk. He and that wife of his seemed more normal in their relations — if you could call it normal to show an increasing indifference toward each other. Sarah was indifferent to everyone but her baby. And how she was spoiling the little beggar. Already, at ten months, he was a tyrant. And he was the image of Sarah's father.

There was Finch now — coming toward the kitchen garden, looking more natural, too — not so gaunt and nervy. Nicholas waved his stick.

"Hi, Finch! Come and see me!"

Finch came up, grinning. "Hullo, Uncle Nick. How are you this morning?"

"Pretty fair. Pretty fair. Oh, I 've much to be thankful for. I 've a new lease of life since Piers's letter came." He took Finch's arm gladly and they walked on down the garden.

"You look nice, Uncle Nick," said Finch. "I like that checked coat on you. Your tie 's smart too."

Nicholas laughed. "This coat is as old as the hills. But the tie is new. Alayne always buys me one on my birthday. Eighty-eight, Finch! Getting to be a pretty old fellow."

"You don't look it. Not since the letter."

"Ha, that made a difference!"

"Gosh, yes . . . Pheasant is so happy that it hurts me to see her. Yet she knows she may never —"

"Just look at the asparagus bed! Is n't it a pretty sight?" Nicholas deliberately interrupted Finch. He cherished the present good and could not face the thought of future evil.

The plumes of the asparagus crowded tall and feathery, still veiled in the silver net of the dew. Little field mice ran in and out of the brown grass.

Pheasant appeared on the path, one of her sons by either hand. The boys were growing fast. They were in happy Saturday spirits and very conscious of their mother's exquisite relief. Pheasant raised her face to the tranquil blue of the Indian-summer sky, smiling and holding fast the little hands.

"Just see the asparagus bed," said Nicholas. "I 've never known it prettier. And by Jove, it 's an old one! It 's been there as long as I can remember."

"That was one crop that was good this year," said Pheasant.

"Look, there 's a monarch butterfly over it!" cried Nook.

"I wish I could catch him," said Philip.

"No." Pheasant spoke sharply. "Nothing that is happy shall be harmed."

"I 'd not hurt him. I 'd keep him in a little box."

"He 'd be a prisoner," said Nook.

"Like Daddy!"

"Don't," cried Pheasant. "Don't say that!"

"That asparagus bed," said Nicholas, "makes me think of what life was when I was a young fellow. I don't know why — but it does."

"I think I know," said Pheasant. "There 's a kind of radiance about it. When you look at it you feel a goodness in the earth and air."

"In those days," said Nicholas, seating himself on his bench, "nothing seemed too good to be possible."

"It 's different to-day," said Finch. "Nothing seems to be too bad to be possible."

"Oh, don't say that!" cried Pheasant. "I do so want to believe in good! And I do. I feel that I am helping Piers when I believe that. I should think you 'd believe it too, Finch, after what happened at Dunkirk. I 've heard you say it was like a miracle."

Finch's mind flew back to the agonizing struggle, the ultimate achievement of those days. The scene came before his eyes, blotting out the garden, the blazing maple trees, the old man on the bench with the little boy on either side of him. He saw Wakefield, himself, the girl, striving together in a kind of trance. He saw the thronging soldiers wading through the shallows, the blazing town, the dying. He remembered how, when they had reached England, they had steered the almost sinking yacht to her moorings and had half-staggered up the hill toward Val's sister's house. They had not been able to find it in the rubble that had been made of the little seaside resort in their absence. The sister had been killed. Finch had not seen Val after that but he knew Wakefield had.

After a little he left the others and went down into the ravine. He crossed the bridge and saw how the watercress fairly impeded the progress of the stream, it had grown so thick. Its glossy leaves had a rich greenness in this, its second crop. But the bullrushes had burst open and their bright down floated on the quiet air. He had a sensuous pleasure in shuffling through the dead leaves up the path toward the fox farm. The leaves were scarlet and gold and mahogany. They were crisp, not damp and sodden as autumn leaves are in milder climates, and a strange sweet scent rose from them.

At the top he saw Althea Griffith walking ahead of him. She was carrying a basket full of watercress she had gathered from the stream. He noticed the way she walked. It was a contrast to Sarah's odd gliding. Althea moved with a kind of delicate vigor, as though walking were her delight.

They had now reached a point in friendship where he could count on a swift glance from her and even a half-smile, but he took care not to thrust himself on her. He stepped on a dry branch and its breaking made her start and look round. Her body swayed, as though in indecision. She took two steps forward, then stopped. Finch walked slowly toward her. He called out "Good-morning" in a matter-of-fact tone.

Now she turned and faced him. He thought:—

"How lovely she is! And what a handicap she 's under!" He liked the straight fair fringe of her hair that almost touched her eyebrows. But he would have liked to lift the fringe and uncover the high white forehead beneath. As he came up to her he asked:—

"Have you heard from Molly lately?"

She answered, as though she had been running:—

"We had a letter this morning."

"Oh. She 's still working hard on the picture, I suppose."

"Yes. Molly works very hard." She looked at him appealingly, as though begging leave to go.

"It 's splendid that she 's getting on so well."

"Yes. She loves the work."

"And how are you others getting on?"

"We 're very happy." She appeared to gather all her strength for the question that followed. "And you? Are you getting better?"

"Oh yes. I 'm pretty fit now, though my eyes still

trouble me. When they 're recovered I 'm going on a tour. I want to make money for the air-raid sufferers. I saw for myself what they go through, you know."

"Yes?" But he perceived that he had brought no picture of suffering to her. Her eyes were on his face with an odd questioning look.

"Will you sit down here a little while?" he asked, indicating a fallen maple. It had been blown over in a gale more than a month ago but still it had drawn on the store of sap that was in it and hid its misfortune from its leaves. Now, prone as it was, it was gorgeous in its scarlet and gold and had kept its foliage longer than any of the other trees, being sheltered in its lowly position. The nest of a small bird still nestled on one of its boughs, and a faint essence of bird song seemed to enliven it.

Without a word Althea put down the basket of watercress and sat herself on the trunk of the tree beside him.

"Why, your feet are wet!" he exclaimed.

"Yes. I was so eager to get the cress I walked right into the stream without thinking."

"I believe you are very impulsive," he said.

"Yes. I have to guard against it."

He thought this over, wondering what she meant. Then he said — "I think it might be better for you to let yourself go."

"Oh, no. I must never do that!" She twisted her long slender fingers together. "It would never do. It 's Gemmel, you see, who tortures us — first me and now even Garda. . . . She can't do things herself and she 's always talking — talking about them. . . . She tries to drive us to do things we ought n't to. She 's always wondering and guessing and, now that Molly 's away and Garda is growing up, it 's worse. I can't tell you what it 's like."

Finch listened to this outburst with a strange throbbing in his pulses. He had always been struck by a sense of mystery in the three sisters, particularly in Gemmel. But what did it mean? He had a sense of shame that this disclosure of Althea's should stir him in this particular way. Perhaps he was too vulnerable to emotion, now that Sarah's spell had been removed. Suddenly, and scarcely conscious of what he did, he dropped to his knees beside Althea and laid his head in her lap.

He did not know what he expected her to do. She was like a frozen stream whose character he could only guess. He felt dizzy from the throbbing of his pulses. He would not be surprised if she cast his head from her lap with the same swiftness with which she might cast aside undesired fruit which had fallen there.

He felt a secret joy when, instead of a rebuff, she laid her hands on his head. They fluttered over it as though in fear, then rested there, caressing his hair, stroking his cheek.

"Oh, Althea," he whispered. "You 're not afraid of me any longer!"

"No. I 'm not afraid."

He raised his face to hers and she bent over him, but she did not kiss him. Nor did he desire her to. What had happened was enough. They did not belong to each other nor could they ever. But it was joy enough for the time that the icy barrier of her shyness had melted and they could be friends.

They heard Garda's voice.

"Althea!" she called. "Are you there?"

Althea stood up. Finch slid on to the fallen tree.

"Althea, I 've something to tell you!"

"I 'm coming."

Garda ran toward them, her face glowing with excitement and happiness. The change had done wonders for her. She was becoming a lovely young girl. As she came up her eyes were bright with curiosity. There was a glint of malice in them too, as though she were treasuring something she had seen, to repeat it to Gemmel.

"What do you suppose?" she said. "Mrs. Whiteoak has been to see us and brought us a basket of purple grapes and a huge bunch of chrysanthemums! Do come and see! She was so sweet and kind! You can see her through the trees, if you look, going down the path." She pointed to where Alayne's lonely figure was visible, descending by another path into the ravine.

Alayne had drawn on an old cardigan of Renny's for warmth. It clung warmly about her, emanating the scent of his tobacco and a certain essence of his vitality. She thrust her hands into the pockets and walked back toward Jalna. She had enjoyed her walk. It was an exercise she had never much cared for but now she made up her mind to do more of it. To-morrow she would go to the stables — and every day after — so that she might send Renny first-hand news of his horses. She would find out things for herself and send them on to him. Perhaps, if she wore this cardigan of his, the horses would feel friendly to her — even feel some connection between her and him. She would begin riding again — go out riding with Adeline. That would be great news for him. In a strange, subtle way she felt that, in doing these things to please him, she was protecting him.

She found Nicholas and Ernest in the sitting room, trying to get the news on the radio. Their two gray heads were close together in front of it while strange, unwanted cries, grunts and squawkings, came from its interior.

Nicholas heaved himself closer. "Let me try! You seem always to think I can't get anything."

"Well, Nick, you can't do anything that I 'm not doing."

"Get out of the way and I 'll show you."

"What are you trying to get?" asked Alayne.

"The news from England," answered Ernest. He looked at his watch. "It 's quite time for it."

"One would think," rumbled Nicholas, as a persuasive male voice came from the radio, "that the entire population lived with its hands in the laundry tub. Soap flakes — super-suds — by Jove, there 's little else!"

He persisted, however, while snatches of serials full of heart throbs filled the room with their woe. At last he gave an exclamation of triumph. "Ha, here we are! Your watch must have been fast, Ernie."

Pheasant slipped into the room. The four listened to the calm recital of air raids and air battles. Their minds were on young Wakefield, who, such a short while ago, had been a mischievous small boy, a sensitive adolescent, in this room. Now, somewhere over there he was sailing in the skies, in daily hazard of his life. Suddenly, startlingly, his name came to them out of the radio. They were frozen to attention. What was the voice saying?

"It is announced that Flying Officer Wakefield Whiteoak — "

"Don't! Don't!" cried their hearts. "Don't tell us that he has been killed!"

Nicholas's large eyes were fixed in apprehension on the radio. Ernest gripped the arms of his chair. Pheasant closed her eyes and her lips moved. The color fled from Alayne's face. All this in a breath! Then the cool buoyant voice continued: —

"— Wakefield Whiteoak, a young Canadian flier, has been awarded the Distinguished Flying Cross for gallantly flying a badly damaged plane back to England after taking part in a raid over Germany. The King personally presented the Cross."

The news went on but no one heard it. This was enough. This terror — this relief! An electric thrill of pride and relief went through the room. They looked at each other, making incoherent sounds to express their emotions. Ernest's eyes were full of tears.

"Wonderful! Wonderful! I was never —" he got out, but could say no more.

"To think of little Wake!" cried Pheasant. "Oh, won't Renny —"

"I 'm glad. I 'm glad," said Alayne. "It will be a great help to Wake."

Nicholas was struggling to get to his feet. "Heave me up out of here," he demanded. "Got to be on my feet." His untidy gray hair on end, his heavy shoulders seeming too weighty for the power in his legs, he stumped about the room.

Adeline must have heard something of the excitement. She came to the doorway and demanded: —

"What has happened?"

Nicholas turned himself about and faced her. He said in a sonorous voice: —

"Adeline, this is a proud day for us. Your Uncle Wakefield has won the Distinguished Flying Cross. It 's been presented to him by the King. Tell her the very words of the announcer, Ernest. I can't remember 'em."

Ernest repeated the words. The grownups listened as though they too heard them for the first time.

Adeline's eyes were like stars.

"Oh, good!" she said. "Oh, good!"

"I tell you," said Nicholas, still in his deepest voice, "we shall beat Hitler. With men like ours — we shall beat Hitler. With a leader like ours nothing can defeat us. What did he say? 'Long, dark months of trial and tribulation lie before us . . . death and sorrow will be the companions of our journey, hardship our garment, constancy and valor our only shield.' Grand words, eh?"

"How well you remember them, Uncle Nick," said Pheasant.

"And yet he says his memory is failing!" said Ernest, very proud of his brother.

Nicholas threw up his leonine old head and went on: —

"'We shall fight on the seas and oceans, we shall fight with growing confidence and growing strength in the air . . .'"

"Aye," said Ernest grimly, "in the *air,* by God!"

Nicholas fixed his eyes on Adeline and went on: "'We shall defend our Island, whatever the cost may be; we shall fight on the beaches, we shall fight on the landing grounds, we shall fight in the fields and in the streets, we shall fight in the hills. We shall never surrender.'"

"Magnificent!" exclaimed Ernest, as though the noble words were Nicholas's own.

"You 've put me off!" declared Nicholas. "You 've put me completely off. I can't remember another word of it."

"Oh, yes, you can, Uncle Nick," said Pheasant. "Please do! It 's grand."

He ran his hands through his hair. "'This Island,'" he muttered, "'subjugated or starving . . . Then our Empire across the seas . . . armed and guarded by the British Fleet, will carry on the struggle until, in God's good time . . . in God's good time . . .'" He could not finish. His voice was shaking. "Adeline," he said, "the future lies with you children. You must remember this day and . . . pledge yourself, yes . . . pledge yourself . . ."

"I will, Uncle Nick."

Alayne brought in the decanter of sherry and they drank to Wakefield. Nicholas was tired. He dropped heavily into his chair.

Adeline went again into the hall.

She found Archer there, staring up at the grandfather clock. He had opened its door and was holding the pendulum motionless.

"If you stop the clock," he said, "you stop time, don't you? I need never go to bed."

She removed his hand sternly from the pendulum. "Let

it go. You can't stop time. No matter what you do. We need it."

"What good is it to us?"

"We've got to have it. Archie, come upstairs with me."

"Where?"

"To Daddy's room."

She took him by the hand and led him up to Renny's room. She closed the door behind them. Then she faced him.

"Archie," she said, "we may have to fight. Uncle Nick says so. We may have to fight — just like Daddy."

"Have they killed Daddy?"

"No, no, but we children may have to fight too, and I think we'd better begin training. Look here."

She climbed on to a chair and took down two double-barreled rifles from the wall. She placed one of these in Archer's hands. He took it as though this were what he had been waiting for since long years.

She opened the window wide. The rich-colored autumn landscape lay before them in peace and majesty. The window faced the east.

"This is the direction they'd come from," she said. "Because England's over there. Now rest your gun across the sill, Archie, and I'll be on the lookout. When I see them coming I'll tell you and we'll fire. We'll shoot them as they come out of the woods and we'll *never* surrender."

He drew his high white forehead into a frown and fixed his piercing gaze on the blue horizon. His small grimy hands gripped the rifle. Adeline's expression was one of watchful courage. The dark red hair framing her face was bright in the sunshine. She felt inside her a gathering strength.